AF445078

A Fading Shadow

Randy K. Wallace

A Fading Shadow
Copyright © 20232 by Randy K. Wallace

All rights reserved. No part of this book may be reproduced or transmitted in any form or by any means without written permission of the author and publisher.

This is a work of fiction. Any resemblance to actual persons, living or deceased, is purely coincidental.

ISBN: 979-8-9871296-2-3
Library of Congress Control Number: 2022949858

This is a revised version of the work originally published in 2006 as *The Banderman Odyssey*.

CHAPTER ONE

From a sky dotted with billowing clouds, the sun shone on the ocean. Jason Ryder stood alone in his secret spot, staring at his reflection in the still water of a tidal pool. His mom had said it was just like it used to be near the pond behind the barn on their farm when she was a child. He'd seen pictures of the old farm, but she'd told him it had been torn down long before he was born.

The pool was a bright shadowy blue with darkened images of the clouds drifting through it. As Jason walked along the beach, he poked at various bits of debris with an old stick he'd acquired long ago. It was his favorite stick, old and worn with time, the gray color wood gets after it's been bleached by countless sunny summer days. It was also unnaturally straight for a stick—or at least any stick he'd ever seen— and it had a strange, spiraled pattern on one end. His mother'd said it was a broomstick, but he'd never seen one made of wood before. The spirals were sure neat, and it was great for poking at things he knew he wasn't supposed to touch. Oily sludge lapped at the shore, the result of the sunken barge that lay just offshore. Mom said that ocean currents would someday clear the deposits, but the sludge had been there as long as Jason could remember. No one seemed to care enough to clean up the mess. But, even so, this was his beach and although it was not what nature would have chosen, it was the only ocean he knew.

Jason poked at the steel blue water of the tidal pool and it swirled up black. He drew an outline of a house in the water. It stayed there for a moment before the water and sludge separated, leaving the pool to reflect the sky once more.

The beach was his favorite place to go, although his mother had forbidden it. Surrounding the house was at least a half a mile of meshed fencing with loops of barbed wire running along the top. He knew his mother hoped it would keep him contained and safe. He could walk up to it in countless places but could only look through. He remembered how happy his mother had been when he was able to point to the signs she'd posted and said, "Danger." In truth, he couldn't read at the time, but his mother didn't appear to mind. She seemed so happy when he was able to point to the signs and say with a wide-eyed determined child-face, "Daanger." She'd loved that.

She'd freak out if she knew he was here, but it was such a great place. The rocks came right into the water on both sides of his hideaway, forming a small bowl around his tiny bit of the ocean. A cave gaped in the crag behind him where eons of waves had washed away the softer material. A small hole in the ceiling led up to the field on the other side of the danger-fence. It was his very own secret exit/entrance.

It truly was a hideout that no one else knew about. The entrance had been formed just a few years earlier during a particularly wet spring. The scree from the cave-in formed a narrow slide into the cave, perfect for a quick entrance. Jason would often pretend to be a commando. He'd run at full speed, slip over the edge and disappear suddenly from enemy view into a world all his own.

Over the past summers, Jason had collected numerous *special items* buried in the dirt from all around the house to create a collection. It contained some of the neatest things any ten-year-old could ever imagine. There were old radio carcasses, glass and plastic bottles, metal containers, Barbie doll heads, ceramics, plates, cups, and toys of every description—all in various stages of decomposition. Jason had his special spot, his neat stick, and the coolest display of 'stuff'. He stood surveying his private paradise, satisfied.

Turning back to the tidal pool, he could see himself framed against the sky in the steel blue water. He sat on a rock and watched the clouds drift by, never having to look up. He poked his stick into the water and created a small black dot in the perfect picture of the shadowy sky. *I should get going before mom starts to worry,* he thought.

CHAPTER TWO

"Jason! Time for lunch," Tate called from the back porch. *Where is that boy?* In her mind, she stressed the word 'is'.

Lately, Jason seemed to be gone more and more often. Up at dawn with only a light breakfast then nowhere to be seen until lunchtime. He was a good boy, but he did love to wander. The only trouble was wandering these days could be dangerous; it could even be deadly.

Tate had put up the danger signs not long after they'd arrived. Jason knew what they meant and usually stayed away. The fences were everywhere, and the only way off the property was through the gate at the front of the house. Jason wouldn't—and couldn't—get off the property unless she went with him. Nevertheless, he loved to collect things and he truly was an ingenious young boy. *Where is he anyway?*

Before Tate had finished going over all the worrisome possibilities in her mind, Jason came running up to the back steps wearing a huge grin. She put her arm around his shoulder as she led him into the kitchen where the previous day's stew simmered on the stove. Jason rolled his eyes as his gait slowed. "Oh, Mom, do we have to have this again? We had this yesterday," he whined.

"You know what I've always told you. Just like my mother used to say, 'Waste not, want not.' And that's just what we're going to do. Wash your hands and get your bottom back in here," she said, snapping a dish towel in his direction as he leapt clear.

***

Jason slouched, then lumbered off to the bathroom. The tap water had a yellowish tinge and reeked of strange unknown things. There were few smells as unappealing. The stench filled the entire bathroom. When the sink was full and after Jason added a mixture of chemicals, the smell was even worse. He hummed a part of a song his mother taught him: "Always Look on the Bright Side of Life."

In the kitchen, Jason found his mom waiting at the table. He sat, and they began eating in silence. The soup was made from rusty cabbage and old potatoes. There wasn't any meat, but it had a slight hint of chicken—probably from a bullion package that had expired years earlier. Jason was hungry and accustomed to eating whatever his mom made. He did his best not to complain. After all, any food was good food. He had gone hungry often enough to know that.

After lunch, Jason jumped to his feet. "See ya, Mom," he said, and made for the door.

"Just a minute, Champ. Get back here and give a hand with the dishes. You're not going anywhere until you help out a little."

"Aw, Mom, do I have to?" Jason said, his shoulders slumped.

"Yes, you have to. Now put the dishes in the sink and wipe off the table."

***

Tate went into the living room, which had been repurposed as a miniature jungle. Here, in the largest and brightest room in the house, she nurtured the plants that formed the staple for their meals. The garden was her priority for a good part of every afternoon. If she had anything to do with it, Jason would grow up to be a healthy young man. For her, it was a matter of fact, not a hopeful possibility. Tending her garden was an essential part of their lives.

She smiled as Jason wiped down the table, rinsed the rag, then skipped to the door. She caught him just in time to renew his sun block and slap his hat on his head. As fearful as she felt, she had to admit over the past few years the world had already begun its recovery. The widespread lack of industry had given the planet a much-needed respite. The atmosphere, like the rest of the world, was on the mend, but precautions had become ingrained in her. There were risks everywhere. It made no sense to add to them unnecessarily. She kissed him good-bye and before he was out the door she said, "Where're you off to now?"

"Just out back, Mom. I'll be back in a while." Then he was gone again.

***

Outside, Jason poked around in the dirt with his stick. If he was observant, he could almost always find something new near the surface. Sometimes it might be the sole of a shoe or a piece of broken pottery. Other times it might be a miniature figurine with Made in China stamped on the bottom. Whatever the find, poking around was what he loved to do, and there was no better pleasure than unearthing some new treasure to add to his collection.

He had asked his mom if there had been a dump nearby, but she said she didn't think so. More than likely, his treasures were probably what was left of the day-to-day trash the previous tenants had tossed out the back door because they were too lazy to take it to an actual dump.

He poked around for a while, but after finding nothing of interest, he headed to the fence. A direct route wasn't possible; the path was obscured by dead blackberry bushes skirting the house. They'd been so overgrown at one time that now the dead thorny twigs were thick and high. It created a natural barrier forcing him to navigate a maze of prickles to get to his passage. When he arrived at the hole, he jumped without hesitation and slid down into the cave.

When he'd first found this place, he had to crawl and dig his way to the beach. But over the months, his sliding, first on his feet and later on his bum, helped create a slide. After countless trips up and down the ramp, it had become smooth and hard. Only the occasional rock stuck out, and he was able to avoid most of them. Unfortunately, today he managed to nail the largest of the stones just below his left butt cheek. It happened on the lower portion of the slide after he had already reached his top speed. The pain left him clutching his upper thigh in agony as he rolled around in the sand.

He was furious and frustrated. But, as the agony subsided and he'd finished writhing and cursing the world, he calmed enough to consider the problem. The rock had been there all along, after all. And if he hadn't blindly leapt through the hole in the first place, none of this would have happened. If he'd removed the stone days or even weeks earlier when it first emerged, this wouldn't have happened, either. The solution to preventing this from happening again was obvious.

Limping out of the cave and onto the beach, Jason retrieved his stick and, using it like a cane, returned to the slide. It was a handy find, because now he used it as a rudimentary digging tool and began clearing around the outside edge of the stone. He hadn't worked long before he realized the removal of the rock would also mean the demolition of his chute. He hadn't progressed far, but he already mourned the loss of his slide. Should he continue or not?

Given the slide was pretty much destroyed, he began again with renewed determination. The stone would not get the better of him. Besides, after a half an hour of steady digging, he had come to a point where the edge of the rock had begun to turn under.

Jason struggled on. With sweat pouring into his eyes and with the rock's face completely exposed, he sat on the stone and wiped his brow on his sleeve. It was at that very moment the rock suddenly disappeared from under him, and he followed. When he came to a halt, he found he was pinned tight in the hole with his legs sticking straight up around his ears. His arms were wedged high over his head, leaving him without leverage. In this position, he could look up into the slide, but no amount of craning allowed him to see the water's edge.

Jason snorted in disbelief. First, the bruise on his leg and now this.

When he thought it could get no worse, it did. He could feel water rising from beneath him. It began to fill the hole and flow around him. He had almost no time to wonder about what kind of pressure he could expect when, instead of being pushed out, he slid even farther into the hole and became wedged even tighter. If getting out before was going to be hard, now it began to seem impossible.

For the first time since he'd discovered the passage to the shoreline, Jason realized how dangerous keeping a secret could be. His mother didn't know where he was, and he had no idea how he was going to get free.

He tried calling out, but he was jammed in the hole so tightly that breathing had become difficult. In frustration and pain, he did the only thing left: he started to cry. With every tear, his energy seeped away until he felt completely drained and helpless. His efforts to lift himself up were fruitless. With a final heave and a sigh, he relaxed in utter exhaustion and despair. It was then that he slip-fell-tumbled farther into the watery hole. He thrashed, banging his back and head on the boulder that had previously fallen from under him. His head came out of the water, and he gasped for air, afraid he wouldn't be able to touch bottom. After a moment of batting at the water he righted himself, relieved to find that the water was less than a meter deep.

With one fear out of the way, a new one seized him. He was in a watery chamber that smelled as if a dozen rotting corpses were about to reach out and add him to their numbers. The only light in the darkness trickled in from the void through which he had just fallen. Gripped by fear, he leapt to his feet and scrambled into the light. Without hesitating, he turned upward and ascended to the surface.

Jason remembered a dream he'd once had in which he was trapped under water. In the dream, he had been vaguely aware that if he should breathe, he would die, so he swam as hard as he could toward the surface. The water pushed against his face as he tore upward, but the surface seemed unattainable. When he felt he could hold his breath no longer, he broke the surface. In his dream, he flew right out of the water. Jason clamored out of his would-be grave and threw himself onto the ground. He lay staring up at the sky, thankful to be alive.

After catching his breath and looking at his watch, he realized he was late returning home. He ran into the house, hoping his mother would assume he'd fallen in the creek rather than thinking he'd crossed the fence. She met him at the door.

"Jason Dennis Ryder, where on earth have you been? I've been calling and calling. Look at you. You're soaking wet and you look like you've been dug out of the ground."

"Sorry, Mom," Jason said, his eyes to the ground as he slipped beneath her stare and into the house.

"Little Mister, hold it right there!"

Jason froze. She reached down and took hold of the bottom edge of his T-shirt with both hands.

"Lift up your arms," she said. "There's no way you're going into my clean house with these on."

The kindness in her voice surprised him as she pulled his shirt up and over his head. She let him pass into the house only after he had nothing on but his underwear and socks. He was thankful she hadn't noticed the bright red circle on his thigh. In his nearly naked glory, she sat him down at the table and placed a cup of water in the microwave. After a minute or so, she added a pouch of prepackaged hot chocolate and set the mixture in front of him.

"Thanks, Mom."

"You stay here and sip on that while I run you a bath. We'll eat when you're clean and then you can explain how you managed to get yourself so darned dirty."

His mom was not someone who forgot her promises. He knew an explanation was going to be a must. He didn't want to lie, but he also knew she'd never allow him to keep his hideout if she knew where or what it was. He would make his hot chocolate last a very long time.

By the time Jason had finished his hot chocolate, it had long since grown cold and the bath was well on its way to being lukewarm. His mom's temper was beginning to flare. Not normally an angry woman, he could tell by her glare that she was close to reaching her threshold for tolerance. Fearing her wrath, Jason downed the last sip of chocolate sludge at the bottom of the mug and ran to the bathroom. While he soaked in the tub, he tossed a million explanations to his dinosaur bath pal. As the prehistoric carnivore ate the last of the throw away ideas, his mom came in with a towel.

"Supper's ready. Time to dry off and get your PJ's on."

Jason ate in silence, praying his mother had forgotten about the explanation she'd said he owed her. Giving her his best wet-cat, sorry look, he tried to appear both miserable and apologetic at the same time. He chewed every morsel twice as many as times as he knew he needed, nursing his plate for nearly a full hour.

It was time for bed when his mother took his plate to the sink, frowning. "Well, that was one of the most painful evenings we've had around here in a long time, but right now it's bedtime," she said.

Could he really be so lucky? It was difficult to contain his excitement as he hurried off to his room. He hoped he didn't appear too joyful as he pulled the covers up to his chin.

His mother looked at him with a half-smile, but then grew serious. His heart sank.

"Jason, you know you have to come right away when you're called. I realize you love digging up the property, but I have to know you're safe. I can't allow you to disappear out back if you can't show you can be responsible. If you say you'll be back by a certain time, you have to be. That's our agreement."

Jason nodded, afraid of what was coming.

"You said you'd play safe and check in regularly. That didn't happen today, and I was worried sick."

The lecture lasted so long Jason felt as if a spanking would've been less painful. When he could hold his eyes open no longer, his mother kissed him good night. She hadn't probed him at all. He fell asleep with mixed emotions. Although she hadn't asked where he'd been, Jason felt as if he'd lied.

CHAPTER THREE

Jason woke to a throbbing pain. His leg felt as if a knot had been tied in it and massaging it didn't seem to help. He pulled down his pajama pants to get a better look. The bruise was big and black. Where the rock had impacted hardest, the skin had been scraped away. Yesterday it was red. Today it reminded him of the road rash he got once when he crashed his bike in the driveway last year. He remembered that afterward, his mom had picked gravel out of the wounds for the better part of the day. His new injury combined a deep bruise pain with the searing sting of a scrape. Jason eased out of bed and dressed. He went about the house hoping he gave no sign of the pain he felt.

When the day was finally over, he got ready for bed, glad to be off his feet. As he undressed, he discovered his pants had stuck to his scrape. It took several painful minutes of wincing at every small advance before he finally got his pants off, his pajamas on and was able to crawl into bed. Was this how it felt to be old, he wondered.

***

During the following week, he stayed close to the house. His mother had demanded it and he was happy to oblige. She'd given him numerous chores to do, and the time allowed his bruise to heal and the scrape to turn into a scab. It also gave her time to restore a little of her faith in him.

Two weeks after the accident, Jason reexamined his buttocks. The scab had fallen away leaving a bright pink patch. It wouldn't be long before that skin would match the rest. Today would be the day. After breakfast, he would gather the courage to ask his mother's permission to leave the house. With any luck, she would end his sentence.

Once he had eaten, disappointment gripped him as she found other chores for him to do. He finished those and wandered around the house trying to work up the nerve to ask when it suddenly occurred to him how silly his fears were. What was the worst that could happen? She could say no, and he would be no worse off. At present, he was only prolonging his punishment by doing nothing. Jason found his mother in the living room. "Mom, I'm really sorry I didn't listen. I was wondering if I can go outside."

Without looking up, she said, "One hour."

He knew she expected he'd stay in his designated area. She was more concerned that he proved he was okay on a regular schedule of her choosing. He wanted to be good, but in this case, he had only one hour of freedom. He grabbed a few things, a flashlight among them, and disappeared through the back door.

At the fence, the smell of decaying flesh filled the air. Peering down into the hole, the entire force of the foul stench hit him full in his face. He held his breath and slipped down the annihilated slide.

At the bottom, he made the mistake of inhaling. Coughing and gagging, he ran to the beach where he took deep cleansing breaths of fresh air. Clearing his nostrils, he debated how to deal with his new discovery. There were only two options: to explore or not to explore, and leaving the cave unexplored wasn't a choice he could consider.

He ran back to the house. As the screen door banged behind him, he called to his mom, "Just grabbing some things from my room," then slipped into his bedroom. He rummaged through his dresser until he found a T-shirt. He took it by the collar and snapped it out, then folded it lengthways three times and placed it over his nose and mouth as a test. Hopefully that would keep some of the stink at bay.

In order to keep his mother from seeing the extra T-shirt, he slipped it on over the one he was already wearing. No need to draw unnecessary attention to himself and invite an interrogation. He zipped out of the house once more, waving as he passed by the kitchen window. His mom gave him a look of warning, so he yelled, "I'll be back on time. I promise!" and then disappeared around the side of the house.

At the slide, he tore the T-shirt off and wrapped it around his mouth and nose. He took a few deep sample breaths. *Better. Much better.* He controlled his descent using his feet as brakes. Bypassing the gaping hole, he touched down at the bottom and rushed out to the beach. He ripped the shirt from his face and breathed the fresher air. A nearly imperceptible breeze from the ocean seemed to push the bad air up the slide like a chimney, which could explain why the stench was so powerful on the topside. Now that he was standing downwind, he could barely detect the smell from the cave.

After he'd recovered, he rummaged through his pack until he found his flashlight. He rewrapped the T-shirt around his face and then returned to the hole. Since his last visit, the water that'd once been trapped underground flowed unrestricted through the entrance, eroding the embankment. Although it had taken a chunk out of his slide, one positive aspect was that the newly formed stream had improved the access and reduced the water level. Jason stepped around the little creek and poked his head inside. Even with the T-shirt over his face, the smell was almost unbearable. He flipped the switch on the flashlight and aimed it inside. Eons of subterranean water had washed away the rock, forming a cavern over a meter high. It stretched so far back he couldn't see where it ended. Nothing within the reach of his beam could be given credit for the stench.

In addition to the rotten smell, there was a musty odor. It was the sour kind that comes from soil that never has a chance to dry—a damp, swampy smell. But there was more. Jason's imagination began to take control. Frantically, he backed out of the hole, scrambled up the slide, and, for the second time that day, ran home without looking back.

When he came through the door, his mother greeted him. Sounding surprised, she said, "Hey, you're back earlier than you were supposed to be."

"I just got bored," he said, hoping she'd chalk his early arrival up to him trying to make a good impression. Thankfully, she let him disappear into his room without question.

He closed his bedroom door and rolled onto his bed. Staring at the ceiling, he let all the possibilities of his new discovery run through his mind. What could be in there? Maybe there was a pirate's treasure, or an underground city. Was there an immense maze of tunnels that, once mapped, he'd find went on forever? What was the best way to go about exploring this new discovery? He might need string just in case he needed to retrace his steps. He would need fresh batteries for his flashlight. He lay there letting his imagination lead him where it would, and his list grew and grew.

CHAPTER FOUR

Before he fell asleep, Jason had come up with a plan for exploring the cave. He'd closed his eyes, but that seemed to give power to his imagination. At some unknown point, his consciousness abdicated, and he dreamed of the treasures he'd find.

***

Jason awoke early, excited. After he finished his chores and morning studies, he put a few supplies into his backpack, including a coat, rubber boots, an extra pair of socks, a knife, his flashlight, and a ball of twine. He found his mother in the living room tending the garden. "Can I go outside for a little while?" he said, tugging a carrot from a flowerpot and brushing the dirt off.

"Where are you off to?"

"Just exploring," he said with a shrug. "Nothing too interesting." *Will the lies ever end?*

"Don't be long."

At the beach, he emptied his pack onto the sand. Underground, it would be cold and wet. He slipped on the extra socks and rubber boots, and donned his jacket. He folded his T-shirt into several layers, converting it into a facemask and tied it around his nose and mouth. He held his ball of string in one hand and the flashlight in the other. With the empty pack on his back and flashlight on, he crept through the opening.

Inside, the ceiling was low, but at the highest point Jason found he could stand up with a few centimeters to spare. The ceiling arced to the floor, creating sides of solid stone. He reached up and put a hand on the rock. Although water wasn't dripping from it, the stone was wet and cold. He peered around the grotto and noticed the high-water marks. They were much lower than he thought they'd be. Apparently, the water hadn't built up enough pressure to flow through the front of the cave. That could be possible if there were other places the water could escape. Now that it could flow in its old bed, the stream had reclaimed its original path, which was the most direct route to the ocean.

Jason stepped across the uneven surface, taking care to keep his weight over his feet. After a complete investigation, it was obvious that the main cavern had no secrets to share and provided no explanation as to the source of the stench. However, he did notice a small fissure at the rear of the cave near the floor. He took one end of the ball of string, formed a loop, and tied it around the stone at the entrance.

He crept along with string in one hand and the flashlight in the other. As the ball unwound, it spun in his hand. He tried adjusting his grip but found that unraveling the string with one hand involved cradling the twine rather than gripping it. When he was no more than halfway to the back of the cavern, he dropped the ball of twine in the water. He reached down to retrieve it. The water was icy cold, and pain shot into his wrist. It was much colder than he had anticipated and now he was happy he'd brought the jacket. Although his excitement and fear were nearly overwhelming, he forced himself to slow down and be more careful.

He walked uphill to the back of the cavern. At the crack in the wall, he got on his knees. The channel was tiny and dipped down into the darkness before turning up hill again. Jason could see no farther than a meter or two into the dark. Giving his head a nod, he thought, *there's nothing left to do but hunker down and start crawling.*

He wriggled into the gap and began the short descent. The passage narrowed even more before it turned sharply upward. He realized his predicament after it was too late. He couldn't arch his back enough to continue on his stomach. Having come into the tunnel downhill and headfirst made backing up impossible. To make matters even worse, the empty pack had caught on the close rocky ceiling. Feeling claustrophobic, he panicked. He couldn't breathe. It was impossible to move forward, and he couldn't wriggle back.

Jason took a deep, calming breath, then another, even though the smell made him feel like vomiting.

He'd have to leave the pack behind. And now that he thought about it, the coat hadn't been such a good idea, either. In this close space and working so hard, he had begun to sweat.

As panic took hold again, his frustration grew. Rational thought was fleeing, but then something his mother told him came to mind. *Whenever you're doing something really difficult, slow down and think. Just take your time. Frustration only makes things worse.* There'd been countless times this little saying had helped him.

He closed his eyes and began to relax. Getting out of the pack proved more difficult than he expected. He couldn't maneuver to get his arms free. But being calmer allowed him to let his mind mull over the problem. There was another way to get the pack off. There were adjustment straps against his chest. The straps could be shortened or lengthened so the pack could be adjusted to fit just about anyone. The clips could slip right off the ends of the straps. Jason rolled an eighth of turn to one side then pulled back and up on the clasp. The strap slipped through and cleared the end of the fastener. He rolled to the other side and repeated the process, which left the pack laying loosely on his back.

He wriggled until the pack lay next to him. The added freedom helped to ease his feeling of claustrophobia. As he lay on the cold stone, his breathing slowed, and he was surprised by how quickly his body began to cool down. Rather than remove his jacket, he zipped it up, reducing the chance it might catch on any a sharp outcropping of some kind. From now on, he would anticipate problems and do his best to avoid any other silly mishaps.

Given the extra space, he was able to roll onto his back and wiggle to the bottom of the dip. From there, he inched his way up the embankment, pushing with his feet. Progress was slow, particularly because he could see nothing but the rock just centimeters from his face. The darkness and his fear made thinking clearly difficult. Earlier, he had imagined a leisurely stroll as he walked down high passages in search of his underground city. Now he realized almost anything, except a smaller passage, would have been better than his current reality. Here he was, making his way forward, not knowing whether the passage would eventually become impassable or end abruptly.

After ascending a couple of meters along the channel, it began to level out and, to his relief, enlarge, which allowed him to roll over once more and look ahead into the dark. He shone his flashlight into the black. The passage continued on for some distance in much the same way with no evidence when—or if—it would end.

Jason looked back. The light from outside had disappeared altogether. He felt as if he were in a tomb. He turned his thoughts forward and commando-crawled through the tiny channel. Even if he'd wanted to, there wasn't enough room to turn around. Forward was his only option.

He continued on for another thirty meters until the passage suddenly opened into a large subterranean chamber where he could stand. Small pools of water were scattered about the floor. He was sure he had come up hill, but, even so, if he were near sea level, the incoming tide could flood the chamber. He should hurry.

Here, the stench was even stronger. He searched the cavern for the source. Beginning at his feet and moving his flashlight beam from one side to the other across the floor, he illuminated every centimeter. The first few passes revealed nothing that could explain the smell, but about ten meters in front of him and to his right, he saw something yellowish white. Was it a pile of bones? That would account for the smell, but bones! Jason's fears grew. If they were bones, who or what had died down here?

Afraid to move closer, Jason examined the heap from where he stood. The longer he studied it, the surer he was he'd found a corpse.

The bones were too large for a dog or cat and too small to be a cow or horse. His stomach lurched. He lifted his T-shirt mask to spit bile onto the ground. What animal was larger than a wolf and smaller than a cow? There seemed to be only one possibility. The bones must be human. Someone had taken refuge in here before the front of the cave collapsed.

A strange weakness began in his ankles and climbed up his thighs and into his stomach. Jason fell to his hands and knees on the cold rock and vomited. For several minutes, he remained crouched on all fours, spitting the acidic taste from his mouth. Each time he thought his stomach was empty, a new wave of nausea surged. When the sensation seemed to have passed, he leaned back on his knees in the dark, still too afraid to move. He glanced down at his watch. His mother would expect him back soon. If there was some other explanation for the mystery of the bones, kneeling on the cold black rock would not provide it. He needed to examine the corpse. If he didn't do it now, he might not have the courage to return. Jason stood and moved closer to the decaying heap.

Upon closer inspection, he could identify at least three separate forms, one larger and two much smaller. A mother and her children? Jason vomited again, spit, and then took another step forward. He had no desire to touch the mass and wished he'd brought his stick.

Two steps more placed him directly over the corpses. Besides the bones, something else littered the floor. Whatever it was, was black and lacked the luster of the surrounding stone. Jason prodded at it with a toe. Immediately, relief flooded over him. What he had supposed were human corpses lay in a pile of black fur. These were animals! Bears were the only species Jason knew of that resembled people in terms of size and bone structure. It was also the only animal that would take such a place as a winter shelter. It was less of a sad story, but still tragic. Jason liked to think of himself as brave, and he regretted that his fear had prevented him from seeing what was now obvious. He did not like jumping to conclusions and, now that he considered it further, to think that a mother and two infants would come into this cave when there was a perfectly good home directly above them, seemed ridiculous.

He pondered a more reasonable scenario. The winter of the mudslide, this bear must have come down here to hibernate. She gave birth during the cold winter months, but with no way out, all three had died alone and in the dark. He could never know if these were the actual events, but at least it was a viable explanation.

With his curiosity satisfied, Jason worked his way around the outside perimeter of the cavern. He examined the walls. There were at least half a dozen openings of various sizes leading deeper, away from the ocean. Some disappeared into the darkness, and others were no more than shallow hollows only a meter or so deep. In numerous places, debris had fallen from above.

He tried to imagine his position underground in relationship to what lay above. He shone his light toward the ceiling. Dripping water created a gentle percussive symphony. He wondered, if there was silence would he be able to hear his mother moving around in the house above?

Jason glanced at his watch. It was time to get back. After one last look around, he crawled back through the fissure.

Getting out turned out to be much easier than getting in. Where the tunnel narrowed and turned down hill, Jason rolled onto his back and slid backward down the little hill. When he reached the bottom, he used his feet to push himself up the embankment and into the first chamber. He crossed the cavern and exited through the hole in the slide.

After a few minutes, he was back home. He slipped into the house and snuck into his bedroom. He stripped out of his dirty clothes before going in search of his mother. As fascinated as he was with his find, he would never be able to tell her about the caves beneath the house. Sometimes he wished he had just one friend his age with whom he could share his adventures.

CHAPTER FIVE

"Jason, it's time to get up," his mom called from the other side of the bedroom door.

Jason groaned.

"None of that, now. Your school day starts in forty-five minutes, so get cleaned up and have some breakfast."

Jason rolled over and rubbed his eyes. He hated weekdays. It meant he would have to suffer through his mother's version of school. Sometimes it felt impossible to understand the point of it all. It wasn't like he was training for a job or anything. *I before E except after C. Ain't isn't a word. If x minus five equals three, x equals eight. Yeah, yeah, yeah.*

Jason knew she'd check on him again in five minutes or so, and, if he delayed, she'd first reduce the amount of time to get ready and, after that, she'd extend his school day. She never wavered, and Jason knew today would be no exception. Reluctantly, he rolled out of bed.

Just as he was tying his shoes his mother peeked in again.

"Oh, good. You're almost ready." She smiled. "I promised myself if you got up right away, I'd make today a special one. I'm kind of excited myself. Hurry up now. I have a surprise for you."

"What is it?"

She smiled, leaving him to wonder. "I'll tell you at breakfast, but you have to hustle. You wouldn't want to have to eat breakfast cold."

One of the staples from their little farm was eggs from their small flock of chickens, who could feed on grass for the better part of the year, and provided most of the protein in their diet. Jason sat down to a plate of scrambled eggs and hash browns. His mom sat beside him.

"So, how about a field trip today? It seems like we've been trapped in this compound for weeks. I think we should get outta here for a little while, have a break. What do you think?"

"Really?" Any escape would be welcome. Jason couldn't contain himself. He leaned forward and shoveled down bite after bite.

"It's settled then. When you're finished here, we'll get going."

Jason helped put the dishes in the sink and looked outside at the weather. Storm clouds had gathered, but that didn't always mean rain. He dressed for the possibility and was ready to go before his mother had finished in the kitchen. "Hurry up, Mom. Maybe we'll find something awesome today," he said, hoping she'd go a little faster. "Where are we going? The sporting good store? The grocery store? A car lot?"

There were no actual car lots in the small town, but there was one place on the way that was packed with old cars. Sometimes Jason could find small treasures under the seats and or in the glove compartments. He had a small coin collection, and most of the coins had come from there.

"Well, a wrecking yard doesn't really qualify as an educational outing," said his mother, ruffling up his hair. "There's really no point wandering around through a bunch of junkers that will never run again."

Jason shrugged. He enjoyed playing there nonetheless. "So where're we going, then?" he said, closing the door behind them.

"The library."

"The library?"

"It's the best kind of field trip. I need some more school supplies. Gotta keep my little genius challenged, you know."

"I don't even like school, and it's 'I have to' not 'I gotta,'" he said, gently correcting her. "Can't we do something else?" Jason kicked a stone into the grass.

Tate laughed. "Mind your manners, now. You can find something entertaining to do while we're there and maybe we'll check out the car lot later. Can you live with that?"

Jason grumbled. He liked to wander around dreaming about the 1996 Ford F-150 4X4. His mom said it was the last year of an ugly body style, but Jason liked the idea of putting whatever he liked in the box and hauling it anywhere he wanted. It didn't matter, though. There was no way he'd ever be able to get it running. At least he could dream.

The library was an unassuming, short, single-story building with a weathered sign on the front door stating its purpose. It was unlocked and had been since his mom broke into it a couple of years earlier. It would have been dark inside except that the entire front wall was made up mostly of large windows. She'd tried to turn the lights on, but the city must have shut the power off to save money or something like that. When she had found the breaker box, all the switches were already in the on position.

His mom would collect books from the dark corners then bring them into the light to see if they were what she was looking for. It would probably take her hours. Jason kicked at a table and wandered into the dark, running his fingers over the spines of books lined up on the shelves. Maybe in the periodical section or the kid's section he could find an old comic to read.

He made his way into the dark where it became necessary to stop every now and again to allow his eyes to adjust. In the far reaches of the library, he found the section he was most interested in. It was almost pitch-black, but by feeling for materials that resembled the flimsy

sort of paper comic books were generally made from, he finally found
what he hoped he was looking for. He filled his arms and made his
way to the light.

He found an empty table next to the window and laid his finds in
the sun. They weren't the comics he'd hoped for. They were something
else: some sort of periodical made of low-quality paper. Instead of staples, one sheet was folded into another. Newspapers. Dang! He'd
found a stash of old papers with *Vancouver Sun* printed in large letter-
ing across the top of the first page. The first one was dated April 7,
2022. On the front page was a photo of a huge crowd of people standing, supposedly on some street in Vancouver. It looked like they were
fighting amongst themselves. There were three distinct groups of people in the picture. The most obvious cluster was a group who were
running and screaming, breaking windows with sticks and rocks. A
second group were uniformed men carrying clear plastic shields,
wearing helmets and wielding clubs. A third was made up of forms
laying at the feet of those who were still standing. Jason couldn't tell
whether these people were alive or not, but the headline made things
clear: Robson Street Riot Claims Thirty.

Although the image was shocking, Jason had never seen so many
people in one place before. As he flipped through the pages, one question became more prominent than any other. *Where are all the people
now?* He'd have to ask his mother later. Jason tucked the newspaper,
and a few others, into his jacket, then returned to the rear of the library, hoping this trip would yield a few comic books.

As he felt around, he heard his mother call, "Are you about ready
to go?"

He gathered what he could and made one last trip to the light, then
they stepped once more into the street.

The sky had gotten darker. His mother looked up. "I think we're
going to have to save the outing to the car lot for another day. I don't
want to risk getting these books wet. Will you be okay with that?"

Jason had treasures of his own to protect so he didn't mind. The
walk back to the house couldn't be over soon enough. He helped his
mom through the door then hurried to his room where he unloaded
his stash onto his bed. With luck, his mother would be too engrossed
in her own interests to begin school.

Jason pulled open an old newspaper, allowing the images to capture his attention. Even the advertisements were interesting. Again, he
was struck by the sheer number of people. There were pictures of
burning buildings and overturned trucks. Another photo depicted a
group of people holding placards. Some of the signs had sayings like
Protect Our Jobs and It's Now or Never. Jason didn't know if he

agreed with that last one. After all, there was always hope, wasn't there?

There were pictures of products boasting slashed prices. Money was something Jason didn't fully understand. His mother had tried to explain it using tokens and an old Monopoly game. He couldn't imagine a time when he'd ever need to worry about it.

His thoughts turned to the town they lived in. So many buildings were abandoned with broken windows. There were a few stores he and his mother frequented that still … well, had stores. It was in these shops where his mother renewed the supplies that she used to grow the plants and purify the water. These were hardware stores. The one remaining department store was where his mother could get cloth and clothing. Sooner or later, though, there'd be nothing left.

Jason continued to flip through the pages until he reached the last section, where he found a series of comics. Since he hadn't been lucky enough to find actual comic books at the library, he savored these. He especially liked Garfield. He'd never had a pet before and wondered what it might be like to have a cat of his own. He sure wouldn't want one like Garfield, though.

Turning the final leaf did not render the newspaper useless. He flipped it over and started from the beginning, rereading the headlines and taking more time to process the stories. Most of them had an accompanying picture. The more important ones were in bigger print.

It didn't take long for him to tire of it, however. Most of the articles seemed like isolated incidents. Some of them were stories caught in the middle: an ongoing investigation of Premier So-and-so, or forest workers continuing to demonstrate in front of the parliament buildings. Other articles matter-of-factly stated that certain events had taken place. Such and such apartment burned down, or this or that person was found in an alley behind a downtown pub. The articles were about problems Jason couldn't understand, people he didn't know, in a time that didn't exist. He laid the paper down beside his bed and rolled to stare at the ceiling. He was still thinking about all that he'd read when his mother called him for dinner. He ate his meal in silence and afterwards helped with dishes. Then he got ready for bed, feeling confident his mother appreciated his efforts. He crawled under the covers and flipped open another newspaper.

***

Once the evening dishes were out of the way, Tate piled her books onto the kitchen table. Jason had already disappeared into his room. For the first hour, Tate was grateful for the opportunity to delve into her reading, but as more and more time slipped by, the more discon-certing his absence became. Normally, he would've come in chattering about what he'd found or something he'd seen. He'd have questions to ask. "What's this, Mom? Did you know about this? Isn't this neat?" She wondered what was going on.

The hour had grown late. Yawning, Tate rose. On her way to her room, she peeked in on Jason. A newspaper lay on the floor next to him, but he appeared to be asleep. Tate dismissed her worries and went to her room. Tomorrow, if Jason was still quieter than normal, she'd try to find out what was on his mind. She pulled the covers around her and closed her eyes. She slept and dreamed of a time long past—a time the world would never see again.

***

The morning sun rose, and the light shining through the window woke Jason. He found his mom tending the garden. She knelt before one of the many flower beds humming some old song Jason had heard over and over again. It was her favorite. "Mom?" He held out the newspaper with the story about the parliament building on the cover.

She turned on her knees to take it from him, and began to read.

"Mom, where are all the people?"

Her eyes suddenly grew wide and rolled back in her head. She slumped to the floor.

Jason staggered back in fright. His first thought was that she'd had a heart attack or maybe a burst aneurism. He'd read somewhere about a woman who suddenly dropped to floor like that. She died.

"Mom? Mom!

He knelt beside her and wrapped his arms around her. "Mom, Mom, Mom," he whispered over and over, tears streaming down his face. With his head pressed against her chest, he noticed it was rising and falling. She was breathing! He eased her head onto the floor, jumped up and ran to the kitchen. From the counter he grabbed a cloth and from the fridge, he took a pitcher of chilled water. He poured wa-ter onto the cloth and raced back to her side. She lay with one leg folded beneath her. If she were kneeling upright, it would have been under her buttocks. Jason helped to straighten her and reached for a sofa pillow to put under her head. He applied the cloth to her forehead and silently prayed she'd be okay.

***

Tate came to and found herself laying on the floor, with a damp cloth on her forehead and a couch pillow under her head. Jason knelt close by; the worried look on his face made him almost unrecognizable.

"Mom, are you okay?"

Tate didn't respond at first. Her gaze circled the room as she tried to reorient herself. She struggled to remember what she'd been doing. When she did, she burst into tears.

"What's the matter? Why are you crying?" said Jason, concern coloring every word.

Tate wanted to respond, but her body was heaving, and she was shaking so badly she couldn't speak. For reasons she couldn't fathom, she couldn't staunch the flow of tears.

Eventually, she did begin to calm down and she struggled to her feet. She used the coffee table first and then the wall for support as she made her way to the sofa. Once there, she beckoned Jason to sit beside her.

When he had joined her, she said, "Jason, why would you ask me such a question?" Her eyes were burning and wet with tears.

At first, he met her gaze. She wanted him to know she was ready to hear anything, but he turned his eyes to the floor.

"I found some old newspapers when we were at the library yesterday," he began.

"I know," said Tate, hoping he heard her encouragement.

"We never see anyone, but there are empty houses everywhere. I guess I never really thought about it before. We don't really know anyone. This can't be the way it always was."

The words seemed to pour out of him, and Tate let him speak. He started with the stories in the papers, but once he got going, he was unable to stop. He told her about the pictures of the hundreds of people fighting, of the demonstrations and the accidents.

When he had finished talking about the newspapers, he went on to tell her about the cave and the beach; he told her about the tunnels. In horror, Tate listened, torn by guilt. After all her efforts to ensure his safety, Jason had still found ways to find danger. As he finished, Tate said nothing. There was nothing she could say. Her negligence could have led to his death.

"You're not mad?" said Jason.

"I'm disappointed. I wish you would've told me you found a way down to the beach. I wish I'd been more careful. Why didn't you say anything before?"

"I was bored, and you would've made it off limits. I can't go anywhere as it is."

Tate sat quiet for a long time. Her eyes felt deep-set and hollow. In the morning, when she looked in the mirror, she could see deep lines etched in her face. She had always tried to remain positive and not let Jason see her concern. She was still too young to be considered aged; the deep lines were caused from worry. They were caused by the way she tensed her muscles at night when Jason was sleeping. They appeared on her face just before mealtime when he was nowhere to be seen and he hadn't answered her call. They came in secret, in the darkness of the night or in the gray light of the hardware store, when she probed around looking for things she'd run out of. Jason rarely got to see what made them but, at this moment, she feared he'd hardly recognize the old lady sitting beside him.

Inside, she struggled, but eventually she turned toward him. "Son, I think you're old enough to know." Taking a deep, shaky breath, she related the story of her childhood and her premature induction into adulthood.

CHAPTER SIX

Tate's Story

Eight-year-old Tatyanna Masterson stood in front of the stove helping her mother with lunch. She stirred the tomato soup while her mother made tuna fish sandwiches. As her mother cut the last sandwich, she said, "That should be good. Go and get the boys for lunch, would you, Tate?"

Tate sighed with the melodramatic quality reserved for eight-year-olds. Then, without leaving the stove, she shouted, "Michael! David! Lunch time!"

"Tate," her mom scolded, "if I wanted you to yell, I could've done it myself."

Tate scowled and trudged off in search of her brothers. They weren't in their rooms, so she went outside.

Her grandfather would never have considered their small plot of land a farm, but they had a barn with a few animals, and her mother had room for a garden. Tate heard a commotion coming from inside the barn. By the sounds of it, the boys were in the loft playing. After covering about half the distance, she stopped and called, "Michael! David! It's lunchtime! Mom says to hurry!" She didn't wait to see if they'd answer. She returned to the kitchen and sat down at the table.

"Did you find them?"

"They were in the barn, playing," said Tate.

"Are they coming?"

"I told them to hurry," said Tate.

"Did they hear you?"

"I yelled."

"Oh my gosh, Tate," said her mom.

Her mom sounded impatient. But then again, she always sounded impatient.

"I asked you to go get them."

"If they want to eat, they'll come." *What's she always so worried about, anyway?*

Two boys came running into the house.

"See?" said Tate, making a sing-songy sound. It was the first Monday of summer vacation. What was all the fuss about?

The boys sat down at the table and waited in their seats while mom brought the soup from the stovetop to the table.

Tate's father appeared at the door. He was home early, and Tate was happy to see him.

***

Several weeks later, with Employment Insurance having run out and the city's population up in arms about the lack of jobs, James Masterson joined the hordes protesting in Victoria, the province's capital.

The following week, the late James Masterson was buried in a cemetery a few blocks from his home just outside the city of Vancouver, British Columbia. If one looked closely at the story on the front page of the Vancouver sun the previous week, Masterson could be seen among the hundreds of protestors laying on the trampled grass in front of the parliament buildings. His name appeared in the same paper in small print in an obituary column that had begun to double in size weekly.

***

Camelia Masterson sat alone in the one room she was comfortable in: the kitchen. The sun had long since set, and Tate, Michael, and David had been asleep for an hour or more, but Camelia was wide awake. Lately, she'd come to hate her bedroom. Her bed was empty and unwelcoming since James had died. The world was falling apart. When she'd attended university, she'd taken what they often called doom and gloom classes. There were predictions that by the year 2070, considering the rate of population growth, the use of fossil fuels, and the pollution of the atmosphere, the world would forfeit its ability to sustain human life on the existing scale. Simply put, people would die. She had hated those courses. They were pessimistic and uninspiring. That was back when she attended university, and everyone knew her as Cam Rusnak, years before she married James. It was during a time when raising a family seemed the most natural thing to do.

Camelia listened as rain pounded on the roof. Now, she felt only regret. She'd been irresponsible when she decided to bring three children into this godforsaken world. Her husband's death had been a harbinger and just the first of a series of tragedies. Following the massive rise in unemployment, the government had been unable to support the jobless and was forced to renege on all insurance programs and social assistance.

Long before unemployment reached a staggering forty-eight percent, businesses began to fold. To recuperate some of what would be lost, retailers offered their products at prices too low to fathom. While luxury items could be had for pennies on the dollar, the cost of necessary goods and services skyrocketed. The price of fossil fuels doubled overnight. Electric companies quickly followed suit. The entire world became locked in a deadly downward economic spiral.

As people's needs rose, so did their discontent. Riots and looting became common occurrences. Unable to survive the recession, some business owners abandoned their buildings, which were then ransacked and eventually emptied.

If anyone could be counted among the lucky ones, Camelia was one of them. Perhaps luck was not the best word to use. She'd been aware of the predictions. Early on, she could tell where things were heading. Following her husband's death, she began to stock up. She filled her house with every kind of non-perishable food she could find.

Now, the months had slipped by. Camelia sat at the kitchen table while, outside, the winter rain poured down. The world raged. And, regardless of her planning and preparation, her family had begun to starve.

She couldn't have guessed how dependent they'd become on the rest of the world for so many essential goods. With transportation systems at a standstill, nothing had come into the city. Every day, the streets were becoming increasingly violent, and food had become impossible to find.

Camelia contemplated the rain beating down on the roof. In the dark and dreary winter season, the drops seemed as unyielding as the fear in her heart. Wiping away her tears, she rose from her chair. She passed by the sliding glass doors to the patio and glimpsed her image. Her clothes hung like drapes, hiding her shapeless form beneath. Camelia trudged down the hall to her bedroom.

***

Tate came into the kitchen. The house had grown quiet since her father had died. Tate's heart was like broken china. Her mother must feel the same.

She found her mom standing at the counter dishing out three bowls from an open can of chili. "Who's not eating?" asked Tate.

Camelia turned and smiled, the edges of her lips barely rising. "Can you go and find your bothers, please?" she said, her voice no more than a whisper.

Her mother seemed to be withering away. All at once, Tate understood why she looked so thin. "I'll be right back," she said, as she went in search of Michael and David. She was almost to the door when she heard a loud thump from behind her. She spun to see her mother laying in a heap on the floor. Tate ran to her side calling out as she went,

"Michael! David! Come quick."

She was laying across her mother's still form, sobs wracking her body, when she heard Michael's voice.

"Tate, what's the matter?"

In the time it took to ask the question, David pulled her away. "Is she going to be okay?" said Tate, wiping at her tear streaked face.

Michael, the oldest, knelt on the floor and laid his head on his mother's chest.

Tate screamed, "Didn't you hear me? Is she going to be okay?"

David wrapped his arms around Tate and pulled her to his chest. "Shhh. You need be quiet, so Mike can listen and try to figure out what's going on."

Tate whimpered.

Michael sat back. "Dave, give me a hand, will you? We need to get her to her room."

"Mom's going to be fine, Tate. I need to give Mike a hand," said David, pushing himself up. "Can you get a glass of water?"

Tate did as she was asked and, trying not to spill, followed Michael and David into the bedroom.

Together, the boys laid their mother on the bed. Tate placed the water on the nightstand beside her.

"She needs to rest," said Michael. "Come on. Let's leave her alone."

Tate hesitated.

"Tate, let's go. Mom needs her rest," said David.

Tate let her mom's fingers slip from her hand and followed her brothers back to the kitchen.

Michael was the first to speak. "I know you guys are hungry. I know I sure am. But we should save the chili for Mom when she wakes up. What do you think?"

Tate nodded, her eyes locked on Michael. David hadn't said anything, so she assumed he agreed. She found plastic wrap in the cupboard, scooped the chili into a dish and stretched plastic over the top. With spoon and bowl in hand, she returned to her mother's bedside, where she sat next to the bed and waited.

Several hours later, Tate woke to the sound of a moan. Suddenly alert, she sat up. "Mom?"

"Tate?"

"Yes, Mom. I'm here. I have some chili for you."

"Tate, you're sweet, but I don't feel like eating."

"Something to drink at least?" said Tate, helping her mom to sit up. With one arm around her mom's shoulder, she offered support as her mother took tiny sips.

Once more, Tate's heart was breaking. Beneath her mother's clothes, she could feel her bones. Her mother weighed almost nothing.

"Can you sit on your own?"

Her mother nodded.

Tate peeled the plastic from the bowl and dipped the spoon into the cold mush. She wished she could warm it, but there was nothing she could do about that. "Here mom. Try to eat a little. We saved some chili for you."

Taking a small part of the spoonful into her mouth, she rolled it around, tasting it, then swallowed.

Tate offered the spoon once more, but her mother put a hand up, waving her away.

"Mom, you have to eat something," said Tate.

"I'll try," she said, her voice crackling, "but I feel a little sick right now."

"A little more water?"

The edges of her mom's lips rose, but as a smile it was a weak and pained attempt.

Tate brought the glass to her mother's lips.

Her mom sipped then waved Tate away with the back of her hand. "I'll be fine, hon. Promise. I just need to rest now."

"But, Mom, I want to stay. I don't want to leave you."

"You'd only be watching me sleep. Why don't you go and see if the boys need any help?"

Tate nodded. Her mother closed her eyes, which suited Tate just fine. She had no intention of leaving. She eased onto the floor, her back against the mattress, and began her vigil.

A few moments later, her mother's breaths grew long and deep. After a half an hour passed and when she felt certain her mom would remain sleeping, Tate rose and tiptoed out of the room.

CHAPTER SEVEN

David stopped at the kitchen door. Tate sat at the table, coloring. Michael was at the sink. Tate looked up when she saw him.

"Is Mom awake yet?" she said.

David ignored her. He strode passed her and took Michael by the arm. Even though he was the younger, he'd always seemed to be the braver of the two. He hauled Michael through the front door and onto the porch. "Listen, you've gotta tell her. Someone's gotta tell her," David said.

Saying nothing, Michael sat down on the steps and slouched with his head resting on his knees. His shoulders hiccupped.

"What's wrong with you? You're the oldest. Do something!" said David. *Why is Michael so weak? Everything is falling apart and it's supposed to be his job to take over. It was supposed to be his job to be the man of the household*, thought David.

The door creaked, and David knew it was Tate. She put a hand on Michael's shoulder. "What's the matter, Michael? Are you okay?" When Michael didn't answer, she turned to David. "What's the matter with Michael, David?" He didn't answer and, in a moment, he heard her footsteps fade away as she went back into the house.

Michael continued to sit on the floor staring at nothing, despondent. David sat next to him, wondering what to do. Then he heard Tate's voice coming from their mother's room. "Mom, something's wrong with David and Michael. They won't talk to me."

David leapt to his feet and screamed as he tore through the house. Michael was close behind, "Tate, no," David yelled.

David found Tate kneeling at their mother's side, holding her lifeless hand, weeping. He put a hand on her shoulder. "Tate, you can't stay here. Come on," he said.

Tate tore her arm from beneath his hand.

David sighed, then eased onto the floor beside her. He could force Tate out of the room, but that would change nothing. If anything, it would create another problem. And there were already more problems than there were solutions.

David kept watch at the edge of the bed until Tate fell asleep, then he motioned to Michael. They slipped out of the room and convened in the kitchen. Michael sat, but David couldn't settle. "There's nothing left in the house. Why would Mom let this happen?"

Michael did what he always did. He said nothing.

David paced. "Come on, Michael. We've got to do something," he said.

"There's nothing to do," Michael said finally.

David's fury spiked. In a stride, he crossed the room, and, with all his strength, he punched Michael on the side of his face. Michael toppled from the chair, then rose in an instant. Michael was much bigger and more muscular, and David suddenly wondered if he hadn't made a mistake. David raised his arms to protect himself and closed his eyes, but the blow never came. When he dared to look, Michael had already returned to his seat at the table.

"Mike, what's the matter with you?"

Michael rubbed his face. "Just give me a second."

David cringed, expecting his older brother to emerge ready to retaliate, but, at the same time, terrified he wouldn't. David knew he couldn't keep the family going on his own. He had less of an idea what to do than a cat would, but at least a cat likely wouldn't starve.

Michael raised his head. "That was a hell of a punch. Remind me not to tick you off in the future," he said, rubbing the side of his face.

David sighed, relieved. "What should we do?" he said.

"I don't know, but it's all I can think about."

"I've been too pissed off to think about much. I keep wondering what kind of genes we inherited. Our dad the coward or our mother the victim."

"That sounds pretty messed up. Maybe you need to see a counselor," said Michael, smirking.

"Oh, shut up," said David. "I have every right to be mad. Mom and Dad had good educations. Dad going to all those protests was nothing but suicide. And what the hell was Mom thinking, anyway? Did she figure she was doing us a favor by slowly starving herself to death and keeping us out of the loop? Where was the logic in that? And what did she think was going to happen when the food ran out?"

"I don't know, but we aren't any better. We let her take care of us and didn't do anything to help. What does that make us?" said Michael.

"Exactly. We're a couple of lazy idiots, and that might be putting it too nice," said David, standing. He crossed to the sink and filled a glass with water. "Is this it, then? Is this how we're going die?"

"What choice do we have?"

David took a swig and peered out the window at a cat crouching in the grass. "Think of all the animals. There are tons of them that don't even know there's a problem in the world. How is it that they can go on living as if nothing's wrong while we sit here and die as if there's nothing we can do? Does that make any sense at all?" David shook his head, disgusted. "How did mankind rise to the top of the food chain, anyway? We're ridiculous."

Michael nodded. "It's true. I never thought about that before."

"I'm not going to sit around here and do nothing. We live in a city. There's got to be something to eat, somewhere." If his big brother wasn't going to step up and take his role at the head of the house, someone had to. David finished his water and threw a jacket on. "You stay here with Tate while I go and find us something to eat. I'll be back as soon as I can."

"Wait a second, Dave," said Michael. "That's a bad idea. You won't be the only one out there. We won't be the only ones getting desperate."

"What should we do, then?"

"We hide Tate, raid Dad's gun cabinet, and go out together. If we don't stick together, none of us will survive."

David nodded. Michael was right. His big brother was back.

***

The following years were quiet ones for Tate. The boys became breadwinners while she took care of the house. Hiding became her routine. They told her that staying inside was the safest thing to do, so Tate remained behind and waited. Each morning, they left the house, not returning until nearly dark, but they almost always came back with something to eat. They never explained the details of how they provided for her each day, and Tate never asked.

CHAPTER EIGHT

As spring drew nearer, each day the sun rose a little earlier. The days were getting longer, and the winter rains were finally beginning to let up. The previous year had been blessedly uneventful. For Tate, boredom was the flavor of the day. She'd long since lost interest in the old toys she'd once been so fond of. Any dreams she might have had were as distant as the sun seemed in winter.

Tate sat in the breakfast nook overlooking the front yard when she heard a commotion coming from behind the house. Was it the boys? No. It couldn't be. It was much too early for their return. She slipped out of her chair and tiptoed to her bedroom window. She parted the curtains just enough to see out. She counted five people, all dressed in black, their heads shaved bald. Most had multiple piercings, but each of them had a tattoo of a skull on their forehead above the right eye, the symbol of one of the many gangs that terrorized the area. The one who appeared to be the leader was more adorned than the others. He wore matching black leather pants and jacket that included silver studs running up the sleeves to the collar. He wore bright silver gauges in his ears, and rings in his eyebrow, nose, and lower lip. A gold chain connected his lower lip and one of his ears. Tate had seen this group before, but always from a greater distance. She let the curtain close. With her back to the wall, she slid down to the carpet and listened. Sweat began to form on her brow, but her body felt frigid. Her heart drummed in her ears, making it difficult to concentrate.

"What was that? Did you see that?" she heard a male voice say.

"Yeah, something from that room over there," said another.

"Hey, I bet there's someone in there!"

"Let's check it out," said yet another.

It was impossible to tell who was talking. Tate sat, paralyzed. They would come in, and, when they did, they would find her.

Her brothers had told stories about gangs like these. They used them to frighten her enough to make her want to hide. They said they'd do terrible things to her if they found her. The sound of the voices grew nearer. The light from the space between the curtains illuminated a small area on the far wall. As Tate watched, the small strip of light suddenly halved. Someone was standing in front of the window looking into the room. Tate felt sick to her stomach knowing there was only the thickness of the wall separating them. She imagined the window steaming up as he breathed against it. Tate's heart rate doubled. It pounded in her ears. She pulled her knees tighter to her chest.

After torturous moments, the patch of light widened again, and the voices moved around the outside of the house toward the garage. Tate gathered all her willpower and scurried along the floor toward her door and out of the bedroom. In the hall, she rounded the corner and slipped into her parents' bedroom. She darted into the closet, closing the door behind her. Using a box of old clothes and the lower shelf as a stepstool, she scrambled to the top ledge and squeezed into the corner.

A moment later, she could hear the hoodlums rampaging through the house, unconcerned about the noise they made or what they broke along the way. She could hear the leader shouting orders to the others, although she couldn't make out the words. She guessed he was sending them on a scavenger hunt looking for anything that might be of value.

She recognized the voice of the leader, the one dressed in leather. Leather-man made certain every room of the house was searched. A girl's voice came from the room Tate had just been in. "No one's in here!"

"Did you check the closet?"

"Of course, I did. Do ya think I'm green or somethin'?"

Tate pulled her knees closer, trying to make herself even smaller. She was trapped. It would be only a matter of time before someone discovered her. What then? There was nowhere to go.

The racket grew louder as gang members moved through rooms on the second floor. Tate waited, sick with fear. She heard the bedroom door swing on its hinges. She heard sheets rustling on the bed and imagined them being flung aside as someone searched under the bed. There was a grunt. The shower door slammed against the wall as someone combed the en-suite.

Tate knew that whoever was in the room had almost run out of places to look. The closet was the only nook left to search. She shuddered. The door opened, followed by an audible click. The bozo had tried the light switch. Of course, nothing happened. There was no power.

"Son-of-a-bitch." It was the girl's voice.

"What's the matter?" called someone from upstairs.

"Nothing. Just can't see a damn thing in here."

Tate huddled with her face scrunched up and her eyes squeezed into slits. There was more racket as the girl thrashed clothes from one side of the closet to the other. A few moments later, the door slammed hard enough to leave a ringing in Tate's ears.

Yet another disgusted sounding voice rang out from upstairs, "Nothing up here. We should get out of here. This is a friggin' waste of time."

Thank goodness. Tate released her breath as slowly as she could.

The girl hadn't bothered to look up, otherwise she would have seen Tate perched on the top shelf.

Having held the same position for so long, her body had begun to ache; Tate slowly turned so that she could lie on her stomach, hoping to find a more comfortable position. As she turned, a shoebox slipped from the shelf and plummeted toward the floor. Tate snaked her arm out, following the box through its descent. It seemed to tumble in slow motion. Her fingers closed on it just as her arm reached its full extension. Saying a silent prayer of thanks, she hauled the box back up, but as she was about to put it beside her, the top slipped from it and dropped through the air. Tate held her breath, helpless as it tumbled, like a dried leaf in the fall, to the floor. The sound of footsteps coming from the hallway paused. Tate held her breath. After a moment, they moved away, and Tate exhaled.

She'd hoped they would've collected what they wanted and left, but no such luck. From the sound of it, they'd piled their loot in the living room. The hours passed as they sorted through it and then proceeded to horse around. Meanwhile, she lay petrified on the top shelf of the closet. After a while, she lost all concept of time. At some point, she must have fallen asleep, because the next thing she heard was someone calling out her name. Groggy, she rubbed her eyes and listened, then recognized Michael's voice. "I'm in here," she yelled.

David must have been the first to hear her, because she heard his voice next. "Mom's room," he said, his voice frantic.

Tate could hear them racing toward her. By the time they crashed through the door, she'd managed to climb out of the closet, stiff and sore.

Michael would have been a senior in high school and always seemed like a giant to her. With his hands under her arms, he lifted her high in the air. When he let her down, he wrapped her in a tight embrace.

David was a short moment behind. "Tate, thank God you're okay. When we called and you didn't answer right away, we thought they took you."

Michael ruffled her hair, saying, "You must have been scared as hell."

"It wasn't so bad after they finished searching the room. It's a good thing I'm small," she said, smiling. They were still alive and still together. That was the best any of them could hope for.

***

As the months passed, Tate's boredom did not ease. Her brothers had no choice but to spend most of each day foraging, leaving her long, quiet days alone with little to do. The one resource left untouched by the gang was the family's extensive library. There was a large section of storybooks that her mother and father had collected, intended to provide them with reading opportunities. Tate could have picked any one of them, but it was her nature to be systematic.

As she took stock, a tear rolled down her cheek. She'd always kept her room tidy, and her mom had seemed to appreciate that. She wiped her face and her thoughts returned to the library. Her mother had arranged the books for easy access. Tate's books were on the lowest shelf. After all, she was the youngest and the smallest. She chose a book from the leftmost point on her shelf.

One by one, she read each selection. When she had read and reread every one of her books, she began to peruse books selected for the boys. Some titles were specific to their tastes, but that didn't mean Tate wouldn't enjoy them. With nothing but time, her desire to learn became insatiable.

Sometime during her twelfth year, craving for something else to read, Tate began to look at the books her mother and father had collected for themselves. One of the treasures was an ancient set of encyclopedias. They were filled with interesting tidbits of information. Books were wonderful. What's more, her mother and father had cherished them. It made Tate feel closer to them somehow. She could imagine her father sitting beside her on the couch with his arm around her as he read one of the countless fairy tales he had collected. She learned about the environment from her mother's old textbooks. She learned about basic construction and home repairs from her father's do-it-yourself books. There were craft books and first-aid books. Although some of the texts were too difficult to read at first, her knowledge grew quickly, and with it so did her understanding. Before long, she'd mastered them all.

One of her other accomplishments, of which she was particularly proud, was a small selection of plants she had begun to grow inside the house. Most of them were useful for one thing or another. She even had a strawberry plant, which provided a special treat now and again.

Her older brothers continued to leave the house on their daily excursions. Almost every day they returned with something for the small household, along with stories to tell. Mostly, they talked about cruel people who took what they wanted from anyone they pleased. They told about those who would do anything to survive. Tate was never certain the stories they brought home were always about others.

She never knew how they managed to provide for the home. The boys said very little about that. These days, scruples were as scarce as food. It was easier to think of her brothers as valiant princes in the fairy tales she so often read. They were the heroes who would travel to the ends of the earth for their sister, and she for them.

Then one evening, during Tate's eighteenth year, the boys were late. She waited patiently for their return. Night came and still they had not come home. That night she cried herself to sleep wondering where they might be.

CHAPTER NINE

Days passed. Each morning, Tate sat next to the window in the breakfast nook waiting for her brothers' return, and each day when they didn't, her sadness grew. Luckily, most of the plants she'd grown were edible. For the first few days, she relied on them for nourishment, holding up, holding on and hoping. But after a week, she resigned herself to the cold truth and allowed herself to cry. Her grieving lasted for days. She ate little. Her new ritual consisted of going to the front window in hopes that they would arrive just as she pulled the curtains aside. Each day, she coped anew with grief and disappointment.

Although she'd developed a decent enough garden, it wouldn't be enough to sustain her permanently. As weeks slipped by, the lack of food in the house became a matter of survival. Staying would lead to the same fate as her mother's, but what she should do, and, more important, where she should go were as yet unanswered questions.

She'd read books from almost every genre, but she had few practical skills. One morning at sunrise, she filled a backpack with what she considered necessities, walked out the door, and began to make her way west toward the city of Vancouver. Along the way, she passed one vacant house after another. Many, like her own, had the useless carcass of a car parked in the driveway. She looked at a license plate: Beautiful British Columbia. *Maybe, once upon a time,* she thought, sadness pulling at her very soul as she read it.

That night, she made her bed in an abandoned warehouse just outside the city limits, but continuous noise disrupted her sleep. The night was filled with high-pitched screams, explosions, and gunshots. After restless hours and near sunrise, she fell asleep wondering, *What on earth am I doing here? Why did I come to the city?*

Just as in her neighborhood, it was the same everywhere. Most people had moved on. If there were people who had survived, Tate couldn't tell. The only evidence that anyone ever existed was in the refuse that had been left behind. She thought about what Vancouver might have to offer as she looked at each empty backyard. There was only devastation here. A breeze rose, and a screen door began a rhythmic tap in its frame. This was a place people fled from and not a destination at all. One thing was both painful and clear: the City of Vancouver was a place to avoid.

Tate stayed the night in an abandoned house and, upon daybreak, turned north and began to skirt the city. She stayed away from tall buildings as much as she could, fearing they might be havens for gangs.

The sun was high overhead when she heard the metallic hollow sound of a garbage can tip over a short distance away. She did not waste time searching for the sound. Instead, she leapt behind a nearby fence and hid. From around the corner of an adjacent house, a medium sized grayish brown dog sniffed its way in her direction. It lifted its head from the pavement, then saw her. Its ears perked, and it hunkered down on the grass.

The companionship of a dog might be a good thing. A dog could offer protection as well as company, something Tate had begun to crave. She called to it. "Here, doggie. Come on, boy." If the dog remembered having ever having an owner before, it didn't show it. Instead, it stared at Tate, not with the curiosity she hoped to see, but with the look of a wild animal. The dog inched forward, drawing back its lips. Other dogs appeared behind it. Tate trembled. Without warning, and as one, they charged.

Tate leapt to her feet and bolted. She had just enough time to make it to the front door of the nearest house. She threw open the screen door and got behind it. The dogs leapt at the door, slamming Tate between the screen door and the solid wood exterior door behind her. They pawed at the bottom and edges of the screen. She tried the doorknob, but the door was locked. In desperation, she pushed against the window in the center of the door, but her weight alone was not enough to break the glass. She would have to do more than push. Summoning all her strength and courage, she put her back to the screen door and pushed away as far as she dared. With a step between her and the window, she threw her full weight into the glass. It shattered inward, and her body followed the shards into the foyer.

Without her to hold the dogs at bay, they clawed the screen door aside and, in a moment, they were at the main door, leaping at the new opening. Tate staggered to her feet and darted up the stairs with the dogs on her heels. Blood trailed behind her as she ran into an upstairs bedroom. At least the blood might give the dogs a reason to linger. She slammed the door behind her just as one of the dogs smashed into it, yelping and pawing.

Tate collapsed, the carpet turning red beneath her. She pushed herself up, pain tearing into her abdomen. She clawed her way toward the edge of bed. The sleeves of her shirt were soaked with blood, but she hardly noticed. It was her side that screamed at her to stop moving. She used all the strength within her, but she finally reached the edge of the bed. She rolled onto her buttocks and propped herself up against it.

The door rattled against the jamb. For the moment, it kept the dogs in the hall. She examined her blood-stained shirt. Her sleeve was streaked with blood from shoulder to wrist, but the bulk of the pain came from her side. She lifted her arm to examine her injury, wincing at the searing sting as she moved.

Everything had happened quickly. She'd had no time to think or exercise caution. The window hadn't shattered into small, harmless pieces. It had turned the window frame into a gaping mouth full of dagger-sharp teeth. When she'd leapt through the window, she'd cut her arm along with all the minor lacerations. Her torso had followed and most of her weight had landed on the lower sill. A long shard must have been poised vertically there and didn't break off until after it was lodged deep inside her belly.

Tate could see the shard poking through her shirt. She could feel it slicing into her with every movement. Blood loss had already begun to take its toll and she struggled against shock and fear. She wondered if the shard was fairly short or if it would turn out to be so deeply embeddded that it would be lethal. She'd read about bleeding caused by such wounds and knew that when she dislodged the glass, the wound might bleed even worse. There was a very real possibility that she could have what the books termed 'deadly bleeding'. She turned her head to see what kind of bedding might've been left behind. There were no blankets, although a fitted sheet lay stretched across the mattress. Blood oozed from her waist, beginning to pool onto the floor. She was running out of time. She reached behind her to remove the sheet, but the fitted corners proved effective in their design, keeping the sheet securely on the bed. She twisted as much as she could, hoping to make her job easier, but searing pain tore at her from deep inside. Sweat poured from her brow, the pain sapping nearly all her remaining strength.

She struggled for what seemed an eternity. With tears streaming down her cheeks, she managed to remove the sheet from the bed. The bleeding from her side had increased. She eased her shirt up to get a look at the injury. The protruding glass was about three centimeters across, providing just enough of a surface to grip. Thank goodness for that. Mustering all her courage and clamping her jaw tight against the coming onslaught of pain, she grasped the glass between her fingers and thumb. She expected it to slide right out. Instead, her fingers slipped off the slimy surface. She screamed as her hand ripped free, causing a new wave of pain. She'd been sure she used all her strength, but the shard hadn't budged.

The blood-coated glass was too slimy. She needed it to be dry. Taking hold of the sheet, she wrapped it around the exposed glass. She leaned back against the bed, hands trembling. She could still hear the dogs just outside the door. The ruckus seemed to have calmed, but she could hear their paws drumming up and down in the hallway. They hadn't given up yet.

"Focus Tate! Focus! You're bleeding to death," she said aloud. She forced her attention to the piece of glass protruding from her side. She took a deep breath and, with everything she had left in her, she yanked on the glass as hard as she could. It came free and instantly blood began to pour from the wound. She was ready with the bed sheet. Taking the corner, she pressed it firmly onto the cut. The cloth turned red, saturated in a moment. Rather than release the pressure, Tate added more fabric to what she already held against the wound. Using one hand to hold the sheet in place, she removed her belt with the other. She slid it around her back and placed the buckle where she could operate it with one hand. After some fiddling, she managed to place the belt so it would tighten over the wound. She cinched it as tight as she could, managing to buckle the clasp before she slipped into unconsciousness. Even as darkness took her, she was certain she'd been too late.

CHAPTER TEN

When Tate regained consciousness, she couldn't lift her head. She awoke on her side in a congealed pool of blood. She gasped at the gore, which had spread across the floor, then she faded into oblivion once more.

When she woke a second time, she was cold and shivering. Her face felt like ice. *It must be white,* she thought before consciousness left her once more.

It was night and too dark to assess her wound when she awoke for the third time. That was something to be grateful for. She was hungry, but alive, and that was enough for now. She tried to move into a more comfortable position, but the pain that tore into her from her side was enough to convince her to remain still.

Careful to keep her torso stationary, she reached into her backpack and took out some of the provisions she'd stowed there. Afterward a few bites, she tried to contemplate her situation, but her thoughts became random and soon turned into dreams.

During her fourth wakeful period, Tate was vaguely aware of the silence that filled the house. The light coming in through the windows indicated it was probably early morning. She could see now the bleeding had stopped, and her bandaging needed to be changed. She eased the pressure from the belt and removed the sheet. The wound was lightly sealed, and she was careful not to stretch. She dragged the sheet around and dug into her pack for a pocketknife. She removed the blood-soaked portion and discarded it. She cut the remaining part of the sheet into large squares to use as clean dressings when she needed them.

The first of the squares she folded into a smaller pad about eight or so layers thick and placed it over the wound. Then she cinched the belt as tightly as she dared. The remaining fabric, she tucked into her pack. Feeling more confident she could avoid reopening her wound now that the dressing in place, she slid sideways out of the mess she'd been laying in.

After positioning herself as comfortably as she could, she again delved into her pack in search of something to eat. The cuts on her arm were mere scratches compared to her abdominal injury. Since each of them had stopped bleeding on their own, she ignored them. Considering the degree to which they'd already begun to heal, Tate imagined that several days must have passed.

As exhausted as she was, there were still other matters to attend to. Her clothes were matted with blood, and she needed a change of clothes if she hoped to reduce the chance of infection. Although she was afraid of reopening the wound, she knew there would be little here for her if she stayed.

There would likely be no food in the house, but maybe it had some useful items to offer. Warily, she rose to her feet and crept around the room. Whoever had once lived here had departed, leaving the furnishings behind. She searched the closet and the dresser. There were a few pieces of unwanted clothing but all in children's sizes. Inside the closet, the floor and shelf were piled with toys and games. There was even some bedding left behind. Tate realized she'd found sanctuary in a child's room. There was still the rest of the house to explore.

She opened the door a crack and listened. The house was silent. Her bravery grew, and she edged into the hall. The blood that had dripped onto the steps had been lapped clean. Warily, she glanced up and down the hall. The dogs were nowhere in sight and the house remained eerily silent.

She kept to the upper floor, investigating each of the bedrooms in turn. In one, she found some clothes that were a bit too large, but they would have to do. At least they were clean. As carefully as possible, she changed, then added a few pieces to her kit, just in case she had an emergency.

Exhausted, she lay down on one of the beds to rest and consciousness fled.

The light was still bright outside when she woke again, but the gnawing in her stomach suggested it was probably not the same day. There was no way of knowing how much time had passed while she slept. As she moved, she noticed her pain seemed less pronounced, but each step stretched her side to almost the point of bleeding again. She made her way to the top of the stairs and stood overlooking the new obstacle. Each step would bring new agony. The stairs were not insurmountable but getting down them would be excruciating and time consuming. Using the rail, she eased down the steps, being careful to lead with the foot on the same side as her injury. In that way, she managed to keep from stretching her healing wound.

Once at the bottom, she stood for a long time leaning against the newel post. She needed to rest, but she was afraid to sit, unable to bring herself to face the agony of standing again. Instead, she leaned heavily on the rail, shaking with every breath.

After a brief rest, she searched the remainder of the house. In the garage, there were gardening tools and a variety of other kinds of equipment that would be useless to a family on the move. The kitchen drawers were filled with baking and cooking utensils. Nothing that remained had helped the family who'd fled, and, by the same logic, there was really nothing that could help her.

By midafternoon, her side demanded she take a break. She scattered her salvage on the coffee table.

Taking the time to recuperate, she sifted through the items she'd collected. Among them was a bottle of disinfectant. Although she'd done her best to keep vigorous movements to a minimum, the task of searching the house had taken its toll. She sat down for a much-needed rest with disinfectant in hand. It would be a nasty and painful business, but there were no doctors to administer antibiotics if the wound were to become infected. She peeled back the matted cloth with clenched teeth and tended her wound.

Satisfied with her handiwork, she contemplated the other things she'd collected. There were too many to keep. She could carry only a small bag and, besides, there would be countless houses just like this one along the way. With careful deliberation, she began to set aside what she considered to be necessary, and even then, she'd have to prune the pile even more. When she was done, she'd chosen to leave behind much of what she'd gathered.

Tate leaned back in the couch. Her bandage was dark with fresh blood. Urgency had been her motivation, but now, having competed her task, she could tell she'd done too much. She rested and pondered yet another problem. Her encounter with the dogs had proven she was unprepared. She needed to be able to defend herself. She thought about finding some sort of firearm, but she could think of several reasons why that would be impractical. First, she had no experience with firearms; she didn't think she could hit anything even if she figured out how to use one. It also meant she would have to find and carry ammunition. Pepper spray might be a good option. She could wear it on a belt or carry it in her pack. Since there was nothing like that in the house, she resolved to keep an eye out in her travels.

With a fresh dressing in place and her pack reduced as much as possible, Tate once more braved the streets of the Vancouver suburbs. Her injury made it impossible to move fast, so she kept close to front yards, scanning the surrounding neighborhood for possible escapes should the need arise. For every new city block, she came up with a new plan that might help her navigate safely through it. Staying close to building entrances was essential. She looked like a silly movie spy, moving from one doorway to the next, always ready to duck inside at the slightest indication of danger. Instead of a cane, she carried a long crowbar that would serve a dual purpose. She could use it for support as well as on any door, or on any dog, for that matter, should she have to.

Tate spent the night in another borrowed bed, with, thankfully, blankets. The day's journey had been hard, and her wound had begun to weep. She cleaned it as best she could, put some ointment on it, and donned a new bandage before laying down in the half-light of the evening and falling into a dreamless sleep.

***

Tate awoke to the morning sun pouring through the window illuminating near-microscopic flecks of dust floating around the room. Her stomach had ceased to beg for food and was now demanding it. Today she'd try and solve the problem of finding nourishment in a city where there seemed to be nothing. She wished she'd asked her brothers about their secrets. She was becoming weaker as her body fed on itself. Soon she'd be willing to do almost anything to stop the screaming demand from her gut.

She left the house and turned toward a small community shopping center. The direction was marked by the too-numerous-to-count billboards and signs common in such areas. As she drew nearer, her fear and apprehension rose. What would she do if she met someone? What would they do?

Inside, she went directly to the hardware store, and from there she checked the sporting goods center. The store had been cleaned out. At one time, guns had stood chained together in a row. Now those chains dangled against empty shelves. Below the counter, where the ammunition was once stored, doors hung open, and the cupboards were bare. The glass counters were smashed and the shelves beneath them were empty. Broken glass littered the floor.

Tate moved to the receiving area. In the backroom was a large bay door, behind which would be the loading dock. Inside, there were still cartons of goods which had arrived but never opened. Somehow, this grab-bag bonanza had been overlooked. She guessed there must have been more than a hundred boxes.

Some were identified by the printing on the side of the box, but more of them were identified as a *pre-pack* by a piece of white tape with the word printed on it in red. There was no clear indication what might be in each one as there were no useful markings on the outside. Because she couldn't know what might be in each box, she was careful to open them all. Eventually, her search was rewarded. Inside one of the pre-packs was a shrink-wrapped pack of six bear mace canisters. She also found some nylon holsters she could attach to her waist. The mace containers were bulkier than she expected; each one was seven inches tall and a little over two in diameter. Tate took three of them and one of the holsters. She put the holster on and placed an aerosol can inside. She also found a pair of small, but powerful, binoculars and a multi-tool that contained a knife, screwdrivers, and a pair of pliers. She put multi-tool on her belt and discarded the pocketknife she'd been carrying. Redundancy was not a luxury she could afford.

Like a gunman, she rested one hand on the bear mace container and felt her confidence rise. She felt armed well enough to stop any attacker.

Tate left the shopping center. It was time to start back to the suburbs in search of a place to rest, and something more important—she still needed to eat.

She knew bear mace was stronger than regular mace and knowing that boosted her courage even more. She wandered into the outskirts. Making her way slowly from one vacant community to another, she investigated every possible location where someone might have left behind a candy bar, a bag of chips, or anything else that could take the edge off her hunger. Each grocery store she walked into was completely devoid of edible products.

In desperation, she decided to explore some of the vacant homes. In the first, she went straight to the cupboards. Nothing. Then she tried the refrigerator. The moment the door opened, she regretted it. The fridge was packed with a multitude of disgusting containers bursting with mold. With the door opened, the room was immediately filled the foul odor once safely contained by a magnetic seal. Tate covered her nose and mouth and left the house as fast as her wound would allow.

She wandered for hours until she happened upon a school. More out of curiosity than anything, she used her crowbar and broke out one of the windows. A twinge of guilt washed over her as she considered for a moment her act of vandalism, but the feeling vanished in an instant. There was no longer public anything. Government was gone.

Tate lifted one leg and slid it through the window. She stood inside a vacant classroom. The walls were bare, the desks were neatly stacked in one corner, and the blackboards were wiped clean as if ready to start fresh in September. She turned to the teacher's desk. Unlike the rest of the room, it was piled high with various papers and books. A computer sat dusty and silent amongst the clutter. Tate crossed the room to the door. The hall was empty and the bulletin boards bare. Her footsteps echoed in the corridor. Most of the doors were locked, but these were classrooms and of no more interest than the first room she'd been in.

She bypassed the office, the maintenance room, the sickroom, and the gym, until she came to the cafeteria. She stepped behind the long stainless-steel counter and into the kitchen area. Ignoring the large refrigerator, she made her way directly to the pantry. Cautiously, she opened the door and was greeted by a scurrying sound in the dark. She pulled the door open and leapt back.

A momentary flash of movement caught her eye as a half a dozen mice scurried for cover. *Good sign*, she thought. On some of the shelves were the deflated remains of bagged goods which had long since been pillaged by the furry occupants. On closer examination, however, there were a few cans and some jars arranged in neat order on the shelves. One plastic container looked like it might contain flour, and another could be sugar. There were also various other containers that looked as though they might be spices of some kind.

Tate began to haul out anything that looked like it might be of use. The tops of the jars and cans were littered with a decade of mouse shit, but her hunger was far beyond caring. A week earlier she would have been disgusted at the thought of eating from any of these tins. Now she did not hesitate. Snapping out a dusty towel, she cleaned off the loose droppings, took the tins off the shelf and continued to dig into the pantry. She stopped when she came to something she recognized: tuna fish. She darted to the kitchen counter and scoured the drawers for a can opener. After a brief search, she found one, chose a can, and cleaned the top as well as she could. The opener pierced the lid and it let out a faint familiar hiss. Before risking a taste, she brought the can to her nose and smelled the contents. It smelled good. She dove in with her fingers. She couldn't remember tasting anything so delicious. She finished the contents of the first can and opened another. It wasn't until she had downed three quarters of the third can that she began to slow.

After she had eaten all she could, Tate turned again to her surroundings. As far as a school was concerned, the quantities of food left behind were insignificant, but for one starving girl, there seemed to be enough to last her a lifetime—certainly enough to save her life.

She stood in the semi darkness gloating over her newfound treasures. Somewhere in the back of the kitchen, an automatic fan of some sort kicked on. She jumped in astonishment. It took her a moment to register the meaning of this wonderful surprise. Everywhere else there had been no electricity. Why would a place like this be any different?

Realizing the implications, Tate looked around for a light switch and found one. The entire kitchen area was instantly flooded in brightness. She turned her attention to the large white doors at the back of the kitchen. It was apparent they were the refrigerator and the freezer. *But which is which?* She didn't really want to open the refrigerator. Even though it had been working all this time, there was no telling about the condition of the food inside. They looked identical. Being unable to come to a conclusion, she resorted to the old fashion method of making her choice. "Eeny meeny miny moe," she started, first pointing to one and then the other. She knew when the rhyme was over, the dreadful task of opening the door would remain, so she proceeded slowly, "catch a—" Then she stopped. Staring right at her was the solution. Beside each of the doors was a thermostat. She chided herself for not seeing them sooner. The first thermostat was set just above the freezing mark. The second was set well below. Her mystery had been solved.

Tate flipped the light switch and walked into the large freezer. It stood mostly empty except for a few small packages wrapped in brown paper. These were completely covered in frost and impossible to identify. Tate looked over everything and then stepped out and closed the door behind her.

After all the searching and the days and days of fasting, she had found food in what she'd thought would have been the most unlikely place. She walked back to the office area. Adjacent to the office was the sick room. In it was a bed. For bedding, it had an old woolen blanket and a pillow with white and gray stripes. The mattress was stained and coverless. Exhausted and with an aching side, she lay down on the cot and was asleep in a moment.

CHAPTER ELEVEN

For the next few weeks, Tate remained at the school. She took time to heal, and advantage of the food stores she had no way to carry. In her boredom, she investigated the building, but that yielded nothing more than a few mostly deflated balls. The staff room turned out to be a gold mine of information. The coffee tables were loaded with pamphlets about every imaginable topic. There were newspapers and magazines. There was a publication called "Teacher." Apparently, teachers had been concerned about their careers months before the school shut its doors to students. They wanted to know what was happening and what they could do about it. Tate organized them according to the date of each issue and feasted on the new information. She finally understood how the economy had collapsed.

There had been other depressions throughout history, but this one had been much more severe than any other. There was a remote possibility that the economy could be bouncing back in other parts of the world, but as far as she could tell, British Columbia had become one massive ghost town the size of three medium states.

While many homes were dark and without power, some buildings still had electricity. The only explanation Tate could think of was that the BC Hydro, the province's power company, hadn't turned the power off to every location before its employees fled the province. It may not have disconnected services to public operations such as hospitals and schools at all.

Tate's spirits rose. With her basic needs having been met and her body healing, she had the time and energy to think about her future. She wanted more than anything to have a home once more. Even a house without a family would be better than a life of continuous wandering. Her home had once been torn from her. Somehow, she would replace it.

Tate had always dreamt of living near the ocean. When she was well enough, she restocked her pack, and, having prepared in both mind and body, she decided to brave the dangers of the world outside once more. She turned her attention to the Sunshine Coast and thus began her journey toward the small town of Gibson.

***

Many years earlier, Gibson had been a small, isolated community locally famous for a television show called *The Beach Combers*. Back then, the only way to and from the community was by ferry, but now a small road wound through coastal forests, making it possible to get there on foot. Even with the new access, Gibson had always had the flavor of a small resort town, never having developed into a large community. It could be the perfect place to start her new home.

Although she'd never been out of the Vancouver area, she still remembered her family excursions to the sunny beaches and beautiful waters. As it turned out, her sense of direction had been good. She did, at least, leave the city traveling the right way. It wasn't long, however, before she was at a loss for where to turn next. The suburbs were a maze, and it was difficult to find her way. The communities were designed to make high-speed travel difficult. The streets twisted among the homes. There were numerous cul-de-sacs and playgrounds connected by trails that passed from one to another. There didn't seem to be any streets that went straight through in the direction Tate needed. She needed a map. GPS and the Internet had made them all but extinct.

It wasn't just old department stores that could be useful. Many other old businesses had treasures to share as well. Now and again, she found useful items on nearly barren shelves. Even gas stations without a drop of fuel still had a gem or two. The map she unfolded was just such a treasure. She sat on the curb studying it and regaining her bearings.

That evening, she found herself holing up for the night in a sparsely populated area. She had reached the outskirts of the city where the distance between houses was greater.

Tate had developed a routine for when it was time to choose a place to stay each night. She started by casing the entire house and checking every window and door. The one she considered at present had been left unlocked when it was abandoned. It didn't matter anyway. Homes that had once been locked had usually already been broken into. The houses perfect for her needs were ones that had drawn little attention. These were often off the beaten path and had not been the target of vandals. A home that had been undisturbed for years would probably be safe for at least one more night.

Nights came and went, and her progress was slow. Away from the city, there were new, unfamiliar dangers to face. Every strange sound brought Tate to a halt, with her ears perked and her legs tensed, readied to take flight.

As days passed, it became harder and harder to maintain a sense of emergency when every alarm was false. In one case it was a stray cat, and in another a bird flitting from one branch to another. In still another, it was a rodent looking for its next meal.

Weeks went by, and Tate slowly relaxed. She became accustomed to the sounds of the forest, like the wind rustling through the trees, chattering squirrels protecting their stash, and the eerie sound of two trees rubbing together. Although her guard was always up, she found she was beginning to see the beauty around her. After all, she told herself, there was more to the world than the dangers it presented. With the city noises far behind, houses were sometimes kilometers apart.

Tate walked, humming an old tune, but her music faded away as she approached a crossroad. She reached for her map. The Town of Gibson still lay many kilometers to the west. There was a small community close by, maybe only large enough to have a gas station and a few houses, but it was ten kilometers out of her way. It would take her the rest of the afternoon to get there and the whole morning the following day to return to this point. It was just too far out of the way to be worth taking a detour for.

Evening found her still hiking along the road. She hadn't come across an old roadside hotel, an abandoned home, or even a broken-down barn, as she had hoped. As the last of the daylight waned, and without the strength to carry her farther, she left the roadside and found solace beneath the overhanging branches of a large spruce tree. She wrapped herself up in every piece of clothing she carried, rolled her pack into a ball for a pillow, and lay down in a pile of dead, brown needles.

***

Morning came and went and still Tate slept dreamlessly. Although the sun was high in the sky, the stranger cast no shadow in the dense forest foliage. Tate was aware of a presence before she was fully awake. She lay perfectly still with one hand on her canister of bear spray. The other she poised to push herself up and roll over at the perfect moment. She breathed shallowly as the stranger moved closer.

She dared not look. In her imagination, the approaching figure was huge. A dozen different possibilities of what it might be, or what it might intend, coursed through her mind, none of them good. Suddenly, in a single swift movement, she attacked. She thrust herself over, popped the safety mechanism, and let loose with the full force of the aerosol spray into the face of her would-be attacker.

In the flash of a glance, she could tell it wasn't an animal. There was a flurry of movement as the stranger's hands flew to his face. He dropped instantly to his knees wheezing and screaming, "My eyes! My eyes! Oh God, my eyes! His voice trailed off as he struggled to breathe.

He stumbled to his feet, removed his hands from his face, and stared at Tate, unable to see. He spun in the direction from which he had come, stumbling out of the trees toward the road. The ditch was nothing more than a shallow swale between the forest and the road, but the man failed to step across it. Instead, he stepped into it. His body lurched forward with his expectation of taking a step onto solid ground. The sudden drop threw him off balance. He stumbled and, unable to check himself, slammed face first into the pavement where he lay, motionless.

CHAPTER TWELVE

Years earlier, it wouldn't have been uncommon to hear Travis whistling. He generally made music everywhere he went. But that was before. A person couldn't go around making so much noise anymore. No one was safe these days. Silence and stealth were his new way of life. Just as he had never been prone to quiet, he had never been a recluse, either. But nowadays, a person was better off alone.

At one time, he'd led a group of teenagers who'd banded together to help one another survive. They called themselves the Castaways. He never intended to lead anyone. It just happened that way. He'd certainly never intended that anyone get hurt. It just happened that way, too.

Part of surviving meant taking. And part of taking meant hurting. It was a mad circle and, eventually, Travis found he could no longer abide by that way of life.

In the beginning, the Castaways were a close-knit group of friends who had gone through school together. They'd lived under similar circumstances and became closer still as their adventures bonded them. But as time went on and one tragedy seemed inevitably to follow another, he found himself the leader of a group of strangers, wondering how he got there. One sleepless night, he took what few belongings he had and walked away from the city.

He was surprised at how good he felt leaving the rot and filth behind. He breathed freely again for the first time in years. There was something better out there and he was determined to find it.

He'd been on the road, traveling west, for the better part of two weeks. He wandered in whatever direction suited him. He figured everywhere was equally likely to be as bad as anywhere else. Whenever he came to a fork in the road, he tried to find a random way to pick his direction. Sometimes he might flip a coin. Others, he might choose the road that looked less traveled. He moved forward, but never back.

It was early one afternoon when he saw a colorful bundle in the shadows of a giant Sitka spruce. Scavenging was a way of life and coming across anything of interest warranted further investigation. Travis left the roadside, crossed the ditch, and carefully approached the pile.

He was no more than two meters away when he recognized it for what it was, a human form. The body lay face down in dried spruce needles at the base of the tree. On its head was a hat that completely covered hair and face. It lacked the normal stench of decay that Travis had come to expect from a corpse. No flesh could be seen; Travis was sure of nothing.

He inched forward.

Without warning, the figure suddenly rolled over and emitted a stinging mist directly into his eyes. He fell to his knees cursing and screaming. His eyes burned in their sockets. He looked around him, but he could see nothing. Afraid his attacker was not finished with him, he struggled to his feet. Tears streamed down his face. His throat was clogged, and breathing was nearly impossible.

As his sight diminished, the blurry form in front of him began to fade. He estimated the direction from which he had come and turned to flee. Light was coming from where the road should be, and he stumbled toward it. Suddenly, the ground disappeared from under him, and his body lurched forward.

He did not hear the sickening dull thud of his head crashing against the pavement. Luckily, he would not remember the fall.

CHAPTER THIRTEEN

Pushing with her feet, Tate scooted away from the man. She didn't stop until her back was against the tree. She sat panting and sweating as the figure lay on the pavement no more than ten meters away. A pool of red had begun to form in a hollow on the pavement beneath his head. In horror, she watched it spread.

If only her brothers were there to tell her everything would be okay. If only her mother were there to remove her grip on the canister so that it would stop spraying into the air in front her. Her fear had its hold on her, and her body shook.

By the time she recovered, the canister lay empty at her feet. She could feel the pulse of her beating heart in her chest and temples. Using tree branches for support, she got up and stepped closer to the prone figure. The pool of blood had grown. The man must surely be dead. She inched closer.

The man's chest rose and fell. He was still breathing. She knew from the warnings on the canister that the product could be extremely hazardous to people. Blindness could be a permanent condition. The directions for a bad reaction had been to rinse thoroughly with cold water and seek medical attention. If the man were to regain consciousness, he wouldn't be able to go anywhere.

She rolled him onto his back. There was a gash on his forehead stretching from his hairline to his eye. Blood continued to stream from it. By the look of him, he was probably in his early twenties. His face was slack and emotionless. Although he looked peaceful now, a mere moment ago who knows what his intentions might've been.

She wondered if she should bandage him. If she did, she might be saddled with leading a blind man around. If he got well enough, he might want to finish what he hadn't been able to start. Leaving him to suffer wouldn't be humane. She had no choice. She would have to finish the job. He was unconscious and would feel nothing.

She reached behind her, unsnapped the leather pouch holding her multi-tool, and pulled it out. She flipped open the knife as one who has become accustomed to using it and placed the blade just below his left ear. A sharp and simple slice into his artery would let the blood flow freely, allowing him to pass into unconsciousness and eventually death. Again, she reminded herself he would feel nothing.

The only evidence of the struggle within her was the shaking of her hand. How could she take a human life? Was this what she'd grown to become? Was this the way the new world was meant to be?

Knowing that it was a mistake, Tate returned the knife to its scabbard, took one last look her assailant, and turned away. She gathered her belongings, hopped the small ditch, and continued west.

She had gone no more than a few dozen steps when the moaning began. The cursed moaning. Why couldn't anything be easy? The sound grew louder. Rolling her eyes, she stopped. Run away or return to the young man's side? Disgusted by her own weakness she returned.

The man lay on his back, staring blindly toward the sky.

"Is anyone there? Please, help me," he said, moaning.

Her feelings of guilt and shame were too much to bear. Putting her pack down, she rummaged through it until she found her makeshift first aid kit. She removed compresses and a strip of cloth. Without wiping the blood away, she covered the gash with a compress and tied the cloth around his head. All the while, the stranger stared up at the sky. He seemed blind and unaware of Tate's presence.

She dragged him off the road and laid him in the grass beside the ditch. She used water from her canteen to rinse his eyes, then placed her pack under his head.

He wore a large trench coat which was covered with pockets, each containing a variety of items. Among these was some food and water. He also carried a rudimentary first aid kit of his own. Tate marveled at the ingenuity. What a good idea this coat was. The many different compartments had freed the man from his need for a pack. The coat looked big and warm enough that it would supply warmth at night. She replaced his belongings and covered him with it.

The sun was low in the sky. She'd get no further tonight.

***

It wasn't until morning that the man regained consciousness. His eyes watered when he opened them, but they lacked that dead blind stare she'd seen when she first decided to help him.

"Do you know what happened to me?" he said.

"Shhhh," she replied. If he couldn't remember, maybe she'd never have to tell him.

"I can't see," he said.

"Stay calm and rest. Here, try to eat some breakfast," she encouraged.

She helped the stranger sit up and put a little of what she had in his hand. He sniffed it. "Thank you," he said, putting it in his mouth. When he had finished, he lay down and before long he was asleep again.

***

Tate awoke with sun streaming into her eyes, its welcomed warmth urging her to begin the day. She contemplated the man on the far side of the campfire's remnants. Her first thought had been to think of him as her prisoner, but that failed to describe their relationship. The word companion came to mind, but that seemed imprecise as well. Oh, well. For now, she would think of him as "the man."

The fire was out, but she knew there might be life left in it. With a stick, she dug beneath the surface and pulled up larger black coals. She pushed them together and, within a few moments, they began to smolder. She tossed a handful of dry grass on top and sank to her knees. With her face close to the coals, she blew softly. Some areas began to glow red. She focused on those, adding just enough wind to encourage the growth of the heat. The red grew, encompassing some of the coals and spreading to others. The grass began to smoke and then began to burn. She put a few twigs on and after a few minutes added larger pieces of wood.

She filled her camping pot with water and propped it on the fire. She had nothing to cook, but, somehow, a hot beverage in the morning seemed to create an easy feeling.

The man stirred.

Tate ignored him.

Small bubbles began appearing along the sides of the pot. The water would be ready soon. Tate reached into her coat pocket and fished out a re-sealable bag. Inside were a handful of tea bags. She removed one of the small pouches. The tiny label indicated the tea inside was lemon. By the time she'd selected her flavor, the water had come to a roiling boil. She dropped the bag into the pot and removed it from the fire to steep. The steam wafted up and she drew the aroma into her nostrils.

The man rolled toward her and rubbed his eyes. "That smells delicious—like lemons," he said.

"Yes, it is, as a matter of fact. It's lemon meringue pie. I'm going to enjoy it with a little ice cream. I would have preferred eggs and bacon this morning, but I don't have any toast to go with it. Alas, who wants eggs and bacon without toast. I suppose this pie and ice cream will have to do," Tate said with as much dramatic expression as she could manage.

"I don't know," said the man. "Pie and ice cream sound wonderfully decadent."

Tate looked up. The man was smiling.

"You know what would go great with pie and ice cream?" he said. "A cold glass of milk."

The man might be playing along, but he also might be making fun of her. Tate couldn't tell. It didn't matter. Having grown up with two older brothers, she had toughened, so she dismissed the potential insult. "I don't have a fridge but give me a moment and I'll fetch the cow. After I milk her, we can have a nice warm glass."

"Oh, if only I had a cow. I envy you." There was a wistful tone in the man's voice. Now he was the one being extra dramatic. Then his voice took on a more serious tone. "Although, if I really had a cow, I would raise a calf. Soon I'd have a herd and before you know it, I'd be eating steak. Maybe even a burger or two!"

"I suppose you'd need some lettuce and tomatoes then," said Tate.

"Well, I guess I can dream. In the meantime, I do have a few stale crackers that might go pretty well with your tea if you don't mind sharing."

"Tea. It's not tea at all! It's … hot apple cider with a zest of lemon. I like to serve it in teacups with handles so small you have to raise your pinky when you drink."

The man rummaged through his coat pockets and produced what remained of a bag of Ritz crackers.

"Those aren't crackers, sir. Those are a delicate French pastry that will pair exquisitely with my *boisson*."

"Bwaasagn?"

"*Est-ce que tu parles Francais?*"

"What are you talking about?" said the man.

"I'm just being silly. *Boisson* means drink in French and '*Est-ce que tu parles Francais?*' means 'Do you speak French?'"

"Oh. I wish I'd understood. I could've said *bonjour*."

"I think you meant *bien sur*," said Tate, shaking her head.

"Yeah, that too. But don't tell anyone. I failed French in school."

"I never would have guessed." Tate wished he could have seen the face she made. "Pass me your mug and I'll pour you some lemon tea," she said.

The man gave her his mug and pushed his crackers closer. "Beware, they're going to be bad. I have no idea how long ago they expired, and I opened them a few days ago. They are going to be so stale," he said.

The crackers were not nearly as stale as Tate had feared. The meal wasn't much, but at least it was something.

***

With the fire out, and everything stowed, Tate put the man's hand on her shoulder and started out. "Watch your step. We're crossing the ditch now," she said, remembering to help him maintain his footing.

Once on the pavement, the man hesitated and turned in the direction he must've assumed Tate was standing.

"What's the matter?"

He adjusted his position. "I don't know if I thanked you enough," he said. "Without your help, I would've been a goner for sure."

"Trust me. I'm not doing anything special here—certainly nothing that deserves thanks."

"I don't even know your name."

"I'm just fine keeping it that way."

"Well, mine's Travis."

"Nice to meet you, Travis," said Tate.

"And yours?"

"Really?"

"I suppose I could just say, hey you. That does have a nice ring to it. I know it's what my mom always preferred I said when I called her. Whenever I would say Mom, she'd stop me and say, 'No, son. I prefer it when you just say hey you.' She was special that way."

"All right, all right! Just shut up already. It's Tate. Everyone calls me Tate. Are you satisfied?"

"That's a beautiful name. It's nothing to be ashamed of," said Travis.

"I'm not ashamed of it. I happen to agree. It *is* a beautiful name. I just didn't want to give it to a crazy, psychopathic, rapist, killer, is all."

"A blind, crazy, psychopathic, rapist, killer," Travis corrected.

"Yeah, that too. Oh, just shut up, why don't you?"

"Do you know what happened to me?"

"No. I have no idea." Tate winced, wondering if she'd ever be able to tell him the truth.

It was a relief when Travis changed the subject.

They walked. Days passed, and Tate continued to care for Travis. He was happy to go in whatever direction she desired with one stipulation: she must never take him back to Vancouver. On that, Tate agreed.

***

Time passed slowly and painfully for Travis. Although he didn't say much about it, he hated feeling dependent. He rinsed his eyes regularly hoping that one day they'd begin to recover.

One morning, as he knelt by a stream and splashed cold water into his eyes, instead of black, it seemed the darkness had taken on a lighter hue. It was too early to tell, but any amount of brightness was encouraging.

Throughout the day, Travis strained to see more. Glancing toward the warmth of the sun, he felt certain he could see its bright outline.

During the following days, the world around him began to take form once more. The faint dark spots on the pavement were potholes. At least he could now avoid them on his own.

He still couldn't remember anything from the day of the incident. Debilitating headaches had plagued him ever since he hit his head on the asphalt. When he wasn't concentrating on keeping his footing, his thoughts were of his strange benefactress. There was something familiar about the color of the coat she wore, and he felt sure she knew more about what had happened to him than she'd admit. Unfortunately, every time he'd asked, she avoided the question and wouldn't elaborate.

More days passed.

Travis awoke. The sky was more than a blur. He could see individual clouds. Images were still hazy, but he could make out most detail. He turned to Tate. "Whew, I'm going to be okay," he said, smiling.

***

The guilt of having injured Travis had haunted Tate since that first day. Now it'd become too much to bear. Although she'd wavered between telling him or not, she could keep the secret no longer. "There's something I need to tell you," she said, unable to lift her eyes from the ground. "I've never admitted it, but I'm the one who did this to you."

"I know," Travis replied, a matter-of-fact tone in his voice.

Tate was stunned. "You knew?"

"I suspected."

"Why didn't you say something then?"

"I thought about it, but it would have felt too much like calling you a liar. I figured I'd just have to be patient."

"I'm so sorry," she blurted. "I was so scared. I thought you were going to kill me. I almost left you there." She started to cry. "Oh, Travis, you can't imagine how close you were to dying."

Travis smiled. "I don't think I was nearly as close to death as you'd like to believe."

"What do you mean?"

"I don't believe for a moment you'd ever do such a thing. I've seen the way you value life and I'm sure if you'd stumbled across me, you would've stopped to help—even if it meant risking your life."

"Really," said Tate, ensuring he could hear the playful challenge in her tone.

"In fact, when you think about it, that's exactly what you did. You had no idea what my intentions were, yet you helped me anyway."

"You mean, that's exactly what I'm doing," she said with a

mischievous smile.

Travis chuckled. "I suppose so."

They broke camp and set out on the road once more. Travis' improved eyesight allowed them to make better progress.

"You know," said Tate, "I've always dreamed of living by the ocean. I was in Gibson years ago, before they built the road in. I wonder what it's like now?"

"What're you going to do once you get there?"

"I don't know. I'm playing it by ear, I guess."

"I've never been to Gibson. Sounds like a nice place to check out along the way." Travis winked.

Tate enjoyed his company. If she had to have a companion, she could imagine worse. She felt relieved when Travis continued to tag along even though his eyesight had returned. Since her brothers' disappearance, she'd missed having companionship. In truth, she felt safer when Travis was around, blind or not. Should she happen across anyone, their strength in numbers, if nothing else, might be a deterrent.

During the weeks that followed, the time seemed to pass quicker. Now that there was nothing to hide between them, their conversation was more open and honest.

Travis was a thinker like her. He strategized about almost everything. His trench coat with its many pockets had fascinated her at first, but, as it turned out, it had its limitations. Travis was frustrated by the fact that it was bulky and he couldn't carry everything he wanted. At some point, he'd said he'd consider returning to a traditional solution. Regardless of how he felt about it now, Tate continued to consider it an interesting solution having numerous benefits.

CHAPTER FOURTEEN

One sunny summer day in the early afternoon, Tate and Travis walked under the arch that marked Gibson's city limits. Trees grew thick and close to the ditch, providing shade on the narrow highway. The town nestled among the hills along the shoreline. The main road followed the curve of the ocean, with other roads branching off, winding their way to other destinations.

The streets were empty and the buildings dark and foreboding. The leaves rustled in the breeze. On the brighter side, the sun felt warm on their backs. The village seemed deserted. They walked up and down one street after another, exploring the little ghost town. It was a scary feeling. On one hand, the community seemed completely abandoned, but on the other hand, Tate couldn't help but feel they were being watched.

Tate knew it was a myth. There was no evidence of such a human ability. Still, her gut feeling told her there were people in this town and they knew strangers were among them. "Are you getting the same feeling I am?" she said.

"That we're not alone?"

"Yes."

"We're not," said Travis.

"How do you know?"

"A face in a window. A moving curtain or shadow."

"Well, that's kinda disturbing."

"Not really. Would it be any different if you lived here and strangers came through?"

Travis was probably right. "You've seen people?"

"A dozen or so, I suppose. I haven't really been counting."

"How?"

"It's easy. Just look ahead for doors with high windows and windows with curtains or blinds. The trick is to *look* without looking."

"So I should be creepy?"

Travis' laugh was more like a whisper. "No, you should be stealthy. Think of it like hunting. The wrong kind of movement can chase your prey away. Turning your head toward the houses guarantees you'll chase away the people you want to catch spying on you. No one likes to be caught looking."

Tate nodded. "I suppose that's true."

"Three houses ahead, the one with the picture window and the burgundy drapes."

"Yeah, I see it."

"See the lower left corner?"

"What about it?" Tate was becoming frustrated and wished Travis would stop treating her like a child.

"Keep watching out of the corner of your eye. That's all there is to it."

As they drew closer, Tate strained to look without looking. It felt awkward and unnatural. The curtain was drawn a little to one side. She expected to see a face, but instead she noticed a branch from some sort of house plant, probably dead, holding the curtain away from the window. "That was stupid," said Tate.

"Not everything out of the ordinary is going to turn out to be someone lurking in the shadows. I'm just saying, that's just the sort of thing you're looking for. Look ahead and be watchful. You'll see something eventually."

Tate became more vigilant. A few minutes later, in the half-moon shaped window over a door, Tate saw a face looming. "I saw one," she said, unable to mask the excitement in her voice. For a moment, she felt a little childlike.

She slipped her hand into Travis' as they combed the alleys and buildings for more evidence to prove they weren't alone. Remembering how afraid she'd been when she first met Travis, she couldn't blame the hiding people. Thinking of those ghosts behind waving curtains as frightened townsfolk helped to ease her fears, and as they walked through the streets, Tate found herself becoming mesmerized by the scenic beauty.

Ultimately, their wanderings led them to the seashore, where they walked along oil-stained sandy beaches and climbed slippery moss-covered rocks. A beached tanker oozed crude oil into the water, some of which had made its way to the beach. But even that was unable to diminish the magic of the moment.

She'd been traveling for so long and had never been anywhere as picturesque and quaint. She could think of living nowhere with more appeal. "This is it," she said.

"It?"

"Yes. This is where I think I'll live for a while. It's beautiful, it's quiet, and it reminds me of a postcard."

"Well," said Travis, pausing as if in thought, "I guess if this is where you want to be, we should see if we can find you a place to live."

Tate decided she should make a home close to the original downtown area if she could, but choosing one was not as simple as walking up to a house and taking possession. With nothing but time, Tate decided to try each one out for a while. Curb appeal was certainly her first consideration, but spending a day or two inside would help her make up her mind.

For their first night, Tate chose a cute little house. After walking through the rooms, she knew it wouldn't be one she would live in, but it made a good temporary base of operation. Each morning, after breakfast, Tate and Travis took to the streets, spending their days getting to know Tate's new community. If they were lucky enough to stumble upon a nicer house, she would remain. If not, it was back to the house from the previous night.

Having a family had always been something she'd dreamed about and, as the weeks passed, she found that she'd ceased to think of Travis as a companion and had begun to hope he'd started to feel the same. Maybe he'd choose to end his wandering and remain with her.

They were strolling along the beach one afternoon when she saw it. She couldn't think of anything that could be more perfect. The house was perched on a flat spot overlooking the ocean. There was a tall fence surrounding it, making it perfect if she planned on having a family one day. She wanted to be sure her children, if there were to be any, would be safe. For herself, she would always have a spectacular view to remind her how lucky she was. If it was vacant, this would become her home. "It looks like a piece of heaven," she said, pointing toward the house.

Travis smiled. "Shall we have a look then?"

They scrambled up the slope, gaining only a little height with each step as they slipped, pushing sand and debris behind them. Laughing and out of breath, they eventually reached the top. The house was, indeed, vacant. Considering the chain link fence, it appeared the property might have been some government-owned facility at some point. The interior was unimaginative, but when Tate flipped a switch in the kitchen, lights came on over the counter.

Electricity was a rare commodity. During the early stages of change, many families had gone bankrupt long before the final collapse. Struggling families gave up phone and garbage services. Over time, power and water followed. If this had been a normal residence, electricity would have likely been nonexistent. Tate smiled in joy.

She roamed around the house, turning on lights wherever she went. She found the thermostat and turned the heat up to 27°C. She wondered about air conditioning, but for now, the idea of sleeping in a warm house in a warm bed was beyond anything she could've hoped for. It'd been years since she'd been in a home with heat.

Her instinct had proven itself. She curled up on the old dusty couch in her new living room with Travis sitting next to her.

He draped his arm over her shoulder. "You did it," he said. "You found the sweet spot."

"It is pretty wonderful, isn't it. No chills tonight," she exclaimed, reaching up and wrapping her fingers around his hand as it rested on her shoulder.

Tate could have invited him to stay, but it wasn't like he could go home at the end of the evening. An invitation like that meant asking him to stay with her from now on. That would mean they'd skip the first date, the first dance, and the first kiss. Tate was scared. What if he said no?

In the time she'd known him, Travis had never mentioned anything about his future other than his plan to travel and explore every new road. She could ask him to stay, but if she did, it could backfire and hurry his decision to leave. So, just like it was in the old days, Tate held his hand and felt encouraged by his arm around her. She could only hope he felt the same. She could only hope he would choose her.

***

From the beach, Travis regarded the building Tate pointed toward. Many of the other houses far surpassed this one in terms of decadent appeal. The steel chain linked fence stood out as its most prominent feature but created a utilitarian impression that seemed to contradict Tate's taste in homes. Other than the fence, the view of the shore from the plateau was the property's greatest asset. From where Travis stood, he couldn't understand why Tate would want this house. Then it dawned on him. She hadn't mentioned it, but if she were thinking about the prospect of starting a family, an impenetrable fence with a large yard, overlooking the beach might be a perfect choice.

Tate was kind, intelligent, and beautiful and Travis was, without a doubt, captivated by her. Under normal circumstances, he wouldn't have hesitated. A woman of Tate's quality was rare even when the world had been normal. He shouldn't pass this opportunity by, but then he thought about his plans to simplify his life and get away from the craziness that'd been all he'd known for so long.

Craziness. What an interesting word. He'd left Vancouver because he wanted something more than the decaying city had to offer. He cared nothing for the people who'd depended upon him. His lifestyle had become unstainable.

And here was Tate, looking forward with a kind of hope and excitement Travis could barely remember. In this desolate world, she had no reason to be optimistic, yet here she was, looking toward the future and planning for happiness. What more could anyone hope to accomplish? That was the real question.

Travis reflected on his journey. When he'd stumbled upon Tate, he'd been wandering for weeks. He'd convinced himself he wanted that life because it promised an existence without responsibility. He thought he wanted to live without having someone depend on him for a change. He had come to realize that when a person's in the company of others, he begins to depend on them, even if that dependence is as simple as companionship. Travis' role in Vancouver had been caretaker for a bunch of misfit young adults with no sense of personal responsibility. They didn't care for Travis other than for his ability to help keep them fed, and he had had no friends among them.

He couldn't remember the last time he'd depended on anyone.

The day Tate pepper sprayed him, everything changed. He'd been independent in every sense of the word. He had no one in his life and he needed no one. But on that day, in the span of a moment, he had become entirely dependent. He'd been forced to rely on someone else for everything. He should have felt weak and frustrated. He could have been angry. But he wasn't. He felt grateful. The time he had spent with Tate had been an absolute reprieve from responsibility. During those first few days of stumbling along the highway, he'd learned what it felt to be cared for, and rediscovered a reason to care. He'd realized that a person cannot live in a void, that people need the reciprocation of love. That was what his previous life lacked and what Tate offered. She didn't even know it.

When he'd followed Tate into the house and she flipped a switch, the house instantly surpassed any appeal all the other buildings might have had. The light seemed to create added warmth, even though the temperature in the room had not risen.

Tate turned the thermostat up and the baseboard heaters turned on. The smell of burning dust filled every room, but it was the smell of warmth and Travis knew it would soon pass.

Tate plopped down on the sofa and dust flew from the cushions. He didn't care. He sat close and threw his arm around her. The possibility that she might push him away never occurred to him. The notion of staying had been playing on his mind for some time. The question was should he wait for an invitation.

CHAPTER FIFTEEN

The house proved to be everything Tate hoped it'd be. It was bright and warm with a beautiful view. After several weeks had passed, she knew Travis would soon choose to leave. She walked from one empty room to another, trying to imagine what it would be like when there was no one left to talk to. She remembered those times when her brothers were out of the house scavenging. She spent the days alone, passing the time, waiting for them to return. When they were there, she dreaded the next time they'd have to leave.

The thought of remaining in an empty house was nearly unbearable. Except for the uncertainty of the future a nomad's life would mean, she might have chosen to go with Travis.

No, she would make a home here and although she'd miss him, she wouldn't leave. These were saddening and sober thoughts, but his choices were not within her control, nor did she wish them to be.

Tate stood in the kitchen looking out over the water. The waves from the rising tide splashed over the wreck just offshore, creating a spectacular display. She had her back to the door when she heard Travis' footsteps behind her. He stopped close enough that she could feel his warmth. If only he'd stay.

Two hands appeared on the counter, one on either side of her. He was so close she could feel his chest rise and fall. Goosebumps rose on her arms. If only he'd stay.

One of his hands moved to her waist and he pulled, willing her to turn and face him. She followed his prompt. His face was so close, there was almost no room between them. Her forehead nearly rested on his chin. She couldn't bring herself to meet his gaze, uncertain of what she'd find there—afraid he was saying goodbye.

His hand rose to her chin and he lifted her face.

Tate closed her eyes, afraid and excited for what might come. Warm lips touched hers and Tate threw her arms around Travis' neck.

***

Tate couldn't remember having had a conversation which culminated in a clear decision about Travis' future. It was something that had been understood between them. In the beginning, he had been an attacker—although admittedly, that had been a gross misinterpretation of his intentions. Later he was her dependent, then a companion, eventually a lover, and now a partner. When the two of them welcomed Jason into the world, Travis became a caring father as well.

It was easy to care for Jason as an infant. Furniture was sparse, and he had all kinds of room to crawl and, later, run. But neither Travis nor Tate wanted a life of confinement for their son. Even the ocean had lost its appeal. The long trek to the beach was a deterrent and the wrecked barge had been seeping oil onto the shore for years. The beach wasn't even a safe place where Jason could play, so it was easier to stay at home. Over the years, the compound had begun to feel more like a prison than a place of safety.

The community wasn't devoid of inhabitants, just as they'd first suspected. Like her, the local inhabitants had a deep desire for privacy, while at the same time harboring a strong sense of community. It was an odd sort of comfort. Just as in Vancouver, the streets were a place of danger. Every now and again, some new stranger would wander into the little town, and usually it was for no good. Tate had become the one peeking through the curtains hoping the stranger was just passing through.

Jason was five years old when she and Travis decided that, once again, it would be better if they found a new home. They depended on what little Tate could grow and what Travis could gather from the stores and surrounding area. They yearned to become self-sufficient. In order to do that, they would need to go somewhere they could farm.

Jason was too young to take on such a journey, so early one spring day, Travis left in search of a better home for the family. He would come back once he had found a suitable location.

Tate waited patiently, but Travis never returned.

CHAPTER SIXTEEN

The hardest part of the story to retell still haunted her dreams. It haunted her in the face of her son, who was growing to be more and more like his father each day. Each contour of his face, and the color of his hair and eyes were wonderful yet painful reminders of the man who had walked out of their lives. The act of remembering was overwhelming and the guilt she felt for letting him go was worse.

After weeks had passed, she'd been haunted by a growing feeling she'd made a terrible mistake. If Travis was not to return, she knew she'd never be able to make it up to Jason.

Days, weeks, and years slipped by. The first year was the hardest. It had been nearly unbearable to answer Jason's daily questions of "When is Daddy coming home?" or "Where's Daddy?". To placate her son, she told stories depicting Travis as a hero triumphing over every obstacle in his search for the perfect home. One day, they would leave Gibson and go to a place where they could live together in safety and happiness. That Tate wanted to believe it so badly made the telling of it easier.

Acting as though Travis was coming home when she didn't believe it herself was one of the most difficult things she'd ever had to do. The only thing harder was bearing the sadness of watching the boy's hope evaporate. She suspected that his memory of his father was somehow tied to that hope, and she feared that, for Jason, his father was a fading shadow.

Eventually, the day came when Tate realized she couldn't remember the last time Jason had asked about his father.

CHAPTER SEVENTEEN

It seemed like only minutes, but hours had passed since Tate had begun her story. As Jason sat in silence, she wondered what he thought of his father. Did he long for him the way she did?

Tate stood. Her stomach growled. Jason must be hungry, too. She went into the kitchen. As she worked, her thoughts returned to Jason's confession. All this time, she had considered this a safe place, when it never was. She put the plates on the table. "Jason, come and have something to eat."

She wanted to say something about how scared he had made her feel, but something about his expression as he sat at the table made her change her mind and she decided not to bring it up at all.

In the following days, she allowed Jason to go nowhere without her. He showed her his slide and the small part of the beach he called his own. She learned about his collection and discovered the caverns below the property. When he'd finished his account, there were no secrets left to disclose. It saddened her knowing that, for him, the magic of their home had disappeared forever.

***

As fall approached, the weather began to cool, accompanied by strong winds and torrential rains. There were no weathermen to tell people about the variations from one season to the next, so predictions about the weather reverted to older methods. On the off chance one neighbor happened to be talking to another, they might reminisce about how hot or cold, windy, or rainy, it had been the previous year. "Did you ever see so much snow?" or "Why, two years ago, the wind almost blew down the old watchtower." Regardless of the talk, seasons came and went.

This year's weather wouldn't be analyzed until the coming year. But when it was, it would be described as the worst ever—especially for the town of Gibson. Normally, the winds and waves were held at bay by Vancouver Island, a land mass that ran about a third of the way up the provincial coastline and stood between Gibson and the open ocean. It took the brunt of the abuse and slowed the winds considerably, but this fall, the island might as well have not existed for the all the good it did. The rains poured down and the wind tossed waves and sludge high over the fence, painting the house and windows with black goop. Tate and Jason lay under siege within the walls of their little home. She had never repaired the roof, or the seals around the doors and windows, so the moisture poured in.

At some point during the winter, strong winds felled a tree across a power line somewhere between their house and the main power supply. The seemingly infinite supply of electricity ended abruptly at the worst possible time.

Without electricity, the house grew cold, and darkness engulfed the rooms long before light left the day. Leaks were too numerous to count. With Jason's help, she moved their important belongings into the one remaining room dry enough to preserve them: the living room. Tate had always maintained stores of supplies including clothing, food, and clean drinking water. Now all of these were running out. She could dry nothing once it got wet. She would have collected water from the roof, but what came from the eaves was tainted by salt and sludge.

Stress and worry continued to strip away Tate's youth. Even when endurance seemed no longer possible, another day came and went. The sun rose and set. One impossible day passed, and another began.

The winter weeks dragged by in slow, painful succession. In addition to the rain, there was the annual shifting of the foundation to contend with. It left doors hard to open and the winter drafts impossible to staunch. It seemed winter would never end.

Six weeks had gone by before the sun broke through the clouds and the winds finally let up. Tate and Jason carried empty jugs to a runoff stream which meandered its way to the ocean about a kilometer north of the house.

She opened the windows and began to reclaim the rooms that nature had borrowed. A little at a time, life began to return to normal.

No longer housebound, Jason spent as much time outdoors as she would allow. He helped her around the house for the first half of the day and then she'd let him play outside in the warm afternoon sun.

***

Their small family was not the only casualty of the winter storms. The water had taken its toll in other ways, too. Below the house, the muck had begun to shift in the ancient ocean caverns, oozing and gurgling its way toward the sea. New, unstable cavities had begun to form under and around the house. As winter slowly slipped by, the danger beneath the house grew.

***

Just when Tate expected a reprieve, Mother Nature struck once again. March winds and rain knocked on the door with the fury of an angry landlord demanding rent, holding the family captive and eroding their spirits. Once more trapped inside with little to do, Tate began to lay plans for the coming summer, reminding herself that spring, and the hope it would bring, were just around the corner.

The long days of winter had given her plenty of time to think. Their home was no longer a safe haven. The fence might have suggested safety at one time, but now she recognized it for what it was: a placebo, a façade of false security. The house was like a Venus Fly Trap. Sooner or later, the apparent safety would prove to be the demise of the unwary visitor. When the weather was warm enough, she'd take Jason and travel east across British Columbia and then into Alberta. Although Travis was gone, she didn't have to abandon their dream of farming and becoming self-sufficient.

The prairies had always been less populated. The ground was flat, and she hoped it would be easy to till. The plains had once supported herds of buffalo and deer. Maybe they would again one day. She knew Travis would have come back if he could. Now that Jason was older, it was time to find a plot of land and build a real home rather than stay and wait for the house to deteriorate around them.

Roadside shrubs had long since begun to overtake the pavement, which itself had begun to look more like a single-hued mosaic. One day, Mother Nature would reclaim all that was once hers, until there would be little evidence of this then-bygone era. The coastline would return to the way it once had been. Only ruins of old foundations among the giant Sitka spruce trees would remain to tell the story.

By the end of April, Tate had gathered the maps and supplies they'd need for their long journey. There were numerous rivers and two mountain ranges to cross before they reached Alberta. The Coastal Mountains would be the easiest chain to traverse. It was early in the year, and it would be the first one they'd navigate, but they'd need to make it over the Rockies before the winter snows began in October. If she was lucky, she and Jason would be in Alberta before then.

***

On an early morning in May, Jason and Tate stood outside their home, looking back for the last time. Tate took stock of their gear. Each of them had on a warm set of clothes and footwear that she expected would last the journey. Although Jason was smaller, he'd have to carry everything he needed and bear his share of the load.

Jason hefted his pack by one strap and threw it over his shoulder. He looked small beneath it. "Are you going to be okay?" Tate said.

"Heck, yeah," said Jason. "Will you?" he added with a wink.

"I sure hope so. We don't have much of a choice." Tate glanced back at the house, feeling like she was leaving something behind, but couldn't put her finger on what. She'd pulled her hair into a ponytail to keep it out of her eyes. She looked over at Jason and made note of the clothing he wore and glanced up at the morning sun. Then it came to her: her hat. It was in the house on the kitchen counter. Of all the belongings she would need, her hat was one of the most important. It would keep the rain and the sun off as well as help her to keep warm at night. She turned to Jason. "Just a second, hun. I'll be right back. I forgot my hat in the kitchen." She ran inside.

Tate felt the front step give a little as she entered the house, but she paid it no mind. After all, she was turning her back on this heap for the last time. The floor shifted under her feet as she made way through the living room and passed the garden she'd soon leave behind. Ignoring the tilt of the kitchen floor, she grabbed her hat and began to retrace her steps through the house.

Before she made it out of the kitchen, the house moaned and then screeched as if in pain.

Tate remembered Jason's description of the caverns below and recognized what was about to happen. She dashed back through the living room, managing a couple of steps before the floor disappeared beneath her. She clawed at the snapping floorboards, scrambling up, but tumbling plants and furniture rained down on her.

***

Jason was standing in the driveway when he heard the house groan. He had no time to feel the smallest pang of worry. The house gave a tremendous lurch and collapsed inward upon itself. He could hear his mother's screams above the sound of snapping wood. The power line anchored to the house snapped free, lashing out in Jason's direction like a giant tongue. He leapt aside. The wire whistled passed him and fell lifelessly in the driveway. The house let out a final sigh as it came to rest in a heap at the bottom of the hole that had once been the oceanside cavern.

At first, Jason stared, shocked and dazed. But even before the wreckage settled, he stripped off his pack and ran toward the house with the fleeting thought that if his father had been there, he probably would've grabbed him by the collar and ordered him to stay back. His father would've recognized the danger.

But his father wasn't there.

Jason ran carelessly toward the collapsed structure.

The roof rested where the floor had once been. He could hear the shifting mud and creaking wood as the building continued its downward path. The exterior door lay on the ground in its frame. Even if he could open it, it would no longer lead into the house. Jason scanned the wreckage for a way in.

The living room window had shattered, leaving its empty frame lined with shards of glass. It gaped like the open maw of a sleeping giant. Jason darted across the wall without a thought and scrambled through the window. The interior walls had been transformed into broken timbers and slabs of plaster laying in all directions. The floor angled deeply into the ground, cluttered with what remained of the walls, the roof, and their old furniture. On hands and knees, he moved deeper into the wreckage.

"Mom," he screamed, over and over again.

No sound returned to him except those coming from the house. He strained his ears but could hear nothing.

He crawled on his hands and knees deeper and deeper into the debris where little light penetrated. He continued to call and search.

Hours passed.

Jason worked himself down into the muck. The thick mud was nearly liquid. It was as though the earth had reached some critical point and ceased to be solid ground. It sucked at his arms and feet, refusing to let go, as if clawing at him to join his mother. He hunched low, avoiding fallen timbers, moving among the shards and splinters. It was then that he saw what he would have mistaken for a mud-covered glove had he not brushed it with his foot as he passed from one broken wall to another. He felt a heaviness in his chest. He was standing right on top of her. His weight in addition to the weight of the wall was holding her submerged in the mud.

"Mom! Mom!" he called as he pulled at her arm.

Most of the material was too large and heavy for him to move. He cleared away enough of the mud to expose her face. Tears ran down his cheeks, landing on hers. He wiped the muck away as gently as he could, staring into her lifeless face.

He called over and over, "Mom! Mom, please wake up." His voice grew quieter and quieter until he finally fell silent.

***

Jason held his mother's hand as he wept in the darkness. As he lay in the cold mud, the sun began to set outside. The rain started again and tiny rivulets began to stream down around him. Still he held on. How could he leave her? She was the only person he'd ever really known.

Long after his hands and feet felt as cold as his mother's lifeless, stiffened hand, he remained next to her, shivering in the dark. Even as the morning sun began creating clouds of rising steam on the pavement, Jason lay underground next to his mother.

She'd always worried about the dangers around them. He'd always known she wouldn't have approved of the chances he took. There was nothing left to care for. Now these underground caverns would be a grave for him after all. He lay with vacant eyes as the hours passed, not caring whether he lived or died.

***

Maybe it was the beetle that scuttled across his leg and disappeared into the muck beside him that finally snapped him out of his despair. He looked dazedly at it as it burrowed its way into the mud. It filled him with disgust. Maybe it was the strength and will to survive that'd been bred into him that made him finally move.

With the afternoon sun pouring down, Jason once again clamored out of the ground and up into a world of light and the living, a broken shell.

The May sun broke the evil spell of the spring rains, but it was not enough to warm Jason. He stood overlooking the wreckage. Everything that once been a house and yard lay abolished.

He turned away and began to walk down the driveway. Behind him, there was nothing. In front of him, the ancient, crumbling blacktop stretched, first to the town, and then to unknown points beyond. Just outside the fence was a squat dilapidated shed. It would never make a home, but for now it could be a place to sleep. If he felt anything at all, his face did not show it. He didn't break into tears or sob. He thought neither of himself nor his parents. He went inside and, without forethought, found a dry, dark corner. He put his back to the wall and there he sat, paralyzed. Eventually, he let gravity take over and his body fell sideways onto the ground.

Darkness fell outside, but Jason didn't notice.

In the morning, the sun rose and Jason lay motionless in the shed.

***

Through the days that followed, the sun moved in slow motion across the sky and the moon followed its path at night. Animals crept in and out of the shed. Some were looking for shelter, others a meal.

A rat edged its way up to his still form. It noticed his body was still warm and moving, so it crept away, disappointed. Later, it came back

74

to see if there was any change. When there wasn't, it disappeared into the shadows once again.

A fly lit briefly on Jason's eyelid. It found some moisture, no doubt looking for a place with plenty of nourishment for its young, but Jason's eye twitched imperceptibly, and the fly moved on.

Eventually, Jason could no longer ignore the pain and weakness that had begun to set in. His body had been slowly taking what it needed from him. His mother was gone forever, and, although he was miserable, his feelings of helplessness and hopelessness had begun to subside.

His mom's survival pack lay in the driveway. It contained many of the same elements of his own. It also included a few other essentials. Jason went through it, separating what he needed.

There were few personal effects in her pack. She'd planned to travel lightly. Jason scavenged the objects that would help him most, leaving the rest. In one pocket, he found several useful items, including a butane lighter, his mother's multi-tool, and a compass. In another was a wax candle, some paper, and a pencil. At the bottom of one of the smaller pockets was a gold locket, studded with diamonds and worn smooth. Jason had seen his mother spend countless hours holding it in her hand, stroking it gently with her thumb. The chain was formed with an intricate design of multiple links that made the metal look ropelike. There was a small metal button on one side. Jason pressed it and the front of the locket opened a little. Although the locket had an antique look to it, the hinge was surprisingly stiff. He pried it open with his thumbnail.

Inside were two pictures. They were of poor quality, having been taken with an old Polaroid instant camera many years earlier. Originally, the pictures were two layers thick with chemistry trapped between them. The pictures in the locket had been split apart so only the paper with the picture remained. Time had obliterated much of their features, but it was clear who each of the people were. Jason had a vague recollection of his father and recognized him. The second picture had much less detail, partly because the image was much smaller. It showed a woman cradling a newborn in her arms. Even as small as the picture was, it was easy to identify his mom. He must be the child.

In an instant, a single, undeniable truth occurred to him. Everything that had happened was his father's fault. Jason tore his father's picture from the locket and threw it to the ground. He snapped the locket closed, put the chain around his neck, and slung his pack over his shoulder.

Whether or not it was his intention, his foot came down squarely on the discarded photo. As he turned to leave, his foot mashed it into the dirt. Jason had turned his back on the house and left the ruins behind.

***

Surprisingly, his pack wasn't much heavier than it had been.

Even though his fingers and toes ached from the cold that had chilled his entire body, his brisk pace quickly warmed him. His stride kept time with the turmoil he felt, while his face was shrouded by the dark thoughts haunting him. Even as the sun rose high in the sky, the trees growing close to the road covered him in a shade to match his demeanor.

At first his sadness and anger were so great it was impossible to discern one angry thought from another. They rushed in, each one overlapping the next. The scenery sped by.

After a time, his mind slowed and, with it, so did his feet. It was true. If it hadn't been for his father, none of this would have happened. His mother would still be here, and they would still be a family.

Jason couldn't remember much about his father, but he must've been the most selfish man who ever lived.

His thoughts felt like they were spinning in ever diminishing circles. Each revolution brought him to one unavoidable conclusion. He and his mother had been about to set out on a journey to find a new home and hopefully the man she loved, and that meant something.

The locket swung and knocked lightly against his chest. It was the one possession she would not sacrifice even though reducing the weight of her pack had been so crucial.

Jason's pace continued to slow.

There were so many things his mother had valued, but it was this locket she chose to bring. Now that she was gone, what was his purpose? Would he travel to Alberta by himself, build a house and plant crops to harvest, alone? The idea was as preposterous as it sounded. Without his mother, there was no real reason to leave home. On the other hand, without his home, he had no reason to stay. Where were his roots now?

His gait continued to falter until he was hardly moving at all. Each stride was shorter and slower than the previous until his trailing foot came to rest beside his other.

Jason stood motionless in the middle of the highway, unaware that he had stopped. In some sort of strange statement, each of his feet rested on opposite sides of the faded yellow line, one eastbound, the other westbound. There, a battle raged inside him. The features of his face were the only indication of his turmoil. Until that battle was won or lost, he could go neither forward nor back.

As suddenly as the emotional storm had come, it left him. Jason wheeled and turned toward the ruins of his old home. He had already traveled more than a kilometer, but that didn't matter. His muscles were warm and stretched. He broke into a dead run.

Even with his pack, he maintained his speed most of the way back and covered the distance in less than half the time. He'd slowed to a fast jog as he came into the driveway. He ran to where his mother's pack was strewn and found the spot where he'd been the moment he turned to leave. The picture had been there at his feet. He scanned the area looking for the tiny photo. It was much smaller than it had seemed when it was framed in the locket, only about the size of a dime. Jason got down on his hands and knees and ran his fingers through the earth. It wasn't there.

Jason stood and faced the ruins. The smell rising from it was as bad as he had remembered when he first discovered his cave. Beyond the heap lay the dark ocean. There was no way to escape the stench unless the wind changed—or he left.

Yes! The wind. Jason put the wind and the ocean at his back. Again he stood over the spot where his mother's pack laid. He scanned the area once more and moved away from the spot, the wind blowing his hair into his eyes. He moved slowly in the direction of the wind, studying the ground from side to side. He had gone almost thirty meters when he saw something pinned under a small rock in the driveway. There, in a tiny crevice between the earth and the stone, was his father's picture. Jason picked up the remains and brushed it off. There wasn't much left of the image and now it included a tear obliterating most of his father's face. Besides the tear, there were scuffs. It didn't matter much. Jason cradled it in his palm before returning it to the locket. It was the only remaining evidence of his lineage.

He glanced once more at where the house he'd grown up in had been. His mother's backpack lay crippled in the driveway. Leaving it there suddenly seemed wrong. It reminded him of the ravaged, looted buildings strewn around town. It was an unfitting reminder that someone had been here.

He gathered her belongings and, with the heaviest heart, put them back in the pack. Each of the smaller items he put into one of the various compartments. He rolled the extra clothes and repacked them as much like his mother would as he could. When he'd returned everything to the pack, he carried it to where the front steps of the house had been. Timbers pointed toward the sky in various directions. Jason picked one and hung the pack on it.

He wasn't running away this time. Unhurried, he turned to go. His heart was heavy with sadness, worry, and regret. As he walked away, the house began to creak. The ground below was still shifting and sinking. Jason could imagine his old caverns filling with liquid mud as it made its way slowly toward the ocean. The board that held his mom's pack began to tilt and then slowly sunk into the pit. It seemed fitting that those things would rest with his mother. Jason wept as he turned to go.

CHAPTER EIGHTEEN

Through the days that followed, Jason walked, his thoughts blurred by pain and uncertainty. The route he would take had been laid out by his mother weeks earlier. She had marked alternate crossings for rivers, but Jason had never been out of his own backyard, and the distances on the map were too great to comprehend.

He woke with the first rays of the morning sun, ate just enough to stave off hunger, and walked on. When the sun touched the ground, he made camp and slept. Morning arrived, and he repeated the process. The days crept by.

Shrubs and trees had grown up along the roadside, providing everything he needed. He recognized most of the edible plants and gathered what he could whenever possible. The towns he passed through he treated with caution and respect. He took what he could use and left as quickly as possible.

More days crept by.

At times, he found himself reminiscing about a happier life. His dreams were filled with images of creating the home his mother had often described. She'd told stories of the time before he was born when the only two people in the world seemed to be his dad and her. Smiling, she'd told him what she imagined life would be like when all three of them were together again. Even though he could barely remember his father, Jason had always harbored a secret dream that the two of them would someday be reunited.

The road had been out of use by vehicles for years and nature was slowly reclaiming it along with everything else. Saplings were taking root in small crevices caused by the frost. In many places, the pavement was so broken it looked more like gravel. Grass and flowers grew thick wherever they could take hold.

The highway wound its lonely way through the wilderness. For the time being, there were no decisions to make, unlike in populated areas, where Jason had to cautiously navigate the mazes of streets. The trees and plants crowded in. Looking ahead, the highway seemed more like a narrow path through the trees than a road. Onward he plodded, sure of nothing.

***

The local wildlife had found its own way back into the world as well. The first animals to return were deer, moose, and elk. Now, neither the encroachment of man nor the constant pressure of hunting and poaching threatened them. Fields and parks that had once been a haven for children grew lush green grass that had never seen the cutting blades of a mower.

First the herbivores, the grass-eaters, returned. The animals higher up on the food chain followed them. A new population had begun to take over—one that was not human, but was, in some ways, more humane. Jason's quiet footfalls didn't seem to alarm the wildlife and he found himself stopping to watch in amazement the habits, antics, and behaviors of the new inhabitants.

The sun passed its highest point in the sky and Jason's feet were hot and achy from the long morning's walk. He sat down at the foot of a large spruce tree and opened his pack to choose from the meager stores there. While he ate his meal in silence, he listened to the sounds of the world around him. He had come to learn the forest was never truly silent. There were constant rustling sounds, like the light breeze causing two trees to rub together, which created a living, sighing sound. Now and then, the cawing of a bird came to his ears from far away. Was it a crow or raven? He heard the awesome sound of wind being pushed rhythmically beneath great wings of a bald eagle long before he saw it swooping down in front of him no more than twenty meters from the ground.

From the corner of his eye, he saw movement between his bent knees. Without moving his head, he cast his eyes downward. A field mouse peeked out from between the blades of grass, oblivious to the fact that he sat just above it. It picked and poked its way through the leaves, investigating anything that might make a meal.

So, this is how mice behave when they're not frightened, Jason thought. He closed his eyes with his head propped against the tree and napped.

A while later he woke with his legs rested, but his back stiff and sore from leaning against the hard tree trunk. He stretched and limbered up before jumping the ditch and walking back out to the road.

It was impossible to imagine traffic ever having been heavy along these thoroughfares. In some ways, it was as if time had reversed itself. Life in the world had slowed down. Only the hardy people remained to eke out an existence in the new wilderness. They'd had to learn to contend with the ever-changing seasons and to live through long, hard winters alongside the wildlife. Those who couldn't learn the necessary skills either perished or packed up and fled south to a warmer, drier climate. It meant, for Jason, a long and friendless journey. He longed for his mother.

With his thoughts inward, and his mind determined, he trekked on. There was no telling when he might come across another living soul.

They would be potential dangers in that event.

He'd gone over his procedure a hundred times. Each of the various scenarios originated from talks with his mother. She'd always said, "You can never be too sure about people. Sometimes they're looking for companionship; other times they're more like predators. You can't really tell the difference at first."

The solution was quite simple: avoidance.

CHAPTER NINETEEN

Jason could tell a village was nearby long before he arrived. Houses began to appear at the roadside and then became more frequent the closer he grew. Besides the increased number of dwellings, some of them seemed better kept—more used. It could also have been the change in sounds. Jason grew more cautious. He moved to the edge of the road and stopped more often to listen.

He heard a cow lowing in the distance. A little later, he heard a hinge squeak. Suddenly, an unfamiliar sound came to his ear. Could it be the sound of children laughing? He strained to hear, but the sounds were still too far away to make them out for certain.

The wind had grown stronger. Blowing at his back, it carried both sounds and smells away with it. He had been on the road so long, part of him wanted to run ahead. He yearned to stop by every house, wave, and say something like, "Hello! How are you today, Mrs. Smith? Isn't the weather beautiful? By the way, your flowers sure look lovely!" Every fiber in his body longed for it.

But he wouldn't succumb to the craving for human contact. The little man that'd begun to grow inside wasn't about to let the boy come out to play. There could be dangers here that he couldn't foresee, so he didn't run headlong and unafraid into the village. He stayed quiet and watched from a distance, like the animals that watched him warily from afar.

***

When Jason drew nearer, he began to see people. He watched them as they went about their normal daily activities, the activities they were bound to, dictated by the changing seasons. It was spring, the planting and growing time.

As he passed by house after house, he could hear his mother's voice in his head. "Be careful, son. Never let your guard down. Some mistakes we only get to make once."

Secretly, he wanted someone to see him. He wanted the town to reveal itself and prove it was warm and welcoming. Maybe it'd be filled with wonderful people who would embrace him and invite him into their homes. It was a secret wish, though, and not one he dared to articulate. Instead, he walked a little more boldly, less concerned about being silent and invisible, challenging someone to step outside and say hello.

To his left, a woman knelt amid ankle high plants arranged in rows. It was impossible to tell what kind they were; probably food of some kind. His mouth watered at the thought. She pulled at plants and placed them in piles next to her. She already had several small heaps along the row she knelt in.

The woman wore blue jeans. These ones had been mended until they seemed like she wore a strange kind of patchwork quilt. It was another sign of the times. She seemed old to him—older than his mother, anyway. It was difficult to tell her hair color. Her head was covered with an old bandana. As she straightened up to stretch and to wipe the sweat from her eyes, Jason darted to the edge of the road and out of sight.

CHAPTER TWENTY

Although the hot sun beat down, spring would soon enough turn to summer. If Hannah hoped to have enough stores to sustain her through the winter, the work must be done. She pulled weeds and placed them in small heaps between the rows. She sighed. There was still three quarters of the garden left to weed before she would be done and her back already ached. She bunched her hands into fists and pushed herself up from her knees. She rose, stretching and turning until the pain subsided. It was then that she caught sight of the young boy peering at her from the woods near the edge of her broken down picket fence. He wore a grungy set of clothes the color of earth. In fact, as she looked more intently, it seemed as though the dirt covering the boy from head to toe might be the stuff that held his clothes together. When she looked his way, he cowered as if he was about to bolt. She smiled inwardly and went back to pulling weeds.

She'd made a lot of adjustments over the previous twenty-five years. She'd survived her own bad luck as well as the looting years. *And* she had survived the mistakes she'd made along the way. She'd learned to grow what she needed and to make use of everything. She'd been a teenager when things had begun to fall apart and, like so many others, she'd spent the best years of her life finding ways to stay warm and alive. She'd never been one to wait for things to get better. She did what she could to make them better herself.

Her community was home to a scant thirty people. Although there were numerous homes to choose from, everyone ended up deciding to stay in a close-knit group. It wasn't how they'd planned it. It was as if they'd gravitated toward each other. These were not the old homestead days. There were threats everywhere and few people had the skills their grandparents had grown up with. It wasn't a perfect community, but it was all she had.

She'd been instrumental in bringing about some of the major changes that had taken place. There'd been a time when the people did almost nothing but squat in their borrowed hovels.

When the banks foreclosed on most of the homes in the area, many people packed up and left, hoping to find employment and a new start elsewhere. Unfortunately, there were no new starts—just more of the same kinds of problems. The original inhabitants had been gone for years. Surely, somewhere there was a vault containing all the documents that proved the ownership of the property. Wherever they were, they would be relics now. The buildings that would contain them were no more than catacombs; time capsules for a way of life as extinct as dinosaurs.

Hannah had decided it was time to clean up the community and the surrounding area. It wasn't that she didn't have enough to do as it was; it was just that she hated waste. She'd lived through so many hard times already. The elements were destroying perfectly good buildings just because the windows were broken. It was heartbreaking to see. She never intended to fix any of them up; she just wanted to slow the decay. There was so much to clean up and that was something she could do.

Somehow, and certainly not intentionally, she'd become a figurehead in the small town. She had no official designation or particular job description. When something needed to be done, she was the kind of person who would get to it and do it. It wasn't in her nature to ask for help or complain. As it turned out, her example was enough to make all the difference. As other members of the community saw the good work she did, they began to pitch in. It didn't really matter whether it was because they felt guilty or because they felt inspired. The work was what was important.

Over the years, a small, almost thriving community grew out of their efforts.

Hannah pulled another weed. She'd be thirty-four in the coming fall and had long since stopped worrying about wayward travelers or what they might think of her. Had she been wearing cleaner clothes, or if her hair was pulled back, she might be considered an attractive woman, but she was long past worrying about that, too.

As far as the town was concerned, truly, there were no riches to be plundered. It was a small, old, and broken town being slowly rebuilt by a weary and broken people. In some ways, by gradually fixing buildings, they were fixing each other. It was a painstaking process. Any careless wanderer would never notice such things and Hannah was beyond worrying about that, as well.

She watched the boy from the corner of her eye as he inched his way along the fence. She wondered where he'd come from and, after toying with the idea, decided it didn't matter. By the look of him, he couldn't be more than ten or eleven years old. She kept her head down and focused on her work. She waited until he was on the other side of the fence across from her, almost to the point of passing by, when she casually called to him with a simple hello.

The boy stopped and stared in her direction. Had she frightened him? He reminded her of a wild animal that was about to bolt. His dark, half squinted eyes followed her every move. She ignored him and went back to pulling her weeds.

The boy watched her for a long time, and she waited to see what he'd do. Finally, after long minutes, he responded.

"Where am I?"

"This place used to be called Harrison Mills. Now? Well, we haven't really decided what to call it." Hannah chuckled, tossing a weed onto the pile. "I just call it home." She pulled another weed before continuing. "What brings your little self all the way out here to the middle of who knows where?"

The boy stood motionless for a long time. She couldn't tell if he was being thoughtful or frightened. His odd behavior created more questions than answers. After the long pause became uncomfortable, he finally answered. "I'm looking for my father."

"Hmmm … we don't get many visitors around here. I don't recall anyone coming through here who I'd think might be your father. What makes you think he came this way?"

The boy stood at the fence in silence.

Hannah changed the subject, "Hey, you look like you could use a bite to eat. How about it?"

Still the boy remained unmoving. She could almost see the argument he must he having with himself. He looked as thin as a rake. What would cause him to hesitate? Whatever the reason, he looked like he could use some help.

"Well, I'm going to go inside to make some lunch. You're more than welcome to join me. I think I'll make some chicken soup and sandwiches. The grain and the chickens are home grown. One hundred percent organic."

Hannah shoved her gardening spade into the soft black soil and rose to her feet. Her spine cracked. She half expected the boy to break into a run at her sudden movement. He didn't. She smiled and then walked toward the house.

Her house was a country style home with a covered porch. There was a small upstairs area built into the gable roof. There was a windowed dormer on each side with a small window on each end. On the main floor, the door from the porch opened into the kitchen and dining area. Hannah swung open the screen door and went inside. It slammed shut behind her, bouncing once against the frame before settling on the latch. She watched through the kitchen window to see what the boy would do. He was still standing by the fence.

Well, if she was going to get the meal ready, she had things to do. She turned her attention to the task of preparing lunch.

The best way to keep food fresh was to eat it fresh. What she didn't eat fresh, she canned for the winter. Two days earlier, she'd butchered one of the chickens. She had chicken dinner twice since then along with some beets she'd preserved and a few of last year's potatoes she brought up from the cellar. Early that morning, she'd taken the bones and remaining meat and put them on the stove to simmer. The smell of the soup stock filled the house.

She used an old wood stove to heat the house and to cook with. She stoked it and added a few sticks of kindling. In a short time, the broth began to boil. She looked out to check on the boy and noticed he'd inched a little closer. Smiling, she reached into the cupboards and pulled out two of everything.

She heard a wooden board creak outside and knew he was climbing the front steps to the porch. She waited until his face was nearly pressed against the screen door before she spoke. "Have a seat at the table," she said. Since her hands were busy, she nodded toward the dining table. "Lunch is just about ready." She cut into a loaf of bread. "I was wondering what I was going to do with all these leftovers," she added with a smile. "What's your name?"

"Jason," he replied, his eyes toward the floor.

"Well, Jason, I'm so glad to have a little company. My name is Hannah." She poured a glass of water for each of them.

Jason seemed reluctant to respond and offered nothing in the form of conversation. *What is such a frightened and withdrawn child doing out on the roads at so dangerous a time?* She tried a few simple questions, but getting anything out of him proved nearly impossible.

When he was finished eating, he took a final sip of water and said, "Thank you so much for the meal. Can I help you clean up?"

"No, thank you," said Hannah, smiling. "Why don't you relax for a while? There isn't much to do."

The boy looked around and his gaze fell upon the sofa in the living room. "Do you mind if I lie down here there for a while?"

"Of course not," said Hannah.

When she'd finished cleaning up and putting the last dish away, she peeked in on her guest. He was fast asleep. She left him and returned to her work in the garden.

***

Jason awoke and looked outside at the sun. Although several hours must have passed, it was still high in the sky. There was still time to get a few kilometers down the road before nightfall if he got moving now. He got up and began his search for Hannah. He found her in the garden. "Excuse me," he said, waiting for her to look up. "Thanks so much for everything, but I really should get going."

"Don't be silly. Why don't you stay for dinner? You could rest here tonight and then be on your way in the morning after you've had a good breakfast."

His heart warmed at the idea. He considered it only an instant before grinning. "Thank you so much!" he said, hoping his hostess could hear the enthusiasm in his voice.

For the remainder of the day, he helped Hannah in the garden and around the house. When the time came for dinner, his stomach was rumbling. He ate everything she placed before him, and she let him help with the dishes afterwards.

When it was time for bed, Hannah escorted him upstairs, showed him where he would sleep, and the bathroom.

"Here's a towel," she said. I hope you sleep well. Just come downstairs whenever you're ready."

Jason smiled. "Good night," he said, as Hannah turned to go. He cleaned up and slipped into bed. The blankets were warm and heavy. Even before he had time to reflect on his day, his eyes betrayed him by closing on their own.

***

It was late in the morning when Jason awoke. Downstairs, he looked for Hannah. She wasn't in the living room, kitchen, or the bathroom on the main floor. When he came to her bedroom, the door was ajar. He called her name. When no one answered, he peeked in. She wasn't there, either. He went to the porch overlooking the garden. There she was, tending the plants. She looked up when she heard the screen door squeak. She smiled, stood, and walked toward him.

"You must be about ready for breakfast," she said. "I didn't think you'd ever get up."

Jason looked down at his feet.

"I'm teasing. You're totally fine. Let me come in and throw something together," she said, stripping her garden gloves from her hands.

Jason ate and discovered eggs were his new favorite food. After breakfast, he should have left, but he felt obligated to help. He could always leave tomorrow.

One invitation followed another, and Jason never found it within him to turn any of them down. Every part of Hannah's home and the village seemed to offer what he'd longed for. The only thing missing was his mother.

***

With each passing day, Jason felt more like a member of the

community. Through the weeks and months that followed, Hannah introduced him, at one time or another, to everyone in town.

The summer days trickled by, and he helped Hannah tend her meager crops. The garden that once contained only sprouts had become corn, tomatoes, carrots, peas, and potatoes. At harvest time, he joined Hannah in the garden once more gathering the vegetables. Preserving them followed harvest.

There was much to do. By mid-October the last of the potatoes had been cleaned, hardened, and stored in the root cellar below the house. She'd cut a hole in the floor a few years earlier. With a spade and bucket, she'd removed enough dirt to create a small hole below the house. She built insulated walls between the house and the cellar. When it was finished it was about two and a half meters long, two meters wide, and a meter and a half deep. There was even a makeshift ladder to get down into it. The dirt walls were shored up with rough pieces of lumber. Along one side of the cellar was a series of wooden bins, each about a meter deep. A large wooden shelf was set against the opposite wall. She put the potatoes and carrots in the bins, while the preserves she stored on the shelves. The natural heat of the ground kept the food from freezing on the coldest days, but kept it cool enough to keep the vegetables through the warmer months.

When harvest was over and the winter rains began to pour, the townspeople kept to tradition. They all gathered in the building which had once been the city hall. Each family brought what they did best. One family brought freshly baked chicken. Another brought potato salad. A third family brought fresh green salad. They laid the food out on old tables set in a row. Everyone brought enough silverware, cups, plates, and bowls for themselves, and together they celebrated Thanksgiving as it had always been intended.

The party couldn't be compared to the gatherings folks had been used to in the old days. Although simpler, this one was much more gratifying. It provided an opportunity to get together, share stories, and be truly thankful that the hardest part of the work was over for another year. It was a time to celebrate the full stores that would carry them through the long winter to come.

Boasting was a natural part of the event. It was a chance to hear how much of each kind of produce families had harvested. Over the years, trade had begun to emerge between them. Hannah hadn't grown hens for laying or butchering, but Edna McLeod did. Their method for exchange was simple: a week for a week. Hannah traded a week's worth of eggs for a week's worth of potatoes. She tried to produce lots of carrots and potatoes so she'd have enough to get the things she needed from those who produced what she didn't. She knew Edna would never see her in need, but it was important that Edna be compensated. The spring months were sometimes scant, but, for now, it was feasting for all.

***

Jason watched and learned. The colder, wetter winter months were a time of hibernation for everyone. It was during this time that Hannah tended to projects she could do inside and around the house. She stopped up drafts as she found them and allowed him to help where he could. His mother had taught him plenty about keeping house, and he wasn't just a child to be taken care of anymore. He was nearly a man, and he could be useful. In the process of helping Hannah, he continued to learn lessons that would serve him well as he got older.

It was as if Hannah had taken over where his mother had left off. It saddened him to realize that his longing for his mother lessened some with the passage of time.

The winter crawled by, and Jason had almost given up thinking about his father. There were times it gnawed at him, but they were short lived. His warm blanket and the smell of a hot breakfast always seemed to get the best of him. He'd begun to make excuses to stay. After all, it was impossible to know where his father had gone anyway.

One early spring night as they sat and ate a quiet dinner together, Hannah said, "What do you remember about your father?"

The question caught Jason off guard; he didn't know what to say. "Why are you asking?"

"People pass through here now and again. Who knows? Maybe something you'll say could jog my memory."

***

It was memories of his mother that came flooding back. Although everyday was easier, now and again he'd find tears streaking down his face when his last memory of her came rushing back, so instead of talking about his father, he began by telling stories of his mother.

As he spoke, he became caught up in all the wonderful things they used to do as a family. He tried hard to remember everything he could about his father, but his memories were few. He remembered being tossed in the air and jumping on his father's back for a horse ride. Most of the stories, however, involved him and his mother. When he could think of nothing more to tell her, he reached into his pocket and brought out his mother's locket and handed it to Hannah.

Hannah opened the locket. Inside were two small pictures. The one of Travis was almost destroyed. She tried hard to look past the rip and the scratches. Even in the picture's poor condition the face looked familiar. The more she thought about it, the more certain she became she'd seen the man before.

"It's hard to tell from this picture, but I'm pretty sure I remember him. If it's the same man, he came through quite a while ago."

Jason's face was a picture of joy.

Hannah wondered if she hadn't made a mistake.

"I'm pretty sure, not certain," she added, but Jason's glow did not diminish.

That night, as she lay in bed, Hannah became even more positive she remembered the man called Travis. If she was correct, she not only knew where he was going, but she knew a great deal about Tate as well.

Hannah decided to keep what she knew to herself.

Sleep did not come for some time. Her memories weren't clear at first, but once she connected the man who'd wandered into town those many years earlier with the man Jason described, she remembered everything. As with Jason, Hannah had been the first person to greet him. It hadn't started out as smoothly as it had with Jason, but maybe that was because in Jason's case, she hadn't seen the young boy as a threat.

Travis told his story from the perspective of a proud father. He'd spoken of the brightest five-year-old he'd ever seen and felt blessed that he could call him his son. She couldn't remember seeing anyone's face glow the way Travis' had. She even tried to convince him he and his family should come to Harrison Mills.

She remembered being a little jealous. Travis was just a year or two younger than she, handsome and intelligent. She remembered being attracted to him and having mixed feelings as he talked about his family. It didn't seem fair that nothing like that had happened to her.

She'd listened to the same story all over again, this time from the mouth of a ten-year-old.

***

As Hannah prepared breakfast, she studied Jason. She could see the contours of Travis' face in his. Her mind spun with questions. Had it been six years since Travis had passed through town? He hadn't returned, so how could he possibly be alive after all this time? Would he recognize his son if Jason were able to find him? Would Jason be able to identify his father? The scratched and torn picture certainly wouldn't be of much use.

During the nights that followed, Hannah was restless. She couldn't imagine Jason being successful with his crazy plan to find Travis. If he followed through with it, he probably wouldn't survive. Not worst of all, but certainly something that weighed heavily on her mind, was the fact that she would have to live with the guilt of sending the boy out into the world and never knowing what had become of him.

With the morning sun, Hannah had come to a painful resolve. This boy was everything any parent could possibly wish for in a child. He needed a home and someone to care for him. She had no choice. She could not allow him to continue his journey. She wouldn't tell him outright that he couldn't go, but neither she would empower him or provide the opportunity.

CHAPTER TWENTY-ONE

Hannah imagined she'd be able to turn his thoughts away from his quest. She knew he longed for a home, and she hoped he'd accept hers as a substitute. But the following days only proved Jason's obsession was far stronger than she could've imagined. Their conversation had awakened something within him. He talked incessantly about nothing else. She tried to change the subject as often as she could, but Jason was relentless.

"I want you to know how grateful I am for everything you've done for me, but I think it's time I got moving."

He spoke to her as one adult might speak to another.

"I know my father was headed east, so I'll start there. There must be other people, just like you who I'll come across that've seen him."

Hannah could barely look at him, but she had to say something. "I know you want to see him again, but if he hasn't come back, something terrible must have happened to him. We are so lucky here. Not many people come through, and it is so dangerous out there. I don't know what I'd do if something happened to you."

"There's nothing to worry about," he said, almost as if he was speaking to a child. "I know what I'm doing. My mom taught me everything I need to know."

"That's not true. She couldn't have. The moment that someone bigger and stronger decides you could serve a purpose, you'll have no choice. Who knows what could happen?"

"I realize that, Hannah, but that's true every day. I've made up my mind. I have to try."

Hannah felt powerless. He'd put her back to a wall, leaving her no choice. "I can't allow it. You're a child and your plan's insane."

"I can do what I want," Jason said, his voice cracking. "You're not my mother, You mean nothing to me!"

Although his sharp words were painful, they were only words from an angry child. "I know you don't mean that," she said.

"I do. My father is out there somewhere and I'm going to find him," said Jason, tears streaking down his cheeks.

Hannah's frustration turned to anger. As much as she might regret saying so, she couldn't stop herself. "You can do whatever you want, but I don't have to help you. If you want to leave here, you'll leave with what you came with."

Jason's shoulders dropped.

It was all right to be angry and frustrated. It didn't matter that he ran upstairs and slammed the door to his room. He'd eventually forget about his crazy dream to find his father and then he'd forgive her. She could find all kinds of ways to keep his life busy and full.

***

There was no way Hannah could've predicted how driven Jason would be or how grownup and independent he'd become. His small frame was a deceptive façade for the independent young man he was becoming.

***

When Jason came down from his room, he'd left the old Jason behind. He was hostile and resentful. He continued to help in the ways Hannah expected of him, but the home he once felt welcomed in had now become his prison.

He ceased to smile. He ceased saying thank you. He felt obligated to pay for his stay by helping, but that was where his responsibility ended.

The weeks passed, but, as determined as he was, he couldn't maintain the stalemate indefinitely. When he could tolerate it no longer, he made up his mind to confront Hannah.

"I'm leaving," he said simply. "You can't keep me here if I don't want to stay. You can lock me in my room if you want, but I'll still leave. I made it this far and I can keep going."

***

There had been no conversation. There'd been no chance to talk him out of it. Jason turned and left the room. Hannah stood dumbfounded. He was right, after all. There was nothing she could do. Hannah retired to her room feeling defeated. If she tried to stop him and urge him see the nonsense of it, it might force him to run away.

***

Jason was thankful Hannah hadn't tried to ground him. Part of him wanted to tell her he loved her and that she had become so much like a mother to him that it was painful. He wanted to say how much he'd appreciated her warm house, comfortable bed, and cozy blankets.

If only his mother had been here with him, they might have been able to make this town their home.

Hannah didn't lock him in his room. She was out of options. Maybe in the morning she could explain things to him. Maybe she could still change his mind.

Sleep didn't come to Hannah that night. Terrible images of what might happen to Jason kept replaying in her mind. She knew he'd spoken truthfully when he said he'd run away. He'd made it this far on his own and he could probably make it a lot farther. The wee hours ticked by. The night sky turned a dark gray and then warmed. Slowly the sun rose and still Hannah had no idea what to do. She wasn't even a real mother. She had never had children of her own, and yet the pain and worry sickened her.

***

In his room, Jason lay thinking. He understood the significance of the wonderful gifts Hannah had given him. She'd never offered, but he knew that, if he wanted, this could be his forever home. It was not out of meanness she wanted him to stay, but if he chose to listen to her, it would mean giving up on finding his father and the chance of reuniting his family. How could he make it clear to Hannah that the cost of staying was just too high? It was something he could never hope she'd understand. With silent tears rolling down his face, he packed his clothes.

CHAPTER TWENTY-TWO

Travis's cell was no metaphorical prison. Lights were out for the night. Without windows, the cellblock was black. The chill in the coal mine did little to stave off the sweat that had soaked into his clothes. He would give anything for a little cool air, but air conditioning was for the privileged, not something afforded to prisoners. He was filthy, and his skin felt sticky. Travis couldn't sleep, although he knew he needed to. The days in the mine were grueling and without his strength he couldn't survive. No one cared if he lived or died, but he was determined to make it back to his family, somehow.

It had been six years since he'd left Gibson. He'd headed east toward Alberta, beginning his journey by traveling to Hope. There he'd connected with the TransCanada Highway. That route had taken him through all the major cities as well as countless small towns. He'd anticipated finding a suitable place to call home somewhere along the way. If Tate and Jason ever decided to follow, they might be able to track his route, and, if nothing else, find out what had happened to him. He remembered hoping to make millions in the software industry and retire by the ocean.

That romantic notion of living next to the ocean had been a fleeting dream, much different from reality. Without fuel for a boat, there was no practical way to fish. Storms were more frequent than he would have thought, and their crops had been limited to what Tate could grow in their living room.

Over the years he and Tate had never argued. There'd never been a need. They were on the same path together, but when they began to discuss the need to move on, disagreement appeared. Tate had spent her youth living in secret and hiding, and, after all the discussion, she felt more comfortable staying behind and waiting for Travis to return.

Travis had spent his young adulthood as a migrant. Since the apocalypse, he had always gone wherever it suited him best.

It made no difference how many times he explained that the supplies in town were running out and the storms were becoming increasingly worse each year. He explained that they couldn't afford to wait. She wouldn't listen. Her only concern was for their young son, and Travis had no argument or assurance that would alleviate her fears.

Tate couldn't be swayed. She'd dismissed the idea of becoming a nomadic family that would eventually settle down when they found the right place. She'd decided that, alone, Travis stood a better chance of avoiding any dangers that might be waiting.

After months of deliberating, Travis had finally conceded that he could travel quicker by himself than they could as a family. He promised to find a less populated location with plenty of space and a long growing season—and return to them.

Once their decision had been made, he didn't delay. He kissed the only two people who meant anything to him and walked out the door. Jason had been five years old.

Travis knew quite a bit about western Canada, and he thought Alberta might provide the kind of environment they needed. He expected to pass through numerous small towns, and he resolved to do what he could to keep an open mind about whether or not each would meet their needs. He didn't wish to go farther than he had to. HE wanted to get back home to Tate as quickly as he could. The information he'd gather would make the journey to their new home quick and direct.

***

Travis traveled for three days before he came to the small community of Harrison Mills, now apparently a ghost town. The stores, like all the others, had been looted and stripped bare. The windows in almost every building were smashed or the doors broken down.

It was overcast and drizzling, which gave the town an unwelcoming feel. While looking for a dry place to spend the night, he noticed a glow coming from the window of a two-story cottage and decided to investigate. He peered into the dimly lit room and saw a woman sitting near a burning candle, reading a book. He scanned the room to assess any hidden dangers, employing all the tactics he'd developed through the years. The woman looked harmless enough.

Although it didn't seem likely to him that a woman would live alone, Travis could see no one else in the house. She didn't appear to be armed and there were no weapons close by that he could see. Travis went to the front of the building and rapped lightly on the door. Instantly, the room went dark. Travis called to the woman, but still there was no response. He heard a small clicking sound from behind him. He was about to turn when a female voice said, "Don't even think about moving." Her tone suggested she was speaking through clenched teeth.

Travis obeyed.

"Drop the pack slowly," she said.

Travis did as he was told.

"Now step away. Keep your hands where I can see them."

He almost laughed when her fingers grazed his ribs as she frisked him, and he jerked. The dark hid his smile.

When she seemed satisfied that he carried no weapons, she said,

"What do you want?"

"I was looking for a warm dry place to spend the night. I saw your light and I decided to ask for your help."

The woman looked at him through narrowed eyes. She bent down, scooping up his pack and motioned him into the house.

Travis could have overcome her at any moment if he'd chosen to, but he sensed she was only concerned about her safety and had no desire to hurt anyone. It was that way with so many people, he knew, and they had every right to be cautious. He allowed her to direct him and waited patiently as she relit the candle. She went from one candle to another until she turned toward him and, for the first time, he got a clear look at her face. She was a good-looking woman, but the deep lines on her forehead and in the corner of her eyes told a story of hardship.

He waited as she eyed him, assuming she was trying to satisfy herself as to whether he posed a threat. She went through his pack compartment by compartment. When she'd finished, she threw it back to him.

"There's the couch. Leave in the morning," she said.

"You won't tell me your name at least?" said Travis.

"Hannah," she said as she went down the hall and disappeared into a room, closing the door behind her. He heard the click of the lock.

Travis slept dreamlessly and woke rested with the sun beaming into his eyes. He thought about what the woman had requested and, honoring her wishes, he packed his belongings. He could still say thank you in his own way. He lit a fire in the cook stove and began to make breakfast. The smells slowly worked their way down the hall and, when she emerged from her room, he was at the door ready with his pack.

Travis wasn't sure whether his hostess would be thankful or furious. He had invaded her privacy by going through her cupboards, although silverware and dishes were hardly private. When she entered the room, a broad smile spread across her face. Maybe she realized he wasn't the predator she'd imagined.

"Well, thank you for the use of your couch."

"I suppose it was probably better than the hard, cold ground to lay on," said Hannah.

"By far." Travis adjusted his pack. "I think it's time I got moving. After all, the day isn't getting any longer."

There was a hint of mischief in the woman's eyes when she said, "Since you went to the trouble of making it, why don't you sit down and have some breakfast with me? You don't quite look up to your journey."

Travis barely hesitated. He laid his pack down onto the floor and went to the table.

Even the night before, in the poor light of the candles, Travis could tell she was an attractive woman. The twinkle in her eye suggested she'd like more if he'd give her a chance, but his faithfulness to Tate was not a thing he would sell for a warm bed and a hot meal, so Travis pretended he hadn't seen it and graciously accepted Hannah's hospitality.

He stayed the day, and during supper she asked him about himself and listened with interest as he told her about his life with Tate and Jason. He hoped she'd be able to tell how much they meant to him so he could avoid any unwanted advances.

Travis had intended to leave immediately after breakfast, but there were a few things around the farm that would be done easier with two people, so he stuck around to help. A few days later, he explained it was time to carry on with his journey. Hannah invited him to stay a little longer, but he insisted on leaving. He had hundreds of kilometers ahead of him and he had to cross the Rocky Mountains before winter.

***

Travis adjusted his arm beneath his head and rolled over onto his side. The sound of snoring from his fellow prisoners filled the cellblock. In the years since his capture, the number of prisoners had ebbed and flowed like the tide. Almost daily, one man, and sometimes more, dropped from exhaustion and malnourishment. Travis had witnessed on too many occasions the unceremonious disposal of the body, as if the man had never been more than a heap of trash.

Travis closed his eyes.

To him, his life was of greater value than any other man might realize. He had a family to get back to and he would not allow Harry, an unrelenting tyrant, to take it. The sunrise would bring another day and then another and still another, and he would do what he must. He would persevere until he found a way to escape or they released him.

CHAPTER TWENTY-THREE

Jason might be determined and optimistic, but Hannah knew something he didn't. If he was lucky enough to come to a town where there was just one road coming in and one road leaving, he could not stray from the path his father had taken. But Hannah was familiar with many towns and most of them, especially those in the lower mainland, were not that small. The moment he made one wrong decision and left his father's trail, there would be no hope that he would ever find Travis. This private knowledge filled her with gnawing guilt and worry.

If she said nothing of Travis, Jason would leave anyway. On the other hand, if she decided to tell him what she knew of his father's plans, Jason would be filled with hope—and leave. Hannah realized there was nothing she could do to persuade him to stay.

She was sure about one thing. Jason would not survive for long on his own, and that was why, when he came downstairs with his pack strung across his shoulder, Hannah met him prepared with her own pack and gear. This wouldn't be the first time she'd been on an extended camping and hiking trip, and she hoped it wouldn't be her last. Along with everything else, she included a high-powered rifle.

"What are you doing?" said Jason.

"Didn't you say you were leaving to look for your father? Since I can't let you leave alone, it leaves me just one choice. We're going to find him together." She could see the relief in Jason's face. A moment earlier, his spirit was deflated. He'd been armed with only his determination and loneliness to drive him. Now he had a companion who happened to know his father as well. In that, Hannah felt relieved.

She left her home with mixed feelings. There were so many things she was unsure of. Today more than any other, her memory of Travis was as vivid as if he'd just been there. She remembered her feelings of disappointment when she'd learned about his family and his desire to return to them. Tate had been lucky to have a man like Travis. As she donned her pack, she felt a twinge of excitement at the prospect of seeing him again.

She was also torn. She'd spent a lifetime building roots and now look at her. She was giving it all up for, in all probability, a wild goose chase. Would she ever see the threshold of her own house again? "I must be insane," she said aloud. All of this for the sake of a child? She closed the door and turned the key in the lock, looking at the grinning boy beside her. She mussed his hair with her hand and reaffirmed her statement. "I absolutely must be."

***

A few short years before, it was common to see vehicles traveling the roads, but those days seemed like a lifetime ago. Once oil disappeared and the economy collapsed, other businesses rapidly followed. The large motor vehicle companies had advertised plans to build and sell electric cars, solar cars, and even hydrogen powered cars, but they'd been unprepared. The economic collapse came too quickly. Even the products available were out of reach by the average person; the same demographics keeping the world running a bit longer. On top of that, in the span of just a few weeks, currency had lost its value.

For a while, people were able to utilize unused reserves at abandoned fuel stations, but those were soon depleted by looters and roving gangs. Evidence of a mechanized world was all around them, but only as a memorial to the way it once was. If she could find an alternate form of transportation, she would. In the meantime, they'd have to rely on their own two feet, just like everyone else.

In the past, the highway to the Town of Hope had been mainly used as a trucking route. There were few communities in the Fraser Canyon, so there were long stretches where there was only pavement and trees for company. There were numerous areas where the road dipped close to the Fraser River. The beauty was breathtaking. The mountains, their peaks covered in snow, lay directly ahead.

There were two main mountain ranges between them and the Albertan prairies. Nestled between the two was a small valley called the Okanogan which used to boast of British Columbia's most pleasant climate and best producer of fruits and vegetables. After that, they'd have to cross the treacherous Rocky Mountains.

If they couldn't find Travis before they reached the Rockies, they'd have to wait until the following spring to cross into Alberta. Hannah couldn't imagine traversing the entire province in a single summer. Once they started over the mountains, they'd have to reach Alberta before the snow began to fall. To add to their challenges, there were many sections of the route where there were winter-like conditions all year round.

Once they got there, the TransCanada Highway would be well marked and easy to follow. This was the main route, so it was likely the same path Travis had taken. The closer they could stay to it, the better. He wouldn't have changed his plans unless he had to, so they'd likely come across any obstacle Travis might have stumbled upon as well.

A rusty, weather-beaten sign claimed they had arrived in Agassiz. Hannah gripped her rifle, hands trembling. "Let me know if you see anything," she said.

Jason nodded, his eyes moving from one side of the highway to the other.

The closer to downtown they drew, the more crowded the buildings became. In the time they were there, they saw no one. If anyone was around, they were staying well hidden. That was just as well. Hannah breathed a sigh of relief when they passed through without incident. She winked at Jason, and he smiled back. She wanted to buffer his fears as much as she could. If he were to become overly worried, it'd make their journey more difficult.

Highway 7 followed the Fraser Canyon, eventually teeing at the TransCanada Highway, but the intersection was still two days' hike away. If they were able to cross the river, they'd pass by a place called Hells Gate where the river narrowed to less than thirty meters.

Hannah looked to her right and the flowing river. It was swollen high above any lines that would've indicated the highest level of the water. In some places, the water flowed almost to the road. By the looks of it, maybe the entire canyon should be called Hells Gate.

Historically, the gorge had been one of the greatest obstacles in opening the province for transportation and commerce. Throughout history, most of the runoff in British Columbia came down this raging river. Some of the longest salmon runs in the world started from places deep within the interior, all leading to this single tributary. Looking out over the water, Hannah shuddered at the thought of hiking Travis' chosen route.

They approached an intersection. A bridge should have been off to the right, but there was nothing but open water. Broken asphalt ending at the water's edge was all that was left of the highway. Looking across, Hannah could see where it resumed on the far side.

Even if the bridge had been intact, Hannah wouldn't have crossed here, but if the bridge were still standing it would've been a good indicator of what to expect from other bridges farther upriver. There might be no way to cross the river upstream. She hoped they wouldn't have to turn back to Vancouver. She led Jason past the washout, saying nothing about the possibilities coursing through her mind. The less he knew about her concern, the better off he'd be. Besides, she tried to tell herself, the missing bridge might mean nothing at all.

They rested that night on the outskirts of town and the following day continued their hike toward the east. The walk was uneventful and they made good time. As the sun set, a large concrete overpass loomed in front of them. A weathered road sign attached to two galvanized posts indicated that the highway split. They had come to Route 1, where one lane led east and the other west. Hannah took them around the corner to the left, then up a small incline into the merging lane of a two-way highway. She had never been on the TransCanada Highway before, but she expected, for a road that would cross the entire country, it would be more … substantial. Jason wouldn't know the difference, though. To him, all roads were the same.

They made camp a kilometer or two north of the overpass. Stunted grass grew on the southwest edge of the highway. After their meal, they laid out their bedding and fell asleep looking at the stars twinkling in the clear night sky. Hannah pulled the edge of her sleeping bag up to her chin. An owl hooted eerily. She glanced over at Jason, but he was already asleep. The long walks had begun to take their toll.

CHAPTER TWENTY-FOUR

Hannah had been trudging with her eyes to the ground when Jason called, "Hannah, check this out." She looked and saw a large opening gaping in the side of the mountain, surrounded by a concrete facade. The entrance appeared to be a perfect half circle with its sides extending to the ground. Jason ran ahead to read the plaque secured to the concrete.

"It says it's called Yale," said Jason.

At one time, the concrete had a smooth finish. Now, in many places, the cement had begun to flake off, revealing a rough pebbly surface beneath. A pile of gravel had begun to form its base.

"This is amazing," said Jason. "I read about tunnels, but this is awesome."

Water ran down the walls in streams and dripped from the ceiling. Amplified by the stone chamber, it echoed, creating a natural symphony.

"Wow, I can't believe how cold it is in here," said Jason, pulling his coat around him.

Hannah allowed him his moment of discovery. It was a short tunnel. The dark bulbs above hung in steal cages. The paint had peeled from them long ago. Now they were red with rust.

Jason held his breath as he ran all the way through. When he got to the far end, he turned around and ran back through again. Hannah took the opportunity to rest a bit while he played. It'd been a long time since she felt youthful, and it was wonderful to see Jason behave like a boy for a change. She'd forgotten how enjoyable the simplest things could be.

"Hey, squirt, there are six more of these and this one is nothing compared to the ones we'll be going through. There's no electricity, so you might even get a bit of a scare." She grinned, realizing she was excited too.

"Amazing," he yelled as he skipped ahead, while the tunnel repeatedly mimicked him in an ever-diminishing volume. "This is so great."

The mountains hemmed them in from every side. The sheer rock faces were works of art, painted in grays, blues, reds and pinks. Like all tourists, it wasn't long before they became complacent to the beauty as one cliff began to look the same as the next. And although the following tunnels were big brothers to the first, they didn't excite Jason the way the first one had.

The constant roar of the river lay somewhere unseen to their right.

"I think we're getting closer to the river. Doesn't it seem louder to you?" said Jason.

"It should be getting closer. We'll be crossing soon. The longest tunnels are on the other side."

Less than an hour later, the road turned sharply to the right and the river came into full view. Jason raced ahead.

Hannah's heart sank as she saw not a bridge, but concrete pilings like fingers of a giant hand poking out of the water on either bank.

She wondered what happened, although it wasn't an important mystery to unravel. The fact was the bridge was gone. There would be no crossing the river at this point. From what she could surmise, part of the rock face had broken off and fallen into the canyon. As the rocks fell, they must have torn away some of the steel and concrete that supported the bridge. With those gone, the bridge had collapsed into the water and been swept away. The debris from the mountain filled in a good part of the original waterway, creating a new waterfall.

As before, the water was well above any high-water mark that had stained the rocks in previous years. There were numerous half-submerged trees along the river's edge. The water was a muddy brown, moving as much debris toward the ocean as the river could carry.

***

Jason approached the edge of the road where the broken asphalt ended. He looked up and down the canyon and peered into the water. His heart sank. If this was the only way across the river, how could they carry on? Would Hannah decide there was no other option but to return home?

He sighed. He'd been determined to make the trip on his own, but for the first time, he realized how dependent he was. He couldn't plan another route, because he had no idea where to go from here. His father's trail ended at this spot.

Jason said nothing. If Hannah decided this was the end of their journey, she'd have to make that statement without his urging. He wasn't going to make it easy on her.

CHAPTER TWENTY-FIVE

Hannah looked out over the river. A week had passed since they'd begun their hike from Harrison Mills. She'd known from the moment they met that Jason was helpful, intelligent, and independent, but their travels had proven his character was much stronger than she'd guessed. Boy that he still was, he possessed all the strengths and virtues some people never developed in a lifetime. A few short days earlier, she'd been contemplating what she'd do if a time came when they were stopped by an insurmountable obstacle. She'd decided then that she'd need to help Jason understand that their effort had come to nothing.

Now that moment had come. She searched her heart. Had she hoped for failure all along? Did she really want to see Jason succeed, or was she just going along with him, waiting for this moment so she could take him back home? A few short days ago, she would've been happy to return to her sanctuary.

But what if ... what if they succeeded?

***

Two days earlier, Jason had come across a dead skunk. He'd never seen or smelled anything like it. Although the smell was enough to gag him, the two of them knelt beside the carcass and examined it. She explained about their way of living and their defenses. Jason listened attentively. He wondered how it might have died. It was so decomposed Hannah couldn't tell, but she had gone on to say she thought skunks had no natural enemies. They laughed together about the importance of staying clean. No one wanted to mess with a stinky person, either.

When they'd left the stench far behind, they made camp. As they sat by the fire, she'd pulled a sliver from his hand that was festering. While she waited for the sun to set, she made a makeshift walking stick. Jason wanted one, too. She picked a straight piece of willow that was easy to work with. After making the stick, she cut a short piece off the narrow end and made a whistle from it. She trimmed it so that it had the look of an ancient flute. When she had the mouthpiece just right, she scored the bark all the way around, then took the piece of wood in both hands and twisted it so that the bark separated from the wood and came away as a little tube. "This only works in the spring, when the sap is running," she'd said. It was the perfect time of year.

She grooved the wood to control the airflow, slid the bark back over the stick and handed it to Jason to try out.

"You can adjust the hole to make it sound the way you want," she said.

Jason seemed to think it was the trendiest thing and spent the entire next day making music—not really music. Noise. He played it until the bark dried up and it wouldn't work anymore. After that, he spent hours making his own.

Hannah's mind returned to the present and she exhaled. She'd been lonely, and her existence had been meaningless until Jason walked into it. She'd forgotten there was more to life than merely surviving it. She'd long since given up on the idea of ever having a real family or friends. She'd settled into the perpetual routine of conquering hardships, but it didn't have to be that way.

From now on, if she was to live, then she'd live well.

From where she stood, she couldn't see Jason's face as he looked out over the raging water. She scanned the river up and down but could see no way to cross. There had been another ancient bridge just up the river, one that was built over two hundred and fifty years ago, much nearer to the water. This bridge hadn't survived whatever catastrophe had befallen it, but could the other have? It had been decommissioned years ago, but that didn't mean it wouldn't support their weight.

Hannah stepped as close to the edge as she could and looked upriver. Unbelievably, the old bridge looked to be intact. She could see the concrete column on the west side of the bridge jutting out of the water. The cables that would have supported the bridge stretched across the river, but they appeared above the surface in only a few places. For the most part, the bridge was submerged in the murky water. From what she could see, the water was too high to consider attempting a crossing there.

Jason turned to her. Now she could see he was distraught, with tears streaming down his face.

"Hey, bud, what's the matter?" she said, smiling.

"I know what you're going to say. You going to tell me it's no use and that we're never going to find him," he managed between hiccupping sobs.

Hannah put a hand on his shoulder and spoke gently. "No. We're not going to give up. There's still hope. The way I figure it, he may have passed over this bridge long before it fell into the river. Even if he didn't, there are other places to cross. We just need to go downstream a ways."

There'd been a crossing in Hope. If that was gone, they'd have to go all the way back to Vancouver.

They sat where the pavement ended, their feet dangling toward the roaring water as they ate lunch. Even on a day such as this, the Fraser

Canyon was a remarkable sight. The lower elevations were covered in trees that gave way to steep slopes. Above those were snow-covered peaks. It was both an awesome and foreboding sight. Their journey had just begun.

***

By the time they got back to the overpass and the highway that led to Agassiz, Jason was tired and sore. "Maybe we should camp here for the night. What do you think?" he said.

"Yeah, I'm tired, too, but Hope is just a couple of kilometers up the road, and if we can get across the river, we can celebrate by sleeping indoors. What do you think about that?"

"Do you really think we can cross?"

"Well, that rickety old bridge was still there, so it's a definite possibility."

"I guess they don't make 'em like they used to?"

Hannah laughed. "Let's hope that's not the case here." She adjusted her pack. "Well, what do you think? Twenty minutes from now we could be on the other side."

"Let's do it," said Jason. The thought of staying indoors was enough of a reason to keep going. As Jason strode onward, he tried to imagine what could've occurred that destroyed two huge bridges. "Hannah?"

"Yes?"

"What do you think happened to those bridges?"

"I can only think of one thing. There is—or was—a dam hundreds of kilometers upstream. If that dam broke, a wall of water would've come down here, which could've destroyed bridges and towns along the way."

"Is that really possible?"

"When they built Kenney Dam, they flooded over a hundred and fifty thousand acres. The damn is about three hundred meters high, and it isn't even made of concrete."

"Holy crap!"

"I'm glad we don't have the Internet anymore."

"Why is that?"

"People migrate toward water. If that damn broke, it would have taken out most settlements along the river, the whole way down. I can't even imagine how many people would have died. If we still had the Internet, we'd have a never-ending play-by-play of the whole thing. Without the Internet, at least I don't have to hear about it every minute of every day."

Silence followed her somber statement. The remaining distance seemed to drag by. The sun dipped toward the trees as they rounded the last corner and the bridge came into view. The water was high, but the bridge was intact.

"Was it worth the effort?" said Hannah.

"Heck yeah! This is awesome. Do you really think we might even get to sleep in a bed?" Jason asked, picking up his pace. With new hope, he forgot about the pain in his feet.

They crossed as the river raged beneath them.

CHAPTER TWENTY-SIX

The first building Hannah noticed after having crossed the bridge was a large, uninteresting rectangular motel with a flat roof. An antique bedframe protruded from one end, giving the appearance it'd been launched into the side of the building, or had been tossed out.

Hannah chuckled.

"What so funny," said Jason.

"That thing has been there as long as I can remember," she said, pointing to the bed.

"The bedframe hanging off the building?"

"Yea. Hope has always been known for its artists. There are wood carvings all over the place here, or at least there used to be. I suppose someone was just trying to be creative with this."

"I don't get it."

"It's a motel." Hannah gave him a look she hoped said, "Duh," and gave Jason a little punch in the arm.

"It's still kind of dumb."

"I guess whether it's dumb or clever is in the eye of the beholder. I've always liked it. What do you say we go inside?"

Jason nodded.

The building was nothing like Hannah remembered. It, like every other abandoned establishment, had suffered from neglect far beyond anything that could have happened under normal circumstances. The door had been torn from its hinges some time ago. The foyer was littered with several years' worth of dry leaves. The fact that they were dry suggested the beds might be likewise. Hannah stopped at the reception desk, thankful it was an older hotel that relied on conventional keys. She grabbed several sets hanging on numbered hooks.

The keys she'd gathered matched room numbers for the main floor, and each was equipped with a conventional lock. There was no point searching past the first room. It was as clean as could be expected after years of sitting vacant. It was complete with beds, pillows, sheets, and comforters. There were dressers, a mirror, and bedside tables. All that was missing were power and room service.

"How about we crash here?" said Jason. "This one has these two huge beds."

Hannah dropped her pack and threw the covers back on the larger of the two. Removing her boots and jacket, she crawled in. By the time she'd settled under the comforter, Jason had done the same. "Don't let me sleep in if you wake up before me. We should get going as soon as we can," she said.

"Sure … okay. But if you wake up first, let me sleep."

Hannah smiled even though she knew Jason couldn't see her in the darkness of the room. "That works."

***

Hannah was sitting on the edge of her bed when Jason woke. He was disappointed to have to leave the comfort of indoor sleeping, but he felt confident they'd hear news of his dad somewhere ahead.

They hiked along Water Street with the Town of Hope on their left and the Fraser River on the right. The river was so high the water threatened to flood the road. Abandoned gas stations and fast-food restaurants lined the highway. After they passed an abandoned car dealership, the highway split, providing three choices: travel west on Route 1, east on Highway 3, or north along Highway 5. Jason looked to Hannah, hoping to see she'd already figured out which way would be best.

Hannah shrugged. "Well, I can tell you we don't want to head west toward Vancouver," she said, pulling out the map.

"This road is called the Coquihalla Highway," she said, indicating the four-lane highway that wound its way uphill. She pointed to the map. "It's a big highway and bypasses the canyon. We could choose this route and drop into Kelowna here, or Kamloops just a bit farther up the road. Kamloops is where we were originally trying to get to. This route will probably make more sense if we want to get to Alberta.

"On the other hand, if you want to track your dad, it might be better to go through as many of the towns as we can," she said as she pointed out the various places along the road.

"What about this other way to … Penticton?" said Jason, hoping he had pronounced it correctly.

"Well, if we cross here, we'll be off of your father's planned route a lot longer."

"Well, then we should head into the mountains, right?" Jason prompted.

"I'll tell you what, Jason. How 'bout I tell you what I know, and you can make the final decision."

"Okay."

"The main problem using the Coquihalla is that it was meant to be an express route. There are no towns up there unless we leave the main road. Even in the summer, there are sometimes pretty cold conditions. We'd have to be prepared for some tough going.

"On the other hand, if we head toward Penticton, we wouldn't be anywhere near your dad's last known destination. On the plus side, we wouldn't be up in the mountains very long and there should be quite a few smaller communities along the way. It might be easier to find food and shelter.

"If you think your dad made it out of British Columbia, then we should go to Penticton. If you think he might still be in or around Kamloops, then we should hike up there and see. Either way, I think the safer bet would be to travel to Penticton. Once we're there, we could decide whether to continue into Alberta or stay in British Columbia. We have to cross the Rockies and this mountain range either way."

After deliberating for some time, Jason finally decided. "I think it would be best to go to Kamloops. If he was never there, we decide what to do then. We need to get back to his route as soon as we can. I know it may be a harder trip, but if we miss him, we'll lose any chance of finding him again."

Hannah nodded. "That sounds perfect. I guess we better get moving."

They followed signs to the Coquihalla and began their long walk uphill. The road was a massive four-lane highway. In the years since the collapse, harsh winters had nearly destroyed it. Frost heaves broke up the pavement and grass grew up wherever it could find a crack.

Between the dips and turns, the road climbed steadily. As they gained altitude, Hannah had expected numerous views of the valley below, but, regrettably, whatever view there might have been was obscured by more hills and trees.

The higher they climbed, the colder the temperature became. They were in a trench where the hills and trees engulfed the sun much earlier than the time of year suggested they should. As the sun disappeared, so did the warmth. The temperature quickly fell below freezing. Shivering, Hannah and Jason huddled around the fire, bundled in jackets which were unsuitable for the clime. It was late May, and, to Hannah's mind, it should have been much warmer. The wind blew cold and, although it was not the case, it felt like it was coming from the north.

They rose in the morning with a renewed sense of urgency. There was no way to predict whether the temperature would begin to warm up or whether it would get worse. They kept their days long and their nights short.

Each evening, when the light began to wane, Hannah had been able to find some form of shelter. Tonight, it was under an overpass, but the night before it'd been a large spruce tree with a soft bed of needles and low laying branches. The benefits of instant accommodation reduced the amount of time it took to break camp. Each morning, she roused Jason with the dawn to share a small breakfast and continue their journey. In the weeks since they'd begun their travels, they had grown strong in body, their skins dark and leathery.

CHAPTER TWENTY-SEVEN

The rain began before dusk; it would be another two hours before it would be too dark to carry on. Dark clouds reduced the natural light, making it seem later than it was. If it started to rain harder, their clothes would become soaked, and if the temperature dropped much more, hypothermia would become a real threat. In the last hour, Hannah had seen no trees, outcroppings of rocks, or manmade structures of any kind. Lightning flashed across the sky in the east and she shuddered, praying it wasn't moving in their direction. "We need to get out of this weather," she said. "Keep an eye out for a good dry place."

"I have been. We passed tons a couple of hours ago."

Hannah could hear the dismay in his voice.

Rain drizzled, slowing soaking into her coat. Water from the grass slapped against her legs and wicked into her boots. She was uncomfortable and knew Jason must be feeling the same. Her toes had grown uncomfortably cold, and still shelter was nowhere in sight. Darkness began to consume the grey backdrop of the storm.

"Hannah, don't you think we should stop soon? It's getting kinda cold," Jason suggested.

His voice shook, and she knew he was colder than he was letting on. They'd been traveling across a large open area and, up until now, she'd been unwilling to leave the road. The sky grew darker and darker.

"Hey, Jay. Hang in there, buddy. If you see anything that looks like it might make a good place to stop, just let me know. I know you're cold, but we have to get out of this weather."

As night fell, the rain changed to wet snowflakes. To make matters worse, the temperature dropped even more, and the snow began to stick to the ground. Hannah had no idea how cold the night might become or how much snow would fall. She began to wonder not how, but if, they'd survive the night.

Hannah's fear grew as she became aware that her body was in no condition to carry on. Her feet were no longer aching. They were now stinging in pain. Her hands were in no better a state, and her soaked gloves were like ice cubes. She tried to zip up her coat even further, but she couldn't grip the zipper hard enough to pull it.

She worried about Jason, too. He trudged along beside her without complaint. He rubbed his hands vigorously together and shuffled his feet, which she assumed was an attempt to keep them warm. She wondered how badly he was hurting.

On the brighter side, the thin covering of snow made the road more visible. Rocks and trees lining the road appeared black, while the road was a light gray strip stretching out in front of them. The contrast between the snowy road and the mountains helped her distinguish objects in the near darkness.

"Well, the snow is good for something. At least I can see a little better," she said, trying to sound optimistic.

A hill loomed ahead. She prayed it would provide the shelter they so desperately needed. "Let's try and move a bit quicker," she said. "Maybe we can get a little warmer. What do you think?" She didn't know if Jason would be able to, but she needed to find a way to increase her core temperature.

Jason responded by picking up his pace and Hannah matched it. It wasn't long before she began to feel warmer and more alert. Even so, her fatigue and soaked clothes meant they wouldn't be able to maintain their pace. Her desperation increased. Every shadow became a possible shelter.

Scrambling up small slopes helped move warmth to her extremities. She hoped it was doing the same for Jason. She knew the act of focusing on the problem at hand would increase their chances of survival.

Every dark spot that might've been a cave or overhanging rock ended up being nothing more than a shadow. A tree turned out to be a scrubby pine offering no protection. Undaunted, they searched on.

Jason tugged at her sleeve. "Look over there, he said, pointing to another small dark area. They left the road and approached a rock face. A boulder had fallen and broken up as it had come down, leaving a path of rock fragments and gravel that stretched out onto the road. Above that, a larger rock jutted out of the mountainside, creating an overhang that protected the void left by the fallen rock. It wasn't a large area, but it might offer some protection from the elements.

They scrambled up the embankment, clawing at the ground as they went. Once under the overhang, Hannah could tell instantly that the ground beneath them was dry, but, being made up of mostly loose gravel and debris from the landslide, not conveniently level.

"I think this is the best we'll do tonight. What do you think?" Hannah asked Jason, glancing around the space.

Jason was already under the overhang. He pushed his back into the rock face and, using his feet, he began shoving gravel out of the way, creating a berm of gravel at the edge and an indent where he could sit without the risk of slipping out and sliding down the hill. Hannah took a spot next to him and did the same. Soon, they had moved enough gravel to level out a small ledge large enough to share.

Unfortunately, they were both wet to the bone and freezing cold.

There were few benefits of living in a world that had fallen apart, but the surplus of certain goods was among them. In her preparation, Hannah had acquired gear of a quality she never could have afforded before the disaster. She unzipped her pack and selected some dry clothes.

It had never occurred to her that privacy was a luxury. She smiled at the thought. Respecting each other as much as possible, they changed and, after wringing out as much water from their rain gear, used it to cover up.

Her boots were soaked so she put an extra pair of socks over her feet and set her boots aside, hoping they'd dry a little by morning. She noticed Jason watching her as she prepared for the night; he copied her actions. They nestled in their stone nest as closely as they could, beginning an uncomfortable and sleepless night.

***

The morning came quietly. Heavy cloud cover subdued the light and there was about ten centimeters of snow covering the ground. Hannah surveyed their surroundings. To the right and left, the road wound out of sight. The slope of the mountain continued below them with only the flat section of the road breaking its decent. The stores in their packs had dwindled and they snacked on what uninteresting fare they could find inside.

"I don't think we should keep going right now," said Jason.

Since she'd met him, he'd had a never-ending supply of ways to impress her. His insight and intelligence were surprising. "I was thinking the same thing. This rock isn't going to make a very good campsite, though."

"There's no wood and those rocks were murder on my back."

Hannah laughed. "That's a fact. We need to take a break and get these clothes dry before they start growing mold."

"Pretty sure mine already have," said Jason, shaking his head and laughing.

"How about we wait until the snow starts melting and then get on with it. We'll stop the moment we find a decent campsite, and then the first thing we'll do is build a fire. Sound good?"

"Sounds good to me," said Jason. "I can't wait."

The drizzle started up again even before the snow had completely melted. The sun passed midpoint in the sky before it finally broke through the clouds for the first time. Hannah wasn't sure they could survive another night without the heat of a fire. She looked up and the sky. "Well kid, I think it's time we made some tracks," she said, standing.

"Sucks, but we gotta do what we gotta do." Jason leaned back to pull one of his boots on and winced in pain.

"What's the matter?" asked Hannah with concern.

"Nothing."

"Hey! None of this male macho crap. Tell me what's going on."

"I don't know. I haven't looked. My foot stings, is all."

The worst thoughts ran through Hannah's mind as she helped him slip one sock off and then another. She expected to see black frost-bitten toes or worse. What she found wasn't as bad as she feared, but it was bad enough. She peeled the sock away from the blister that had become an open wound.

The skin had been torn away from the ball of Jason's right foot. The blister was soggy and raw. The torn skin was just a flap. After having spent the last two days wrapped in a wet sock, his foot looked old and wrinkled.

"Is it bad?"

"This must have really hurt." Hannah shook her head and furrowed her brows at Jason. "Why didn't you say anything last night?"

"To tell you the truth, I didn't feel anything until this morning. I was hoping it wasn't bad. It didn't really hurt until I tried putting my boot on."

"It's bad, all right. If you can't walk, then we can't get off this mountain," she said, digging into her pack.

She brought out bandages, gauze, and ointment. She cleaned the lint out of the wound and used a pair of fingernail clippers to get rid of as much of the dead skin as she could. Afterward, she applied some antibacterial medication and wrapped the wound as best she could.

Jason's subsequent limp punctuated their need to find a suitable shelter. In his condition, he wouldn't be able to hike for a full day. She hoped their afternoon walk would be a short one—not that they had much choice.

Hannah hoisted her pack onto her shoulders and started out. As she walked, she reflected on the preparations she'd made. She hadn't thought to bring materials for an emergency shelter because she'd expected to find numerous vacant houses along the way. Of course, she hadn't planned to go over the mountains, either. Even so, she hadn't realized how little civilization there'd be in the mountains of British Columbia.

The hours wore on. Jason's limp worsened.

Hannah looked at the sky. The clouds had disappeared, and the wind had subsided, making for one of the warmest afternoons in several days. Eventually, it even became necessary to tuck her rain gear into the straps of her pack, allowing some of her wet clothes to begin to dry. But the sun had begun to dip to toward the horizon, and they wouldn't be dry by tonight. The clothes she wore wouldn't protect her when the temperature began to drop.

Their path took them ever uphill. No matter how high they climbed, it always seemed as though she could look up and see more mountains. She wondered how much higher they'd have to go before they'd finally begin their descent on the other side. Would there ever be a place where they could look out and see the remarkable green valleys she'd imagined?

Hannah had always considered herself an outdoorsman, but she'd gained a lifetime's worth of knowledge about outdoor life with their recent experiences. It was a little late, but she was beginning to get some clear ideas about what would be necessary to cross the Rocky Mountains. Unfortunately, they had only what they'd brought along with them, so she would just have to find ways to make do. One thing had become clearest of all: the need to make better progress. The summer would soon end and they could not afford to be in the mountains when fall arrived and snow began to fall in earnest.

Jason had limped the entire day without complaint. Although he must be in great pain, he kept going. Maybe it was because he was afraid if he became a burden, Hannah would choose to turn back. On the other hand, maybe he was so quiet because he was a driven young boy who wouldn't let a little pain get in the way of something far more important to him. Either way, she respected the fact that he showed such inner strength.

It was nearly dark when they finally came across an outcropping of rock partially hidden by a thick grove of trees. Among the living trees were a number of dead falls. There were even some trees that were dead but still standing. It was perfect. The rock would make a good shelter and there was plenty of wood for a fire.

Hannah started a fire about two meters from the stone face. The previous day's rain had saturated all the wood that was laying around. With her hatchet, she cut a piece about a foot and a half in length. Holding it upright so that the point of one end rested on a log, she started to cut kindling. The first chips were wet, but soon she reached the dry inner wood. Once she amassed a small pile of dry tinder, she used a knife to make much finer shavings. She collected some larger material and stacked it close by, so she could add it as the fire grew.

The fire lit easily and soon the rock wall grew warm as it began to absorb the heat. Even during the night, when only embers remained, the wall would continue to provide warmth.

Jason kept the fire burning while Hannah devised a way of hanging their clothes to dry.

Days passed and Jason's foot healed. The campsite served them well. Hannah woke up early each morning to hunt. Rabbits were abundant and provided a good source of protein. Although she didn't have to go far for rabbits, she'd hoped for bigger game, like a deer, mountain goat, or sheep. If she could bag one of those, she'd be able to use the time to dry some meat and replenish the non-perishable supplies that'd be essential to continue their journey.

It wasn't until Jason's foot was mostly healed that he was able to join her on short hunting excursions. One morning, she came across several sheep grazing at the edge of the road less than a kilometer from their camp. She took careful aim and dropped a large one with a single shot. She removed the hide and kept it. Once it dried out, it would make something warm to lay on. Tanning would have been a valuable skill, but there was no point wishing for it. When the opportunity arose, she'd add that ability to her repertoire. In the meantime, they took the meatiest portions from the carcass and left the rest. Even before they finished, a bald eagle came to rest in a nearby treetop, surveying the spoils it would soon enjoy. Laden with as much meat as they could carry, they returned to camp.

They spent the remainder of the afternoon preparing a kitchen of sorts, then filleted the meat for drying. The rock face made a perfect backdrop. There was plenty of warmth and the smoke from the fire would add a bit of flavor to the meat as well.

They took turns stoking the fire and kept it going through the night. It took several more days, but when the meat was dry, it was more like leather than meat. Hannah wrapped it in a clean T-shirt she sacrificed to the cause. She knew she'd be able to replace it in the next town easily enough.

She tossed another log onto the fire and leaned back against the warm rock. "How's your foot feeling?" she said.

"Pretty good. It barely hurts at all."

"Do you think you'll be able to hike pretty soon? I was just thinking we should probably get back to it. There's a long way to go."

"It's a bit painful to walk on, but I'm sure I'll be fine."

"And you think you'll be able to walk on it for a whole day?"

"I think so. It does feel good, just a little tender—probably because it's brand-new skin."

"Promise me you'll let me know if it starts feeling bad at all," said Hannah.

"I will."

"That's not good enough, Jason. You don't have to be macho about it. We can't afford to be laid up again."

"All right! All right, I promise." Jason stirred the fire with a stick.

Hannah squinted her eyes and cocked her mouth to one side, trying to look both serious and funny at the same time. "You better," she said, and ruffled his hair.

"What does macho mean?"

"It means acting manlier than necessary."

A few minutes later, with their belongings tucked into their packs, they turned their backs on the camp that had served them well. The sun was shining once more, and the cool mountain air was not nearly as biting. The world was a beautiful place without the misery of pain. Hannah resolved to make a better effort to ensure they remained in good health. It was too long a journey to tempt fate and risk disaster a second time.

***

During the days that followed, Hannah stopped regularly to check Jason's foot, which showed no sign of getting worse. They made good progress while unseen eyes watched from the brush. The big cat studied the pair from the top of a rock. It stood without flinching, camouflaged in the dry brown scrub.

***

Hannah knew they were being followed. She hadn't become aware of it all at once. Among the noises of the wilderness there were the normal rhythmic sounds of the woods that followed them along their path. The trees rocked and swayed in time with the breeze, creating a continuous, predictable, and monotonous symphony. But now and again another noise, out of place with the other sounds, not loud or scary, but different enough to draw her attention, had become a periodic addition to the music. She could've easily dismissed it as her imagination playing tricks on her.

A pebble bounced down the slope from above, and Hannah swung her head to follow it, but she saw nothing. She looked to Jason to see if he'd seen anything, but he smiled back, apparently unaware.

Hannah's feeling of foreboding grew. Sometimes the strange sounds seemed to come from her left, while other times they seemed to come from her right. After hours of seeing nothing, she'd begun to feel silly and paranoid. Then a sudden movement caught her eye. A bush was swaying out of time with the rest of the forest movement. Had it been a squirrel or a bird? "Jason, did you see that?"

"You think we're being followed?" Jason said.

"I'm not a hundred percent sure, but, yeah, I do. Something is following us."

The hours trickled by.

They watched the roadsides more carefully from then on, but there was no further sound or movement. As time wore on, Hannah's feelings of tension grew. The hairs on the back of her neck stood up. She felt primitively in tune to her surroundings. Driven by fear, she picked up the pace.

The sun was on the downside of the afternoon and there were still a few good hours left before nightfall, but Hannah didn't want to be caught unprepared in the dark. "I think we should set up camp a bit earlier tonight," she said. "How about we start looking?"

"What about over there?" said Jason, pointing to what looked like a suitable area. It reminded Hannah of the camp they'd had when Jason's foot was healing. If offered a similar rock, an abundance of dry wood ,and an area open enough to provide some advance warning should something appear out of the woods unexpectedly.

It was one of the few times Hannah'd felt in real danger and she wasn't quite sure what to do about it. "This looks like a great spot," she said.

In the meantime, Jason worked diligently to ready the camp area. "What do you think's following us?" he said.

"I'm not even sure we're being followed. But I think it'd be wise if we were careful," she said with a slight smile, hoping he'd believe her.

***

There was still an hour left before dark once they'd finished preparations, so they gnawed at jerky and thought about ways to defend themselves during the night. The rock provided protection from behind. On one hand, it would leave them nowhere to run. On the other, it would force any predator to approach from the front. Hannah hoped that fire would be enough of a deterrent.

"Maybe we should put dead branches all around the edge of camp. If something sneaks up, we might be able to hear it," suggested Jason.

He seemed excited about the idea and, Hannah had to admit, it wasn't a bad one. A bonus was that it'd keep him occupied for a while. "That's a great plan," she said.

By this time on any other evening, they would've both been sleeping. Hannah peered into the woods. Nothing moved. She sighed. Waiting for something to come crashing out of the brush was the hardest part.

"Do you think we should take turns keeping watch tonight?" said Jason.

Hannah nodded. "That's probably a good idea."

"I'll take first watch, then."

"No. Tonight that'll be my job, but I promise to wake you up in plenty of time so I can get enough sleep for our walk tomorrow. How would that be?"

"I guess."

"Growing boys need their rest." Hannah smiled, hoping it would ease Jason's disappointment.

Darkness fell, and Jason settled in while Hannah took over the job of feeding the fire—and watching.

***

Beyond the firelight, an occasional glint from glassy eyes flickered and the hours passed. Hannah's eyes grew heavy. Betrayed by her fatigue, she drifted off to sleep.

***

The fire began to die. Soon there would be nothing left but charred embers. The beast crouched, watching. When the fire was no more than a faint red glow, it rose.

Its body hovered centimeters from the ground. It moved forward making no sound. The female prey's body shook, and she stirred in the barely visible light from the fire. The animal froze, its eyes fixed, unblinking.

***

Hannah awoke to the chill of the cold night air. Jason lay curled in a tight ball, sleeping soundly. She had no idea how long she'd slept, but the sky seemed a little brighter. Maybe it'd be light in an hour or so. With a nearby stick she poked at the embers, and a cloud of sparks rose into the air. She drew a pile of hot ash together and added a couple of smaller pieces of wood. Before long, the fire leapt to life and began to pour off heat. As the warmth increased, Jason unfolded.

***

The cat lowered itself to its belly and settled down to wait.

***

Hannah looked toward the sunrise. An hour ago, she was sure the sun would peak over the mountaintop at any minute, but the sky still looked as dark as it did when she'd first woken.

Another hour passed and still there was no change in the sky. She began to wonder if she'd slept at all. She shook her head. She was going to be tired tomorrow. Hannah threw another log onto the fire.

After several more hours, a faint reddish glow from the east began to light the sky. Hannah tended the fire as the sun rose. The world was encrusted in a sparkling white frock.

Jason stirred and rubbed his eyes. "You never woke me," he said, sitting up.

"I guess I never really got very tired. I couldn't sleep," she said, lying.

"Did anything try to cross the barrier I made?"

"Not that I know of," said Hannah. "I didn't hear anything."

Jason walked around the perimeter, inspecting it. He interrupted her thoughts a moment later when he called, "Hannah! You should come here."

She was at his side in a moment. The sun was already starting to take the chill out of the air and, in a matter of minutes, the leaves that were now frosty would look coated with dew. Jason pointed at the matted shape of a footprint in the grass. An area the size of two of Hannah's fists was devoid of frost. She reached down to touch the earth. It was still unnaturally warm. Whatever had been standing there had disappeared just moments earlier. She looked back to the fire only twenty meters away and shuddered.

They scoured the area for more tracks but were unable to find a clear imprint. Those they could make out suggested that the animal might have been a small black bear or possibly a cougar. After a quick breakfast, they broke camp.

***

By midmorning the frost had disappeared altogether. Except for the foreboding feeling that haunted her, it was a perfect mountain morning. The contrast between the blue sky and mountain peaks was stunning. Birds were everywhere and surprised her repeatedly whenever they exploded out of the grass in front of them. Occasionally a ground squirrel sat chattering and then barked angrily at their approach.

When they stopped for a brief lunch, Jason said, "I've been watching all day long and I haven't seen or heard anything."

"Me either. Maybe whatever it was just bedded down for the night and that was all. There's probably nothing to worry about." Hannah hoped her words would be enough to placate Jason, but nothing could persuade her to stop watching. It would require more than a day without any signs to convince her there was no threat.

CHAPTER TWENTY-EIGHT

A month earlier, the big cat's fur was sleek and thick. Back then, she'd had her winter coat and didn't notice the cool night temperatures. Now her fur was mottled and patchy, as she cast off her heavy coat.

She rose from her resting place as the woman at the fireside began to stir, then wandered away some distance before she stopped to sniff and paw at a field mouse hole in the ground. A small rodent scurried into the open. Her heavy paw came down swiftly accompanied by an audible crunch. She went back to the hole to dig out the remaining occupants, completing her morning snack. Afterward, she made her way up among the rocks where she sat perfectly camouflaged, eying the travelers.

She watched as her quarry gathered their belongings and broke camp. The road ran north and south along the east side of a wide gully. The cat backtracked south and then up the slope, making her way among the rocks as the travelers meandered along the road, sometimes ten or fifteen meters below.

Throughout the day, she did what she did best. She was a shadow: silent, constant, and unnoticed. The sun grew hotter as the day wore on, and she continued her pursuit.

It would not be long before she would catch them unwary. The big one looked like it might have some fight, but she was interested in the little helpless one. She would wait.

***

The shadows lengthened, and the warmth of the sun slipped away along with the light. Jason made camp and started a fire. "Should we keep watch tonight?" said Jason, as he threw another stick onto the flames.

Hannah nodded.

"Can I take first watch this time?" He could be helpful if Hannah would let him. He wanted her to feel like she could count on him, to feel like she didn't need to take care of him all the time—like they were companions and Hannah wasn't just his babysitter.

"Sure," said Hannah.

Unlike the previous evening, there was no trace of hesitation in her voice. He hoped her reason for agreeing was that she had faith in him and not because she felt there was no threat.

Jason added fuel to the fire as Hannah settled down to sleep. It wasn't long before he could hear her breathing deepen. An hour slipped by, and the fire began to die. He stoked it and listened to the night sounds. There was a light breeze rusting the leaves accompanied by night's symphony. Jason shook himself awake and threw another branch onto the fire.

***

The cat's hunger was nearly unbearable. It hadn't actively hunted since it began following the humans three days earlier. It stared, unblinking, at its quarry. The night wore on.

The hunter and the hunted became entwined in a strange kind of dance orchestrated by flames. In the dimming light of the dying fire, the cat raised its body and began its slow crouching advance.

The boy stoked the fire and watched it as its warmth and brightness grew.

The cat retreated and settled to its belly once again.

And the dance continued this way: the fire dying down, the cat growing bolder, the boy stoking the fire, the cat melting into the darkness, again and again.

***

Jason would have preferred to have kept watch the entire night, but he was tired and knew that if he were to fall asleep, Hannah would likely never trust him again. And if he managed to stay awake, she probably wouldn't see his heroic gesture as anything other than a boy playing at being a man. Staying awake the entire night would gain him nothing, so after he'd stoked the fire for the fourth time, he nudged Hannah awake. "It's time for your watch."

Hannah yawned and stretched. "How early is it?"

"I don't know. I know it's been a few hours, though. I think maybe half the night."

"Sounds good. Thanks," she said, yawning and stretching. She stood and walked several laps around the campfire before settling in front of it with her palms to the warmth. "I've got this. Get some rest."

Jason nodded and crawled into his sleeping bag.

***

On the fourth night, the clouds parted to reveal a full moon. Eerie light bathed the trees and rocks. The firelight didn't reach into the night the way it had on darker nights. The cat got to her feet, no longer looking with longing eyes at the small boy. She gave no thought to the danger of the burning flames. It was time to feed.

Flames sparks into the air and the wood popped, covering her sound as she crept nearer. A twig snapped beneath her paw and the cat stopped. Although the big one sat crouched by the fire, it didn't look in her direction, so she moved forward, only pausing at the slightest movement from either form.

As time wore on, she crept nearer. When she was close enough, she tensed, preparing to pounce. The muscles in her legs tightened and rippled. Without sound, she launched herself into the air, her eyes locked on the soft flesh of the big one's neck.

She came down on four paws, reared up on her hind legs and came down hard.

***

The cat's attack surprised Hannah. Huge white teeth and an open maw flashed in the firelight. She brought her arm up to stave off the attack and, instead of her head or neck, the cat's gaping mouth clamped down on her forearm. She didn't feel the cat's teeth sink deeply into her flesh. She only felt the pressure and the brute strength of the beast as it tore her arm out of its way.

Hannah rolled sideways, but the cat was quicker than she imagined. It batted at her. The five-centimeter-long claws shredded her jacket and ripped into her skin. Her adrenalin flowed. Instead of pain from her tearing flesh, she felt only a tug on her arm. Using her feet against the cat, she pushed herself away, but, again, the creature was on top of her, tearing for her throat. Hannah spun sideways, and the cat missed its target.She felt its teeth sink into her shoulder.

Though the battle had lasted only seconds, Hannah's strength was already slipping away as she bled from half a dozen wounds.

The cat repositioned itself to attack again. Hannah wheeled backwards, warding it off with her feet as best she could. The cat worried her from side to side, preparing for a final assault, then lunged. There was nothing she could do to stop it as it flew toward her.

Suddenly, a large branch appeared in front of her. Jason was swinging it back and forth across the cat's path. The cat landed awkwardly and turned away from Hannah to its attacker. Jason brought his stick around and positioned it between himself and the cat. The cat batted it away hissing, but Jason was quick, keeping the stick between them.

Hannah's right arm was nearly useless. She reached to her belt and took her knife from its sheath. She struggled to her feet and took a position next to Jason.

They faced the cat, screaming. Jason slammed the branch onto the ground in front of it. Then he brought the branch down hard on the cat's shoulder and neck. The cat stumbled back, shook its head, and spun toward Hannah. Then it leapt again.

Hannah fell back under its weight, her knife in hand. She thrust upward as her back hit the ground.

***

Jason watched in horror as a growing pool of blood seeped from beneath the two still forms. The cat was as big as he, and heavier than he thought it'd be. He pulled hard and was finally able to drag it to the side.

Hannah lay still and lifeless. In the darkness, Jason couldn't tell if she was breathing or not. He put his head to her chest, hoping to hear a heartbeat, but through her jacket, he could hear nothing. His own chest hurt with the thought that she was gone.

Then he felt a warm hand on the back of his head.

"Give me a hand, will you?" she said.

Congealing blood from her wounds was everywhere. Her torn clothing was saturated. It was impossible to tell how badly she was injured. Even in the subdued light of the fire, he could see how pale she was. He tried to talk to her, but her words were slurred, and her sentences made no sense. He tried to think clearly, but it was so hard. Images of his mother clouded his judgement. The possibility that Hannah might not survive made the task of helping her almost too much to bear.

Jason pushed her into a sitting position. She almost fell over. He righted her and unzipped her coat. He hoped he wouldn't have to cut it off her; now more than ever, she'd need it to keep the cold at bay. But he couldn't get to her wounds while it was on. He hurried, feeling as though his clumsiness was wasting precious time. Hannah was slipping away and he was too slow to stop it. He fought to remain calm.

Her right forearm was injured. Using his knife, he slit the coat from the cuff to the elbow. There were several clean puncture wounds. Although the coat sleeve was drenched in blood, the wounds seemed to be clotting on their own. There wasn't a great deal of blood loss there. The worst must be coming from elsewhere. Jason was sick with fear. Already, too much blood had been lost.

The cat had focused its efforts on Hannah's upper body. He continued to search, pulling at the coat, balancing Hannah, and fighting against time and despair.

He pulled the coat from her shoulders. His hand came away covered with fresh, warm blood. He worked quickly to cut and tear through her clothing so that he could get a clear view of the wound. The cat had bitten Hannah more than once in her shoulder. Some of the puncture wounds were clean, neat little holes, while others had torn deeply into her flesh. It was these he was worried about.

One of Hannah's injuries was high on her right shoulder at the base of her neck. It was from there that the blood poured freely, covering his hands as he worked. He reached behind him, grabbed Hannah's backpack, and rummaged for the first aid supplies. He pulled out the extra cloth and compresses. He passed one long strip of cloth under her left arm and brought it over her right shoulder. He folded a compress into a small square and pushed it against the wound where the bleeding was worst. He cinched it tightly and tied it off.

He moved to her other injuries and began putting bandages on them as quickly as he could. By the time he had finished dressing her wounds, he was cold. He could only imagine how she must feel. Her head was slumped against her chest, and she looked uncomfortable, so he helped her into a prone position. He took what warm clothing remained and covered her as best he could. There was nothing more to do except sit by and keep watch. He was comforted as he watched her chest rise and fall in regular intervals.

The fire blazed. Jason waited.

CHAPTER TWENTY-NINE

Midmorning came and went before Hannah began to stir. She opened her eyes and squinted against the sunlight. She tried to move but winced in pain. Jason gave her a piece of jerky and she took it weakly. She put it in her mouth and tried pulling off a bite, but didn't have the strength.

Jason took it and tried tearing it apart with his hands, but the jerky was too tough. In the end, he took it between his teeth, bit off a chunk, and gave it to her. She was able to get down a few bites before exhaustion overtook her and she fell asleep.

He was suddenly keenly aware of the crisp mountain air. It had a biting quality that gnawed at them, and when the wind came up, not even the fire could keep them warm. He spent his days keeping the fire blazing and making sure there was enough food and water available for the times when she woke.

By the evening of the third day, he was so worn out that he could no longer remain alert. He built up the fire and decided to take a short nap, promising himself he'd wake up at the slightest noise. He sat down close to Hannah, closed his eyes, and was asleep almost immediately.

****

Jason bolted upright at a sudden popping sound. It was dark except for the fire. He spun his head to the left to where Hannah had been resting. She wasn't there. Scared, he scanned the area. He was overwhelmed with a sick feeling that something terrible had happened. It sucked the air from his lungs. He fell forward on his hands and knees, wrestling with the need to vomit.

He sat back on his haunches, taking a gulp of air, willing his stomach to settle, and trying to wake up. What was that, on the other side of the fire? Obscured by smoke and flames, he could see Hannah crouching, warming herself. She fed the fire gingerly with her left hand. The other she held motionless next to her body. She smiled weakly at him.

"Hey, kid, I don't think I could have done a better job myself. Thanks."

"The fire?"

"No. My bandages, silly."

"You shouldn't be moving around," he said, hoping she could hear the concern in his voice. He moved to lend a hand. "I'm sorry I slept for so long. You need to get some more rest."

Hannah laughed lightly. "Jason, I couldn't sleep right now even if I wanted to. My back is killing me." She tried stretching a little. "Tell you what, I'll keep the fire going and you get a bit more rest."

Jason pulled his jacket tighter around him. He returned to his rough bed, lay down and closed his eyes. He woke in the morning with light from the sun shining in his eyes. Hannah had already cleaned her wounds, reapplied her bandages, and was working at mending her torn jacket, which was beginning to look like something from the fourteenth century with its large stitches made of thick material cut from the cat's hide instead of thread. The lines of stitching crisscrossed here and there as she connected the material in any way she could. It wouldn't be water repellant but when she was finished, the stitching held, and for the most part it looked like the coat would do the job it was intended for.

They maintained the camp for several days as Hannah's wounds healed, keeping careful watch and making sure the fire was always burning.

When her wounds had healed enough, they continued their journey. Every now and again they came across old, weathered signs that had long since been left to the whims of Mother Nature. Some had rotted and fallen into the foliage. Others would last for another winter or two before they, too, succumbed to the ravages of the mountain climate.

They passed a dilapidated sign stating they were at an elevation of a thousand meters. They continued to hike up one steep hill and down the next, dipping and rising, turning and twisting. Midsummer had arrived, but that high up, it didn't matter, Hannah and Jason plodded on, their food stores dwindling.

It was a difficult decision to postpone their journey to replenish their food supply. Hunting would prolong their time in the mountains and preparation would take precious time as well. According to the map, the remainder of the trip looked like an easy hike that would take only a few weeks, but there were numerous areas where spring floods would have either washed away the road or left it submerged. Still other portions had possibly been obliterated by avalanches.

Their clothing was beginning to wear out. The fact that Hannah's jacket had been shredded and repaired didn't help. As the days passed, the never-ending stresses on garments not meant to withstand this kind of use and abuse was taking its toll. Jason's knees had been peeking through his pants for weeks. The shredded material began centimeters above his kneecaps and didn't stop again until part way down his shins. In the olden days, his attire may have been stylish, but now it was just impractical.

"I don't want to, but I can't see a way around it. I think we need to find a place for a long-term camp," said Hannah.

"Long term?"

"Long enough to gather more food."

"Can't we wait a little longer?".

"I wish we could, but if we don't take care of our gear, or we run out of food, we might not finish this trip."

"Well, how about we walk and hunt? If we get a deer, we can set up camp then?" said Jason.

Hannah smiled, nodding. "Sounds good," she said.

"In the meantime, maybe we could play a game."

"What kind of game?"

"See who can see the next kilometer marker first."

***

It turned out to be a great game, helping them keep their minds occupied as well as gauging their speed. It also helped them calculate the distance remaining. Hannah had kept a rough calendar in her head to keep track of how much time remained before the weather began to cool. She estimated they were able to make between forty and fifty kilometers each day. Unfortunately, there'd been many delays along the way and there had been many days where traveling was slowed by conditions out of their control. From what she could tell, it'd been about a month since their journey began. With the delays and backtracking, they'd averaged about twenty kilometers a day. They needed to pick up the pace if they were going to reach Kamloops by fall.

Weariness was another factor, and it was beginning to have an impact. Wild game proved to be scarce at these high elevations, and there never seemed to be a decent place for a campsite. They trudged on, eating the last of the sheep.

As supplies disappeared, Hannah's spirits continued to fall. They climbed a south facing slope that looked like a comfortable place to rest. As they basked in the sun, eating quietly, a small herd of mule deer walked out onto the road just below them. A light breeze blew against Hannah's face, telling her that the deer wouldn't be able to smell them. Hannah could hear their hooves on the pavement. Without taking her eyes away from the deer, she popped her remaining jerky into her mouth and reached slowly for the rifle propped against her bag. Jason sat unmoving.

Periodically, the deer looked up from grazing to check their surroundings. The wind held its direction, allowing the hunters to remain undetected. Hannah operated the bolt. There was a slight click as the round popped up from the magazine and into the chamber. To her ears, the sound of metal against metal seemed loud enough to startle the herd. So did the beating of her heart. Hannah used the palm of her hand to rotate the bolt down into the cocked position. The deer continued to feed, unaware.

Hannah slowly raised the rifle to her shoulder. Using her bent knee as a rest, she leveled the gun and brought a deer into the cross hairs of the scope. She was about a hundred meters away, so she didn't have to compensate for elevation. The gun had been sighted for this distance. The light breeze would be of no consequence. The target held its position. Hannah squeezed the trigger.

Form the corner of her eye she saw Jason jolt as the gun thundered next to him. Hannah jacked another round into the chamber as the herd darted in every direction. Her focus remained on the deer she'd fired upon.

While the other deer scattered, her target remained. The impact of the bullet had shaken its body. She knew she'd hit it. The animal staggered and fell, rolling sideways into the ditch. It bounded to its feet momentarily, as though it had tripped, and leapt away in the direction of the rest of the herd. Hannah hoisted the rifle up ready to send another bullet in its direction, but the deer's body went limp in midair, and it fell into the grass, motionless.

Leaving their packs, Jason and Hannah raced down the hill. There was no moment wasted contemplating the lifelessness of the beautiful animal before them. There was no remorse. Animals were a source of food. They were sustenance. This wasn't a basket of berries, but it was a harvest nonetheless.

Hannah moved to the throat of the deer. She slid her knife through its skin and flesh, and with one motion, cut through most of the soft membrane of the neck. Blood began to flow freely, and Hannah moved to the lower part of the animal.

With Jason's help, she made three incisions that looked like a capital I. The top connected the front hooves across the animal's chest. The bottom connected the rear hooves. The last cut ran the length of the body and connected the two lines.

Within an hour, the hide was laid out flat with the hair down. With Jason's help, they placed as much boneless meat on it as they could salvage. Hannah hadn't chosen a particularly large animal. They needed to be able to carry what they harvested, and she didn't relish the idea of waste. By the time they'd gutted and de-boned it, what remained was less than half the original weight.

Hannah glanced around. There'd been no time to consider how she'd prepare the meat or where they'd have to move it. She'd need to make a fire and create the materials for preserving it.

Directly up the hill from where they stood were their packs. Beyond that was a protected area nestled among the trees. It would be a perfect environment for the chores that lay ahead.

As they dragged the meat uphill, she thought about what she would do with the raw hide. They stretched it flat among the rocks. "I'll get started here, if you go back for the packs," said Hannah.

When Jason had finished collecting wood and starting a fire, he went to work helping Hannah cut the meat into thin strips that would dry quickly. He took green boughs from the surrounding evergreen trees and threw them onto the fire to create the smoke needed to add a little flavor. They used nearby willows to create lattices to support the meat so it would dry in flat strips.

Tired after the long day's work, they feasted on fresh, mouthwatering venison.

Together, they maintained the smoky fire and continued to dry the meat through the night. Hannah wasn't particularly worried about the recipe. Her main goal was to get as much moisture out of it as she could. It had to dry thoroughly enough to keep. All their effort would be for nothing if the meat rotted in their packs. It would be even worse if they ended up sick from the bacteria that grew on it.

In the following days, she gave Jason the job of tending the fire and taking care of the jerky while she turned her efforts to the clothing. There were ways to turn the hide into leather, but she could also use it as it was just as well.

While it was still moist, she cut patches from it for the knees of Jason's pants. She poked holes along the edges a few millimeters apart. The hide would shrink so she laid them out to dry. She worked at them periodically to try and keep them from turning rock hard, though it didn't help much.

She pegged the rest of the hide down in the grass on the slope. She was amazed how much warmth could be garnered from the sun, given the right conditions. A few days later, the hide was mostly dried.

Hannah retrieved her rolls of thread. She first doubled and then quadrupled long pieces. Using her largest needle, she sewed her new patches onto Jason's jeans with the hair on the inside.

It was during her repairs that she noticed how much Jason had been growing. The clothes that once fit well were now beginning to ride high on his ankles. His shirtsleeves rested a few centimeters higher than his wrist.

When she'd first met him, he'd come up to her chest. Now his head came to her chin. These days, it was easy to see the contours of Travis' face in his. He was quickly growing into a handsome young man.

When the hide was finally as ready as it would ever be and the meat stored safely, they donned their packs and left their camp to continue their journey. They'd burned another week of summer. Already dark clouds settled on the mountain peaks, while clear blue skies accented the eastern skies. They were in a race, and their lives depended on them winning.

***

As their elevation dropped, the cold mountain climate gave way to typical summer days. The sun rose warm in the morning and that warmth soaked into them all day long.

There always seemed to be a light breeze in the mountains. That, and the fact that they were always moving, was enough to keep the mosquitos and other flying insects away. The evenings, too, began to feel warmer.

With the weather in their favor, finding places for camping was easy, so they used every moment of daylight they could. It was late summer when they stood at the top of a hill so long it seemed to drop into oblivion. There were no more rises to break their view. The downward trend lasted for as far as they could see. It was too early to tell, but from where they stood, it looked as though they were standing on the brink of the end of their journey. Hannah fought the urge to run, knowing they were likely still days away from the nearest settlement. Nevertheless, against her conscious will, her pace quickened.

CHAPTER THIRTY

In the early fall, the raggedy pair wandered into the ghost town of Kamloops. The weather hadn't yet turned cold in the valley; the days were still long and warm. The hills were scattered with orchards producing the Macintosh apples British Columbia had once been famous for. The season was over, but Hannah and Jason were able to find the odd late blooming tree. Their bodies craved a diet containing any kind of fruit or vegetable, so they took the best they could find and carved away the parts that were inedible. They feasted and then continued their march toward what they hoped would be civilization and a warm welcome.

The city wasn't as deserted as many of the communities in the lower mainland. The echo of children playing in the back alleys and parks danced on the wind. It was a good sound—a sound of hope. They crept through the streets. While there was evidence of habitation, Hannah knew the city sported only a small part of its original population. Without the roar of automobiles, the streets were almost silent. Caution was always the best practice, and Hannah felt sure they were becoming experts.

They moved slowly, hoping to remain undetected.

Suddenly, the streets became silent. The warm, welcoming sounds were gone. Hannah's hopes were destroyed in an instant. Along with the sudden silence, the potential of new dangers compounded her fear. It seemed apparent they'd been spotted, and this city had a contingency plan.

A message must have swept through the town. Hannah imagined children being rushed indoors by fearful mothers. A new and deadly threat had just entered their secluded community, one worth hiding from.

Hannah looked down at her hands. Her fingernails were packed with dirt and her hands were the color of mud. She ran her hands from her face into her hair, where her fingers became entwined in the knotted snarl that had once been comprised of individual strands. It had never occurred to her to reflect on how they must appear.

It might seem to the townfolk as though they'd stepped out of time. Their clothes were ragged, torn, and patched in the oddest ways. They were more a combination of animal and old world than products of this one. Jason looked like a comic book Cro-Magnon man.

Hannah's spirits fell as quickly as the noise in the streets. She became acutely aware of the pain in her shoulders from the long trek and carrying her share of the extra load of the recent addition to their provisions.

Hannah shucked the pack from her shoulders and collapsed onto the sidewalk in front of an old department store, her back to the wall as she sat in the shade of the awning. After a short rest, she'd figure out what to do next. Until then, it felt good to get the sun off her back.

After what felt like hours but surely wasn't, Hannah unzipped a side pocket in her pack and took out a water bottle. She took a swig and passed it to Jason. He looked at it indifferently at first, then casually accepted it.

"What do you think, big guy?" said Hannah.

***

Jason glanced from one end of the vacant street to the other. If he hadn't been there to hear the noises of the children playing, he could have easily imagined the town was unoccupied. "I didn't know it'd be this hard. I thought it would just be a long walk. If you hadn't come with me, I would've been dead ten times by now."

"Easy," said Hannah. "Don't be so hard on yourself. That big cat would have been the end of me if it hadn't been for you. This wasn't a trip anyone should've tried alone."

"That's my point, Hannah. It's been so long since I saw my dad, I can hardly remember what he looks like. How can we ever hope to find him? Why did I even try?" he said, tears beginning to form in his eyes.

Hannah pulled her pack from between them and slid over to Jason's side. She wrapped an arm around his shoulder and pulled him close.

Jason let her, then closed his eyes with the familiar smell of her smoky, dirty clothes filling his nostrils.

"You don't have to wonder what he looks like, Jason. You're his spitting image," said Hannah, giving him a squeeze.

CHAPTER THIRTY-ONE

Harrold Grimond, better known as Harry, was a mountain of man. He stood in the decadent living room of his mansion, drinking wine and looking out over his orchards through an enormous picture window. There were three entrances leading to various parts of the house, each guarded by pairs of armed men. A fireplace adorned the west wall, its stone chimney exiting through the ceiling.

The quiet was shattered by a skinny, short wisp of a man who ran into the room, yelling, "Harry, Harry!"

Harry turned at the sound of his name and extended his free hand, hoping to slow the little fellow, but instead of coming to a halt in front him, the man slammed into his open palm, crashed to the ground, and spilled Harry's drink. Even as Harry shook the wine from his dripping fingers, the little man babbled.

"Two men just came into town. There's a big 'un and a little 'un. Ah saw 'em just walking down the streets like they owned 'em!"

"What are ya goin' on about, Fidjitz?" said Harry, taking the small man by the collar and hauling him to his feet.

"Ah swear. Ah'm telling you! Two of the ugliest looking no-good-down-n-outers just came out of the mountains. Ya know no one ever comes that way! They must be real tough! Hurry up, Harry. They're coming down main street and they're almost right in town."

Harry looked at the men standing unmoving at the door. "Well, what are you waiting for? I pay you to do next to nothing most of the time. Gear up!"

The guards darted out of the room.

Fidjitz tugged at Harry's sleeve. Annoyed, Harry yanked his arm away. "Enough!" he said. His men returned, along with several others. "How many times have we done this?"

No one moved.

This time he yelled. "What're you waiting for? You know what to do!"

They followed Fidjitz along the streets until he came to an abrupt stop. "They're probably just up ahead somewhere," he said.

Harry gave a nod and the group split in two. One disappeared into the shadows of nearby buildings. The other slipped into the alleys.

"Show me where you last saw them," said Harry.

Fidjitz stopped at the next intersection and peeked around the corner. He pointed up the street. The strangers were sitting on the sidewalk in front of the department store. Harry glanced around at second story windows. At least a half of a dozen other town folk were watching. By the looks of it, they were quite the pair. The bigger one was armed and Harry could see how Fidjitz had come to his conclusion. If he judged them only by the clothes they wore, they weren't the savoriest of people. Harry dropped to one knee, and, looking at Fidjitz, put a finger to his lips.

Fidjitz nodded, following Harry's gaze.

For a long time, Harry studied the strangers, who sat a hundred meters up the street. His men had taken positions around them, and, until he gave his word, they all remained in an odd sort of stalemate.

From where he knelt it was impossible to tell much of anything about the two. He could see one rifle and two medium sized backpacks. The wide brimmed hats on their heads covered their faces. They sat in the shadows, making them even more difficult to assess.

Suddenly, the big fellow moved his pack aside and scooted over to the smaller man. The littler one leaned against the big man.

Fidjitz elbowed Harry and pointed.

Harry's eyes had already begun to narrow. He was trying to look past the bulkiness of their clothing as well as the dirt and shadows hiding their faces. The longer he studied them, the more he understood. What was that glistening on the little one's face? Were those tears? Harry looked closer. "Damn. This is stupid," he said.

***

A movement in the corner of her eye drew Hannah's attention. She'd expected someone would see them and they'd eventually be observed. She'd have done the same. She scanned every door and window, as well as the corners of every building within her view. Now and then, she detected fleeting movements among the shadows. Jason sat up and became more alert. Hannah stood and walked to the center of the street.

"What is it with you people? Have you forgotten what hospitality is, or are you all just a pack of cowards?" She intended to sound confident, but her voice cracked from the strain. She walked back to where Jason sat on the sidewalk.

A stout man, well over two meters, and maybe in his late forties, strode down the street toward her. He walked past her to her pack and picked up the rifle from where it rested. "No, lady, we haven't forgotten about hospitality, but please don't confuse caution with cowardice." With the rifle resting in the crook of his elbow, he patted the stock with his opposing hand. "I'll just hold on to this for the time being, if you don't mind. And, by the way, welcome to *my* town. You might recognize it. It used to be called Kamloops."

Hannah eyed the big man. In a way, she recognized herself in him. She, too, had fashioned her own town from the remnants left to her by a bygone society. Even back home, she would never have taken wandering strangers lightly. She would've been quick to put the safety of her town above anyone who happened through, no matter how needy they appeared. It wasn't unreasonable to expect the same from these men. They couldn't know she was a respectable woman who deserved to be treated with dignity.

The man raised a hand in air. A moment later, a squinty-eyed squirt of a man joined them as armed men appeared from nearly every visible doorway and began to advance. Ultimately, they were surrounded by twenty menacing figures. Hannah looked from one face to another. Their blank stares offered no clue as to their intent. She hoped she was looking into the eyes of a group of citizens concerned about their community and not some rogue militant group.

The big man broke the silence. "What brings you two all the way out here … and through the mountains, no less?"

"We're just passing through. We were hoping to get some rest, clean up, replenish our supplies, and be on our way," said Hannah.

"Where're you comin' from? We ain't seen nobody come from the mountains in years," said the man who resembled a weasel.

"We started out from Harrison Mills," Jason said.

"Never heard of it," the weasel said with a sneer.

He sounded rude and he struck Hannah as a nasty little man. "Like I said, we've been traveling for weeks. We probably made a big mistake coming the way we did, but that's just how it goes, I guess. It was the shortest route."

"You're pretty lucky," said the big man.

"Yeah, we figured. I'm surprised we made it this far. We've been in more scrapes than I can count. I'd be more than happy to tell you all about it, but we were just getting ready to have some dinner," said Hannah.

He smiled. "You haven't said where you're headed."

"Alberta."

"I can't believe you want to leave beautiful British Columbia. Doesn't that make you a couple of traitors?"

Hannah couldn't tell if he was serious or not. She chose to treat him as if he was kidding. "Just looking for a better way to live is all," she said, hoping he'd appreciate her refusal to back down.

"Well, here's the deal. I still don't know what to make of you, so, if you don't mind, I'll just hold on to this for a while," he said, indicating her rifle.

With as much sarcasm as she could muster, Hannah said, "I probably won't be needing it any time soon anyway. I've already got this wonderful warm feeling swirling around inside me. I can tell what a cozy little town this is, and I can hardly imagine ever wanting to leave." She continued with hardly a pause. "Listen, it seems like you can do one of two things. You can either shoot us, or you can pretend there's still a little hospitality left in this godforsaken country and offer us something to eat and maybe a place to clean up."

The man smiled, but his eyes were as cold as a reptile's. "I guess that's almost exactly what I was trying to decide. The truth is, lady, there's one other option I was thinking about. We could take everything you're carrying with you and send you packing on your way."

"That would suit me just fine. We made it this far. I'm sure we can keep taking care of ourselves … without your help," said Hannah.

"I can't help wondering how you're going accomplish that. Look around you," he said with a sweep of his hand. "Everything as far as you can see belongs to me. It's true, you can help yourself to anything, but then you'd be stealing from me, wouldn't you? And, frankly, I can't have that."

"People don't generally question my integrity," said Hannah, feeling her face warming. "Just hand me my rifle and I'll forget we ever set foot in this stink hole. We'll be out of here so fast that by the time you're asleep tonight, you won't even remember we were here."

"Listen, Mister, you can't even imagine how dirty and tired we are. We just want to sleep where it won't snow on us," said Jason.

Hannah's suspicions rose when the man's features softened. When he responded, it was as if he had flipped a switch.

"Well, you sure as heck must be one tough pair to be travelin' on those high roads. Fact is, we've never seen anyone walk out of those mountains." He patted Jason's shoulder. "I'll tell you what. Our little community isn't nearly as hostile as it seems. I'll lend a hand to a couple of fellow Canadians," he said with a sweeping hand toward Hannah and Jason. "Heck, I'll even invite you to my own home for dinner."

Hannah gathered her things. She had no choice.

"By the way, everyone in these parts calls me Harry."

Hannah put her hand out for her rifle.

Harry pulled it away. "We'll see how things go," he said, turning back in the direction they'd come from. The small crowd parted, and Hannah and Jason followed Harry through the gap, with his personal guard trailing. The skinny man followed behind them all. He reminded Hannah of a mangy dog.

They left town, going west. After walking for nearly ten minutes, a manor appeared ahead, looming over the town. Hannah guessed it was their destination. It was an impressive building, and one Hannah suspected Harry could never have afforded in his previous life.

The guards stayed with them until they mounted the steps of the massive home. Then everyone, except the skinny man, melted away. He remained at Harry's coattail even as they walked to the door. Without acknowledging him, Harry closed the door between them, leaving him standing alone outside. Maybe he slept on the porch, Hannah speculated.

Harry led them to the kitchen. "Why don't you have a seat on a real chair for a change. I bet you haven't enjoyed one of those in a while," he said.

Hannah was surprised to see him pop a couple of mugs of water into a microwave oven, punch a couple of buttons, and turn it on.

"Hey, Maggie!" he called. "Come down here and meet our guests."

Hannah heard movement above them. In a few moments, she heard the sounds of footsteps pounding on a staircase. A gaunt-looking woman who Hannah guessed to be in her late forties, wearing too much makeup and a bright red dress overloaded with frills, poured into the room. She reminded Hannah of a saloon hostess from an old western movie. Judging by the sound that her hurried steps had made on the stairs, Hannah'd expected to see an excited and happy person. Instead, the woman's eyes were lifeless and fearful, like a mongrel that'd been beaten its entire life.

"Maggie, these are our guests." Harry paused as if he'd forgotten something. "Oh, my," he said. "I don't even know your names."

Hannah offered her hand. "Hello. I'm Hannah and this is Jason."

Hesitant, Maggie looked to Harry. After his nod, she accepted Hannah's hand and shook it.

"There," he said, an insincere smile showing off white teeth, "friends already."

The microwave dinged, and Harry put the steaming cups on the counter. He opened a cupboard and brought out a container of instant coffee and a package of hot chocolate.

Hannah's mouth watered. She was surprised to see so many of the familiar conveniences she'd been accustomed to as a child.

"Your curiosity is obvious. Why don't you let Maggie show you to your rooms and you can freshen up? Later, you can ask all the questions you want. I'm quite proud of our little northern treasure. I'd be happy to tell you all about it over dinner."

Maggie led them upstairs. "Here's your room, Jason. Inside, you should have everything you'll need. I'll find something clean for you to put on, but I hope it's okay if it won't fit."

"Whatever you have'll be fine," said Jason, smiling.

"Can you give me a moment while I help get him settled?" Hannah said.

"Sure. Will you be long?"

"No. Just a minute or so." She followed Jason into the room.

"Holy crap," Jason exclaimed. "There's a bathroom in here. This is amazing. I've never seen anything like this before."

"I need you to focus for a second," said Hannah, taking him by the shoulders and bending forward to look him in the eye. "Try to keep your belongings as accessible as you can."

"Clothes, too?"

"Probably not. Just everything else. I don't trust Harry is all. For now, we need to be careful, okay?"

"Sure."

When Hannah returned, Maggie was still waiting in the hall. There was only one word to describe her get up: bizarre.

"Yours is just a few doors down," said Maggie, walking ahead and stopping in front of another room. "I hope you'll be comfortable," she said with a small smile. "I *know* I can find something you can wear."

"Thank you," said Hannah. She closed the door and left her clothes on the floor beside the bed but took the rest of her belongings to the bathroom. She'd be damned if she'd let Harry take any more of her things.

Hannah turned the water on and let it run until steam began to fog the glass. She stepped inside and adjusted the temperature until it was as hot as she could stand. She let it flow over her head, across her face and down her body. Satisfying dark mud flowed into the drain. She put generous amounts of shampoo onto her filthy hair and kneaded it into the knots. She washed all over, savoring every moment.

Half an hour later, Hannah emerged feeling clean and with her hair free of tangles. She found a dress laid out on the bed. She picked it up and held it in front of her, looking at her reflection in the full-length mirror. She'd expected it to be another old western special, but this was a tasteful summer dress. Maggie had also supplied her with a pair of leather sandals. Either Maggie was intuitive or just lucky, but Hannah liked this style.

She smiled. The sun was inviting, and she felt invigorated.

After she fixed her hair, she picked up her bag and took it downstairs. It was so disgusting that she didn't want to touch it. She hadn't noticed before, but now that she was clean, she could tell it reeked of campfire smoke and old sweat—not a pleasant combination. The pack was more dirt than fabric.

There was no one waiting for her when she stepped into the hallway, so she started downstairs. She followed sounds coming from somewhere below. On the way through the main living area, she saw Jason's pack and dropped hers beside it. She listened at the door while giving the living room a quick inspection. All the furnishings were beautiful solid wood pieces.

From the great room, she passed through an extra wide arch into the dining area where there was an antique table that looked as though it'd never been used. Tucked underneath was a series of matching chairs. In the center of the far wall were two large ornate swinging doors. She could hear voices from behind them. She listened for Jason's, but his wasn't among them; it sounded to be just Harry and the woman he called Maggie. She chose the door on the right, and it moved freely as she put her weight against it. It opened into the kitchen.

Harry and Maggie stood beside an island counter in the center of the room. A third person Hannah had never seen before was busy preparing a meal. She half expected an air of tension in the room, but there wasn't any.

Jason was nowhere in sight. Hannah's heart began to beat a little faster, but she remained composed and hoped neither of them would detect her agitation. If Harry or Maggie noticed, they didn't show it.

"Where's Jason?" she asked, as calmly as she could.

"My goodness, don't you look absolutely marvelous? Doesn't it feel good to get out of those old dungarees?" Harry said, ignoring her question.

Skipping pleasantries, Hannah asked, "Has Jason come down yet?"

"Isn't he just the most precious little boy you've ever seen? Harry said, directing the question to Maggie.

Maggie's lips turned up into something that was supposed to be a smile, but her lack of emotion made it clear she was only smiling because Harry expected it.

"Maggie and me never could have any kids. We tried and tried."

"Yes, Jason is very special." Hannah couldn't imagine why Harry wouldn't answer her question, but before she could press him further, Harry continued with his own agenda.

"Where's his father? A boy and his mother shouldn't be out travelin' all alone. I'm surprised a pretty thing like you would even dream of such an unbelievable adventure."

Hannah was becoming distraught and there was no way she could hide it. Harry was clearly getting some sort of satisfaction from torturing her, but she couldn't figure out what.

As if reading her thoughts, he said, ending the suspense, "Jason's just out in the backyard. Come on. Let's go see what he's up to. I thought he might prefer to play while he waited for you."

From the kitchen, they went through a mudroom. The back door opened onto a porch and a huge backyard that Hannah guessed to be more than four acres. Near the center was a large tree. Hanging from it was an old tire swing where Jason swung. He looked up when the screen door slammed shut. The moment he saw Hannah, he leapt from swing and made a beeline toward her. She hugged him tightly. Then she held him out at arm's length. He had been provided a shirt, jeans, and a brand-new pair of running shoes.

He spun in place with his arms out to show off his new apparel. "Hannah, look at these. Have you ever seen anything so great? I wish my mom could've been here to see this. She would just flip!"

Harry raised his eyebrows. "And all this time I thought you two were mother and son. Were you being sneaky, Hannah?"

This time Hannah had no doubt about Harry' smile. There was no warmth in it. She might as well have been looking into two black beads. They reminded her of a rat's eyes. She feigned confidence. "I guess if you'd asked and I told you that he was my son, you could say I was misleading you. Jason's more family to me than anyone."

Then she caught Harry staring. Her dress exposed the injuries caused by the cat. The scars were still a deep red. One ran from her elbow, up her arm and disappeared beneath the capped sleeve of her dress. The other, more severe looking of the two, zigzagged along her shoulder and up her neck.

"If it hadn't been for Jason, I'd be cougar food instead of standing here getting the third degree from you."

The maid came onto the porch. "Dinner's ready," she said.

"Now, that's perfect timing," Maggie said.

Hannah couldn't understand why their host and hostess were behaving so strangely, but decided that until she could figure out what was going on, she'd keep Jason as close as possible.

By the time they'd finished their meal, the sun had set. The sky was a beautiful red and purple burst of color that lit up the horizon in the west. Under other circumstances, it would've been picture perfect.

"Harry, we appreciate your hospitality, but we should probably find somewhere else to stay," said Hannah.

If Harry heard her, he gave no sign.

Hannah was fed up with whatever sick game Harry was playing. She needed to make herself understood, but she knew she had to find the right words. She wanted to be forceful, but not confrontational. She thought she understood how a fly in a spider's web felt.

She couldn't help feeling if she pushed too hard, she and Jason could end up prisoners. In fact, they might be already.

The skinny man came bursting into the room, ran to Harry ,and began whispering something in his ear. Harry's face was a dark mask.

When the man had finished speaking, Harry gave his fake smile and said, "Maggie, why don't you show our visitors where they'll be sleeping tonight? I'll be back in a bit." He left without saying more.

Hannah felt trapped. She worried if she decided to run, Harry had enough men to track them down. For now, they had no choice. She and Jason gathered their bags and followed Maggie upstairs. Maggie motioned Jason inside his room and closed the door behind him. She did the same for Hannah.

"Sleep tight, dearie." Maggie said as she closed the door.

Hannah heard the ominous clicking of the door's lock. She hurried to try the handle, but, as she feared, it was locked tight. She could hear Maggie moving away. There was a pause in the sound of her footsteps. The woman was too far away to hear, but she was probably stopping to lock Jason's door as well. Her suspicion was confirmed a moment later when Maggie cackled as she descended the steps, "Sleep tight, y'all."

Jason must have figured out what had happened. Hannah could hear him banging and kicking at the door. Perfect. Maybe he would keep it up for a bit.

She hadn't noticed earlier, but the windows were barred. It took her only moments, however, to see an easier way out of the room. Though the door had been modified so it could be locked from the outside, whoever had made the changes had overlooked a very important aspect of most interior doors: the hinge pins were on the inside of the room. Hannah dug through her pack until she found the multi-tool she always carried. Using the awl, she slammed it up into the hinge to drive the pin out. A couple of hits with the palm of her hand sent a sharp pain shooting up her arm. She needed something with a little weight to strike it. Using her foot, she broke off a leg from the vanity.

With her makeshift mallet, she made short work of her task. A few moments later, the door was off its hinges. She retrieved her bag and propped the panel in its frame before moving down the hall. She hoped it would fool anyone giving it a glance.

She ran to Jason's room. He was still hammering on the door. Hannah feared he'd start screaming if he thought she was Maggie. "Jason," she hissed. "It's me, Hannah. Calm down".

"Hannah, she locked me in! Help me. We've got to get out of here. Hannah? Hannah? Are you still there?"

"Jason, shhhh. I'm right here. Get your things together. This'll take me a minute."

This time she used a screwdriver to pry the doorjamb away from the frame. It was held on by only by a few small finishing nails. She wasn't concerned about getting it off in one piece, only about getting it off near the knob. With the wood clear of the latch, she used her knife to open the door.

Once inside, she tossed the bits of the doorjamb onto the bed. After closing the door to make their escape less immediately obvious, they crept to the main floor. The lights were still on throughout the house, and all was silent, making it impossible to tell where anyone might be. The living room was empty. Light was coming from beneath the dual swinging kitchen doors. Hannah took Jason's arm and pulled him to the left side of the door where they stood with their backs against the wall, listening. Still she could hear nothing. With her left hand stretched out flat against the door, she pushed against it, opening it just a crack. She could see about half the kitchen. It was empty and silent.

Hannah let the door slip closed and shifted to the opposite side of the door. From there she could see the rest of the kitchen. It too, was empty. Relieved, she motioned Jason to follow.

Hannah heard footsteps coming from the hallway. She tugged Jason through the door and slipped into the kitchen. Without hesitating, she ran out the exterior door, easing the screen door in place behind them.

They slipped into the night.

CHAPTER THIRTY-TWO

A few kilometers west of the city, nightlights flooded the fields surrounding what used to be the Kamloops Regional Correctional Centre. Each of the prison cells was part of the original structure, but there'd been numerous additions and modifications since it'd first been constructed. Its current function wasn't significantly different from the original, except that it no longer contained criminals.

All the bunks had been removed. Maybe it'd been because they'd run out of linen. Maybe it was because they wanted to be able to put as many people in a cell as possible. Then again, maybe it was to reduce disease. No one inside knew.

Travis Ryder watched his cellmate stand facing the bars with his face pressed between two of the cold, hard, metal cylinders. A normal sized man's cheeks would have been resting, one on each of the adjacent bars, but his cellmate was skinnier and smaller than many children. Travis imagined he'd probably paid for it with a lifetime of being teased, taunted, and tormented.

The bars were far back on his face. Only his cheek bones were stopping him from passing through, and that by just the thickness of his skin. Like a ring one size too small, a little more pressure would be all it would take.

He'd been Travis' companion since they'd first thrown him into the cell, so he had no idea as to the number of times Ajax had tried to escape this way. The little man wasn't a fast learner, but he was persistent. He twisted his head, first one way and then the other, all the while pushing as hard as he could. The metal scraped against the sides of his face. Although the pain must have been horrific, Ajax pressed harder. His cheekbones cleared the bars, and suddenly his face passed through. His ears followed.

Travis shook his head. He probably should have done something about it, he knew, but he would have thought Ajax would have learned by now.

Ajax's triumph was short lived. He suddenly realized he could neither get through the bars, nor could he go back. Already, his injured face had begun to swell, and his ears were now acting like fishhooks. When he tried to pull back into the cell, his ears and the bones of his face held him fast. Panicked, he began to yell. "Tavs! Help! Help me, Tavs!"

Damn, Travis thought. He should never have let it get this far. Travis shook his head. How many times had Ajax pulled this stunt? He'd stopped counting. Eventually, it would get him killed. Travis wondered why this had to be his problem.

In the past, he'd tried to calm Ajax. He'd tried to find something to act as a lubricant so he could slide his head out. There was next to nothing in the cell, so there was nothing Travis could do to help. The man was a damn fool. "Stop screaming," Travis said through clenched teeth.

"I can't! It hurts. It hurts bad!" said Ajax, wailing.

With this kind of racket, the guards could come at any moment. "If you don't shut up, I promise you, I'm gonna kick your ass," said Travis.

"Please, Tavs, please. Get me out! I wanna get out," said Ajax.

"Well, you're not getting outta there by yelling, and the guards will be here any minute."

"Oh, no! No guards. Please Tavs, help me! Help me!"

Travis' temper flared. If the guards came, they would remove Ajax in pieces. "A promise is a promise," he said. He took a step back and kicked. His foot came to an abrupt stop against Ajax's crotch. "Now shut the hell up," he said.

Ajax slid to the ground and lay motionless, his head trapped on the other side. He knelt whimpering and clutching his ass.

"Stupid shit. I bet you licked a frozen metal pole when you were a kid, too," said Travis. "What the hell do you think you're doing, screaming like that?" Part of him wanted to leave the berating at that. He might have, if it had been the first time Ajax had done this. "You know what they'll do if they see you like this, don't you? They'll solve your problem, all right. They'll take your head right off." Travis snapped his fingers to make his point. "And what's worse, they'll probably take mine as well. You know they will." Travis exhaled. You are so stupid. I can't believe you can't figure this out for yourself."

The main door of the cellblock creaked open and a bright light spread across the floor. The elongated shadow of a guard began at the door and stretched to the other end of the block. Silence replaced the normal din when, as one, all the prisoners seemed to cease breathing. For a long time, the guard loomed in the entry and Travis knew it'd been Ajax's noise that'd brought him.

Apparently satisfied nothing was amiss, the guard departed. A hydraulic closer eased the door shut, returning the cellblock to near darkness.

The guard hadn't stuck around long enough for his eyes to adjust. Ajax was damn lucky he hadn't been seen.

Travis leaned back against the wall. There wasn't much to talk about in a cell shared with a man whose language was as limited as Ajax's. The most he ever said tended to be in situations such as these. Travis began speaking in a low thoughtful tone. "I like you. I really do.

Usually, I don't mind taking care of you, but this is getting ridiculous. You never learn."

Ajax continued to whimper.

"I really don't understand how you got this far. I know you want me to help you out of there, but your face is too swollen. Anyway, you're just going to end up right back in there. One of these days, someone is going to put a bullet in your skull. I don't want that, and I know you don't want it, either."

Travis closed his eyes, leaving Ajax with one last thought. "Just shut your trap and stop your damn whining. You'll just have to wait until the swelling goes down a little."

Ajax's noises softened, but he continued to moan.

"Shut up. Otherwise you can stay there 'til breakfast."

Ajax closed his mouth.

Travis knew they kept Ajax around because of his size. If it wasn't for that, they probably would have done away with him long ago. They worked in the coal mine during the day, and he could get into places bigger men couldn't. He'd listen to Travis, so they kept them as cellmates.

As frustrated as he'd been, Travis felt bad for kicking Ajax. He was the size of a child and mentally handicapped to boot. Nonetheless, some days he hated the man, partly because they'd never be able to have a normal friendship.

As the hours passed, Ajax lay on the floor with his mouth gaping, oblivious of the small puddle of drool that'd begun to form in front of him.

The night wore on and the temperature dropped. It was cold at night at the best of times, and Ajax's teeth began to chatter loud enough for Travis to hear. Usually, when the two of them got cold, they'd huddle together. The clothes they wore weren't intended to do more than offer basic protection. Any prisoner, including Travis, could drop dead and no one would mourn. Those who died were the lucky ones; as far as Travis knew, no one had ever escaped.

Travis listened to Ajax shiver. The colder he was, the better. When he was cold and tired, he tended to make less of a fuss once the time came to free him.

Exhaustion and near hypothermia were the only substitutes they had for sedatives. After he felt enough time had passed, Travis went to Ajax's side. "Be still, now and I'll try to get you out of there," he said in a hushed tone.

Ajax remained calm.

Travis lifted his head and squared it to the bars. He pressed Ajax's ears hard against the side of his face and fed them through the gap.

Ajax's whimper grew louder as the pain increased. Somewhere in his brain, he seemed to know the precarious nature of his situation. Pushing hard and steadily, Travis forced Ajax's face back through the bars, peeling Ajax's beard away as he went, taking a layer of skin along with it. When Ajax was freed, there was no ceremony or rejoicing. Travis left him to his own devices and retreated to his corner. He needed to get some rest. The morning always came too soon.

***

The night ended, yet there was no hint of sunshine in the cellblock. Without warning, the door at the end of the hall opened. Three burly figures lumbered between the cages. Except the occasional glimmer reflecting from their eyes, they were no more than silhouettes.

Travis yawned. It was still too early for the regular morning routine. From somewhere down the hall, Travis heard a key as it was inserted into a barred door. There was an audible clicking sound as it did its work. A door swung on rusty hinges. A few moments later, the three guards returned, dragging a reluctant figure between them.

No one talked about why this sort of culling took place. Some of the prisoners thought they did it to keep the remaining prisoners frightened and well behaved. Travis was pretty sure the real reason was because the unfortunate ones hadn't or couldn't work hard enough. He didn't care. The person being dragged away wasn't him, and that was what mattered.

Travis sat with his back to the farthest wall. Ajax scooted closer and leaned against him. Travis put a comforting arm around his shoulder. Even Ajax seemed to understand that whoever'd been taken wasn't coming back.

Travis closed his eyes. The long years of imprisonment and labor had begun to wear on him. He had little patience, and he was growing weary. How long would it be before they came for him one of these cold mornings? He hated himself for mistreating Ajax. "I'm sorry," he said. "I promise I'll never kick you like that again."

The door opened. A woman with a cart, accompanied by another with a ladle, came down the hall. There were no trays, bowls, or flatware. The trolley stopped in front of each cell and the serving woman deposited a ladle full of wet gooey slop in a heap on the floor. It wasn't because the glop landed on the floor that made it nasty, but the fact that it was a gooey, thick, white mass of vile consistency and taste. Travis was grateful the servers dropped the meals in the same place every day. That was something. It also made that part of the floor sacred. Neither he nor Ajax ever walked on it, and Travis kept it as clean as he could.

They ate. With one hand, Travis fondled an ivory-colored bone dangling from his neck. Years earlier, there had been a third cellmate. His name had been John and the bone had come from him.

One day, while working in the mine, John had lost two fingers beneath the sharp edge of a spade. Travis never understood what his thinking had been when he brought them back to the cell. Maybe he'd hoped he'd be able to get them reattached. Whatever the case, he kept them.

It hadn't taken long for his hand to become infected and useless. Soon afterward, he became sick and weak. When his uselessness matched that of his injured hand, the guards had come and taken him away. Like everyone else they removed, John didn't return. The only thing he left behind were two fingers.

Travis smiled. Here he was rolling a human bone between his own fingers, and he'd thought John was crazy. Now he wore the bone around his neck to remind him of how precarious life could be.

Each morning, after the kitchen staff served the gruel, the guards returned to take the prisoners to the mine. Once their doors were opened, prisoners created two columns. In the main hall, inmates from other wings joined them, creating one enormous assembly.

Ajax was in no condition to work. "Stay here and stay out of sight," Travis said. Ajax had barely eaten, and Travis was confident he hadn't slept all night. If the guards found him, Ajax might not be in the cell when Travis returned from the mine.

The door opened and the morning routine began. They marched out of the prison, through security gates, and into the blinding light. The workforce was composed of a hodgepodge of men, women, and children. They followed the road out of the compound and marched for fifteen kilometers to an old open pit mine called Ajax.

Ajax wasn't the name Travis had given his cellmate. He surmised that, because Ajax didn't know his own name, the guards had given him one of their own. Ajax had been what they called him when they'd first met, so that's what Travis called him, too.

At one time, the mine had produced gold, but there were large coal deposits as well, which was excavated and taken to the east side of the mine where it was stockpiled. It was how they produced heat and electricity for the town. The reserves were already enough to supply power for decades.

It was grueling work that tended to lower life expectancies. Individual shafts had been dug at the bottom of the pit near the water level. The shafts brought new kinds of dangers, including gas pockets and cave-ins. Death at the mine was a regular occurrence.

Travis looked up and down the ranks, as was his habit, but few looked up. There seemed none among them with the spirit to do more than follow orders. Most of the prisoners were frightened and bewildered. Their faces wore a broken look that he'd long since grown accustomed to. Most of the men and women standing around him were already corpses just waiting to be buried. One or two of the prisoners met his gaze, but their eyes betrayed them. They were no more than human husks.

A coughing noise came from behind. Travis turned to see a man throwing up and wondered if he was sick or simply scared. When Travis had first arrived, he'd considered forming alliances and friendships, but he quickly learned how futile an idea it was. There was no point getting to know anyone, so the man's name didn't matter.

Travis's gaze found his feet and he thought back to when he first got there. They'd stripped him of everything he owned, leaving him with only a set of clothes like the rags he now wore. When they decided his clothes should be replaced, then, like his food, they threw them unceremoniously into a pile on the cell floor. The only belonging he could call his own was the bone hanging from his neck from a cord he'd fashioned from the fabric of his shirt. He stroked it while he wondered what kind of man he had become. The beater of helpless handicapped men on the brink of death? He hoped he was more.

The group was moving, tearing him from his thoughts. He couldn't afford to fall behind. That mistake had proven fatal for many. He glanced up at the clear blue sky and his thoughts turned to God. He didn't know whether to pray or curse. He wasn't sure it even mattered. The only thing that he knew for certain was that part of him still clung to survival, still held out for some hope of escape. He had to see Tate once more.

CHAPTER THIRTY-THREE

It took an hour and a half to walk from the prison to the mine. They came to the edge of the hole and Travis didn't give the seemingly bottomless pit gaping before him a second look. He braced himself for the knee-pounding descent that wouldn't end until he reached the entrance of his mineshaft. Most of the prisoners were seasoned and were no longer emotionally and physically affected by the routine. New prisoners tended to be wide-eyed and nearly paralyzed with fear. There may have been a third group of those who were biding their time, hoping for an opportunity to flee, but this group was either too small or too wise to let themselves be known.

Travis was one of this third group. He had often toyed with the idea of flight, but, looking around him, he knew the prisoners would be no help if an opportunity for escape presented itself. And, alone, there was no hope.

Kamloops was the closest town. To make matters worse, they used dogs to hunt down escaped prisoners. Travis wondered what he might look like to everyone else. He was no pinnacle of strength. His cell had been his home for so long he struggled to remember his life before it.

Soon he would reach his mineshaft and begin work, but, for now, he found himself longing for home. What had become of Tate and Jason? Facing the daily task assigned to him was one thing, but when his memories came flooding back and the fear that something terrible might have happened to them, it made the idea of carrying on almost unbearable. He blinked away tears welling.

Travis' thoughts shifted to Ajax.

Through the years, he'd never been able to teach Ajax much. Admittedly, he'd never really taken the time to try to understand why that might be. It seemed pointless. He could've had worse company, to be sure. Ajax would often respond correctly when Travis spoke to him, proving he had some ability. But, in many ways, he had more in common with a mutt than a human being. Travis had become both his teacher and his guardian. There'd even been the occasional tender moment. In a small way, Ajax had become a friend.

Enough of that sentimental crap, he told himself. His cellmate was a gibbering idiot without the sense to keep his head in his cell. He shook his head with a faint smile. One thing about Ajax, he never gave up.

Maybe Travis had learned something from Ajax after all.

The group had wound its way down the switchbacks to the mine. The time for dreaming had ended. Now it was time to work.

The prisoners broke into smaller groups, and Travis entered his tunnel. The mineshaft wound this way and that, following the thin veins of coal ore wherever they ran. Lanterns lined the rock walls.

Travis's crew consisted of himself and nine other men. He expected them to be one short, but as always, they were ten. Had they replaced Ajax already? Of the original group of ten, only three remained. Besides Ajax, the other was a hard man named Jared. Travis was pretty sure he hadn't yet resigned himself to his fate.

There were never women or children among them. Boys were used in other mine shafts in much the same manner as Ajax. When the boys became men, they'd replace those who had died or were killed.

Since the quality of the ore couldn't be determined in the darkness of the mine, the women were employed outside to sift through it.

They reached the end of the tunnel and broke into two groups. Travis picked up his shovel and began to fill his buckets. As soon as he finished, a man picked them up and began the long hike out of the mine. Throughout the day, they switched jobs as necessary. Whether he was shoveling or hauling rock, it was backbreaking work. When the day was over, the long walk back to the prison would be as close to a break as he'd get. Eating and sleeping weren't really breaks.

There were two wagons waiting at the entrance. Each team would fill one. There was no point finishing early since they were required to mine for the full duration, regardless. The real goal was to finish on time and avoid the penalty of failure. 'Work steady. Fill the wagon,' was Travis' motto. Three hundred buckets full was what it took.

Travis could still remember his first day. There'd been no warmth from the other prisoners. They were far too tired and too overworked to care— unless he didn't pull his weight. Then they cared. Then they cared plenty.

There'd be hell to pay if the crew failed to meet quota. First, there was the payment the guards would exact, but then there was the payback owed to Jared. Travis couldn't blame him. It was one thing to be saddled with a couple of greenies and then have to follow them around and make sure they didn't get themselves killed. It was worse still to fail to meet quota because of them.

Today was one of those days. The new crew members seemed fit enough, but they looked more scared than anything else. If it'd happened to them like it'd happened to Travis, they'd been lulled into a false sense of security before being captured. They'd been wined, dined, and showed what a wonderful little town they'd stumbled into. They were given a hot bath, fresh clothes, a hot meal and a comfortable bed. Unfortunately for Travis—and, he guessed, the rest of them—the bed hadn't lasted the night.

The new men had closed their eyes and had fallen asleep to visions of sugarplums until they were rudely awakened only to find they were tied hand and foot. They were dragged to a wagon and dropped off in a dark cell with nothing to look forward to but a hard day's work and, eventually, a bullet to end it all.

That was what had likely happened to Ajax. There was no point feeding what couldn't earn its keep. If he made it through today, he'd probably find a new cellmate waiting for him.

Another bucket was full. He had ten more to fill before rotation. His turn on the pick was next, a harder job by far. The crew could only fill the wagon as fast as a man could dig.

Travis was fortunate. At least these newcomers knew enough to get their asses in gear. There wasn't anything else to learn. Work your ass off and make it through the day. Even an idiot could do that. Hell, Ajax had been proving that for years.

The day wore on like every other day before it. They loaded the wagon and hiked back to the prison in the dark. Although it still took hours, the hike back always seemed shorter. Travis wondered if he'd find Ajax in the cell when he got back. He hoped he would.

CHAPTER THIRTY-FOUR

Travis crossed the cell to the back wall. His eyes adjusted to the darkness. His chest ached a little at the thought his cellmate might be gone. "Ajax, you in here?" There was no answer. "Where are you, little buddy?" Travis scanned the room, but the cell was empty. Travis sat and hunched forward, his elbows on his knees and his hands carrying the weight of his head. He was supposed to feel nothing, but he couldn't help himself. Ajax was gone, and it could only mean one thing.

As a man, Ajax hardly qualified. Everything he'd done in his life had amounted to nothing. Travis had tried to talk to him, but Ajax had no memories. The fact that he had parents was inescapable, but Ajax had no recollection of them or any name they may have given him.

Maybe the first time Ajax had been greeted as if he was anything other than a beast was by Travis when he'd been thrown into the cell.

He'd never been able to teach Ajax to say 'Travis'. The closest he ever got was 'Tavs.'

Ajax had very little understanding of the world around him. Whatever ailed him made it nearly impossible for him to learn anything new. His knowledge and understanding of the English language were rudimentary. The guards called him Ajax and Ajax understood it referred to him.

Travis sighed as he reflected on his earlier behavior. He would've liked to have been the model of patience, but he wasn't. When he was feeling angry and frustrated, he tended to call Ajax an idiot. It seemed to make no real difference to Ajax. He didn't know what an idiot was anyway. Travis often justified his bad behavior imagining he was nicer to Ajax than anyone else, but he knew there was no excusing his poor conduct. Ajax couldn't help who he was. His disabilities weren't a matter of his choice. Hurting Ajax had been akin to beating a child or a dog. Travis felt ashamed.

What was most frustrating about Ajax was his inability to remember anything. Ajax's short-term memory seemed to last just a few minutes, just shy of the time it would take a normal person to put those thoughts into long-term memory.

For no reason other than his own personal optimism, Travis was convinced if Ajax had been brought up in a normal home, he might have overcome some of his challenges. Travis needed to believe that. If he hoped to help Ajax, he had to trust his work could come to some good.

Travis smiled as he reminisced. In some ways, it had. Progress had been slow and difficult, but when Travis compared Ajax's abilities of today to the day they met, there had been a significant improvement. A residual bonus had been that his work with Ajax gave Travis something to keep his mind focused on something other than the laborious task of working in the mine.

Although learning was difficult for Ajax, one thing Travis was sure he knew without a doubt was that captivity was a harsh and unpleasant way of living. On a nearly daily basis, Ajax tested the bars. Travis could imagine him thinking if only he could get his head through, the rest of his body could follow. It was never that Ajax tried that bothered Travis. It was that Travis had to rescue him each time. He didn't enjoy being the cause of the pain Ajax suffered during the reversal process, but he especially didn't like the worry of what would happen if the guards found Ajax stuck there.

Ajax seemed to understand that escape was simple, that the only way out of the cell, and the prison, was through those bars. Travis had to admit, if he could get his head through, he might have done same thing. After his head, there was just the chest and pelvis left to squeeze through. Yeah, if there was a chance, Travis would try.

Even though scars that Ajax would never be able to explain covered his body, suggesting a sad and painful past, Ajax was a happy soul until the end. He didn't talk much, but his smile was infectious.

He'd miss Ajax.

CHAPTER THIRTY-FIVE

Ajax waited until the guards were gone. It'd be a long time before the hall door would open again. He placed his face firmly against the bars and began to work his cheeks from side to side, forcing them forward with each push. Part of him was familiar with this. His cheeks were still raw from the previous evening's ordeal. He couldn't remember much, but he remembered being this far and knew he could do it again. He worked his ears through, and the rest of his head followed easily.

He rested.

This was as far as he'd ever gotten before. Tavs had always been there to help him after he'd calmed down, but Tavs wasn't here this time.

When he'd relaxed a little, he stood as tall as he could and turned his body sideways to the bars. He started first with his arm and then his shoulder. His shirt added too much thickness, so he removed it and let it fall to the floor. Using the same technique as he had with his head, he slowly inched his upper body between the bars. He exhaled as much as he could and forced his chest and ribs to flex as he pushed himself through the narrow opening. With each painful movement, he shoved his way farther between the bars.

Ajax took shallow breaths. There wasn't room for his chest to expand enough to allow his lungs to fill with air. When he thought he could stand the pain no longer, the last of his ribs finally passed through. He contorted his stomach and slid through up to his hips, then he collapsed to the next cross member. For a long time, he lay there, half in and half out of the cell.

He was still resting when he heard heavy footfalls drawing closer. The sound was coming from somewhere on the far side of the door. He'd been making too much noise. Ajax panicked. He was stuck. There was no going back. He couldn't push with his legs as he had before. The most he could do was wriggle his lower body while pulling against the floor.

Ajax twisted and cocked his hips. He focused on just one hipbone at a time. He could feel the skin peeling away as he progressed, but adrenaline and fear counteracted the pain.

The sounds of the guard grew closer.

With a lurch, the widest part of his second hip cleared the bars and the rest of his body followed. Ajax stood and proceeded to the door. After a couple of strides, he remembered to grab the clothing he'd shed and then he ran toward the door.

He looked through the window in time to see a guard on the other side. The door swung inward, and Ajax slid behind it. He stood silent, barely breathing, with less than a foot between him and a man who'd put him back in the cell—if he didn't kill him instead. Ajax held his breath. The guard stood for a moment, then turned around. The door swung closed behind him.

Ajax didn't know how long he waited behind the door. He kept important ideas in his head by replaying them over and over. The image he now replayed was of the guard walking down the long corridor. In Ajax's mind, he kept walking over and over from one end of the hallway to the other. When he could hold onto the image no longer, he looked through the little window again; he had to stand on the tips of his toes to see outside. The hall was clear. He slipped through the door as quietly as he could.

Nothing was familiar to him. He needed to get out and it wasn't going to be easy. The urgency of leaving the building had already begun to fade. Ahead were empty corridors. Behind him? He turned to look. There was a large metal door with a small square window in the center. He went to it and opened it; it led to his cellblock. The memories flooded back. He cocked his head. Had someone from inside the cellblock hissed at him to go? Maybe it was only one of his thoughts. Either way, he listened to the voice and went.

Somehow, Ajax's feet managed to lead the way. He didn't trust his memories. They were quiet shadows, more like dreams than reality. As if some inner instinct had taken control, he followed his intuition. He didn't second guess or waste time wondering which was the correct path. He stayed low and left the building as quickly as he could.

Once outside, Ajax sprinted toward the trees. He found a hiding place in the brush and rested. The prisoners returned, chains clanging, and Ajax watched them march by.

CHAPTER THIRTY-SIX

Maggie came into the living room and found the door to the kitchen still swinging on its hinges. She thought of their guests and ran to the foot of the stairs. She could see the first bedroom. The door was closed. She turned toward the kitchen. She slammed through the door to be greeted by silent stainless-steel appliances. She ran to the exterior door and yanked it open. She was just in time to see the gate swing lazily closed.

She spun on her heel and raced upstairs into Jason's room where she saw the door molding laying on the bed. *Damn*. Harry was going to beat her, or maybe worse. He might kill her.

She ran up the hall to Hannah's room. With key in hand, she put one hand on the knob. The door overbalanced and fell into the room. Maggie's face paled. Like a sleepwalker, she stumbled to the bed and slowly sat.

***

Harry returned to a still, silent house. Maggie could normally be heard mulling around somewhere. He was hesitant to call her name, for some reason he couldn't identify. He started in the kitchen then went from room to room on the main floor. The house was empty. Something was wrong. He reached into his pocket and pulled out a metal object about ten centimeters long. With a flick of his thumb, he transformed it into a knife. With his back to one wall, he looked up the staircase, then back into the living room. Step by step, he worked his way up the stairs.

It occurred to him that he might have underestimated the woman and the boy. He scanned the rooms as he passed them until he found Maggie sitting on the bed. There was nothing to be said. She'd failed him. He left her there—she could rot in that room for all he cared—and went downstairs, turning off the lights along the way.

CHAPTER THIRTY-SEVEN

Hannah and Jason fled into the street. An occasional light illuminated a window here and there, but otherwise all was black. Jason tried to run ahead, but Hannah blocked him with her arm. She looked right and left. For as far as she could see in both directions, the streets were bare. Hannah nodded to the west. "This way."

"But this is the wrong direction," said Jason.

"Yes, it is," said Hannah. "We told Harry we were heading toward Alberta. When he finds out we're gone, we might not be able to get out of the city going that way."

"So we go west and then around?"

"Not much of a plan, but we don't have time for a better one."

They raced toward the outskirts of the city.

There was no time to choose their next destination. They needed to get to a safe place that would allow them to take some time to think and get reoriented. Making the hardest decisions under the most adverse circumstances seemed to have become a way of life. Hannah had discovered long ago it was a skill that could be developed and honed.

They ran for an hour before slowing to an effortless jog. Regardless of the fact there was no evidence a search party had been formed, she wanted to be a safe distance from Harry before she looked for a place to rest.

The streets formed a standard grid, so it was easy to keep track of the general direction and distance they'd traveled. Even as her mind raced, she knew they were at least a couple of kilometers away from where they'd started, and that was comforting.

Now she could start to think about a place to sleep.

There were numerous houses and most of them seemed vacant. It would've been nice to have been able to slip into any one of them, but she had no idea how populated the area had become. She wouldn't risk entering a dark house only to discover it was occupied.

They hurried through the unfamiliar streets, and then beyond. Eventually, the city houses began to thin.

Tired, worn out, and on the verge of collapsing, they stumbled into a barn. Feeling her way into the dark interior, Hannah found a supporting post near the center with a ladder attached. It creaked and moaned as they climbed up. Although the loft smelled musty, remnants of dry hay still littered the floor.

Hannah rummaged through her bag until she found her old clothes. She was still wearing the summer dress and had been unpleasantly exposed to the cold breeze flowing between her legs as they sought freedom. They were dirty and worn, and it pained her to have to put them back on, but she knew she'd get no sleep dressed as she was.

"Hannah, that's gross," said Jason. "Those old clothes stink bad."

"Tell me about it."

"Were we really that dirty?"

"No," Hannah said, with a pause for comedic effect, "you were worse. Now be quiet and help me pull some hay together."

Hannah had no idea how long they'd been running, but it was long after dark. And it wouldn't be long before the morning sun began to rise. Part of her dreaded the light, but she'd welcome its warmth. Without the convenience of phones or radios, Harry would be at a disadvantage—if he chose to start a manhunt at all.

The moment her head touched the hay, Hannah replayed the evening's events in her mind. She could hear Jason's deep breaths above the rustling noises of the mice and other rodents sharing the barn with them. Questions filled her mind. There'd been no time to become acquainted with the town, so there was no time to develop allies.

The burning question was why had Harry deceived them with false hospitality and then locked them in their rooms? Close on the heels of that question flooded others: Why had town's people surrounded them when they arrived? What were they planning on doing with them once morning came? Where did the electricity come from? Everywhere else there was none. The province was shutting down, but from what she could tell, Kamloops still enjoyed the comforts of the old world. There were so many riddles to unravel. Too many.

CHAPTER THIRTY-EIGHT

Hannah woke first. The barn was an ancient old style one with a loft above and individual stalls below. The roof was a gridwork of beams and ancient shakes. She could see the sky through a multitude of holes in the roof. In one section, a beam had given way and part of the roof littered the floor.

Hannah inspected the ladder they'd used the night before. It looked like some kind of animal had eaten almost all the way through many of the rungs and she was amazed they'd made it up safely. She thought about the bale elevator she'd spied on the floor nearby. For safety's sake, when the time came, she'd drop it to the ground and use it instead.

Among the many possessions in her pack, Hannah had a pair of binoculars. She'd considered getting rid of them because she rarely needed them, but today she dug them from beneath everything else and looked out over their surroundings. They were high enough she could see a little of the town and adjacent area. They were west of the city center by several kilometers. Across the valley on the opposite hillside, she could make out even rows of trees, likely an orchard. There were other flat areas that looked like they might be cultivated fields. Some might be corn while others looked like they might be some sort of grass crop. There was even evidence of livestock grazing on higher slopes.

She was amazed at the apparent organization it must've required to pull off such industry. Her wonder was punctuated by the rumbling in her stomach, but she'd have to ignore it for now.

Even with the binoculars, the city was impossible to appraise. From her perch, the city streets were out of her view. Except for the wind rustling the leaves of nearby trees, everything was silent. Out of the north, from somewhere in the hills, a black plume of smoke rose in the air.

Someone, she couldn't remember who, had mentioned no one had come out of the hills in a long time. Since they'd tried to capture her, maybe there'd been others. She returned to her bed. Jason was still asleep. By the look of the sun and the feel of its warmth, it was about midmorning. She lay back down and tried to piece the puzzle together. She must've been more exhausted than she thought. Before long, she began to dream.

CHAPTER THIRTY-NINE

A clamor from below snapped Jason out of his deep slumber. What was Hannah doing down there? He was about to yell down when he saw she was still asleep beside him. Someone was in the barn. He placed his palm over her mouth. Her eyes flew open. Then she heard the noises, too. Jason removed his hand, and they lay, barely breathing. There were at least two men below.

"I don't know why we're here. It's not as if they're going to hang around. Besides, if they were heading toward Alberta, they wouldn't have come this way," said one.

"They're probably long gone. You see anything back there?" inquired the other.

"Nope, nothing."

"Check out the loft, and we'll get outta here."

"You must be joking. Go up there yourself. Just look at that ladder. No one could have gotten up there without that thing crashing down."

"Listen, you useless sack of crap. Get your ass up there and check it out, or I'll end this argument with a bullet right here and right now!"

The second man grunted. There was a pause followed by a creaking sound that could only be caused by his weight on the lower rungs. Jason could hear him as he ascended the twelve-foot ladder adjoining the two floors. He sat motionless as the distance closed. Jason saw a shock of hair appearing through the hole in the floor. He would wait just a moment more. When whoever it was, looked up, he'd jump to his feet and knock him backward through the hole. With any luck, it'd disable him and give them a chance to escape. Either way, they'd go down fighting this time. Every muscle in his body tightened as he readied himself.

The man's hand reached for the last rung. He clasped it firmly and began to draw his weight upward. Suddenly, there was a snapping sound and the shock of hair disappeared. Jason saw the man's arms flailing above his head as he dropped out of sight. He must've managed to get a hand on the next rung down for there was no immediate thump on the ground below. A moment later came the sound of more breaking, until Jason heard the thump he'd been hoping for. The only way up was now in ruins.

"I told you it was too damn rotten to carry anyone's weight."

"Shut up and give me your hand," said the other.

A man grunted and Jason could imagine him struggling to his feet. There was a brief huff of disgust followed by the sound of retreating footsteps. Jason waited a few minutes before edging his way to the opening and peering below. He watched as they moved toward an adjacent house. Jason smiled with satisfaction. One of the men was favoring his leg.

"This couldn't have worked out any better. They'll move their search somewhere else, and, as long as we stay out of sight, we should be fine," said Hannah.

"What should we do next?"

Hannah handed Jason a strip of jerky. "I don't know yet."

"Dad could be here. You know that, right?"

"I thought about that, too."

"Are we going to look for him?"

"I don't know, Jason." Hannah turned away.

"We're going to make sure he's not here, right?" He wanted to sound stronger, but his voice in his own ears sounded to him like he was pleading.

"I said I don't know what we're going to do. That's all it means." Hannah pulled at her jerky.

His dad had come this way. Jason could feel it. "I don't care what you do or don't do. I'm looking for my dad—alone if I have to," Jason snarled between clenched teeth.

Hannah's eyes narrowed, and her face clouded. The last time he'd spoken this way, Hannah'd wanted to keep him against his will, but this wasn't the same. He'd never seen anger in her eyes before. He was suddenly afraid of what she might do.

"Young man, we all get angry now and then, but I have never deserved this kind of treatment, in the past or now. I will not tolerate it."

Unable to meet her gaze, Jason looked at the ground. "I'm —"

Hannah interrupted him. "This is the second time you've treated me badly. The first time, I let it pass, but now I wonder. Is this the way you spoke to you mother, too?"

Hannah was right. He could never have imagined treating his mother the way he'd treated Hannah. Her only sin was that she wasn't his mother.

She came back and put a hand on his shoulder. "If you have an idea that won't land us back where we just escaped from, I want to hear it. I think you know I didn't come this far only to turn back. If that was true, I'd have left you in Hope."

There wasn't anything Jason could say, so he said nothing.

"Give me a hand over here," said Hannah, standing over the elevator.

"What is that thing?"

"They used bale elevators to get the hay into lofts. I think it'd make a great ladder, don't you?"

"Then what?"

"That's the thing, isn't it," said Hannah. "Judging by the treatment we got earlier, and that search party, it won't go as easy for us if they catch us again," said Hannah, as she scanned the area below.

***

Hannah considered everything she knew about British Columbia's geography. Kamloops was no mystery. On the valley floor, a river coursed with several bridges spanning it, but there was no reason to cross it. That'd only take them farther north.

Unfortunately, their options had become limited. They could circle south through Kelowna, or go north through Valemount, but either direction would take them away from the route Travis would most likely have taken. They had little chance of finding him as it was. If they changed their course, they might as well give up. Obviously, in this town full of enemies, they couldn't approach anyone on the street and ask them if they'd seen Travis.

As the morning passed, Hannah agonized over their situation. The only option seemed to be to pass through Kamloops and carry on as planned. Perhaps the next town would be friendlier. And maybe Travis had made it through this God forsaken hole. She could only hope. "We better get some rest," she said.

"I'm not tired."

"We can't go anywhere during the day, so we need to rest now."

"What are we going to do?"

"Maybe your dad got past Harry. If he did, there might be news in other towns along the way."

"We're not going to talk about this?"

She could understand his frustration, but she'd be grateful when she was no longer his target. "That's what I'm doing, and if you'd you like to know what I've been thinking, this is your chance." As the words left her mouth, Hannah instantly regretted snapping.

Jason's eyes dropped to the floor. When he raised his head, he seemed calmer. "Yes, please," he said.

"Staying here may be safe for now, but we won't get anywhere if we do. We can't talk to anyone because we can't risk Harry catching us again. If he catches us, I doubt he'll make the same mistakes again. Sticking around Kamloops is too dangerous, and for all we know, your dad wasn't even here."

"So you think we should leave?"

"I think we have just as good a chance of finding answers in the next town. We can certainly hope for better hospitality."

Jason said nothing, so Hannah carried on. "Those are just my thoughts. I figure we need to travel at night regardless of any decisions we make." Hannah knew Jason wanted to stay and search, but, as much as she wished their journey could end there, she couldn't imagine how they could avoid Harry.

"I'm fine," said Jason.

Hannah could see he wasn't. She knew why he pouted, but she refused to pander to him. If he had something to say, he'd just have to come out with it.

Eventually he did. "I'm fine. But it's so damn frustrating. I have no proof, but I feel sure he's here."

"That's a definite possibility, but even if he is, how are we going to find him?"

"What's the next town?"

"Chase is about sixty kilometers up the road."

Jason thought for a moment. "If we can't find anyone who saw him in Chase, will we come back here?"

Hannah hadn't planned that far ahead. Maybe Travis *was* here, but she didn't want to commit to returning.

"We'll come back here, right?" Jason insisted.

Hannah shook her head and sighed. There was no point in trying to foresee the future. It might never come to that, and if it did, well, hopefully she'd have time to figure something out. "Yes, Jason. If we don't find anything in Chase, we'll come back."

"Okay then."

The evening came and went, and the sun sank in the sky taking with it the last rays of light. They dragged the bale elevator to the edge of the loft and pushed it out. It reached the halfway point, teetered for a moment, then slid to the ground.

Hannah waited until the moon rose before they descended onto the dampening grass. At the bottom, she stood and listened. She could hear nothing except normal night sounds, so she led the way toward the highway.

Cautiously, she stepped into the open. She could see nothing and in this light she and Jason would be as invisible. Hannah put a hand on his shoulder. She didn't have to remind him to keep quiet.

They'd gone far to the west of Kamloops and Chase lay to the east, with the city between them. They'd have to double back the entire distance plus put the city behind them from the east before first light. Hannah had no way to predict Harry's security practices, but she imagined he probably didn't patrol this far out at night. He may have soldiers stationed closer to the city. She hoped if there were patrols, she could count on them being lax.

Less than an hour had passed when she was paralyzed by the sound of voices. She could see nothing, but guessed there must be at least a dozen people moving toward them. Besides voices, there was the distinct sound of shuffling feet and the occasional clang of metal.

Hannah grabbed Jason's arm and pulled him into the tall grass next to the road. A soft glow joined the sounds: lanterns.

Suddenly, Jason rose out of the grass. Hannah jerked him down. Whoever it was, it sounded like they were moving quickly and with purpose. The lights would soon be upon them.

There was no time to hesitate. There certainly wasn't any time to discuss their course of action. Hannah grabbed Jason's arm, expecting to lift him clean off his feet. With his arm firmly in her grip, she whirled, tearing him with her as fast as she could move. Two steps away from the highway, the ground fell away beneath her feet, and they slipped down an embankment that'd been hidden in the darkness.

Hannah slid to a halt. She clamored back to the brink of ditch and watched as wave upon wave of chained men and women, sandwiched between guards, trudged by.

With each passing prisoner, more questions rose in Hannah's mind, the most pressing being could Travis be among them?

After they'd disappeared, Hannah scrambled up to the road. She followed, staying outside of the light. Their answers were marching away into the darkness.

CHAPTER FORTY

On a buckboard, Harry arrived at the mine as the sun began to rise. He hopped down and stood overlooking the great expanse of the old open pit as the sky brightened. This was the key element to his empire, and it'd been ten years in the making. It stretched a full kilometer across and measured three hundred meters to the surface of the lake below. There was no telling how deep it might be. Harry had no way of pumping the water out or draining it, so he employed traditional mining strategies. Wherever there was evidence of a coal vein, his workers dug shafts. Even now, they milled about like ants. Some moved in and out of the shafts carrying buckets of ore, while others manned the horses that periodically brought up wagonloads of low-grade coal ore along the spiraling roadway. The mine was a bustle with activity from the lakeshore, all the way to where Harry stood. The visible manpower was impressive, but the greatest concentration of the workforce slaved away far beneath the surface where they used rudimentary tools to mine.

As impressive as it seemed, even Harry could tell that the mine wouldn't produce ore for much longer. It didn't matter. The electric grid powered by the coal had a limited lifespan of its own. It was toss-up as to which one would last longer. Soon electricity would truly be an extinct luxury—maybe even in his lifetime.

Before the economy collapsed, he'd been a successful entrepreneur.

But then the economic bottom fell out for the whole world. He could never have imagined the new opportunities world strife would provide. Now he lived with more security than he'd ever hoped to gain. The power he wielded and the control he had over the lives of those below him was intoxicating.

***

Fidjitz didn't like the fact that he appeared to be a nervous little man. He couldn't help the way his hands shook whenever he got excited. While he both feared and adored Harry, it was Harry's way of life he envied. The man could do anything he wanted.

Fidjitz' job was to deliver information. He did his job well and he did it with enthusiasm—two qualities that seemed to please Harry. What Harry didn't realize was that by giving Fidjitz his mandate, he'd made Fidjitz a powerful man in his own right. Harry was his weapon and there was nothing more satisfying than putting Harry into action.

If Harry was his gun, that meant Fidjitz was the man with his finger on the trigger.

It might seem to Harry that Fidjitz' happiness stemmed from Harry, but that was simply Harry's misinterpretation of their relationship. This was a very good day for Fidjitz. Today he was going to do more than just point the Harry gun. He was going to use him to kill someone he had come to hate.

Part of Fidjitz' job was to identify any potential threat to Harry or their way of life. Sometimes the threat was as simple as someone too willing to express a moral code contrary to Harry's design.

Fidjitz was a gatherer of information and evidence. When he shared it with Harry, he came to think of it as loading the Harry gun. He fed the information in like ammunition and the Harry gun always made the same predictable decision. There was no trial, no publicity, no ceremony, no proclamation, no lecture, and no leniency. Fidjitz pointed and a man of his choice disappeared.

A week earlier, Fidjitz had picked just such a target. He'd been contemplating the woman for a while. As he played back the events leading up to this moment, he felt giddy with glee.

She would have made a nice one. It was supposed to be natural. She was supposed to fall in love with him. Granted, no one ever had, but that was the old Fidjitz. This was the new one. Now he had an important and prestigious job. Now he was the second most powerful man, if not the first, in the entire community—maybe even the second most powerful man in the whole world. He figured she'd be pleased to be with him. He'd been sure she would be. How could she not? He could offer her freedom.

That day was more vivid a memory than any he had. He'd felt confident. His posture was perfect and his confidence high as he approached the woman carrying her bucket of ore. He'd looked into her eyes with his offer of life.

He was supposed to have started a new existence with his beautiful companion. Like the storybooks, they were supposed to live happily and contented forever after.

That was the way it was supposed to have happened. It was supposed to have been his moment.

It might've been his scruffy mat of filthy hair. It might've been that his few remaining teeth looked like small black pebbles, or that when he smiled, the stench from his mouth was almost toxic. It could've been that he was just a skinny runt of a man and that every piece of clothing, no matter what size, seemed to hang off him, making him look a bit like a scarecrow.

Where there should have been adoration, the woman's eyes told him she was repulsed.

Fidjitz had said nothing. He'd recognized the obvious the moment she turned toward him. His mouth had gaped. The words he'd rehearsed only moments earlier were gone from his mind. Thoughts about a future with this woman had vanished as if they'd never existed. He'd turned away, vowing the woman would pay for the way she made him feel. She'd pay for thinking she was better.

Now, standing next to Harry, he stood at the edge of the mine. He'd aimed his gun and it stood poised, ready to fire. It was with satisfaction and pride that he literally handed Harry the high-powered rifle. Shells were hard to come by, so they were never wasted.

***

The woman walked out of the mine carrying a bucket of ore. Without warning, her body flew backwards and landed motionless on the ground. Those who stood near gawked. A moment later, the rifle's report echoed across the pit.

***

A few people looked skyward, possibly to see if they could tell from where the bullet had come, but Harry was too far away, and, besides, he'd already handed the rifle back to Fidjitz and was climbing onto the wagon.

Workers carried her corpse to the end of the pier and threw it into the water unceremoniously. The woman was of no consequence, really. And now her name was forever lost.

Work continued.

***

After placing the gun in the wagon, Fidjitz climbed up next to Harry. Already, he'd forgotten her.

***

Harry slapped the reins against the horse's back. He wondered at times about the information Fidjitz provided, but it really didn't matter. Fidjitz would never break the one rule Harry had given him: make no mistake that came with a cost. Simply put, if Fidjitz didn't provide information in a timely manner and an uprising took place as a result ... well, Fidjitz would make that mistake only once.

Harry drove the wagon to the cornfields. He pulled on the reins, bringing the team to a halt alongside the barbed wire fence. On the other side, a crew of men and women harvested corn while guards looked on.

Harry had made the trip in order to observe a particular slave. He was a tall man whose muscular body rippled in the sun. He worked separate from the others, suggesting that he'd removed himself socially from the group.

Harry watched from his perch until the slaves were given a water break, which was what he'd come to watch. There was large drum of water with a spigot on the bottom. Hanging from a small chain was a tin cup. As the workers lined up, Harry could discern a rudimentary pecking order.

A shorter, stockier man raced ahead, reaching the barrel before the others. He'd clearly disrupted the order. He filled the cup and lifted it to his lips, but before he could drink, the tall man was beside him, yanking his hand away and spilling the water. The mug bounced at the end of the chain, where it swung, as the tall man squeezed the hand that had held it. Even Harry could hear the grating sound of bone against bone. The stocky man dropped to his knees.

The taller man picked up the dangling cup, filled it, and drank. He filled it a second time and guzzled it down as well before dropping the cup for the next person in line.

When the last of the workers had their drinks, the injured man gingerly lifted the mug and drank. The guards hustled them back to work and the day carried on as if the altercation had been nothing out of the ordinary.

Harry nudged Fidjitz.

Fidjitz hopped off the wagon, crawled through the fence, and crossed to one of the guards. They exchanged words.

When they had finished, Fidjitz returned, occasionally looking as if to judge Harry's demeanor. Fidjitz broke into a jog, hoping Harry hadn't gotten upset. He tripped in the dirt, fell, jumped up, and hurried on without bothering to brush himself off. When he got to the fence, he pulled the barbed wires apart and quickly slid through. The top wire snagged his shirt, while the bottom wire caught hold of his pants near his crotch. He let go of the top wire to focus on detaching the bottom wire when more barbs entwined in his shirt. He looked up at Harry.

Harry didn't soften his face, hoping his look drove icicles right through Fidjitz. Fidjitz grabbed the top and bottom wires again, spread them apart and stepped through. Harry chuckled at the look of pain on Fidjitz' face as the barbs from the bottom wire tore into his leg. He ran to Harry and apologetically climbed onto the wagon.

Harry clucked the horses into motion.

CHAPTER FORTY-ONE

The following morning, Harry arose some hours after the sun and gorged himself on a late breakfast. Like a ravenous animal, he shoveled in bite after bite while Maggie stood motionless against the wall behind him. He would never offer a compliment, and although her vacant look gave her the appearance of being barely aware, she moved as if she could read his mind. She cleared dishes and provided second helpings without direction. Her makeup did little to conceal the scar on her cheek that Harry had given her many years earlier. He'd intended the wound to be a lesson, but it had actually served to add another enemy to the growing list.

With breakfast out of the way, he retired to his recliner and nursed his coffee until a knock came at the door. He gestured to Maggie, and she showed two men in. One was the guard from the previous day and the second was the taller man who had ruthlessly crushed the hand of another for taking his place in the water line.

Harry didn't bother to acknowledge them as they entered the room. He continued to sip his coffee, a commodity that was almost impossible to attain. As it neared the bottom, he swirled the contents, saying. "I need a top-up." When Maggie returned, he added sugar and fresh cream. Then he deliberately stirred the coffee while the two men waited as if made of stone. Only the occasional slurping sound could be heard as Harry drank his hot beverage. If his visitors felt as if they lived only by his will, then his performance served its purpose. The guard was in no danger, but Harry knew he had a reputation for being impossible to read. He hoped they knew they couldn't predict when he would make someone an example. The guard's demeanor suggested he was well aware of that fact and had no intention of becoming one of those ufortunate souls.

Harry took a final swallow of coffee and addressed the slave, ignoring the guard. "What's your name?" He hoped the contempt he made every effort to convey wouldn't be misinterpreted. No man must forget his place.

Although the man didn't cower, neither did he have the countenance of superiority that he'd displayed in the field the day before. He was smart enough to know he was no longer at the top of the pecking order.

"Sturge," he said without embellishment.

Harry nodded and raised an eyebrow. "Well, Sturge, you've come to a crossroad. I've brought you here to give you a chance to step up in the world. What do you think of that?"

"I don't know."

Harry laughed. "Getting out of the field doesn't sound good to you?"

"Maybe. It depends on the offer."

"You're shrewd, I'll give you that." Harry paused as if in thought, but he was really waiting for effect. "Here it is. You can go back to the fields and pluck corn, or you can work for me."

"How is that any different than what I'm doing now?"

Harry turned to the guard. "Maybe I don't need him. Take him back to the field."

The guard stepped forward and took Sturge's arm.

"Wait," said Sturge.

Harry eyed him. "Well?"

"I apologize. Please."

"An attitude will get you killed, boy. Be warned, because this is the only one you'll get."

Sturge nodded. He adjusted his stance and his expression softened. Harry hoped he knew the words were nothing more than a statement of fact.

"I've been watching you, and I think you might be useful to me. And, of course, it does provide certain benefits." Harry paused. When Sturge said nothing, he continued. "If you work for me, you'll move from the hole you're kept in and into a house I'll provide for you. You'll go to work each day and do the tasks I give you—any task I give you." Harry held the man's gaze with eyes as dull and lifeless as a shark's. Neither the guard nor the prisoner uttered a sound.

Then Harry's face relaxed into a broad smile suggesting, *don't get to close because I might bite your hand right off.* He motioned to a chair. "Sit down."

He nodded toward the guard. "You can leave. I'll let you know when I need you." He didn't know the man's name, and he didn't care.

CHAPTER FORTY-TWO

Hannah and Jason followed the prisoners for the better part of an hour. The mass consisted of both men and women of every age. Each one of them appeared worn-out and defeated. Their clothes were no more than filthy rags. Hannah had never seen a hardened criminal before, but none of these people fit her image of what one might look like. The world of her younger days had been focused on political correctness and human rights issues. What she saw in front of her made her feel sick to her stomach. Her heart raced, and her head pounded. Maybe Travis had never even come through here. Maybe he had—and hadn't survived. Hannah kicked at a pebble, resolving that if she could do anything to help these people, she would.

The sound of the prisoner's shuffling feet was enough to drown out any sound she and Jason were making, but they were cautious, nonetheless. She was vaguely aware that, somewhere off to her right, a river flowed alongside the road like parallel ribbons winding along the valley floor.

Without slowing, the prisoners made a sudden turn to the right and continued along a narrower road. They walked for another kilometer in the darkness before lights began to peek through the trees lining the road. As they grew nearer, Hannah could see the grounds of a huge compound. There was a high fence with loops of barbed wire strung across the top surrounding an enormous complex of buildings. At one end was a large open space devoid of buildings and brush. In the corners were square towers that reminded Hannah of rooks in the game of chess. On the far end was a series of concrete buildings. There were windows, but each was barred.

She grasped Jason by the arm and yanked him into the brush. She dared go no farther. The lights in and around the compound lit up the prison, its yard, and a good deal of the space between where they crouched at the fence. "We can't risk getting any closer tonight," she said. "We don't know what we're up against."

When the last of the prisoners disappeared, Jason said, "What do we do next?"

Hannah didn't reply immediately. She was listening to the repeated sounds of metal clanging against metal, a noise that could be nothing other than cell doors slamming shut.

She moved a short distance to several large trees which were close enough together they could almost be considered a thicket. "Let's camp here and tomorrow we can try to figure something out," she said, letting her pack fall to the ground.

Fatigue had settled deeply. It seemed every part of her body ached. The journey had been so long and hard already, and it was unlikely to get easier in the days to come. She dropped to ground and nodded to a space next to her, inviting Jason to join her.

She wondered how he felt. He'd been a true trooper and had rarely complained. A more driven young man she'd never met. She rolled her head in his direction until she could feel the rough bark against her cheek. "Jay, my boy. Remind me again why we're sitting outside of the quite possibly only functioning prison in the country—which happens to be in a town where we've had nothing but troubles?"

Jason didn't respond for a long time. She wondered if he'd fallen asleep. She wouldn't have blamed him if he had.

"You can feel it, can't you?" said Jason. "He's here. Or he was. I just know it."

"Maybe."

"We could've been right beside him. And if we'd been at Harry's any longer, we'd be in there right now," he said, nodding toward the compound.

"If there was anywhere your dad could've ended up, this is probably the place." She sighed and mussed Jason's hair. "It's your call, kid. I've come this far, and I'm game for whatever you wanna do."

"If there's a way to find out what happened to my dad, I have to try. After all this, I just can't stop now."

"I'm glad." Hannah shut her eyes and ran her fingers through her hair. "I can't believe what's happening here. Those poor people," she said, pulling her bag into her lap. She toyed with the zipper but didn't open it. Hannah knew she should eat something, but the thought of it made her feel like vomiting.

"What are we gonna do?" said Jason.

"I wish I knew."

Hannah prepared a makeshift bed. *At least it's better than a rock ledge in the snow*, she thought. "It looks like this is it for the night. We'd better get some sleep if we can."

Jason opened his pack and pulled out the bits and parts that would turn the hard ground into a passable bed. His breathing deepened long before Hannah's mind slowed enough to let drowsiness overcome her. Learning about the prison was one thing, but even if there was a way to sneak inside without getting caught, then what? And how could they bring an end to Harry's immoral empire and his horrible crimes against people? She knew she was smart enough to figure it out, but the hours passed and she came up empty.

CHAPTER FORTY-THREE

Harry rubbed the sleep out of his eyes and tossed the covers to one side. Maggie would remain asleep for at least another hour. Mornings and Maggie had never been the best of friends. She'd wake up with puffy eyes, knotted and disheveled hair; the wrinkles crisscrossing her face reminded him of cracked clay baked in the heat of the midsummer sun. A few years ago, she was all he could think about. Now, he found the sight of her repulsive.

She'd wandered into town and, like he did with everyone else, Fidjitz brought her to him. It was his nature to make quick decisions when it came to women, and when he saw her, he knew she would be his. Lately, he couldn't figure out why he kept her around. She'd never relished his dream. She'd never fallen in love with him.

"Send someone for my horse. Make sure it's here by the time I'm ready," he called to the guard on duty downstairs.

***

It took Harry the better part of an hour to reach the mine, but he didn't mind. It gave him the opportunity to enjoy the results of his years of hard work. Everything, in every direction, for as far as he could see, existed because of him.

From the edge of the giant pit, Harry looked down at the swarm of activity, orchestrated for the sole purposes of holding back the tide of chaos and keeping the lights burning at night. It was easy enough to justify. He'd created a community, a way of life. Where would these people be without him? The question took more time to ask than to answer, because the answer was: nowhere.

Hannah and the kid crossed his mind, but only long enough to dismiss them. They meant nothing. The horse gave its head an impatient shake. Harry took the reins and turned it toward town.

CHAPTER FORTY-FOUR

Hannah woke with a start to discover Jason tugging at her sleeve. His face wore a just-woke-up groggy look, but he wasn't looking at her. He was staring wide-eyed into the brush behind her. Hannah turned and followed his gaze. Sitting on his haunches, making him look more in common with an animal, was a skinny, half-starved-looking man. His hair was a tangled shock with dirt and leaves everywhere they'd stick. His clothes were no more than rags. And wherever there was a hole—and there seemed to be more hole than cloth—an injury peeked through.

Although his overall appearance and attire were dreadful, they were not nearly as fearsome-looking as his face. Large chunks of skin and swaths of his beard were missing, revealing oozing flesh. The wounds began at his temples and worsened as they progressed to his jawbone. Blood, now dried, had saturated what was left of his shirt.

His eyes were vacant, and Hannah wondered whether he had special needs or if he was insane. She expected him to attack or bolt at any moment, but she couldn't figure out which was more likely.

What ensued was a standoff of sorts. No one moved.

CHAPTER FORTY-FIVE

Travis returned to his cell to discover it was empty. He thought there might be more blood on the floor than when he'd left. His eyes were drawn to the bars. He wondered what'd happened as he ran his fingers over the discoloration he found there. It was dry to his touch. He applied pressure, and his finger and came away wet. He wasn't surprised to see it was tinged red.

He visualized Ajax forcing his way between the bars. Considering his previous injury had yet to heal, the amount of blood wasn't surprising. In addition to the blood on the inside of the cell, there was a puddle on the floor in the hall just beyond the bars.

The evidence suggested Ajax had been able to get his head through. Once he managed to get his wounded face through the bars, he would've been tired and in pain. Travis surmised he'd probably rested his face on the floor, thus creating that particular stain.

Travis ran his fingers through his snarled hair. He knew Ajax wouldn't have been able to get very far once he escaped from the cell. He might've been lucky enough to remember the way out of the building, but he wouldn't have had the knowledge and forethought to avoid the guards and find a safe place to hide.

The door opened, and the evening meal arrived. Travis ate in the silence and solitude of his cell. His thoughts returned to Ajax.

No matter what happened, and no matter where Ajax was, Travis hoped he was okay. Dead or alive, any fate would be better for him than to merely survive in this cell. Sometimes Travis thought even a bullet would be better.

Travis retired to his corner and considered Ajax's admirable tenacity. During the years he'd spent with Ajax he'd witnessed astonishing stupidity. Now, all those moments stood in shadowed obscurity when compared with the strange respect with which Travis now regarded him.

As he fell asleep, the one thought he'd take with him into morning was *Go, Ajax*.

As he slept, Travis' dreams took him back to Tate. His mind replayed the pleasant sunny memories of the coast, Tate and their son Jason. In his visions, Travis watched him grow up and discover the world.

As dreams sometimes do, the events unwound to reveal a story of tragedy rather than one of hope. He struggled to save the lives of his loved ones. Through the night, he tossed on the cold floor.

He awoke to the light from the cellblock door and the normal sounds of the morning. His mind burned with images of disaster.

With each passing night, the weight of his guilt and regret grew heavier. With every passing year, Jason was another year older, and he was afraid Tate would lose faith.

Travis yawned and thought of Ajax. Although the little guy had been exasperating, Travis was glad he hadn't shared his cell with anyone else.

CHAPTER FORTY-SIX

Ajax awoke in the underbrush as the early morning sun peaked over the horizon and poured into his eyes. Unfamiliar with his surroundings, he shook his head and wrinkled his forehead. He should be in the cell with Tavs beside him, but he wasn't. *Where is Tavs, anyway?*

He'd wanted to escape. He could remember that much. But he wouldn't have gone anywhere without Tavs.

Ajax looked around. How could have escape meant he would leave Tavs behind? That was impossible. *I wouldn't have left without Tavs. No way. Without Tavs, what will I do? Where will I go?* A sense of dread awakened as Ajax's eyes darted from left to right. *Maybe I should run as fast and as far as I can.*

Two strangers lay asleep no more than a meter away. *They must have been there all along and I just forgot. They must be friends.* Ajax stared and waited.

If he'd learned anything, it was to wait and see.

His cheeks hurt. He touched one side but jerked his fingers away. The pain was horrible. *I wonder what happened to my face.*

***

Jason's initial fear gave way to curiosity. It wasn't so much that the man looked crazy or dangerous. Odd, yes, but more bewildered than anything. "Who are you?" Jason said, with a tone he hoped wasn't at all threatening.

The newcomer didn't respond immediately. His eyes turned toward Jason and the edges of his mouth turned up in a broad smile, a smile so wide that his eyes became nothing more than thin slits. It reminded Jason of a dog greeting its master after a hard day's work. The fact that the man said nothing accentuated the strange circumstance.

The long uncomfortable silence continued, accompanied by the steady surreal stare from the man Jason had begun to believe might be a lunatic after all. Where was he from, and what had caused his strange injuries? Jason glanced toward the prison. By the looks of the man's clothing, he certainly could've come from there.

Jason pointed to the man and then to the prison, saying as slowly as he could, pronouncing each word carefully, "Did you come from over there?"

The newcomer followed his gaze to the prison and back to Jason, his expression never changing.

Hannah, rousing, repeated the question. She touched the man's shoulder and pointed to her own eyes with two fingers. The man followed her fingers and looked at her. "Did you come from the prison?"

No response.

"Maybe he doesn't speak English," said Jason.

"It's possible, but I don't think that's the problem. Even someone who can't speak English would at least try to communicate or indicate he understands," said Hannah.

"Well, he doesn't seem like much of a threat," said Jason.

Hannah raised her eyebrows and shook her head. "We need to look after ourselves right now. He was fine before we arrived, so I can't imagine why he wouldn't be fine once we're gone. If he came from there," she said with a nod toward the prison, "he must be more resourceful than he looks."

Hannah's logic seemed terribly flawed, but Jason couldn't imagine taking care of him, and at the same time deal with all they needed to do. Jason sighed, putting an arm around the man's shoulders, "You have to stay here. Don't follow us." The man stared blankly, so Jason repeated, "You need to stay where you are. Stay here. Stay." He said each word slowly and deliberately, hoping the man understood. It seemed to be working. When they walked away, Jason looked back. The strange man remained standing among the brush, smiling and waving as he watched them leave.

Jason helped Hannah cross a barbed wire fence tangled with willow and poplar, then looked back one last time. Still the man stood among the trees, smiling as if nothing was out of the ordinary. Jason couldn't shake the feeling that, for the man, this might be a normal day.

When they were out of sight of the prison, Jason tugged on Hannah's sleeve. "You know he could be in there, right?" he said.

"Uh-huh," Hannah said without looking in his direction.

"Why are we walking away, then?"

"Right now, I'm hungry," she said.

Jason was sure he detected frustration in her voice.

"There's a strange little man back there who's seen us, and I'm not sure what to do about that," she added.

As he wondered what she might mean by that, his stomach growled. Maybe finding something to eat should be their priority, but he couldn't shirk the feeling that leaving the man behind was a heartless mistake.

CHAPTER FORTY-SEVEN

Their encounter with the stranger weighed heavy on Hannah's mind. She led the way in silence, moving south through a hayfield covered in short sharp shards of grass. Their path followed a ridge overlooking the river.

Jason had said nothing regarding the prison, which was a relief. Still, she had no idea what to do next.

Suddenly, the familiar noises of horses, the creaking sound of wagon wheels, the grunts of workers, and the periodic snap of a whip sounded across the field. Hannah dropped to the ground. There was no need to tell Jason to do the same. Although the stubble cut into her hands and knees, her ears were tuned to the activity laying just over the knoll.

Side by side, they inched closer to the crest of the hill. At first, she could see only the sky, but as they drew nearer, an orchard came into view. Soon, she could see workers scattered throughout, but she couldn't tell how many there were.

The wagons had flat beds with short sides. Pickers carrying baskets of apples came and went in a steady stream. Once the wagons were loaded, they were hauled away to be replaced with empty ones.

Guards were on duty, prodding anyone who paused or who wasn't moving as quickly as they should.

Looking at the bounty before them was almost more than Hannah could bear. A glance in Jason's direction caught him mid gulp. Her mouth had begun to water, too. By the look of it, the workers must've just begun their work. Every tree limb drooped with the weight of the fruit it bore.

Hannah crept away from the hilltop. If only they could move around to the opposite side of the orchard, they could collect as many apples as they wanted. She glanced back to the hills above them to the east. From what she could see, they were void of human presence. Behind them, the slope ended at the base of a shallow creek bed, now dry through the summer months. It would provide the perfect cover for them to reach higher ground with little risk of detection.

They wound their way up the ravine until it leveled off near the top of the hill. They could see the entire orchard and most of the valley. The orchard looked no bigger than a small field, the trees no larger than berry bushes planted in tight rows, and the workers resembled ants.

Beyond the orchard was the town and even from where she stood, Hannah recognized the building that served as Harry's home. *Just another prison*, she thought. She shivered.

Scrambling along the hillside was the easy part. Moving quickly, it took less than an hour to skirt the orchard. An abundance of ripe apples were hanging on lower branches.

"At least we don't have to climb for them," said Jason, smiling.

It took only a matter of minutes to gather as many apples as they could carry, and they turned again to the hills.

They came across a small out cropping of rocks that looked as though it would offer cover. Sitting on the uphill side with their backs resting against a large boulder, they feasted on apples. Hannah couldn't remember tasting anything so wonderful. "Don't eat too many," she said. "You might regret it later."

"I probably will," said Jason, taking an enormous bite.

Hannah laughed.

When Jason had eaten his fill, they continued east along the ridge. In order to travel east toward Alberta, they had to pass close by the town. As it grew nearer, the view revealed one vacant street after another. The lack of activity reminded her of every other community they'd been through.

Hannah led the way along an ancient path, steering Jason away from the prison. For now, her only concern was to get away, and she couldn't afford to give up the opportunity to travel during the day when they could make decent time. If Travis had ever been there, he was either long dead or long gone. In a few hours, Kamloops and all the dangers it held would be far behind them.

***

Ahead, the path wound around a large bolder that perched on the downhill side of the trail. As any child might, Jason ran to it, and laying both hands on smooth surface, he vaulted around it, landing on the far side.

Suddenly, he lost his balance on the steep slope and began backpedaling to regain his footing. He scrambled up the hill, as the rocks and turf tore loose under his feet, tumbling down the slope. His hand found purchase on a half-buried rock, but it pulled free, and he began to fall down the hill.

He tumbled backward and, as he dropped, unable to stop the toppling or find anything to dig his heels into, he wondered fleetingly how badly he'd be hurt when it was over. Suddenly, he felt a sharp tug on his arm and his descent came to a halt. Hannah had managed to wrap her fingers around his wrist. "That was close," she said, smiling. She gave a quick yank and he scrambled back to the trail where the ground was more stable.

He lay panting, afraid to look down. No sooner had he regained his breath then he heard voices from below. He rolled to his side and peered down the slope. Between tall blades of grass, he could see three men sitting around a flat rock. Cards were strewn across it; they were playing some sort of game. Jason could make out the shape of binoculars hanging from the straps on one man's neck. They'd probably heard him, but he prayed Hannah had pulled him back before either of them had been spotted.

Jason glanced over at Hannah but realized she could see nothing from where she crouched. Her expression was quizzical at first, but then her eyes widened as she heard the voices, too.

Jason felt paralyzed as he waited to be discovered. When the sound of voices faded, he hazarded another look over the edge. The dust had settled, and the men had returned to their game.

Whoever had planned the defense of the community had placed the outpost in an excellent location. The men were positioned on a flat section of the hillside hemmed in by boulders similar to, but smaller than the one he and Hannah now hid behind. Their location provided cover as well as a view of the main road leading into the city. Anyone entering the valley by this route wouldn't see the garrison until it was too late.

It had been nothing more than good fortune preventing their detection. Unfortunately, now they were pinned.

With firsthand knowledge of the Harry's tactics, Jason felt his hatred for the man rising. Harry would continue to prey on unwary travelers. As for himself, he was tired of being afraid, of being chased, and he'd had enough of being held against his will. The thought of sneaking around hoping to avoid these men was more than he could bear. With his back against the hill and his feet against the boulder, he pushed as hard as he could. Even though it was his intention, he was still surprised when the giant rock gave way and began to roll down the hill. Without the boulder, there was nothing left to hide behind. Jason looked at Hannah. Her expression was one of utter shock as their only cover disappeared below them.

The cards forgotten, the men had only enough time to rise from their seats. The boulder quickly gathered speed. On its third bounce it shattered into several smaller pieces and knocked other rocks loose, transforming what had been a single giant rock into a landslide. One of the men was pointing up the hill, but before he could say anything to the others, a bouncing boulder stuck him in the chest and took him off his feet, crushing him instantly. A moment later, the landslide buried him along with any thoughts he may have had.

The two other men were quicker. They dove toward opposite sides. One leapt clear, avoiding the bulk of the threat, but turned in time to see his remaining companion swept away by the falling rubble.

As the last of the boulders passed him by, he stood in the settling dust looking toward Hannah and Jason. He raced toward the flat stone where a rifle leaned.

He leapt to a rock, but it twisted beneath his body. He lost his footing, and his feet flew out from under him, launching his body into the air. He tried to right himself, but his feet were already high above his head. He reached out to try and break his fall, but there was no flat place for his hand. Jason watched it snap beneath his weight.

His breaking arm did little to slow his descent. The back of his head was the second point of impact. His body came to a halt crumpled between the rocks where it remained motionless, his limbs twisted at unnatural angles.

Jason rose, but Hannah stopped him with a hand on his forearm. For a long time, they waited to see if the man would move. When it seemed clear they were out of danger, they picked their way through the debris to the man's side. Blood poured from a wound in his head, but he was conscious. He wore a long-sleeved shirt, but it didn't hide the bone sticking through it.

He looked at them, almost apologetically. "I can't feel my legs. Please, help me."

Jason's stomach lurched. He turned away and threw up.

***

The man was bleeding from his head and nose. It was obvious he had a back injury of some kind, and Hannah knew they shouldn't move him. They couldn't provide medical care, to start with, and even if they could have, he'd probably spend the rest of his life in a rusted wheelchair—if he lived at all.

Before she finished her thought, he began to choke. Hannah couldn't tell whether he was choking on blood or his own tongue. She wanted to help, but the man lost consciousness. She reached for his wrist and felt for a pulse. It was there, but weak. A moment later, it was gone altogether.

Hannah stood, but Jason reached for her arm and doubled over, a fit of convulsions taking control of his stomach. "You all right?" she asked.

He cocked his head to one side and then nodded weakly.

"You don't look okay."

Dropping his face into his cupped hands, Jason began to sob. "I was mad, but I didn't think. It's my fault they're all dead. I wanted to crush them."

Hannah helped him to his feet.

Jason used his sleeve to wipe the vomit from his mouth. "I didn't know it would be like that," he said. "I just didn't think ...," he said.

Hannah wanted to comfort him, but she didn't know what to say. She knew she could have said, "They would've taken us back to Harry, or, worse, would've killed us," but those words felt to her like they would justify his thoughtless action. To berate him seemed heartless. So she squeezed his shoulder and said nothing.

As Hannah turned to leave, it occurred to her that Harry might assume the death of these men wasn't an accident. If he determined that and assumed it was them, he might seek retribution. These men had been armed. She could use that to her advantage. "Wait here," she said. "I'll be right back."

"Where are you going?" said Jason, the pitch of his voice elevated. "Please, Hannah. Let's just get out of here."

Hannah didn't want to stick around anymore than he did but, ignoring his plea, she scrambled back to the outpost and the rock where the men had been playing cards. They hadn't had time to pick up their rifles. The stock of one of them had been snapped in two. When Hannah picked up the second, she was surprised to see it was hers. The scope was broken, but other than that it looked to be fine. It was loaded, but she didn't see any extra ammunition lying about. She picked her way among the rocks to the closest body. She rifled through the dead man's pockets. Finding nothing she needed, she moved to the second. The boulder that struck him had pulverized his entire torso. She found ammunition strung on a makeshift bandoleer, now soaked with the man's blood. She unclipped the buckle and pulled until it came free, removed the bullets and put them into her pack. She was almost finished when she heard rocks shifting behind her. She turned to see that Jason had joined her.

Tears were streaming down his face.

"They would have killed us, you know," said Hannah. She felt guilty. The deaths of these men shouldn't have bothered her, but they did.

"This rifle belonged to my father. It was one of the few things I still had of his," she said, hoping it explained why she was robbing the dead. She stowed the last cartridge.

Their return trip to the path led them near another of the men. The butt of a revolver jutted from his jacket. Jason stopped to look closer. With the speed of a chicken pecking at seeds, he reached out and pulled it from its holster. Hannah was surprised Jason didn't search the man for extra bullets, but she was relieved he hadn't. With a little practice he would be out of rounds, and she wouldn't have to worry about his safety or the safety of anyone else.

This had been the first outpost they'd seen, but the odds were that if there was one, there'd be others. They were probably set up at all the entrances to the town. How many was the only real question. Three? Four? Ten? There was no way of knowing.

CHAPTER FORTY-EIGHT

Fidjitz came crashing through the kitchen door, yelling as he came. "Harry! Harry! Come quick! There's an emergency!"

Harry ignored him. In his world, there were no emergencies. Everything could be taken care of in due course, and, in his experience, there was never anything that couldn't be taken care of. Harry finished his toast as he sipped his tea. When he was finished, he huffed as he stood. "Can't even enjoy breakfast in peace," he said under his breath. "Now, what's this damn emergency that can't wait?"

Harry followed Fidjitz outside. Like an excited dog, Fidjitz ran a little way ahead and then back just as quickly. He ran ahead again and back.

"Ya gotta come quick, Harry!" His voice was almost cracking.

Harry glared at Fidjitz. He hoped it was enough to tell the man it was time to stop making such demands. Still, Fidjitz kept ahead of Harry, leading him along as fast as he could.

They passed through a latched gate and entered the alley bordering Harry's backyard where a team of horses and a wagon awaited. The back of the wagon was covered with an old tarp. Fidjitz waved and pointed to the wagon. Harry walked forward and pulled the tarp back revealing the bodies of three men. Harry knew them all. The biggest of the three had been a good friend of his.

He turned to Fidjitz and demanded, "Explain this."

"Wuh, wuh, we don't know what happened. When we got to the post to relieve 'em, it looked like some kind of landslide fell on 'em. We found 'em in the rocks."

"Who's up there now?"

Fidjitz stuttered. "B-b-ret and Danny stayed up there. They sent me back with the bodies. They sent me to see you, Harry. They said be quick, so ah was quick. Ah came as fast as ah could Harry. Ah hope—"

"All right, all right! Shut up."

Fidjitz's mouth snapped shut as he swallowed back the sound he'd been about to make. His whole body contracted.

"Did you bring all their belongings back with them?" said Harry.

Fidjitz nodded.

Harry poked through the contents in the wagon. He noticed the empty holster and the missing rifle, but said nothing. He turned toward the house.

"Harry?" Fidjitz said.

A look of contempt spread across Harry's face.

"Harry … what do you want me to do with the bodies?"

"Dipstick! What do we always do with the bodies? What the hell do we *always* do with the bodies?" Harry turned away once more, ignoring the bewildered look in the man's eyes.

***

As Harry walked away, Fidjitz curled his lips and mocked him. He hated these sorts of jobs. Harry flew off the handle as often as not. If he dumped the bodies as he was ordered, Harry might change his mind by morning and Fidjitz could find himself laying in the ditch along with these unlucky sods.

Fidjitz untied the horses and climbed onto the wagon. He clicked his tongue and slapped the reins on their backs to get them to move. This wasn't good at all. Fidjitz shook his head and mimicked Harry one last time. "What the hell do we always do with the bodies?" he said, his upper lip curled up to his nose.

CHAPTER FORTY-NINE

Hannah and Jason crossed the main road and into the western hills, keeping a careful lookout as they went. Hannah'd seen plenty of violence and carnage over the past few years, but she didn't know of any way to minimize the impact on Jason.

They'd traveled several kilometers, and it was beginning to get late. Jason had spent the day fondling the handgun he'd taken from the dead man when he should've been helping to watch for potential dangers. Hannah couldn't tell if he was just fascinated by it, or if something else was going on. So far, he'd said nothing about his traumatic experience.

It was earlier than normal, but if she found a place to camp for the night, maybe she'd have a chance to talk to him and try to help him deal with the feelings with which he was most certainly contending.

None of the houses on the outskirts of the city were inhabited. She wondered whether that was by Harry's decree. She suspected it sure wasn't by chance. She worried that Harry was somehow using buildings like this as traps. She'd have chided herself for being paranoid, but paranoia had saved her on more than one occasion.

They stood in the empty yard of a beautiful home that had fared well through the harsh winters. The city stretched out below them. As the sun began to sink over the hills, lights blinked on across the valley, giving them a visual picture of where the population was centered. Hannah thought about the penitentiary and wondered about the prisoners detained there. Could the prisoners be counted on to fight if the opportunity arose? It was hard to imagine that they would, conditioned as they no doubt were. Hannah wondered if Harry would ever be challenged.

Other lights appeared. She could see firelight coming from the outpost they'd fled earlier. The sight prompted her to search for evidence of other outposts. Together, she and Jason were able to identify three other probable sites.

The final glow came from where they'd first met Harry. It was probably the outpost that had detected them in the first place. She smiled, remembering they hadn't been recognized as a woman and a boy at first.

Although she was only guessing, the locations of the fires were good to know. "Shall we?" she said.

Jason nodded and together they walked to the front door, turned the knob, and went inside. As it turned out, the house was not entirely abandoned. A terrible rancid stink assaulted them.

"Oh. my gosh!" said Jason. "What is that smell?"

Hannah recognized the stench immediately. It was a packrat's nest. By the intense smell of the place, there was likely more than one, and the rats had been living there for years.

***

As they moved from one room to another, Jason continued to caress his gun, trying to appear to be prepared for anything. It felt like a game he used to play at home, but he was holding no toy, and he knew this wasn't a game.

"There's not much more to do. Why don't you search this room while I check out the rest?" said Hannah.

"I'll make sure nothing'll surprise us in here," said Jason, though he didn't want to admit he was afraid there might be someone other than the rats in the house, and he didn't want to be alone.

There wasn't much to look at. He looked in the closet and under the bed, but the room was empty. He could hear Hannah moving around somewhere deeper inside the building. Suddenly, he heard a scurrying noise. It was coming toward him. In the darkness, whatever it was appeared to be the size of a football and it was racing straight at him. Jason pointed his weapon and pulled the trigger. Nothing happened. He pulled it repeatedly, but the trigger wouldn't move. The thing scurried between his feet and disappeared through the door. Sweat dripped from his brow and stung his eyes. Jason wiped his face with his forearm, but it only made the stinging worse.

It was too dark to see why the gun hadn't fired, but now that the danger was passed, he was glad it hadn't. In his panic, it hadn't occurred to him it might be an alarm to the townspeople who were looking for them. How many angry enemies might the shots have brought? Jason looked to the ceiling and silently counted his blessing. He ran his fingers over the cold steel one last time, then stowed the gun in his backpack.

Hannah came back from her rounds. "Looks good," she said. "We can spend the night here."

"Here? How can you say that? This place is filthy. And it's infested with rats." he said, his voice shrill.

"It's perfect," she said.

Even in the dark, it sounded like she was smiling. "How can you say that?" he said, protesting. "I'd rather sleep under a tree."

"Look around you, Jay. When do you think was the last time anyone set foot in here? Even if they came in for a quick look, how far would they go and how long would they stay?"

Jason recognized a rhetorical question when he heard one, so he didn't respond.

"There's a fairly clean room in the back. Follow me," said Hannah.

They walked passed a couple of large rat's nests, one spilling out of a closet and onto the floor. The nest looked like it was made mostly of mattress stuffing. It was more than a meter deep, and Jason wondered how long it had taken them to build it and how many rats lived there. Nor was it the only one that size in the house. There were two others on the main floor and probably more upstairs. Just because Hannah was right, didn't make the thought of staying less revolting.

Hannah led him into a back bedroom that, as she'd said, wasn't nearly as filthy as the rest of the house. There was an old-fashioned bedframe with wires stretched across with springs at each end. The fact that there was no mattress was probably why the room was so clean. There was neither food nor nest-building material.

***

Hannah dropped her belongings to the floor and sat down on the bed for a much-needed rest. It had been a shocking day for both of them and she wanted to determine how badly shaken Jason had been by his ordeal. His normal upbeat demeanor was absent. His head hung down, and all she could see was the locks of brown hair on the top of his head. "You want to talk about anything?" she said.

Silence was her only answer.

Hannah could almost hear the cogwheels of his mind turning. It was uncharacteristic of Jason to refuse to speak when something was bothering him. He was usually so direct. Maybe he was trying to get his thoughts together, she mused. So she waited.

Painfully long minutes passed before he spoke. When he did, his feelings came out all at once. In the time that she had known him, he'd never ranted, but she listened without judgement and did her best to process all she was hearing.

"What are we doing here, Hannah? What are we risking our lives for? I killed three men. We left that man behind at the prison even though we knew he couldn't take care of himself, and, by the look of him, he was probably just lucky to have escaped. And if those wounds on his face aren't taken care of, we both know they could get infected. Even I know that. I pushed that boulder off a hill because I wanted to hurt those men. I didn't even think about the consequences.

"I don't even remember where we've been. I couldn't get back to the prison if I wanted to.

"I saw a rat running toward me and tried to shoot it. I didn't even think what would have happened if the gun had gone off.

"I killed three men today, Hannah. I *killed* them. That rock looked like I could push it and I wanted it to crush them. I wanted to destroy them. I did it, too. You didn't do it, Hannah. *I* did it!" Jason's tears flowed. He wiped his face on his sleeve.

During the silence that followed, Hannah could have spoken, but she had no idea what to say. It seemed the longer they travelled together, the more dependent upon her Jason grew. She hadn't realized he'd come to feel their reason for being on this journey had ended. His confidence seemed crushed. She wondered what she could say, what he needed to hear, what he needed.

She decided to follow her gut. "Are you finished feeling sorry for yourself? Anytime you want to be done with all this whining about how horrible you are would be just great!

"Now that you've told me how you feel, let me tell you how I feel. You're right about some things and we need to see what we can do about those. But you're wrong about some other things. So let's be realistic.

"First of all, we've all done some very terrible things out of anger. Most of the time we're lucky and nothing bad happens because of it. But you need to see what happened for what it was. It was an accident. A strong wind or a heavy rain could have knocked that rock loose on any stormy day. Come on Jason, how strong do you think you are?

"Second, we both have fears. We've been facing dangers since we started this journey. Being afraid all the time is exhausting.

"You're right about the man we left behind. I'm worried about him, too. I truly hope that nothing bad has happened to him. It's been bothering me ever since we left this morning and I already decided we should get back there and see if we can find him.

"You're a good young man, and I'm very proud of you. If you don't mind me saying, we have an impossible job ahead of us and we're going to have to be damn tough if we hope to live through it.

"Now, if it's all the same to you, I need to get some sleep. Tomorrow we're going to need every ounce of strength we have." Hannah hoped tough love was the right way to approach the situation, but this was no time to start coddling him.

Jason crawled onto the springs and scooted to the wall. Hannah lay down beside him. The moon rose, casting an eerie light in the room. A rat moved across the floor, staying close to the wall. Hannah hissed at it, and it scurried away. She closed her eyes and the next time she opened them it was to the morning sun shining into the room.

They started their morning with an apple. By midmorning, they had come full circle and were standing outside the barn where they'd spent the night three days earlier.

Long before midday, they reached the road that was used to move prisoners to and from the worksite. There was no sense staying out in the open any longer than necessary. A horse whinnied from far away. Hannah ignored it. "Let's stick to the brush," she said.

Hopefully, the man would still be where they'd left him. She hoped he hadn't been recaptured.

***

It was midafternoon by the time they arrived at the prison. Jason began to search the brush for any sign of the little man.

Hannah nudged his arm. "Let's split up," she said. "We'll have to hope he didn't wander off."

"Hey, Mister," Jason said, calling as quietly as he could.

No one responded.

"Jason! Come over here," said Hannah.

Once at her side, he could see trampled brush, so he supposed the man had stayed for a while, but, looking around, Jason couldn't see any anything to indicate whether the strange man had been taken by force or if he'd left the area on his own.

Jason's shoulders felt heavy. He was weighed down by a deep sense of guilt. He hung his head and returned to the spot where they'd made their bed before. He pulled an apple from his pack and rolled it around in his hands. He was hungry, but he had no desire to eat it. Somehow, the feel of the smooth red skin was soothing. He toyed with it a while before returning it to his pack. The palm of his hand fell on the butt of the gun.

He took it from its hiding place to look at it. The pistol had a revolving cylinder to hold the shells. He found the safety and flipped its position. There was also a release lever that allowed the cylinder to flop to one side for loading and unloading the bullets. Jason operated the mechanism and the cylinder fell open to reveal a series of brass disks. All the holes were full. He put his finger on the side of the cylinder and rotated it quickly. It spun freely with a series of audible clicks. He snapped the cylinder closed and admired every element of the weapon. It was the first revolver he'd ever seen and the feel and weight of it in his hand was like magic.

He had an unbearable urge to experiment with the weapon, desiring to experience the exhilaration of pulling the trigger, feeling the recoil, and hearing the explosion. He noticed when he pulled the trigger slowly back a small lever moved up and forced the cylinder to turn. It seemed obvious to him that it would stop when the next bullet aligned in the barrel. He also noticed that the top trigger moved back as well. It reminded him of a small hammer. He anticipated that when the cylinder was in the right position, the hammer would release and slam down on the end of the bullet. Jason was mesmerized. He continued to pull the trigger and the hammer continued to move slowly away from the bullet.

Suddenly, a hand came across his and squeezed it lightly.

***

Hannah didn't know how familiar Jason was with the weapon, but she'd assumed he had some understanding of it, considering he was comfortable with the rifle she carried. Watching the fascinated look in his eye told her she'd assumed more than she should have. She sat down next to him and gently took the weapon from his hands.

She examined the pistol for a moment before she found and released the catch holding the cylinder in place. She turned the barrel up and let the shells drop into her palm.

"Here you go," she said and dropped them into his open hands. She pointed the pistol away from her and looked down the barrel to see that it was clear. She then used her thumb to return the cylinder to its closed position.

She turned the weapon first one way and then the other, then she pointed it away and slowly pulled the trigger until the hammer released and slammed forward with a loud clicking noise.

Then, with her thumb on the hammer, she pulled the trigger back. "See the cylinder moving?" she said.

Jason nodded.

When the hammer reached its farthest position, there was a click and it locked into place. "Now it's ready to fire," she said. "If you pull the trigger, it will release the hammer and fire. That is what they call a double action revolver. The cylinder revolves and there are two ways to fire the weapon."

Hannah spoke in a whisper, as if they were having some kind of secret meeting. "These weapons are much more dangerous than a rifle in a lot of ways. But somehow, they're also more fascinating. Look at how short the barrel is. A weapon like this is easy to hide, but it's also very easy to point in unplanned directions. It's important to be extremely careful. To be honest, the best place for this gun is probably with the man you got it from." Hannah didn't want Jason to feel reprimanded, but she hoped her words would give him a sense of respect for the weapon.

Hannah continued, "I noticed you found the safety. Because it was on, you know the previous owner used it. You should, too."

Jason nodded.

"I took the bullets out of the cylinder so it would be safe to show you about the gun. You should never handle a loaded weapon unless you plan to shoot it. This particular pistol is called a forty-five. It gets its name from the caliber. Look on the back of the bullet. The information is also on printed on the side of the gun. That way you can make sure to use the correct ammunition for it."

Jason looked at one of the bullets. One of the markings was the number forty-five.

"These guns are famous for the damage that they can cause. They're also incredibly loud. In the old days people would wear hearing protection when they used them," she said. "I hope you remember everything I've said."

Jason nodded but didn't look up.

"The best way to use the gun will probably depend on the situation you're in. I don't see a problem with you keeping it, but I suggest you put those bullets in one pouch and the gun in another. We haven't needed it so far and we probably never will."

Hannah placed the weapon in Jason's hands, on top of the bullets he already had, hoping to punctuate that the gun was a little too much for him to handle.

Unfortunately, the visual statement she was trying to make was lost when they heard the sound of breaking twigs and brush behind them.

***

Jason instinctively grabbed for the gun, but instead of pulling it up and pointing it, he ended up juggling it from one hand to the other. As he did, the bullets fell onto the ground at his feet.

Hannah was already facing the direction from which the sound had come. By the time Jason managed to stand, with the gun under control, he was pointing the empty weapon, with the cylinder flopped open to one side, at the very man they had come to find.

Under other circumstances, it would have been funny. As it was, every ounce of strength he had left in his body drained. He plopped to the ground, spent. He looked up to see the stranger mimicking his expression. Forgetting his epic firearm failure, he smiled. Again, the man mimicked him.

While the stranger stood unspeaking, Hannah pulled an apple from her pack. Without hesitation, the man took the apple and began to chew on it. In a flash, he was finished, seeds and all. Hannah offered him a second, and then some water as well. He took it and began to drink deeply. He drank so fiercely, she had to pull the flask away. He followed it with his hands but made no attempt to take it back. Hannah offered him a third apple and he took it, too. This time, he ate slower.

When the man was finished, he walked to where Jason sat in the grass. He crouched in front of him and studied his face. He shifted his weight to look at Jason from one side, and then he changed his position again, so that he could get a good look at the other. Jason let him look at him, and even when the man reached out to touch his face like a blind man might, Jason let him. When the man seemed satisfied, he sat back, continuing to gaze at Jason. "Tavs," he said. He paused for a breath, then repeated the only word he had yet uttered. "Tavs."

CHAPTER FIFTY

Harry paced from the kitchen door to the picture window overlooking his empire and back again. A brand-new fist-sized hole adorned the wall next to the fireplace. After the bad news about the outpost had been delivered, he'd lost his temper in a way he couldn't recall having happened before. Luckily, when he'd punched the wall, he'd hit the space between two boards rather than a stud, and created a hole instead of a shallow dent and a busted hand. Fuming, he continued to pace, adding to the wear in the already threadbare carpet.

The big man who'd been killed was the closest thing he had to a best friend. They'd built the community together, back when the town was being overrun by people moving across the province looking for greener pastures. Many came, looted, and left. Others stayed, but not always as useful members of the community. Oftentimes, they were parasites who wanted nothing more than to leach the community dry.

The solution had been simple. There had been much to do to rebuild the community, and little manpower to accomplish it. It made sense to utilize the prison facility to control the transients and use them to help build the community in the process.

For Harry, the community was more important than anything else. The world would never develop any kind of normal social structure on its own. If the community were going to grow, then the people who lived here would have to make it happen—regardless of the cost.

At first, he felt bad about having to make life and death decisions. Ending a person's life wasn't an easy thing. But after a while the simple truth became obvious. The world would be a better place without those who refused to work to improve it.

And so the imprisoned transients who complied and were docile were transformed into useful members of the community, and everyone enjoyed the benefits. There were lights at night, food on everyone's tables; even those who lived in the prison received three meals a day and a place to sleep.

His original plan had involved re-educating the workers and bringing them back into useful service within the community. He'd always thought that once he gave them back what they'd lost, they'd regain a sense of purpose, and they would grow to love him.

But, instead, most of them became angry and resentful. They'd learned to hate the community and everything it stood for. Very few had proven to be the kind of people he was looking for, and those who were, he identified before they ended up behind the prison walls.

It was a good system and it worked well, at least in Harry's mind. He now lived in a world where he enjoyed the freedom to act on what he believed in. The fear and respect from the town's people were bonuses, even though he knew he was feared more than he was respected.

Still, he was troubled. The death of the guards hadn't been a freak accident. Someone else had been there. The missing weapons were proof of that.

He thought back, but in all the past years, there wasn't a single instance where an outpost had been caught off guard and decimated the way this one had been.

People came looking for an easy meal and a soft bed. They came to loot and to steal. They didn't come looking for a fight.

Harry played possible scenarios in his head, and in each one there was one constant: that boy and woman who'd somehow managed to elude capture. Harry could imagine them poised behind the rocks, and he could see them creating the avalanche. What he imagined infuriated him, but the scenario didn't end there. The intruders had descended from the hill to the outpost. They walked among the bodies and had gone through their possessions. They weren't only murderers, but thieves as well.

He slammed his fist into the wall, punching another neat hole just below the first.

CHAPTER FIFTY-ONE

Jason awoke to the sun warming his face. He yawned, stretched, and worked the crick out of his neck. The cracking sounds coming from his vertebrae reminded him he never wanted to get used to sleeping on the ground. Even the most uncomfortable bed was better than this.

"Look who's finally waking up," said Hannah, from somewhere behind him.

It took him a moment to realize their guest wasn't anywhere Jason could see. He rolled in Hannah's direction and gave a questioning look.

Hannah nodded to his left.

The man was sitting with his back to a tree, a goofy looking smile on his face. As much of a burden as he would probably become, Jason couldn't help but like him right away. Maybe because, being very tiny, he more closely resembled an oversized action figure than a real person.

The air was still and the sky a bright blue. It was shaping up to be a beautiful day, which was something, considering their circumstances. Jason yawned again and rubbed the sleep from his eyes.

His glimpsed a movement from the corner of his eye. Almost on their own, his hands flew up in time to catch an apple sailing through the air in his direction.

"Nice catch," said Hannah. "As soon as you're ready, we should get moving."

As they walked to the river, he wondered about their new companion. Where had he come from, and what was he doing out here all alone when he seemed unable to fend for himself?

The man walked along carefree and smiling even though the skin on his face had been stripped away. It was raw, red, and looked to Jason like the pain must be agonizing. Except for the fact that his years were given away by the wrinkles and the crow's feet etched into his face, he was more like a child than a man. There was a story trapped inside of him, of that Jason was sure. He wondered if he'd ever find out what it was.

By midmorning, the man had still said nothing more than "Tavs."

"So, you like the word tavs," Jason observed, thinking that perhaps it was the man's name.

However, upon hearing it, the man became agitated and began to repeat it over and over excitedly.

Well, that wouldn't work. Maybe Tavs wouldn't be such a good name after all. It might become frustrating if, every time Jason tried to get his attention, he responded by chanting his own name. It'd be even worse if they needed him to be quiet.

Jason spent the rest of the morning trying to think of an appropriate name. Something about the man made it seem that even when he sat still it looked like he was about to spring. In some ways, he resembled a mystical forest creature. Jason wanted to work his personality into any name he'd choose for him.

As he discarded one name after another, it occurred to him that the process might be inappropriate. He was trying to name the man in the same way a person might name a pet. On the other hand, Jason needed something to call him, and the man was certainly not going to help him figure it out.

Smiling at the man, Jason said, "I bet if elves existed, they'd have looked just like you. How about if we call you Elvin? I think that sounds good, don't you?"

The little man smiled.

"Okay, then," said Jason, "from now on, you're Elvin."

Elvin smiled dumbly. Jason wondered if maybe his new name sounded familiar in some way or if it was because he'd tried to make his voice sound friendly. Either way, the man seemed to accept his new name, and Jason liked the sound of it.

"Hannah, I've decided on a name. We're going to call him Elvin."

" Did you ever think that he might already have a name?"

"I've thought about that, but do you think he's going to tell us what it is? I think we need to call him something. Hey, you isn't going work very well."

"Elvin sounds totally fine," Hannah said, smiling.

CHAPTER FIFTY-TWO

Faydra pulled back on the reins, and her horse came a stop. She slid from the saddle and dropped lightly onto the ground. Except for the missing bodies, signs of the carnage was everywhere. Blood that had once pooled in seemingly every depression in the rocks was now reduced to dried brown splotches.

Another crew of watchmen had already been assigned. The new outpost was approximately a hundred meters downhill from the old one. The men had been instructed to leave the site alone, but it hadn't stopped them from investigating. In the two days since the accident-slash-murder, the entire area had been polluted with tracks from every fool who felt the urge to test his Sherlock Holmes skills.

Fallen rocks from above created an area of loose scree beginning just above the outpost and ending on the level ground some thirty meters below. Playing cards were still scattered about. A lunch that had never been eaten had become rank after spending days baking in the sun. Faydra poked around, but she could find no evidence that the events were anything other than an accident.

Unfortunately, calling it an accident was not a part of her job mandate. Ultimately, it was her task to locate the culprits: a boy and a woman. She might be on a wild goose chase, but that didn't matter much since Harry might have finally lost his wits. Rumors had been circulated over the past few months suggesting that he was out of touch—and out of his mind.

Faydra skirted the area searching for any sign that there had been others present besides the now-dead guards. The trail leading to the outpost should have been most recently disturbed by the horse and wagon used to move the bodies, but there was also a second set of tracks that overlapped the first. The path from the main site to the wagon was littered with footfalls and scuffmarks made when the bodies were dragged out of the rocks.

Faydra scowled; it was a tracker's nightmare.

She moved up the slope to where the rockslide had originated. It was steep going and there were traces of foot traffic going both up and down the hill, indicated by the way the toes or heals dug into the soil, respectively.

She continued up the slope until she reached the trail where she found an indent in the ground that could only have been caused by a tremendous weight. It was there that the rock that caused all the damage must have rested. The rock had never had a firm seating on the hill to begin with. It was amazing it hadn't fallen sooner. Faydra considered herself an excellent tracker, but even a master couldn't have made sense of the mess she was now examining.

What she *could* glean from the outpost confirmed her thoughts. There were just two possible explanations. One, it was an accident, or, two, the men had been murdered. The more likely of the two was that it was an accident, just as the men who discovered the bodies had first reported. Those same men had probably taken anything of value before reporting the deaths. Of course, they'd never admit to it. They'd have hoped that Harry wouldn't have noticed, and, as far as they knew, he hadn't.

If it was her job to make assumptions, her investigation would end here.

The woman and the boy had probably hightailed it out of the valley as quick as they could. They were lucky to have escaped in the first place, and were probably long gone.

If it became necessary to track them, she would. Harry would never approve of a half-baked investigation. As it was, she didn't have anything more than guesses and Harry wouldn't appreciate hearing about those. He could easily come up with those on his own. He'd want to be sure. And, if he couldn't be sure, then someone's head would no doubt be on the chopping block. If there was one thing Faydra knew, it was that that head wasn't going to be hers.

The solution to her problem was in the missing guns. When she found the guns, she'd know what had happened.

CHAPTER FIFTY-THREE

It took Faydra an hour to get back to town. She made mental notes of the orchards and the corn crops as she passed them. Harvest was in full swing, and the ripening crops were the easiest meals available. If the woman and the boy were still around, they'd probably frequent one, or both, of those places. Something to watch for should she have to.

She strode to the building that had become known as Central Appointments, the agency used to ensure all the most important needs of the community were being met by assigning personnel. Records of the schedules of workers throughout the city and about the prisoner population were kept there.

Central Appointments had records about every crew, its members and where they were assigned. There were also records for the small militia that was deployed in emergency situations. The ranks of these men were maintained through a boot camp filled with conscripted recruits, both young and old. Manpower was a commodity as much as anything else.

Faydra approached the counter. The office appeared to be vacant, and there was no sign posted suggesting when the secretary would be back.

She peered over the counter. A young woman sat at a desk, thumbing through some papers. Faydra drummed her fingers on the counter. The woman looked up with little interest until she recognized her visitor. She almost turned her desk upside-down as she rushed to the counter. Faydra's reputation for not tolerating slackers was well known.

"Faydra, I'm so sorry. What can I do for you?"

"Tell me where I can find the crew that was on the southeast ridge the day before yesterday," she demanded.

The secretary flipped through a cabinet of folders and pulled out one with the words *Outpost Duty* scrawled across the top in pencil.

She thumbed through entries until she found the schedule titled *Southeast Outpost*. She followed the rotation until she found the entry she was looking for. She read the names for Faydra. "Cornwallis, Dempsey, and Frankie."

Faydra glared at the receptionist, waiting. There wasn't anything more frustrating than having to deal with visionless peons who were good for nothing more than preening and smiling. This receptionist was one of these people.

Suddenly, the receptionist's eyes widened as she realized that more was expected. She flipped through the remaining pages and pulled out another schedule. This one was not a list of names, but a list of places and times. The receptionist located the words *Northeast Outpost* and looked at the line just below it. "They're roving on the northeast side of the city today. They've just started their rounds."

Faydra swore under her breath and turned to leave.

The secretary called to her retreating back, "They're scheduled to be at the northwest outpost in three days."

Faydra stalked out of the building without looking back. There wasn't much more to do until evening. She certainly wasn't going to wait three days to talk to Cornwallis.

CHAPTER FIFTY-FOUR

Faydra would be damned if she'd chase across the countryside for three days. All three, Cornwallis, Dempsey, and Frankie, would be home later and she'd find them in their respective dwellings. Faydra made a stop at the stables to collect a fresh ride.

No one expected her, but that didn't matter. She entered the stables and approached the first person she came across. *It's got to be a rule. Why can't I ever find the person I'm looking for?* The stable hand was a young woman in her early twenties; just some girl with a horse fascination. Not even worth talking to. Faydra walked along the stalls, taking the time to evaluate each horse she passed. The perfect horse would be one that looked a bit scruffy, a little worse for wear, and maybe a little older to go along with her outfit. If she happened across the fugitives, it would best if she looked like someone passing through the area instead of a local.

She found an ancient mare with a scar that stretched from her forehead to her jaw, likely from getting tangled up in a barbed wire fence at some point. Perfect.

Faydra opened the stall, took hold of the horse's halter, and led it out.

The stable hand approached, opening her mouth—in protest, Faydra presumed. Faydra gave her a menacing glare, stopping her short.

The young girl turned on her heal and retrieved a saddle from a nearby sawhorse. Faydra waved her away and picked the grungiest piece of leather she could find. *Careful girl. Another mistake might be your last.*

After Faydra selected the tack, the girl saddled and bridled the horse then handed over the reins.

CHAPTER FIFTY-FIVE

Faydra rode to Cornwallis' house first, arriving before he did. She knew a woman lived with him and probably a couple of varmint kids as well. More bugs.

She tied the horse to the fence and walked to the top of the porch steps where she sat and waited.

She could hear scurrying and whispering from inside. The woman was probably rushing her children to safety. Faydra smiled. Maybe she thought the spawn of the devil had arrived. If Faydra had kin, it was the boogeyman. And between the two, she was infinitely more dangerous.

***

By the time Cornwallis made it home, it was dark. He'd been riding all day, but the horse had to be returned to the stables each evening, making his commute two hours a day. He was filthy, exhausted, and felt defeated.

Although he slouched with fatigue, his frame straightened the moment he recognized the figure sitting on his front steps. "Faydra." It wasn't a greeting as much as a startled exclamation stating the obvious.

Faydra didn't respond. Instead, she stood up and motioned him to sit.

Cornwallis was well aware he was insignificant in her eyes. Even though he was in charge of a small group that included two other men, he was barely more than a delivery boy. His deliveries included anyone who was a new arrival in town. It was beyond his understanding why Harry's long arm of the law was sitting on his front step. He would have preferred otherwise, but he was certain his surprise and fear were written clearly across his face.

He walked wearily toward the woman and sat where she indicated. He'd thought he was exhausted before, but now he felt as though he'd aged ten years since walking through his own front gate. He realized he might very well might be walking to his own execution. There seemed little rhyme or reason to such things here.

He was thankful when his unwelcome guest got straight to the point.

"Cornwallis, you are so right." She bit off the over-stressed final T. It was as if she were reading his mind. "It is very possible that you are already a dead man. But no matter what happens, you can make a choice. You might even be able to make a difference."

With downcast eyes, he waited for her to continue. When she didn't, he raised his head and met her glare. He knew she was trying to intimidate him, but he thought, *if today is my last day, I can at least face it with dignity. If this bitch wants to make me believe my life is about to end, I won't give her the satisfaction of seeing me crumble.*

"Let's talk," said Faydra. "I want you to tell me everything you know about the dead men you found. It would be in your best interest not to leave anything out."

Cornwallis exhaled, relieved, then spent the next half hour telling Faydra everything he could remember.

When he'd finished, Faydra left. She never asked him if he'd told the truth. She hadn't threatened his life. She hadn't warned that if she found out he'd lied to her she'd be back. She walked away without a word, untied the horse, mounted and then, to the road in front of her, she said, "Cornwallis, do yourself a favor and take the day off tomorrow."

***

Intimidation was Faydra's life's work, and she was damned good at it. If any of the other men had fingers that need pointing, she would need to move quickly. She couldn't allow them the opportunity to get their stories straight. If she got to them before they got to each other, she might be able to avoid an execution or two, maybe even three. Harry wouldn't question her judgment, and loyal men were hard to come by; he needed to keep as many of them around as he could.

CHAPTER FIFTY-SIX

As Faydra had expected, there were candles burning in Dempsey's house. There were power curfews in place to conserve the precious commodity. It looked like Dempsey was abiding by the law.

Faydra tethered her horse for the second time that night and strode up to the front door. She pulled her hand back as if to knock, paused, changed her mind, and opened the door as if she were entering her own house.

Dempsey sat on the sofa drinking something—possibly beer. There were some skills that would never be lost.

Unlike Cornwallis, Dempsey lived alone. He'd taken off whatever work shirt he might have worn and was now wearing a mostly brown, once-upon-a-time white T-shirt. A pair of suspenders held up a grungy pair of pants that fit him like a sack. As a man, he was revolting.

Faydra did nothing to hide her disgust. If anything, she tended to use it as a tool; one of many that she could expertly wield. The less self-worth Dempsey had, the greater her power over him would be.

Faydra approached her target as he attempted to stand. She placed a boot on his chest and pushed him backwards into the couch, an easy task while he was off balance. It required no strength but was very effective. By the look on his face, Dempsey was impressed. She laid it out plain and clear for him. *Nothing but the truth so help-your-rotting-carcass,* was what she hoped her look said. Dempsey seemed to think so.

Their conversation was short. Everything he said matched up with Cornwallis' story, but the information she was looking for was absent. *How could it be possible that these three men are that obtuse? Are they that stupid?*

She left Dempsey with the same advice she'd given Cornwallis: "Stay home tomorrow." The fact that he was still alive should be enough to make him feel fortunate.

CHAPTER FIFTY-SEVEN

As she rode, her thoughts drifted to her chores for the following day. The order of her visits in these situations was always in a predetermined ranking. It began with the man running the crew and ended with the one with the least seniority. If there were any additions or revisions to the stories, they usually came from the man at the bottom. Frankie would be the key. He was also the one who brought the bodies back to Harry. If he had a story to tell that was any different than the one she'd already heard, Dempsey and Cornwallis would be getting another visit.

It was late, and she wanted to get an early start so she could get to to Frankie's before he left for work in the morning. Fortunately, the house where she kept her belongings was along the way. She left the horse in the backyard enclosed with a wire-meshed fence. The area was over gown with brush providing good feed. In the morning she'd drop down to the river and let it get something to drink. She removed the saddle, bridle and blanket, before turning the horse loose.

Inside, she stripped and crawled into bed. She needed sleep.

***

Faydra woke before dawn and prepared for the ride to Frankie's. She hurried knowing if she missed him, it'd make her job harder.

She arrived at Frankie's front step just at sunrise. Inside, she could see Frankie preparing for his workday. Faydra walked up behind him as he stood at the kitchen counter. She coiled her fist and slammed it hard into his back where his kidney would be. Frankie lurched back and upward in pain, slamming his head into the cupboard. The impact cut his head and blood began to pour down his forehead and into his eyes.

She dragged him backwards while he was off guard and threw him into one of the kitchen chairs. It rocked precariously, but he managed to check himself and balance it without falling over backwards. In a fluid motion, she grabbed a towel from the counter and threw it at him. It landed in a heap on his head, covering his face.

Frankie took the towel and wadded it to staunch the flow of blood. "Faydra," he said. When he had pressure on the wound, he looked up. She could see he was afraid.

She paced back and forth, letting his fear work on him. The more anxiety he felt, the better. It always made her job easier. When she was sure he'd waited long enough, she posed her first question. "Where is it?"

Frankie repeated the question in a bewildered, almost childish tone. "Where is it?" His voice cracked at the end. Faydra could see his confusion. The question his face asked was "Where is what?"

If she had to guess, she didn't believe the previous two men had scripted their stories. If they had, they were a lot craftier than they seemed.

Already she could surmise that Frankie was much less intelligent than Cornwallis or Dempsey. The most likely story she expected to uncover was that Frankie had swiped the gun and was hoping no one would notice.

"You know why I'm here, Frankie?"

Frankie shook his head. "No."

"Oh, come on. You know I can't believe that. You got to have some idea about why I'm here."

Frankie held fast to his blank look.

"Let me level with you Frankie. Here's the simple logic. I'm here … right?"

Frankie nodded.

"And if I'm sitting in this rot hole of a kitchen, there's a pretty good chance that you won't be walking out of here when we're through. You feeling me?"

Frankie nodded. Sweat poured down his face.

"Now here's the twist. Are you ready for it?" She didn't wait for a response. "I'm privy to a bit of important information and I'm not about to tell you what that information is. I need to decide whether you'll lie about it or not."

Frankie gave no response.

"You still with me?"

Frankie nodded.

"This is what you're going to do for me, Frankie. You're going to give me the information I want. You're going to read my mind. If I decide that you're on the up and up, you might live through this. But if I don't believe you're being altogether truthful …." She stopped there. There really was no point continuing.

***

Frankie worked hard to try and come up with whatever it was that Faydra wanted to know. There wasn't much he could say. He often broke the power curfew. That was worth a public flogging, but nothing more. Other than that, the only other serious thing that happened was taking the bodies back to Harry. It was impossible to believe that that could be what she wanted to know about. He was supposed to take them to the dumpsite straight away, and he did that. It was scary enough having to deal with Harry face to face. Faydra was even worse.

"Faydra, I really didn't think it was that big of a deal. I always get home late and sometimes it's just easier to throw a light switch on rather than dig up a candle. Even when I do use—"

Faydra cut him off. "I don't care one iota about the damn electricity. Tell me what else you've been getting your filthy hands into."

Frankie thought hard. The only thing that he could think of was the nasty business of finding the bodies on the southeast ridge. He began to tell her everything he knew.

It didn't take Frankie long to see that this was the story Faydra wanted to hear. He tried hard not to blame anyone else. If today was to be his last day, it didn't need to be anyone else's last day, too.

***

By the time Frankie had droned on through most of his story, Faydra was convinced of two things. First, Frankie was guilty of nothing—at least, nothing serious. Second, someone else must have been at the site. Whoever that had been was also responsible for taking the pistol and the missing rifle.

Frankie was in mid-sentence when she stood and turned to leave. Passing through the door, she stated for the third time, "Take the day off." The screen door bounced once against the doorjamb before the latch clicked into place.

I guess I'm going hunting for a couple of fugitives.

CHAPTER FIFTY-EIGHT

Hannah was well aware they'd been impossibly lucky no one had detected them yet, and she also knew their luck wasn't likely to last much longer. Another day was already shot and now she had Elvin to contend with as well. Although they'd left nothing behind at the outpost that might suggest it was anything other than an accident, it wasn't a stretch to imagine Harry would be looking for an explanation for the deaths of his men. Hannah didn't like making assumptions about what Harry might or might not think, but if she were to be cautious, she had to assume he was looking for them.

***

Jason could tell Hannah was brooding. He could've waited around for her to tell him what was bothering her, but it wasn't in his nature to play games. He and Hannah were peas in a pod that way. His mom had been like that, too. If something was on her mind, it didn't take her long to say exactly what it was.

Jason was about to ask, but then she spoke.

"Listen Jason, it's great and all that you named Elvin, but we're not much farther ahead than we were two days ago … maybe even farther behind."

Jason laughed. "You make it sound like Elvin's a pet." His mom used to warn him against naming strays. "Once you give them names, they're almost family," she used to say. Since there was no guarantee they could feed them, he'd never had any pets as a child.

"Jason, this isn't funny. We're not playing a game here."

"Of course not," said Jason, "but Elvin is a real person, and he needs our help."

"We know they use some of the prisoners to harvest apples. We know there are many more prisoners than the ones in the orchard, but we have no idea where they go, and now we've missed them again."

"What are you getting at? Do you think I'm not trying hard enough?" Jason spat, feeling blamed.

"All I'm saying is we need to focus. Right now, we don't have any kind of plan. We have a little information, but we haven't even decided how to use it. What if Harry and his men show up this morning? I don't want to be caught off guard, and I won't be a slave for that maniac." She shook the rifle as if to punctuate her point.

Jason nodded and sighed. "What if we get an early night's sleep tonight and wake up before the prisoners leave? We can follow the group that doesn't go to the orchard."

***

They spent the rest of the day hiding in the brush. Once the prisoners had been herded out of the compound in the early morning hours, no movement came from the prison. Hannah found this to be both a relief and a frustration. There was little to fear during the day, but neither was any knowledge to be gained.

By the time the prisoners got back, it was late in the evening and too dark to determine anything about where they'd been or what they'd been doing during the day.

As the prisoners disappeared into the building, Hannah arranged her bedding. If she and Jason were going to be able to rise early enough to follow in the morning, they'd have to get some rest. "Tired or not, we need to try to sleep," she said. "There's a lot to do in the morning."

Hannah closed her eyes and in moments she could feel her breathing begin to deepen.

CHAPTER FIFTY-NINE

Faydra returned to the scene of the avalanche and climbed to where the boulder had once rested, where she contemplated the various paths the woman and boy might have taken. If she were them, she would've stayed on the game trail they'd come in on. She walked slowly along the track, scanning for signs. It wasn't long before she found the evidence she was looking for. They hadn't doubled back at all. After the rock had fallen, they'd returned to this point and continued on.

Faydra followed.

***

Faydra stood on the front steps of an abandoned house. She could see the trail she'd followed both arrived and departed from the same spot. The fugitives were no longer there, but they'd spent the previous night somewhere inside. She looked up at the sun. There was still a good hour of light; enough time to investigate before darkness made seeing impossible.

The front door led into the living room. There was an old sectional sofa surrounding a huge television. A packrat infestation had destroyed the room. In one corner, the debris was piled over a meter high. *How many rats does it take to make a nest this size?* The stench was almost unbearable. Faydra raised a forearm to cover her nose and breathed through her mouth.

She moved from room to room, but each one seemed worse than the next. Maybe the fugitives hadn't stayed here at all. There were just two doors left to investigate. *If there isn't a decent place to sleep behind either of these, I'm sleeping outside.* She pushed the door open and sighed in relief. Someone had scrounged what they could from other areas of the house and placed everything in this room.

Faydra flopped onto the bed and closed her eyes. There was nothing else she could do today, so there was nothing that would keep her awake.

***

She woke at first light and reexamined the footprints. If it had been her, and she had narrowly escaped an outpost, she would've left town as soon as possible, but she'd found nothing to suggest that these two were leaving the area.

There was no reason to take the risk of them seeing her sooner than she wanted, so she untied the horse and left it to find its own way. She'd continue the rest of the way on foot.

The trail led her into the brush, but by the look of their efforts, they must have been more concerned with being seen than being tracked. It was easy following the broken twigs and crushed underbrush through the willows and shrubs. It couldn't even be called tracking. They might as well have paved the way. The fact that they'd passed this way twice made it even easier.

Faydra arrived where the creek intersected the river and exchanged her 'paved' trail for the paved road. It'd be harder to track them if they'd stayed to the road but at least it was easier walking. Anyway, she reminded herself, tracking wasn't about following a continuous path of signs. It was all about knowing the terrain, understanding the quarry, and predicting where they were going.

Since they were trying not to be seen, they'd be sticking close to edge of the road or traveling in the woods. The road to her right led into town. The road to the left led to the penitentiary. If they were heading toward town, other security forces would eventually pick them up. Besides, it was hard to imagine them being as foolish as to go back to town. So she followed her instincts and turned toward the penitentiary. It was still early. If she was wrong, she had plenty of time to double back.

CHAPTER SIXTY

Hannah looked in the direction of the prison. She imagined without artificial light that, inside, night and day would be indistinguishable. On the outside, the sun hadn't yet risen, and she had no idea when the gates would open. She gathered Jason and Elvin and moved to the highway where all the prisoners would have to pass before being taken to their individual work sites.

Hannah looked east. The sky was beginning to brighten. One by one, the stars disappeared. Jason seemed tired. Hannah knew he needed more sleep, but there was nothing to be done about it. For as long as they remained in this godforsaken town, restful sleep was not among their options.

Elvin, on the other hand, was awake and alert. If the prison had been his home, this might be his normal waking hour.

Suddenly, Elvin's eyes widened, and he cocked his head slightly to one side as if listening. He turned his face northward toward the prison. Then Hannah heard it, too: a distant growing rumble, as if something or someone was drawing nearer. Hannah looked to the east as the noise grew louder. It was as if the rising sun had been accompanied by thunder.

Hannah waited, her gut churning as fear rose to her throat. She looked toward Jason and saw he was doing everything he could to ensure that Elvin remained low and out of sight, but Hannah wondered if his efforts might be useless. She held a finger to her lips and gritted her teeth, hoping to communicate how imperative it was to be silent.

Jason grimaced, lowered his brow, and then shrugged as if to say, "I know, but what more can I do?"

That look did nothing to ease her apprehension.

The clamor grew louder as the prisoners drew closer. There were hundreds upon hundreds of shuffling feet, accompanied by the sound of horses and rattling chains. Occasionally, a man barked orders, but Hannah could make out none of what was said.

It was almost light when the prisoners came into view. Elvin huddled behind Jason with fear in his eyes. Two guards led a column of prisoners four wide, stretching back as far as she could see. Armed guards flanked the procession on both sides. It took several minutes for the entire group to pass by.

It was difficult to make out individuals, but Hannah did her best to get a look at the hundreds of people passing before her. Almost beyond hope, she scanned the crowd for a glimpse of Travis. Judging by the expression on Jason's face, he was hoping for the same.

Almost the entire group had passed by when suddenly, Elvin began to point and chant, "Tavs, Tavs, Tavs."

Together, Hannah and Jason turned toward him and pounced, giving him no chance to say more, smothering any sound as they landed on top of him. The one thing she'd feared most had happened. The guards had already been alarmed and it would be only moments before they would be there to drag them from their hiding place.

Hannah and Jason waited in silence. Elvin lay motionlessly beneath them. The moments ticked by, but no one seemed to have noticed the sudden commotion in the trees. Hannah waited until the prisoners were gone and then rolled to one side. She took her weight off Elvin and released the breath she had been holding.

When the commotion faded into the distance, Hannah rose and parted the brush. The trio stepped cautiously onto the road. She looked both ways then followed the procession at what she hoped was a safe distance. Eventually, they came to a T in the road where the group split in two. The larger portion turned south and bore toward the hills, while the smaller group turned toward the valley floor, toward the orchards and the apple harvest. What was so important that Harry would dedicate most of the works force to its effort? She didn't know, but it had to be an important piece of the puzzle. When the small group was out of sight, they followed the main group into the hills.

The road became more winding and turnoffs became fewer and fewer until it became apparent there'd be no further splitting of the groups. Wherever they were going, it would be as one large body.

Hannah noticed that Elvin was becoming increasingly agitated. She looked up and realized how dangerously close they'd gotten to the rear of the procession. Fortunately, it'd been Elvin who'd alerted her, but if he didn't hush, he might alert them as well.

"What's up, buddy?" said Jason, hoping to comfort and calm him.

"It's okay," Hannah said. "You're safe with us,"

Elvin covered his ears, stomped his feet, and began spinning in circles. Hannah had no choice. Unless they stopped to deal with their miniature adult and his tantrum, someone was bound to notice.

Hannah took his arm and pulled him to the side of the road. "Shhh," she said in as soothing a tone as she could muster. "You need to be quiet."

As the prisoners disappeared up the road, Elvin began to relax. When he was calm once more, Hannah led them out onto the road.

After several repetitions of the behavior, Hannah realized it was the proximity to the prisoners that was causing it. He was like a human alarm. Every time they got too close, he became more agitated.

She couldn't be certain where Elvin had come from, but having escaped from the prison made perfect sense when she considered the wounds on his face, the thicket where they'd found him, and now his reaction to the prisoners.

The prisoners walked for more than an hour until they came to a wide spot in the road where a number of wagons and horses waited. The crew was swiftly loaded on the wagons in groups of ten and the horses started off at a trot.

It took all of Hannah's physical reserves to keep up. Elvin, on the other hand, had no difficulty maintaining an easy gait. Hannah was amazed at his level of fitness. Luckily for her, the waggoneers never demanded that the horses run faster than a trot. She wondered why they hadn't collected the prisoners at the prison; it would have saved a lot of time, not to mention human energy.

Less than a kilometer later, the road ended at a large opening in the trees. The ground seemed to fall away abruptly, and the lead wagons disappeared from sight. As curious as she was, so far there was nothing to tell her what the prisoners' destination might be.

Hannah stopped at the edge of the wooded area surrounding what appeared to be a canyon. Hannah and Jason had taken but a few steps when they realized Elvin wasn't following. Jason beckoned to him, but Elvin retreated into the brush where he cowered. Hannah shrugged. The drop-off was close, and it'd be safer if they investigated without him.

Hannah and Jason crouched low and approached the edge of the canyon as far as they dared. When they were as close as they could risk on foot, they dropped to their bellies and crawled the remaining distance.

Looking into the abyss, Hannah's eyes grew wide. Before her was the maw of a gigantic open pit mine. She'd seen pictures in old National Geographic magazines but had never before seen one in real life. From this perspective, it looked like a giant empty, almost black, ice cream cone about a quarter of a kilometer deep and more than a kilometer wide. There was a small lake at the bottom. She could only guess at how deep it might be.

The prisoners had already diminished to the size of ants, yet they were no more than halfway to the bottom. Hannah's heart when out to the workers who would slave away for the entire day just to be taken back to the prison and caged for the night.

She rolled on her back and looked at the sky. Was there no end to the atrocities man could inflict on one another? After a moment, she stood and walked back to the woods where Elvin was hiding. Jason casually pulled a couple of apples from his pack and tossed one to

Hannah. They no longer tasted as good as they had two days earlier, and they'd do little to hold back the pangs of hunger, but they were still better than nothing. He tossed one to Elvin, and Hannah half expected him to drop it, but Elvin had been eyeing Jason from the moment he started rummaging in his pack and he caught it deftly.

For a few minutes, the only noises were crunching sounds as they devoured their meager meal.

Jason pointed toward the mine. "What's that?" he said with a full mouth.

"It's an open pit mine of some sort. Over the years, they've hauled all the dirt and ore away until there's nothing left but this big hole."

The real question was what they were mining. In all the pictures Hannah'd seen, it had been for molybdenum or gold, but neither of those would have much use in today's world that she could think of. Maybe molybdenum, but almost certainly not gold.

Across the road, there were mountains of tailings, and beyond that there were mountains of rock. Somewhere, there should be a facility of some kind for refining whatever ore they were removing.

They were about to investigate when the sudden appearance of a team of horses cresting the hill sent them scurrying into the underbrush. As the wagon rolled by, the solution to the mystery occurred to Hannah like a gunshot. Coal. Of course. They were using coal to fuel an electric plant somewhere. Hannah scanned the horizon until her eyes rested on a faint plume of smoke rising in the distance. She pointed toward it. Jason's gaze followed her finger.

"What is it?"

"I think it's an electric plant. It's the reason for hot showers and microwave ovens," was Hannah's quick reply. "We may as well get some rest. They'll be here until the day is over is my guess."

CHAPTER SIXTY-ONE

Although no evidence of the fugitives could be found on the asphalt surface, Faydra knew people on foot tended to obey the rules of the road. She kept a careful watch for signs that the two had slipped into the ditch.

Once she had passed beyond city limits, it became even easier to follow their trail. Fewer side roads for her to eliminate reduced the number of possible routes they might have taken. She often looked ahead, knowing they were probably moving slowly. She could stumble upon them at any moment. Bent, broken, and trampled foliage provided reliable information about how long the fugitives had spent in any given spot. Just because the boy and the woman were two days ahead of her didn't mean they were very far away. She'd prefer it if it were she who discovered them and not the other way around.

Faydra arrived at the prison close to noon. The trail led into a grove of trees near the entrance. Even without a trained eye, it took no more than a glance to tell they'd spent a significant amount of time here. Apple cores littered the ground. The grass was matted. She combed the area. There were indications that there were more than two people in the group, which was a new development. Who was this third person and where had they come from? What sort of a threat might this new person turn out to be?

There was a trail leading to the south. She assumed if she followed it, it would take her back to the outpost or the orchard.

A second set of recent tracks led from the underbrush and seemed to follow the direction of the prisoners. There was no doubt this newest set of tracks included the third member of the party.

The new tracks overlapped those most recently left by the prisoners. They were definitely following the prisoners. There was no chance the woman and boy could pose any real threat to Harry or the community. The longer she followed them, the more convinced she was that Harry had set her on some goose chase.

Faydra debated between waiting for them to return and continuing along their trail. After short consideration, she decided it would be best to find them on their travels as opposed to being discovered in their hideout. She'd gone to great lengths to look the part of a vagrant; she wanted to be welcomed into the group. It wouldn't do to risk suspicion before she had a chance to gain their trust.

Faydra scanned the area once more to ensure she hadn't missed any important information and then set out on their trail once more, knowing she was only an hour or two behind.

CHAPTER SIXTY-TWO

According to Hannah's estimation, it would be five or six hours before the inmates started their return trip to the prison. The captives would be tired, and their pace would likely be slower, which would hopefully provide her and Jason more time to prepare.

Ideally, if Travis was among the prisoners, they could locate him and get him out without a fight. But if things led to a skirmish, she doubted she could count on the prisoners for help.

They wound their way along the road toward the prison, walking in silence and making good time. Hannah rounded a blind corner and lifted her head in surprise. Her first instinct was to duck into the woods, but it was too late for that. The woman had already seen them. To try to hide would only make them look foolish. Instead, she dropped her rifle from her shoulder and let it rest in two hands with the barrel pointing at a spot in the road near the feet of the stranger who was still almost a hundred meters away. Her clothing suggested she was a wandering traveler. It seemed a bit strange to Hannah. How had the woman managed to avoid detection? Maybe she was just lucky. Hannah shrugged it off. There were so many strange things in the world and there was no point questioning every one of them.

It was the stranger who spoke first. "Hey," she stated in tone suggesting she was weary from traveling.

Before Hannah could offer any words of caution Jason returned her greeting. "Hi," he said. "Are you from around here?"

"Nah." The woman nodded toward the east.

"You're not from around here?" Jason asked.

Hannah watched the woman's reactions carefully, but if there was anything she was trying to hide, she was doing it well.

"No. Just traveling around, looking for a good place to stop," said the stranger.

"If you're looking for town, you're going in the wrong direction," Jason said.

It didn't seem to Hannah that Jason was about to give away any crucial information, so she let him continue without interrupting.

The woman's eyes rose, and she began to smile. "You mean there's a town close by?"

The woman seemed genuine, but in all Hannah's experience she'd learned it was never a good idea to believe anyone was what they claimed. Considering where they were and where they'd come from, it struck her as unlikely that this woman wouldn't know there was a town close by. Coming from the east should have meant she would've had to have passed through town, in fact. Hannah didn't want to confront her, but something felt wrong. She hadn't said much, but even in that she was trying too hard.

The stranger was feminine in some ways, but she had a stance Hannah associated with a man. Her appearance didn't seem to fit the helpless woman she was trying to portray.

Maybe the woman didn't deserve this level of scrutiny. Maybe it was she who was trying too hard to find something wrong where everything was right. "Yes, there's a town. You didn't notice it?" said Hannah.

The woman didn't hesitate. "I've been traveling all summer long. Most of the towns were completely deserted. I've been heading west trying to find somewhere where I could find a reason to stay. Originally, I'm from Edmonton, but that place has been taken over by a bunch of thieves and cutthroats. I had no choice. It was either leave or die. I spent the summer crossing the Rockies and just came through Penticton not long ago."

The woman hadn't answered Hannah's question and was edging closer with every word. Hannah continued to press. There was something tickling the back of her mind. Was it bothersome that the woman hadn't asked any questions of her own? Or was it the fact that she was traveling alone? "You're alone?" said Hannah.

"I am now. My husband was killed a few weeks ago. A big cat got him. There wasn't anything I could do." She turned her head toward the road as if the pain was too great. If she was pretending, it was a good act.

She slowly raised her head. "Are you going into town?" she said.

"If I were you, I'd turn around and go back the same way you came. If you're looking for a place to call home, this isn't it," Hannah stated matter-of-factly.

"I don't know if I can. I've been traveling so long …."

The itching at the back of Hannah's mind persisted. She couldn't put her finger on it.

"If you've been traveling so long, where's your pack, food, and extra clothes?" said Jason.

Hannah watched the woman's reaction, but all she got was a scornful smile.

"Listen kids, if you'd been traveling half as long as I have, you'd know there are lots of places to crash. Clothes and everything else under the sun has been left behind in every little carcass of a shack. All you have to do is ask the pack rats to step aside and give up a little space. All I need is this." She lifted the back of her shirt to reveal a bulging lumbar pack.

Suddenly, as if a switch had been flipped, the woman became furious. "I don't know why you think I'm the one with something to prove. You come up on me in the trail and you grill me like I'm dangerous. Have I done anything like that to you? Have I suggested you're less honest than you look? No, I haven't," she said, answering her own question. "But maybe I should. You three look like the unlikeliest group I can imagine. One little boy, an old woman, and a retard."

Hannah, seeing Jason's temper flaring, wondered why all new meetings seemed to go the same way. They seemed to start off fine and then, invariably, something always went wrong. The woman's sudden verbal attack caught her off guard. All the internal alarms that had been chiming were suddenly forgotten. A moment earlier, she'd wondered what the odds were that a big cat had also attacked this woman or why her clothes weren't in worse shape than they were. Now she wondered why she'd ever questioned the woman.

It didn't matter anyway. The stranger could've dismissed all the questions Hannah had for her. There were a thousand reasons and explanations, all of them feasible. There was something wrong about this woman, but Hannah was unable to see it. "Listen, I'm sorry if it sounds like we're giving you the fifth degree. We've been through a lot, too. And to tell you the truth, it's a heck of a lot easier to be alone than to run into anyone. You'd just complicate our lives if you joined us, and it looks like you can take care of yourself just fine. I can't say it's been great meeting you, but we're going this way." Hannah nodded down the road beyond Faydra. "And you're going that way." She used her thumb to indicate the road behind them.

"You're right. These are the hardest times for people and instead of being warm and friendly, the first thing we do is turn on each other. My name is Faydra and if I don't have to travel alone … if I could travel with some decent company, it would make my life a whole lot easier."

Hannah held her ground. "Faydra, it's been nice meeting you, but we're on a different kind of journey. We're not looking for the next wonderful town right now. In fact, there is an excellent chance that we'll be buried right here, and I really don't think you want to be a part of that."

"Why don't you let me be the judge of that?"

Jason was still standing with a menacing look, though his features had softened somewhat.

Having faith in people was as much a curse as a blessing. A person's character has a way of shining through and Faydra would prove herself in time, but the risk that it would be too late loomed large. Hannah found her mind wandering back to the prison.

Faydra chattered like a magpie. From the stories she told, it was clear she could hold her own in terms of survival. If they allowed the woman to join them in their travels, Faydra wouldn't be another person to babysit. In some ways, Hannah looked forward to spending a little time with someone who might turn out to be a kindred spirit. She decided to let the woman stay, and sort it out if need be later.

***

As they walked, Hannah began to ignore Faydra's ramblings, and her thoughts returned to Jason and their plan.

She couldn't just walk away from Kamloops leaving hundreds of prisoners enslaved by Harry, but she had no idea about how to free them. Even if she could, it was probably not enough to stop him. For as long as unwary strangers traveled the roads, Harry would flourish.

The sun was sinking fast. In addition to all the other problems she faced, Hannah had to accept that whatever plans she made, it would take days before she could put them into action.

The long pauses in conversation created by Hannah's thoughts didn't inspire Jason to fill them. He hadn't warmed up to their new traveling companion, and from what Hannah could tell, he had no intention to. He walked in silence, always maintaining his serious look. The miles passed beneath their feet until the lights of the prison came into view. Hannah led the group off the road into the sanctuary of the brush.

Faydra didn't seem to mind Jason's sullen attitude and pressed Hannah with questions. "You seem like you've got something pretty heavy on your mind. If it's not too personal, it seems kind of strange that you'd be hanging out in front of an old penitentiary." Darkness had fallen, and the automatic lights of the prison lit up the surrounding field shedding a little light into the thicket.

She responded to Faydra as if coming out of a trance. "Hmmm … yes … they are heavy thoughts," she said. "But if you want to me to tell you that this place is the perfect place to settle and rebuild your life, I can't do it. As I said, all I can do is suggest you head south, find the first safe place you can find and spend the winter, wait 'til spring and then keep heading south. Since you came from Edmonton, I can tell you that there's nothing west of here. Like I said, if I were you, I'd go south."

After hours of being silent, Jason finally spoke. "If you go down there," he said, indicating the town, "you'll probably be back here by morning, and we can watch you march down the road with the rest of the prisoners."

"Do you know how absolutely crazy that sounds?" Faydra said in disbelief.

"I'd never have believed it myself," said Hannah. "I certainly didn't expect it. We wandered into town just like you did. We're lucky we're still free."

"What happened?"

Hannah told her how they had been cornered and finally invited to dinner by Harry. She told Faydra how odd the man had seemed. She described the events of the night they escaped and those that followed. "Maybe they thought we wouldn't try and get away … probably because all they see is a woman and a young boy. I guess it's understandable." Hannah gave Jason a nudge. It was enough to get a forced smile from him. Maybe she'd finally broken him out of his sulk.

"It's great that you got away. What keeps you around now?" said Faydra.

The light was gone from the sky. Hannah had no desire to respond. Fortunately, the returning work crew interrupted their conversation. Their stomping feet were the most prominent sounds in the darkness. Moments later, the leading prisoners came into view, effectively suspending their conversation until the last of them passed by.

Jason watched stoically as the men, women, and children trudged into the facility. Elvin's behavior had transformed from the dull detached look he normally wore to being mesmerized as he mouthed the word 'tavs' over and over again. When the last of the prisoners were out of sight, Hannah turned her attention once again to Faydra, "That's the reason right there." She nodded toward the fading cloud of dust which followed the prisoners into the building. "How can I leave here knowing what's going on? Life's barely worth living as it is, and I can't bring myself to be a part of destroying it. Who would I be if I didn't try to help?"

"Maybe they like it this way," Faydra said.

"How can you even think for a second they like their lives? Didn't you even look at them?" Hannah returned. Already the dust cloud was no more than a memory.

Faydra shrugged. "There have always been the have and have-nots. Me? I've always been a have-not. What makes you think you're going to make a difference? Even if you release all these people, do you think you're going to make their lives better by doing it? They have a roof over their heads and food in their bellies. That's something at least. It's more than you have."

Hannah was appalled. "Do you really believe that crap?"

Faydra began to laugh heartily at Hannah's outburst. "It doesn't matter, Hannah. What are you going to gain by getting caught? You'll get caught and that'll be that."

"Humph," said Hannah, shaking her head. "If that was all there was to it, you might be right. But it's not just that. We're looking for someone, and we think he might be here." Hannah motioned toward Jason with her head. "That young man right there? He's the reason I'm here. I said I'd help him, and I will … or … I guess I'll die trying."

"Why?" Faydra seemed honestly bewildered.

"I've been wondering about that myself. Each time I come up with the same answer. Family. I've only known Jason a few months, but I feel like we're connected." Again, she used her eyes to refer to Jason. "His father came this way and there's a good chance he came through here. If he's here, then someone might know him. I have to believe the key to where he is is here."

"All right, Hannah, you're going to find this man, free him, free the community, kill Harry…and then what?" said Faydra.

"Maybe you're right. I can't even imagine doing all of that. I don't have any intention of killing anyone. It does sound completely crazy. I'd be happy if we can just find Travis and get out of here."

"If he's here," Faydra finished for her.

Jason's eyes had narrowed again, doing nothing to hide his distaste for Faydra.

"It's what we're about. We'll do what we can," Hannah finished. She hoped the tone in her voice was enough to communicate she'd ended the conversation.

There was another long silence until Faydra once again broke it by pressing the issue again. "So what are you going to do next?"

"Maybe it's best we don't talk about it, Faydra. I can't risk that you'll talk me out of anything we might do. We need to get some sleep, anyway," said Hannah as she prepared the ground where she'd slept the previous night. "You'll probably want to decide what your next move is going to be. Jason and I already know what we're planning to do."

Again, Hannah left the conversation with nothing left to be said. She was relieved when Faydra was quiet at last.

Jason had remained silent during the entire conversation, and Hannah was grateful there had been nothing Faydra said that motivated him to speak. Turning her back to everyone, she closed her eyes and tried to fall asleep. Her busy mind fought her. She resented Faydra for her pessimistic perspective. It made her task much harder. As she thought about some of the ludicrous things Faydra had said, a sick, unarticulated feeling that the woman would report their whereabouts and be the ruin of them began to form inside her.

CHAPTER SIXTY-THREE

Hannah woke in time to watch the early morning procession wind its way out of the compound. She imagined the guards who'd been left behind would settle down for a long day of doing next to nothing. Giving them an hour should be plenty of time. If anyone remained in the prison it would probably be as a precautionary measure and to provide the food services necessary to keep the prisoners alive. Hannah hoped she'd find the number of people at the facility negligible.

Hannah looked over at Faydra. Her eyes were closed, and her breathing was deep. As far as she could tell, Faydra was asleep. She was about to step out of the thicket when Jason stirred. *Damn.* She put her index finger to her lips. He rose and came quietly to her.

"What are you doing," he whispered?

"Someone's got to check out the layout of the prison. I need to know more about what's going on in there … how it works," Hannah replied.

"I can do that," said Jason, his eyes lighting up.

"No, Jason, someone needs to stay behind and look after Elvin. I was counting on you to do that for me."

"What about her?" Jason queried with obvious distain in his voice.

"I don't know. Maybe she'll move on when she wakes up. If we're lucky, " Hannah paused, "who knows, maybe she'll be useful for something."

"Hannah, we should stay together. I don't want you to leave me behind," pleaded Jason.

"Listen, buddy, I'll be back soon."

Hannah could see he was reluctant, but he watched her walk away nonetheless. There was no indication that anyone was watching the road, and the gate from which the prisoners had departed stood gaping. It would remain that way until they returned.

Hannah ran through the main gate and then quickly to the wall. She stayed low, trying to keep out of the sightlines from every possible vantage point. She was counting on the likelihood that no one was watching, but she didn't want to end her expedition before it started. So far, there was no movement in or around the compound. As far as she could tell, it was deserted. But there were hundreds of prisoners, so there must be some number of staff working somewhere.

During the time that she and Jason had spent in the thicket, she'd seen no deliveries. Along with staff, there would have to be regular shipments as well. Hannah didn't know what to think. There were more questions than answers.

As she approached the building, it was immediately apparent where the prisoners emerged from each day. From the gates, the tall razor wire that lined the fences jutted directly to the building making it impossible for her to skirt it. The windows were high on the wall, too high for anyone to jump and reach. They were protected by bars set too close for anyone to escape through. In some places, the windows were broken, and she could see glass littering the ground. *Those must have been busted from the inside.*

There were faint sounds that seemed to come from inside the walls, but below her feet, suggesting a basement. There might be a guard close by and Hannah tried to be prepared for it. She peeked around the corner. A large bay door had once sealed the entrance. At one time it would've been able to be opened and closed to secure the building, the door was now gone, leaving a gaping void. The bent and broken mechanism that had been used to operate it was still there. Without a functioning door, it was impossible to lock the facility. Hannah passed through the doorway and into a large garage.

It was clear why no one would be around. The building couldn't be secured from inside this warehouse sized room. The ceiling was at least six meters above her head. About halfway up the wall, a catwalk encircled the entire area. The concrete floor had begun to succumb to the elements and was a maze of deep cracks. The individual slabs of cement had heaved from winter frost, and plants had taken root wherever they could. Even moss found homes in the shaded areas. The only light came in from the yawning bay entry.

In light of the neglect, Hannah moved with more confidence. The prison wasn't functioning in all the glory it once had. At the back of the loading bay was a narrow steel door. Even from ten meters away, Hannah could tell it was open. There were no other doors in or out of the area, making it the only place the prisoners could have come from. Hannah had been worried she'd have to wander around the building for hours trying to figure that out. Fortunately, their daily path was easily discernable. It had probably been years since any cleaning had been done, making the floors virtually dust free where it was continuously traveled.

On the other hand, filth had accumulated in deep rows next to the walls, which included whatever had blown into the building through the doorway over the years since the main bay door had been ripped from its rails.

Beyond the door was a reception area of sorts, but it, too, was vacant. Hannah had never been in a prison before, but she imagined she might be standing in the area that would have been used when the prisoners were first brought in. She envisioned a busload of convicts arriving.

They would've been escorted off the bus after the big bay doors were securely closed behind them. From there they might've gone single file through the steel door and waited as their belongings were checked in. At some point, they would've been cleaned, and their clothes exchanged for prison issue.

Hannah moved cautiously through the hallways. She passed various doors. One was marked Supplies. The knob turned easily, but the door was held closed by a hydraulic door closer. She pushed hard, and the old stiff cylinder slowly gave. The light from the hallway provided enough illumination in the room to see it was nothing more than a custodian's closet, just as the sign stated. One wall was covered with metal shelving holding various industrial strength cleaning products. The opposite wall was lined with a assortment of cleaning machines that had once been used to clean, polish, and wax the floors. Among them were several large buckets. Brackets on the walls held mops. Like everywhere else, everything was covered in a thick layer of dust. No one had been in this room for years—probably not since the facility had been shut down. A vertical steel ladder was attached to the wall at the back of the room and rose through a hole in the ceiling, possibly leading to the roof.

Hannah left the room and went back out into the hall. She wasn't concerned about finding the prisoner cellblocks. The most traveled hallways probably led directly to them. She was more interested in discovering the whereabouts of whatever guards might have been left behind. Hannah strained her ears for any movement or noise. Her efforts were rewarded almost immediately. From somewhere ahead she heard footfalls and jingling keys. She raced back to the supply room. She carefully held the door handle open as the closer pulled the door shut to avoid making noise when it came in contact with the door jam. Someone passed by and she could hear heavy boots thumping on the floor. Soon, the noise disappeared into the distance. She waited for complete silence before peering into the corridor once more.

The man was either returning from an errand or leaving to go on one. If might be useful to know which it was. She walked down the hall in the direction he'd gone. The hallway was about three meters wide and seemed to go on forever. There were various doors leading off from either side. Of the ones she checked, most were locked. Hannah explored the hall as quickly as she could. At the end of the corridor, it T'd. It was evident that both were used to some degree.

She continued from one hallway to the next, letting her ears do more of the guiding than her eyes. Soft, far-off sounds acted as both compass and alarm.

The corridor ended abruptly at a large steel door with a small window high in the center. Thin reinforcement wires crisscrossed inside the glass. The door swung easily as she pushed on it, revealing a series of steps down into a dark chamber lit only by the light coming from the open door. Hannah stepped forward. She felt as if she were walking into a lion's den. The hallway continued, but now it was lined on both sides by small three-sided compartments. The fourth side of each of the chambers consisted of a wall of iron bars. The entire area reeked of mildew and old sweat. Hannah gagged and breathed through her mouth. As she'd expected, the cells were empty.

Out of curiosity, she examined one, but there was nothing to see. Any furnishings had been removed, leaving only a vacant room. If there had been working toilets, they, too, had been removed. There were still holes in the walls and a toilet flange in the floor. There was no evidence of the bunks that must surely have existed at one time. They had probably been removed because of the filth and disease they would have become homes to. Hannah shivered at the thought. Having seen enough, she turned to leave.

She was about to put a hand on the handle when she heard the sound of footsteps and voices coming from the hall. They were still far off. She walked to the top of the platform and stood on her toes to look through the window. She could see nothing. The sounds of boots on concrete grew closer. Images of guards on their way to her hiding place made her feel a wave of panic. There was nowhere to run other than the hallway through the door and the individual cells behind her. She moved to the hinge side of the door and stood with her back to the wall. The footsteps grew louder still. Hannah closed her eyes and waited for the door to swing open.

CHAPTER SIXTY-FOUR

Faydra watched through barely open eyes as Hannah walked up the hill toward the prison complex. She waited until Hannah disappeared before she went through the normal motions of waking.

"Good morning, Jason," she drew out the word 'good' in her best 'I-just-woke-up' voice.

Jason looked at her indifferently and nodded.

That worked. She didn't like him, either.

She walked over to Elvin nonchalantly. Jason had already dismissed her. She knew he was still miffed because if it hadn't been for her, he wouldn't be stuck waiting for Hannah to get back.

***

Though he wouldn't have put anything passed Faydra, Jason was caught by surprise when she slammed the heel of her hand into the bridge of Elvin's nose. Elvin dropped like a stone, unconscious. Jason was stunned but was still able to reach into his pack to find the pistol that lay at the bottom. He silently cursed himself for not carrying the gun in his coat pocket. His hand found the butt and pulled it free, shaking the backpack to the ground. He brought it up in one smooth action and was ready to fire, but he was still much too late.

Faydra had too swiftly moved from where Elvin had fallen. Her hand came down hard and grasped his fist, pinching his fingers against the metal. The power in her hands was astounding. She squeezed hard on his fingers, smashing them into the grip of the pistol. At the same time, she stepped to the side and away from where the bullet would travel if the gun were to fire. She twisted the revolver away and, with a flip of her wrist, tossed the weapon into the woods. She continued to put pressure on his hand and twist his arm at the same time. He had no alternative but to turn his body until she had his arm held firmly behind his back and his hand pinned between his shoulder blades.

Although the pain robbed his knees of strength, Faydra hauled him to his feet using his arm as leverage. From her back pocket she produced a short length of cord. One end had been prepared with a loop tied with a slipknot. Faydra slipped the loop over Jason's free hand and pulled it tight. She added his other hand and deftly bound the two tightly together. Jason winced in pain. A wicked smile spread across her face.

By the time his hands were secured, Elvin had begun to stir. He sat up rubbing the bridge of his nose. If he understood or was upset about what had happened, he didn't show it and when Faydra began to march Jason up the hill, he dumbly followed along.

They arrived at the prison gates and Faydra walked through as if she'd been there hundreds of times before. Without hesitating, she continued through the main reception area and directly to the office that doubled as a staff room for the few guards who remained behind during the day. One of those guards sat at a desk with his feet propped on top, a surface that had long since ceased to be used for its intended purpose and was now just a glorified ottoman.

When Faydra dragged Jason to the desk, the guard jumped to his feet and stammered apologetically while ignoring him and Elvin.

"There's a woman roaming around here. I want her found," Faydra commanded.

"Yes, ma'am," said the guard who had been lounging. As she'd predicted, he rose so fast he almost fell over in the process.

Pushed along by two guards, they left the room and followed the main hall, passing several wings along the way. Jason kept watching Elvin's expression. If he recognized anything about the place, he gave no indication.

At the end of the hall, a guard unlocked the door and opened it, revealing some sort of interrogation room. Once inside, Faydra retrieved the cord from Jason's wrists.

The bigger of the guards pushed him into a chair with such force that when he landed, both he and the chair slid into the corner and toppled over. Jason's elbow slammed into the concrete wall.

He recovered in time to see the same man throw Elvin to the floor. Faydra stood in the doorway looking indifferent. Jason rose from the floor and glared impotently, alternately massaging his elbow and his wrists.

The guard said nothing as he turned to leave. He slammed and locked the door behind him with an audible click. Jason picked up the chair and sat, defeated.

CHAPTER SIXTY-FIVE

The seconds dragged by as Hannah hid in the empty cellblock. Blood pounded behind her eyes, and the sound of her own heartbeat throbbing in her ears made it nearly impossible to focus as the guards drew closer. She strained to listen and forced herself to calm down. Certain the sound of the footsteps was getting farther away, she moved to the window to peer down the corridor. A small group of people were walking away from her. Two were guards. One of them was Faydra. Hannah's heart sank as she recognized Jason and Elvin. Jason's hands were tied firmly behind his back. She was saddened to see that Faydra walked freely. They'd been betrayed.

It would only be a matter of minutes before the guards would be scouring the facility looking for her, and it was safe to assume that Faydra knew her way around. They would've blocked off the main entrance as soon as Faydra had come through. Leaving by that route was most certainly out of the question.

She slipped through the door and into the main hall. As quickly and quietly as she could, she returned to the supply room. The door was equipped with a dead bolt. On the inside of the room, there was a safety knob for operating the lock. On the outside, the lock could only be opened with a key. Hannah turned the bolt and locked the door. Her fears were proved valid when she heard the quick heavy footsteps of two guards hurrying along the corridor. The sound of their steps paused briefly at regular intervals. They must be checking doors, she concluded. They stopped at the door of her storage closet. There was a twist on the knob and a sudden yank. Seemingly satisfied that the door had been locked all along, the guards moved on, leaving Hannah in the dark and silence.

It was still early in the day and the main body of the prisoners wasn't due back for hours. Hannah turned a mop bucket upside down, padded it with a few cleaning rags, and sat down to think.

CHAPTER SIXTY-SIX

Having locked the boy in the interrogation room, Faydra made her way back to a more comfortable office. She'd leave it up to the guards to find Hannah; it was nearly impossible for the woman to free herself. There were only two exits and both of those were carefully controlled. It was Faydra's turn to sit with her feet up. A self-satisfied smile spread across her face while the building bustled with activity.

As the hours slipped by without progress, Faydra's patience began to fade. It didn't seem reasonable that in a near empty facility it'd take so long to find a single person. Hannah wouldn't have been able to evade the guards who were searching for her this long unless she knew they were looking for her. *That's the answer, isn't it, you crafty hag? You already know we're looking for you.*

Faydra stood and went in search of the nearest guard. When she found one, she pulled him aside. "She knows we've got the boy."

The guard looked at her wide eyed and confused, "What?"

"Listen, you idiot," she said, speaking to the man in a sharp staccato, "she's here and she knows we've got the boy and his stupid friend. She's hiding in here somewhere. Find Mac and tell him to come and see me."

When guard didn't move immediately, Faydra shrieked, "Now," accompanied with a look that inspired the guard to run in the direction he believed Mac might have gone.

CHAPTER SIXTY-SEVEN

Hannah sat in the dark with her head resting in the palms of her hands. There would be no stopping the search. Eventually, she knew, Faydra would try to use Jason as leverage. There was no point wasting time wondering how she'd hurt him or what she'd force him to do when he could take no more. If Hannah stayed where she was, they'd eventually find her.

Locating Jason would have to be her priority. With guards combing the building, moving through the main hallways would be too dangerous. She stood and circled the room in frustration. She had no options.

The only direction left to explore was the ladder. It was a time for action, not hiding. She had no idea what she'd find at the top. The sign hanging beside the ladder that read Maintenance Personnel Only wasn't much help.

She placed a hand on the rung just above her head and started up. She half expected a locked hatch somewhere above her and hoped that wouldn't be the case. The ceiling was about three meters from the floor, and she was relieved when she passed through a rectangular opening surrounded on three sides by a railing. She sighed, pausing at the top. It was dark below, but darker in the room she was about to enter. The only light came from the small window in the door of the custodial room which did nothing more than turn the attic entry into a dim hole in the floor. It did nothing to show what the loft might contain.

She stepped from the ladder to the second floor. If it was the furnace room, there was still hope, although none of the noises associated with working machinery were present. She felt along the nearby wall for light switches. She finally found them only to discover that they were already in the up position. She flipped them down just to be sure. Nothing. She'd have to explore in the dark. At least it was only darkness she was facing and not an impasse just yet.

Starting at the switch panel, Hannah felt her way along with one hand on the wall and the other stretched out in front of her as her eyes. For the first meter there was nothing but flat bare wall, then her hand came abruptly to cold metal. She followed the object around to the left and pushed against it. Although it didn't move, the metal gave slightly. It felt to her like the typical light gauge material furnaces were often made from.

As she moved, she began to picture the room in her mind's eye. Even in the dark, she could almost visualize its dimensions and contents.

When she reached the end of what she believed had been a bank of furnaces, the wall continued for a few meters. Then it turned sharply to the left once again. The next wall was about four meters long and bare. As expected, it turned once more to the left. She knew she had come almost full circle since she could see the faint light from the entrance a few meters away. She resisted the urge to hurry. She didn't want to miss anything. It was beginning to feel like she was in a dead-end room.

It wasn't until she had almost reached her starting point that her progress was halted when her shoulder slammed into a metal outcropping that missed her face by centimeters. Whatever it was, it was made from much heavier gauge steel than the furnaces. She backed away slightly and began to feel around more carefully. She could feel more rungs. Either there was another level or roof access.

Hannah didn't hesitate. She grabbed the nearest bar and began her ascent. She reached high above her head with each step to feel for obstacles or the ceiling. She had ascended about twice her own height when she came to the end of the ladder. A sealed hatch blocked her way. She felt around the edges for a latching system. Her fingers found it and she searched its shape to learn how it operated. It was some sort of cam system attached to a thirty-centimeter-long lever. She positioned herself so she was secure and pulled the lever toward her. It didn't move. She gathered her resolve and pulled harder. The lever remained as if welded. Hannah feared the worst. It was locked. Having failed her first attempt, she tried pushing on it. Again, it didn't give. Frustrated and out of options, she threw her weight into it. The lever creaked. Encouraged, she shoved it as far as it would go.

Feeling confident that the latch was open, she took another step up and shoved her body against the door. With all the strength in her legs, she pushed upward. At first, it was as if she was pushing against a solid wall. Then, slowly, the door began to rise.

She pushed the door until it was perpendicular to the roof. Light flooded into the room below. The roof stretched out like a parking lot covered in tar and gravel. There were no fences up here, which made sense since below there was no part of the building that wasn't surrounded by the high razor wire fence. Even if a prisoner made it up here, the entire roof could be seen from any one of the towers. Escaping from here seemed out of the question for anyone.

From the open hatch, Hannah stood almost dead center of the building. She could only pray that she could find Jason and free him before she was discovered. Hannah returned to the ladder and resigned herself to returning to the room she'd just left.

She took one last quick look around and descended. Although it was still gloomy in the corners of the room, with the roof access open, it was easy to see everything that had been hidden from her earlier. For the most part, it was just as she thought. The place was the central furnace room for the complex. There were more than a dozen furnaces lining the walls, each with its own duct. They formed two groups separated by a narrow passage. In the dark, Hannah had missed that hallway when she'd navigated the room the first time.

There were a full twenty-four individual furnaces. The second set stood back-to-back with the first set in the center of a room. Each was labeled. One read Laundry; another East Cell Block. Hannah looked for anything that might indicate the interrogation rooms. Eventually she came across one called Conference Rooms. She shrugged. It was worth a shot.

Hannah took to the ladder once more and went down to the maintenance room below. The shelves were littered with piles of rags and cleaning products. At the end of the shelf at about chest high was a bin. At first glance, the contents were no more than a bunch of junk. In desperation, she looked closer and found some potentially useful items. There was a role of masking tape, a scraper of some kind, a cheap multibit screwdriver, a hammer, and an old pair of pliers. She slid her hand through the center of the roll of tape and stuffed her pockets with the other tools. She tucked a bundle of old hand towels under her shirt and hurried back up the ladder.

She returned to the furnace with the words Conference Rooms printed on the metal tag. She could reach the top, but she wasn't tall enough to get up to the ductwork fastened there. Once again, she went back to the supply room. This time she brought up the pail she'd used as a chair. She turned it upside down and stood on it. It gave her the height she needed to get a knee up.

She scrambled to the top and balanced beside the duct. Once she'd removed the screws, she took out the ones that held the ninety-degree corner piece to a longer straight section that disappeared through the wall. Half an hour later, she wrestled the four-foot section of metal ducting to the floor.

Next, she went to work with the rags. Using the razor knife, she cut them into strips. She used a square knot to attach each one to the next. With each additional strip of cloth, her rope grew by about twenty centimeters. When she had finished tying the last of the rags, her rope was about four meters long. She coiled it and draped it around her neck.

Before exploring the duct, she returned to the hatch leading to the roof. The sun was bright; she was worried that the light coming from the outside might attract someone's curiosity, so she pulled the door closed.

She wasted no time getting back up on the furnace, which was easier now that the duct wasn't blocking her way. She worked her way into the square metal tube and began to wriggle toward the conference rooms.

It was fortunate that the building had been built during a time when dedicated furnaces were installed to control the heat in various rooms. The advantage for Hannah was that the duct would lead directly to the rooms she hoped to get to. She maneuvered undetected through the complex, crawling on her stomach with as much care as she could.

CHAPTER SIXTY-EIGHT

The prison was in turmoil, but Faydra didn't care. The work here was beneath her. She'd brought the quarry this far. The incompetent guards could handle the rest. At least she could enjoy watching them as they stumbled around like the bumbling fools they were.

Guards had been posted at each exit. The two remaining guards had been given the task of searching the entire complex. They'd already gone through all the large rooms and hallways. Anything that was locked had been ignored with the assumption that the fugitive had no keys.

The second search had been much more thorough, based on the possibility that the woman knew she was being hunted and had been lucky enough to avoid them the first time. They started from one end of the building and worked systematically throughout. Each room was searched thoroughly before passing to the next.

She could always call for reinforcements, but Faydra knew that, for the sake of these men's lives, it was imperative they solve the problem without involving Harry. His wrath carried unpredictable consequences that were never pleasant.

The hours trickled by.

CHAPTER SIXTY-NINE

It was pitch black inside the ducting and Hannah found it difficult to maintain a sense of time and place. To make matters more complicated, the ductwork didn't lead to the conference room. It led to conference rooms, plural, which meant the conduit would certainly branch off at some point. In all likelihood, since they were connected to the same furnace, the rooms would be fairly close to one another.

Hannah continued working her way noiselessly along the hollow tube knowing any sound she made might echo through the halls. She mouthed her mantra repeatedly. *One knee forward and then the other. Check the sides for junctions. Be quiet.* She'd find Jason.

After countless repetitions, she reached her hands out to touch the sides, but, instead of metal, she felt nothing. She slipped forward and pawed at the space in front of her. Nothing. She continued forward until she found another single duct. With a little further exploration, she discovered she had her choice of three passages. Fortunately, she'd planned for such a situation and had decided to start from the left and work to the right. She removed her jacket and placed it behind her in the heating duct where it would serve as her marker to let her know when she had found her way back.

She turned left and counted each forward movement so she'd at least have some idea of how far she'd need to go on her return trip. When she reached seventy-three, the ducting suddenly made a sharp right turn and brightened.

The source of the light was no more than six meters in front of her. She stopped to listen but could hear nothing. She forced herself to avoid negative thoughts. The facility was enormous and there were twenty-four furnaces and twenty-four series of heating ducts to check. She'd check every single one if need be. She crept toward the opening as if guards occupied the room and were expecting her. She reached the grating and investigated the room. There was a stainless steel table in the center and a large mirror on one wall. She craned her head in all directions to try and see as much as she could. The room was empty.

Hannah attempted to return, but although the space was large enough to crawl in, it was too small for her to turn around. She began the arduous task of backing out the full distance she'd crawled forward. Eventually, she made it back to the intersection and worked her way down the second of the three passages, where the result was the same: an empty room.

Once in the third duct, Hannah could hear Jason's voice even before she could see the light from the vent. By the shadows on the floor she could tell that there were at least two people in the room. She prayed Jason was one of them.

Elvin was the first to come into view. He sat at the table with his head down. She inched closer until she could see Jason standing in front of the door. Although she was crouched only a short distance away from the very people she was looking for, she could do no more until she found a way to get their attention without causing a commotion.

CHAPTER SEVENTY

Jason stood looking into the hallway. The door was locked, but there were no guards in sight. It had been hours since he and Elvin had been brought to the room. Earlier, he'd heard a conversation between the guards and Faydra. The whole place was locked down and everyone was searching for Hannah.

Jason liked problem solving, but they had taken everything from him. The room was barren except for two chairs and the table. There was a vent in the ceiling, but it was too high to reach, even on his tiptoes. Of course, Elvin was no help whatsoever. He might as well have been a two-year-old.

Jason sat at the table across from Elvin and stared at the floor between his feet. All hope ebbed away. Then he noticed what appeared to be fine flakes of snow pouring through the air onto the floor. He looked up. It was coming from the vent. Jason watched the dust floating down, expecting it to lessen and then stop altogether. Periodically, it would abate for a moment or two but then it came again.

Jason looked, but could see nothing. He hefted the chair onto the table and jumped up to take a closer look. It was just a dark hole. But when a raspy whisper came from inside, he was so alarmed he nearly fell from the chair.

Although her voice was barely audible, he recognized it immediately. "Hannah?" he whispered.

Elvin looked up from his chair, seemingly happy at the new activity, but, as usual, he said nothing.

There was no time to waste. Hannah examined the vent cover. Two clips held it in place. If removed, it had to be pushed up from below until it snapped into place. Hinges of a sort held the other side. Hannah positioned the screwdriver tip against the vent cover over one of the clips. She hammered down on the handle with the palm of her hand. The clip separated from its clasp. She repeated the process on the other side, and the vent swung down, releasing another shower of dust.

"Step back a second, Jason," Hannah whispered. Jason backed out of the way, and Hannah crawled through the opening until her head hung in the room. She gripped the ledge tightly and let her body drop through the hole. She landed on the table next to Jason.

"It's so good to see you!" said Jason as he wrapped his arms around her. Hannah hugged him back, but she was already devising a way out. The guards would be back, and she had no way of knowing when.

"Jason, I want to get us all out of here, but it's going to take some doing."

"Let's go," Jason said, clasping his fingers together to create a lift for her foot.

Hannah grinned. "Not just yet. There's more we need to do."

***

Hannah hopped off the table and went to the window. It was reinforced glass, and they wouldn't be able to break it, but that didn't matter. She grabbed the chair Jason had been standing on by two legs and placed the other two against the floor. Using all her weight, she pushed down, and the legs gave a little. They didn't bend a lot, but she thought she could make it look like the damage had happened when the chair was bashed against the window.

Next, she shooed Elvin out of his chair and put it on the table and climbed up. "Jump up here," she said to Jason.

In a flash, Jason was standing beside her. "Sit here, would you?" she said.

Jason did as she asked.

Hannah climbed first to the seat and then to the back using Jason as a counterweight. On her tiptoes, she was able to get her head up inside the ductwork. With a small leap, she transferred her body up into the shaft and wriggled in. Next, she rolled over on her back so that her feet dangled out. It was hard, but bending as much as she could, she was able to sit up at an odd angle with her neck completely craned over.

"Jason, I want you to pull the table over to the window, then put the broken chair on top of it. Put all of the furniture over there."

"What for?"

"Just do it. It'll be clear in just a minute. We don't have time for me to explain everything."

The table made a horrible scraping noise, but there was nothing he could do about that. He moved as quickly as he could. By the time he'd finished, Hannah had already stretched out her homemade rope and let the coils dangle to the floor. She wrapped the rope around her wrist and braced herself in the duct with her feet. At least the knots would help make the climb easier.

"What about Elvin? We're not going to leave him here, are we?" protested Jason.

"No. Now hurry up."

"Shouldn't Elvin go up first? That way I can help him."

"No, Jason. I need you up here first. Now get moving," Hannah hissed.

Jason grabbed the rope and scurried up. Once he got into the duct, there wasn't much room. He wriggled over Hannah.

"I'm going to try and get Elvin to climb the rope. I need you to go back the way I've come."

"I don't know where to go."

"Let me finish. This is important, Jason. I don't want anyone getting lost. My coat is back there. We're going back using the tunnel my coat's in. If I can get Elvin up here, I want him between us. You need to make sure he goes down the right tunnel."

"Got it," said Jason, disappearing into the dark.

Hannah turned her attention to Elvin. If anything were going to go wrong, it'd be now. He might not understand how. He might not understand her directions. "Elvin. Come. Now." Hannah ordered. If Elvin had been a prisoner here, he'd want to escape. Hannah was relieved when he raced over and took hold of the rope. A moment later, he had his full weight on it and had begun to scale it.

Thank God he was scrawny. And, fortunately, he was also quick. A moment later he was scrambling past her and into the dark. She prayed Jason would be able to lead him in the right direction.

With Elvin out of the way, Hannah lost no time pulling the rope up. After that, she reached down for the vent cover and pulled it into its frame. It made a bit of a racket, but the clips snapped into place. Even if Faydra ultimately figured out where they'd gone, she hoped her tactics had bought them some time.

She rolled to her stomach and began edging her way back toward the furnace room. When she arrived at the junction, neither Jason nor Elvin was there to greet her. She felt for her jacket, but it was gone as well. She could only hope that they'd made it safely back to the furnace room.

Hannah shuffled her way through the dark. Suddenly, from far away, there came a loud clanging noise. Hannah felt the duct bounce beneath her. Her heart jumped to her throat. She could do nothing but go as fast as she could.

Although she covered the distance in less than half the time it had taken her the first pass, it felt like it took too long. She was anxious and afraid. She stopped once or twice to listen, but the ducting was stable again and all was as silent as before.

She scurried forward and was surprised when the ductwork took a sudden, unfamiliar, sharp downward turn. Something had happened, but she had no idea what. She stopped instantly, feeling around her in all directions. From what she could tell, a seam in the pipe had torn loose leaving a gaping split in the duct just in front of her. The whole thing dipped to the ground at forty-five-degrees. She couldn't judge how far it was to the floor or how much farther it might be to the furnace room. She hadn't considered the possibility that it wouldn't support the weight they'd put on it.

She whispered as loudly as she dared, "Jason." She waited impatiently for a reply, but she got none. It seemed obvious that the tube had collapsed under the load of Jason and Elvin, and down was the only place they could have gone.

Hannah suddenly realized she might not make it back to furnace room. As silently as she could, she continued headfirst downward. She used her arms and legs to slow her decent by putting pressure against the metal sides.

She cursed the absolute darkness. There was no way to tell where she was or how close to the Jason and Elvin she might be. There was nothing she could do but continue.

When she reached the bottom, her hands slid out onto cold concrete. She was on the floor, but where? "Jason," she hoarsely whispered.

This time she heard him reply. "Over here."

She moved forward in the dark, but before she had completely cleared the ducting, she banged her head against something metal. A low metallic ringing sound filled the air. Hannah reached out with her hand to feel in front of her. She followed the object both right and left. She had indeed returned to the furnace room, but the weight of Elvin and Jason in the final portion of the ducting had caused it to collapse to the floor.

She called once more in a harsh whisper, "Jason, where are you?"

"Over here," he repeated quietly.

They were close. She crawled on her hands and knees until she collided with something warm and soft. It was Jason's leg.

"Are you two, okay?" she said.

"I think so. Where are we? What happened?" said Jason, a quiver in his voice.

"Everything's fine. You're exactly where you need to be. It must have been a damn scary thing to be in that pipe when it came crashing down." The darkness prevented Hannah from being able to estimate Jason's state of mind or see whether he nodded.

"What are we going to do now?" Jason said.

"I've got kind of a plan, and if it works out, we'll get out of here. If it doesn't, we're going to be in a lot of trouble."

Hannah described where they were in the building and where the exit was. If no one had come rushing in on them when the duct broke free, they probably hadn't heard it or couldn't find their way to it. There was still the fact that even though she'd tried to divert the guards with the bent chair in the interrogation room, there was really only one escape route and they had taken it.

"Jason, can you give me a hand?" said Hannah.

"What do you need?"

"Sooner or later, someone's going to figure out where we went. If they try to follow us, maybe we can slow them down if we can close off the end of this heating duct."

"Good plan," said Jason.

Hannah led the way back to the fallen ductwork, and using their combined weight, they were able to crush the sides and flatten the end creating a dead end in the pipe. They worked at it until it was smashed flat. Then they folded the flattened end up as much as they could. If anyone followed them, that should stop them for a while.

CHAPTER SEVENTY-ONE

A loud metallic clanging sound echoed throughout the complex. Faydra leapt up and ran into the hallway. If the prison had been functioning as it once had, the place would've been buzzing with activity as personnel rushed to find an explanation for the noise. Unfortunately, there were only four men available and two of them were stationed at the exits. The other two were wandering around somewhere, supposedly looking for the one person who was likely responsible for the commotion.

I guess I'll have to investigate myself, she thought, as she began walking in the direction from which the sound seemed to have come. She hadn't gotten far when one of the two remaining guards found her. "The prisoners are gone," he said breathlessly

"The prisoners escaped?" she said. "How the hell is that even possible?" She fumed as she listened to the variety of improbable scenarios the guard suggested. She almost knocked him over as she pushed past him to get to where Jason and Elvin had been held. She stood in the open doorway, looking into the room. "And this is exactly how you found it?" she said.

"Yes ma'am. Well, almost. The room was locked and empty. The table and chairs were stacked against the wall just in front of the door. We had to push them out of the way to get inside."

One of the chairs had been nearly destroyed. It appeared as though it'd been used to hammer against the bulletproof glass of the two-way mirror or the window in the door. As Faydra studied the room, she could draw only one conclusion: the situation in front of her made no sense whatsoever.

The obvious solution was that, somehow, Hannah had made her way back to the cell and released the prisoners. That was what the guard had suggested and, in that much, he wasn't wrong. However, his explanation didn't feel right. Hannah would have had to have stumbled upon the room and found a way to unlock the door or pick the lock. She couldn't have piled the chairs and table against the door and then closed it behind her. If the miracle of being able to locate him wasn't enough, she would've had to have slipped past the guards who were searching for her—and all this in a building she'd never been in before.

If she had managed to free them, that meant there were three fugitives wandering around the prison.

Faydra pulled the one good chair from the table and sat down to think. She let her eyes comb the room. She was accustomed to finding and decoding the most minute clues. She was rarely stumped, and she was determined this would be no exception. She looked up at the ceiling and noticed the vent. She stared at it for a moment.

From her new vantage point, she let her eyes roam around the entire room. Eventually her focus landed at her feet. There she pushed a small pile of dust from side to side with her boot. She casually used her toe to draw the dust together from all sides, formed a small pile, and she spread it out again. She repeated the process as she considered the problem at hand. Then her eyes lit up. She examined the duct with new understanding. She didn't know how they got to the duct, but she knew they hadn't escaped through the door.

She crossed to the table and pulled it to the center of the room. A moment later, she pulled the grate free and raised herself to her full height. Still she couldn't see into the hole, so she chinned up into the opening. From her new vantage, the signs were obvious. The surface should have been covered with an undisturbed layer of dust, but instead it was a riot of scuff and drag marks. There were large deposits here and there where the dust had been pushed around. A good portion had ended up on the floor where she discovered it.

The security guards would never be able to fit into the small space, but the boy, the woman, and that runt of a man could have. She jumped down and hurried to the nearest guard. "They're in the vents. I'm going after them. Be ready for my signal."

She returned to the vent with one of the guards who boosted her up. She reached the intersection, and after one failed attempt, she worked her way down the correct shaft. When she'd gone thirty meters or so, she stopped to listen. From far away she could hear faint voices. Knowing she was on the right track, she hurried along as silently as she could.

She arrived at a broken section but could hear Hannah and Jason talking quietly in the dark. Everything was working out perfectly. She'd catch them off guard. They didn't stand a chance. She slithered down the shaft undetected.

As she approached the bottom, it suddenly narrowed. She tried to work her way backwards, but she couldn't get enough leverage and the descent was too steep. She cursed herself for having fallen into a trap. Someone had sealed off the end. She was able to make a little progress with each effort, but when she relaxed even a little, she slid once more to the bottom of the shaft.

***

Hannah was startled to hear someone in the heating duct. The only person who could have figured it out and followed was Faydra.

Hannah huddled against the wall and drew the others near, hoping Faydra hadn't detected them before she slid into the trap.

Faydra struggles subsided, then she spoke. "I know you're out there, Hannah and Jason. This little trap was very clever. I never would've expected it from you."

She was putting on quite a show. Her voice had a silky quality. If Hannah hadn't known better, she might've even believed her.

"Help me out of here and I'll make sure they go easy on you. I can do that, you know. Harry trusts me. He and I built this town together. Help me out of here and I'll make sure you're treated like royalty."

Jason whispered, "She made us believe she was traveling from Edmonton. We help her, and we'll be stuck mining coal."

"And if your dad's here, any chance of saving him will be gone, too," said Hannah.

Then to Faydra, "Faydra, I'm sorry, but we're not going to be able to help you."

Faydra responded with venom. "The guards are going to find me. They're waiting for me to tell them where you are." There was a slight pause and then Faydra began to yell, "They're here. Get your asses in here."

Hannah rushed to silence her. "Shhh and I'll help you. Just be quiet."

Faydra quieted again.

"Move to one side so Jason and I can free you." She waited for Faydra to follow her instructions. There was silence for a long time. Hannah still held the screwdriver tightly. In the dark, she raised her arm slowly. Her coat whistled as her sleeve cut sharply through the air. Her arm came down in a swift arc with all her weight and power behind it. The screwdriver penetrated the metal and carried on into the vent the full length of the shaft. Faydra thrashed briefly inside her metal tomb and then became still. Hannah stood and returned to where Elvin and Jason were sitting, leaving the screwdriver protruding from the metal vent.

"Hannah, what happened?" whispered Jason.

"Nothing. Everything's fine," she said in the dark.

CHAPTER SEVENTY-TWO

The guard listened for Faydra, but without knowing where she'd gone, it was impossible to follow the piping. The heating ducts sometimes ran with the hallways and sometimes they didn't. He waited patiently for what seemed like a very long time. He was about to give up when he heard her calling from somewhere far away. He raced in the general direction, but her calling ceased almost immediately. He walked farther in the same direction, hoping to get some indication of where she might be, but no sound was repeated. He continued to wait for another hour before he gave up. Whatever she was up to, if she needed something, she'd get it. Faydra could take care of herself.

The only thing he could do was prevent the intruders from leaving the building, and the easiest way to do that was to maintain patrols at both entrances. Sooner or later, they'd have to come out of hiding.

CHAPTER SEVENTY-THREE

Hannah kept watch while Jason rested. She could've slept. She knew the prisoners would make so much noise coming into the building they all could've been sleeping soundly and still they would've been woken, but there was no point taking chances.

The prisoners were brought in, fed, and put to bed. Using the open upper hatch to keep track of the light outside, she lingered. She'd wait until the sun began to rise before attempting anything.

The night was almost over when Jason stirred and spoke. "Hannah, I can't sleep."

"That's okay," she said. "It won't be much longer." The sound of a deeply drawn breath came from Elvin's direction. *At least one of us can rest*, she thought.

When the night sky began to brighten, Hannah decided it was time to put their plan into action. The prison was as silent as a tomb, but it wouldn't be long before the prisoners would be woken for another grueling day.

Jason rousted Elvin and he followed, if not eagerly, at least willingly.

Although the hatch didn't provide enough light to navigate by, there was still a faint glow from the maintenance room below. Hannah led the way down the stairs where she waited for Elvin and Jason to catch up.

From what little they could see from the small window, the corridor looked to be clear. When all three of them had assembled, Hannah turned the knob on the deadbolt and opened the door. Together they moved into the hall. Hannah turned to Jason. "Wait here quietly," she said, then tiptoed to the main entrance. She leaned around the corner as far as she dared and peered down the hall. A guard was stationed outside, but he appeared to be asleep—not that it mattered.

She hurried back to Jason and Elvin. They moved together up the hall toward the cellblock Hannah had been in the previous day. She looked to Elvin's expression to see if he recognized it, but there was no indication that he did.

Near the entrance was a control station used to lock down the cells. It was vacant. Apparently, once the prisoners were brought in for the night, there was no need to keep anyone on duty there.

Hannah walked to the console and flipped the switches that would open all the cell doors, then she rushed down the hall to the cellblock. She pushed the door open and stood facing the dark room. She'd expected the captives to recognize their freedom. She'd expected that they'd already be moving out of their cells. Instead, they simply stood in their compartments, not moving. She wondered if this was too much like their regular morning routine.

CHAPTER SEVENTY-FOUR

Travis woke with a start to the clanging sound of opening cell doors. His body clock could tell it was an hour or more earlier than normal. They hadn't yet been served the morning slop.

In some of the other cells, prisoners began stirring at the unexpected sound. He had no more than gotten to his feet when the main exit door of the cellblock swung open. Instead of a burly guard, the silhouette of a woman was framed in the doorway. Slowly, other prisoners came forward to stand at the threshold of their cells.

The woman spoke with authority. "Do you want out of here or not?"

If the woman had a plan, she didn't take the time to share it. Some of the prisoners walked out of their cells into the corridor, Travis among them. He could see the uncertainty on their faces, although he was surprised to see so many come forward as quickly as they did.

"Who are you?" said Travis.

***

A man spoke. In the dim light, Hannah could see his beard was full and matted with dirt. She cringed internally at the thought of what kind of animal life it might contain. She hissed back, "Do you think we could discuss this later? We need to get out of here together, and we need to get out of here now!"

"What about the others? Did you free them as well?"

Hannah couldn't see the point of stopping to answer his questions when it was action that was called for. The whole rescue idea was turning out to be more difficult than she'd imagined. "I guess so. I opened all the cells I could. Are you coming or not?"

***

Travis turned his attention to the prisoners in his block. He needed to motivate them to move as one. He called, "It's time to go, everyone! Let's get out of here. Follow me!"

Understanding slowly dawned for many. First, there was a quiet stirring, then, in a few moments, it grew to a low rumble.

Intuitively, Travis understood that the woman intended them to overrun the guards. He called to her over the growing clamor, "If you're going to make this work, you're going to need everyone."

Without hesitation, he ran past Hannah and out the door. His cellblock was not the only one in the complex. There were others, each filled with captives. He raced from one to the next, announcing the impending freedom for all and calling on someone to lead. He didn't wait to find out who. It might be no one, based on what he'd observed in the past. He left them to their own devices and moved on.

By the time he made it to the last of the blocks, his efforts were almost unnecessary. In the last cellblock, the group was already organizing and as soon as the doors opened, many charged out. Travis forced his way back into the hall where prisoners were milling about. Even in the growing commotion, there was no indication these people would do anything that would help their plight. They'd just as likely allow themselves to be rounded up and returned to their pens.

In a last-ditch effort to motivate the prisoners, Travis yelled as loudly as he could. He swung his arms madly in the air and raced through the crowd. Slowly they began to move, and then, like cattle, they started to stampede. The guards realized what was happening, but it was too late. Their orders were lost in the chaos and noise.

A single pistol shot thundered in the corridor, but before the guard could fire a second, he was pulled beneath the weight of the mob that flowed toward the exit. The hoard boiled down the corridor. Someone fell and was trampled beneath the mass. Travis led on. He raced past the woman who had released them, but ignored her. Freedom was only a doorway away and it would be his.

***

The crazy-looking bearded man raced past Hannah. The masses of prisoners followed, already out of control. She recognized her opportunity and took it. She plowed in among the forms, knowing perfectly well the dangers of losing her footing. Jason huddled in a nearby doorway with Elvin beside him looking bewildered.

"Hurry, Jason! Take my hand. Hurry," she yelled.

With Elvin close by, Jason leapt into the flood of prisoners. He grabbed for Hannah's hand and pulled Elvin along. Struggling to maintain his footing, Jason served as the tether between her and Elvin. Should either of his hands fail, someone would be lost. Hannah held on tight. She willed him to follow.

Another deafening gunshot pounded in her ears. Hannah didn't see where it had come from; she focused on keeping up with the mob. A man beside them lurched forward. Even before his body began to crumple, deep red oozed from his chest. His arms flailed as he tried to maintain his balance. Falling forward, he grabbed Elvin. The crowd was relentless as it pushed forward. Hannah held onto Jason with all her might, but Jason was unable to hold the weight of Elvin as well as the man who pulled him down. Hannah saw Elvin's hand slip away, and he and the dying man disappeared beneath the surge of the stampede.

Hannah turned her attention forward. She still held Jason's hand. His purple fingers poked out of her fist. Together, they were swept along.

When they reached the exit, Hannah looked back. The guards were nowhere to be seen. A few bodies lay scattered. She imagined the guards were among them. The crowd reached the gates and raced on. In the hallway, they had become a mindless mob, but once outside, they seemed to move with a purpose. They didn't scatter as Hannah had expected they might. Instead, they swarmed toward town.

It only took a few minutes to empty the prison and then all was silent. Hannah turned to Jason. "What should we do about Elvin?" Jason said, tears welling in his eyes.

Hannah nodded toward the building.

They carefully went into the bay. There were fewer bodies than Hannah had expected to see. A handful of prisoners had not survived, but none of the guards had made it out alive.

***

In the corridor, there were even fewer casualties. The bodies of Elvin and the unfortunate prisoner lay where they'd fallen. Elvin's still form lay beneath the man who had pulled him down. Jason raced to him and pulled the dead man away from him.

Hannah knelt, taking Elvin's hand in hers.

Although tears flowed from his eyes, there were none in Hannah's as she concentrated. Jason followed her gaze to Elvin's wrist and realized she was feeling for a pulse. He searched her face for her reaction. The tension in her face suddenly disappeared and was replaced by a smile.

Elvin coughed, and his eyes flickered open.

"Come on, buddy. We need to get out of here," said Hannah.

Elvin staggered at first, but in a few moments, he was moving as if he'd never fallen.

They were only minutes behind the main body of the hoard, but it was as if they were passing through a war-ravaged landscape. Not every house had been broken into, but those that had been were nearly destroyed. Windows were broken and belongings strewn in the yards. In some cases, the inhabitants lay motionless on their porches or in the grass. On one front porch, a woman wept, clutching her children. Far ahead, the crazed mob had split and raced along various streets. The town was at the mercy of the tsunami it had created.

It was unnecessary to track them. She already knew their destination. She followed them to the big house with the large tree and the tire swing in the backyard: Harry's house. Hannah ran to the window and peered inside to see four men enter the room. Harry had no chance. The first man through the kitchen door picked up a lamp from a nearby side table, brought it over his head, and swung it forward in a smooth sweeping motion. His entire body followed. The heavy lamp connected squarely with Harry's forehead. There was an audible crack as he fell in a heap. The three others tore through the rest of the house. Then, as quickly as it started, the violence was over.

Suddenly, the bearded man from the prison walked casually though the door. He walked over to Harry and bent down beside him. It looked to Hannah as if he was almost disappointed he'd missed his chance for revenge. He reached forward and placed his thumb on the side of Harry's neck. Hannah could tell from his reaction there was no pulse.

Hannah and Jason moved around the side of the house and entered through the back door. When the man heard their footsteps, he turned. His quick reaction reminded Hannah of a wild animal.

"I guess I owe you my gratitude," he said. "Thank you."

"Oh? Why is that?" said Hannah.

"Aren't you the one who opened the cells?"

"Aren't you the guy who wanted a description of the plan when you were supposed to be helping with the escape?" said Hannah.

"You're right. I guess that was me."

If a sheepish grin hid behind the beard, Hannah couldn't tell.

"Sorry," he said. Then he saw Elvin. "Ajax! You're alive!"

"Ajax?" said Jason.

"Yeah. Ajax, you finally made it out." He turned to Hannah. "We were cellmates and one morning he was just gone." Travis ruffled Elvin's hair.

Elvin smiled saying, "Tavs!" in the excited tone they'd become familiar with.

"His name is Ajax, then?" asked Hannah.

"I wouldn't know," said Travis. "That's just what they always called him."

An awkward moment followed, and, with nothing more to say, Hannah prepared her departure. "Well, I'm glad you made it out," she said, but then she paused. It suddenly occurred to her that she still needed to find Travis and this man was as good a start as any. "Before we go, there was something I was wondering," she said.

"What is it?"

"Maybe you can help me." She beckoned to Jason.

Jason understood immediately and began to rifle through his pockets, producing the locket he'd brought from home.

"Actually, we're looking for someone. We think he may have passed through here," said Hannah.

"We didn't get a chance to get to know very many people, but I'll help if I can." said the man.

"We're looking for a man named Travis Ryder," said Jason.

The man's gaze shifted between Hannah and the boy. His eyes grew wide and then, as if all his strength left him at once, he fell to his knees.

"You know him?" said Jason.

"I haven't heard that name in years. I guess you could say I know him."

"Where is he? Do you know what happened to him?"

Travis stood slowly. "I know him," said Travis, "because he's me."

Jason stared in disbelief.

Hannah took Jason's arm and moved him behind her, a mother protecting her child. Anyone could claim to be the long-lost Travis Ryder. The man in front of her was easily thirty pounds lighter than the man she'd met years earlier and his beard covered most of his features. Hannah couldn't imagine what this man's motives might be, but she hadn't come this far to be duped by a stranger.

Elvin stood next to the man repeating "Tavs" under his breath.

"Why does he keep saying that?" asked Jason.

"It's the closest he ever got to being able to say my name," Travis said, smiling.

Hannah wasn't convinced. "I knew Travis Ryder and you look nothing like him. If you're Travis, you should know who I am," she said.

The man studied Hannah for a long time before saying, "I only met one person before I got captured and was trapped here. I stopped in Harrison, and I met a lady there. Her name was Hannah."

"Dad?" said Jason and threw his arms around his father's waist, the locket dangling from his fingers.

EPILOGUE

Travis stood, first looking at Hannah and then at the boy who was his son. He'd awakened to freedom, a moment he'd never dared imagine. Every obstacle that had been in his path was suddenly removed. Now he stood face to face with a son who had endured unimaginable hardships to be standing before him. Tears flowed from his eyes.

It was a bittersweet moment. His son was alive but his beloved wife, the person who'd kept him alive all these years, had been killed. And he'd been reintroduced to a woman who had done more in such a short time for his son than anyone ever could.

She'd left her home to escort Jason across the province. Travis could see the affection between the woman he met only once and the son whose childhood he'd missed. He could tell she was happy to see Jason reunited with his father, but there was pain behind her eyes as well. Did she feel stranded once more without family or home? There was no circle. He stood with Jason and she with Ajax.

Travis turned to Jason. "Where to, son?" he said.

Jason reached over and took Hannah's hand as if it belonged in his. He hugged her, then looked at his father and said, "I'm going wherever you two are going."

About the Author

 Randy Wallace was born in Oregon and then as a child moved to Canada. His family arrived at a treed property with no access to electricity, running water, or telephone. Randy grew up helping turn a piece of wilderness into a farm. These meager beginnings shaped his life, his teaching career, and, later, his writing.

A Fading Shadow was originally undertaken as an exercise to encourage his students to brave their own writing, and it proved successful. His agreement to share his writing if they'd share theirs was a strong motivator for both Randy and his students.

In 2008, Randy's 19-year career as an educator was cut short when he suffered a debilitating brain bleed. Of the original effects, short term memory challenges and the inability to divide his attention remain. He continues to work at improving his functionality.

Randy has a wide range of experiences and talents that lend themselves to the realism of his writing, from working in his father's sawmill to learning how to operate logging and farming equipment, to managing a trapline with his older brother, an endeavor that required countless hours of planning and spending hours in freezing temperatures traipsing along snow-covered trails.

Randy's book titled *#9 Grundpark Road,* a fantasy adventure, is also published by All Things That Matter Press.

Links along with some of Randy's other writings can be found at www.randykwallace.com.

Randy can also be reached through:
www.goodreads.com/randykwallace
www.facebook.com/randykwallace
www.twitter.com/randykwallace
www.Instagram.com/randykwallace
www.linkedin.com/in/randy-wallace-18342a9
www.justajot.blogspot.com
www.randykwallace.blogspot.com

www.ingramcontent.com/pod-product-compliance
Lightning Source LLC
Chambersburg PA
CBHW051512150726
47997CB00001B/223